CHRISTOP

The Devil's Face

Christopher Artinian

CHRISTOPHER ARTINIAN

THE DEVIL'S FACE

Copyright © 2024 Christopher Artinian

All rights reserved.

ISBN: 9798335796507

CHRISTOPHER ARTINIAN

DEDICATION

I've dedicated a book to her before, but she is the one who keeps me going, who makes all my dreams come true. To Tina.

CHRISTOPHER ARTINIAN

CHRISTOPHER ARTINIAN

ACKNOWLEDGEMENTS

She gets a dedication and a mention in the acknowledgements. That's how much I utterly depend on her. She's also the woman who let me have a polytunnel which has given me a new lease of life. Tina, I will never be able to thank you enough for all you do.

Thanks so much to the guys across in the fan club on Facebook (now called Christopher Artinian's Safe Haven). You rock!

Massive thanks to my editor, Ken. His help and guidance are priceless. And a very, very big thank you to the wonderful Christian Bentulan for another great cover.

And, last but not least, thank you to you for buying this book. Your continued support makes a world of difference.

1

NOW

Katie Wilson entered the dining room with a proud smile on her face. The Christmas decorations had come down this very day and the house was back to looking spick and span. That's how she liked things, spick and span. She was like her mother that way and her mother before her. Home and family were everything to Katie, and although that was an old-fashioned concept to many, she didn't care. Home and family were the two things that made her happy.

She placed a plate in front of her husband, Donald, then each of her two children, Calum, twelve, and Alison, who was thirteen going on thirty. *What on earth is she wearing?*

Katie was determined not to rise to the bait. Alison had way too much of Auntie Pauline's free spirit in her, but she wasn't going to let this mealtime descend into a pitched battle like the one on Christmas Eve.

"Dinner won't be long," she said, turning and heading towards the door.

"Something smells good, anyway," Donald replied.

Katie paused at the entrance and turned. "Yes, and it would have smelt good a lot sooner if you two hadn't been out all day in that croft."

Sheepish grins passed between the father and son. "I've got to show the boy how to work the land. It will be his when we're both sunning ourselves on a beach in the Bahamas."

Katie laughed and shook her head. "Och, what am I to do with the pair of you?"

She was about to turn once again when there was a sudden rumble and the whole house shook. Panicked expressions appeared on all their faces for the briefest moment until the lights went out and she and the two children let out startled screams.

The rumble stopped after a few seconds, but the lights didn't come back on. Katie's heavy breathing could be heard from the doorway and she let out another short, sharp scream as a hand grasped her arm.

"It's alright," Donald said, sensing her fear. "It's just a power cut."

"No. What was that almighty noise?"

"Hold on to the frame, I'll be back in a minute."

Katie held the doorframe tight. It was a shameful thing to admit, but even at the age of forty-seven, she was afraid of the dark. She would frequently drift into slumber with a small light on, claiming she had fallen asleep reading, but Donald knew better. He knew there was something about the dark that chilled Katie to her soul.

She had told him of childhood trauma. Visits in the dead of night by a figure; no, not a figure, a vision … more than a vision. Something impossible, inexplicable, terrifying. A thing. A thing that she could feel sitting at the foot of her bed but materialising inches away from her face at the same time. A thing that would whisper the words, "You can't run away. You can't run away," over and over as if it was some kind of demonic spell. The rest of the room would be black, but the malign face staring at her through the darkness would somehow possess the dimmest illumination.

If this wasn't horrifying and traumatic enough, there was always a prelude to its appearance. *The creeping*, Katie called it. *The creeping*—a slow, unnatural vibration rising from her toes, up her legs to her torso and beyond, freezing her, paralysing her, stopping her from screaming, fleeing, even so much as closing her eyes. When *the creeping* began, she knew she was at the mercy of this malevolent creation. She knew that she would have to suffer whatever it did, whatever it put in her head.

When the visits ended and her body was released, she would go charging into her parents' room, crying her eyes out, refusing to return to her own bed.

Donald put these episodes down to night terrors because the alternative was way too frightening for good Christians to contemplate, but in the mind or not, he knew she was still terrified to her core.

"Here," he said, flicking on a torch and guiding her to the table where their two children remained wide-eyed and still shaking from the thunderous sound.

"What was that, Dad?" Alison asked, the façade of the punky young woman she wanted to be suddenly shattered at her feet as the frightened girl she was came to the surface.

"Err … um … I don't know," he said, placing the torch on the table and lighting one of the candles he'd grabbed from the same drawer. He let the wax drip, forming a spot on a side plate that Katie had laid out for a crusty roll. He placed the base of the candle in the gluey mixture, and when he was happy that it would remain upright, he did the same with the other three.

It was only a small table, the centre extension had been folded away after Boxing Day, and the torch and four candles provided more than enough light for them to see one another's faces. The children still looked startled, but Katie was drained of all colour as she sat bolt upright in her chair. Her eyes were cast beyond the meagre flames into the darkness. Her mouth was open a little, almost as if she was talking under her breath.

Oh, dear God. Please, no. God, no. God, no, no, no. The creeping. It's happening again. The creeping.

"It's freezing in here," Alison said, and for the first time, Donald and Calum noticed it too.

"What's happening, Dad?" Calum asked.

"I … I think we might have experienced a minor earthquake, that's all."

"An earthquake?"

"They do happen from time to time in this country. Just minor ones mind."

"Yeah," Alison confirmed. "I heard there was one in Morvern a few months back."

Donald nodded. "That's right. They were talking about it at the livestock sales in Dingwall the last time I was there. Didn't do too much damage, but people felt it alright." He looked up to the ceiling. "I'd better check the roof, make sure we're not missing any tiles. And the sheep. I should check on the sheep."

"Mum? Mum, are you okay?" Calum asked. Katie continued to stare into nothingness and now her lips were visibly moving, despite the fact that no sound could be heard.

"Mum, it was just a little earthquake. It's nothing to worry about." Alison said the words despite not being too sure herself. The sudden drop in temperature worried her and she wondered if a fissure had opened up beneath the floorboards, allowing the cold air from outside to chill the house. She'd heard how Ronnie McClintock's cottage had succumbed to subsidence and half the kitchen had almost collapsed after the big storm last year.

Donald hesitated. His urge was to head outside to check on the property, but he sensed the worry in his

THE DEVIL'S FACE

children's voices and he looked at his wife. *She's in shock.* He glanced around the dimly lit dining room. The pictures were still hanging straight on the walls. There were no visible cracks or other damage. *Dammit. Katie's more important than a few loose tiles.*

"Look," he said, taking charge, trying to grab her attention. "I know you're a perfectionist, but that joint will be done well enough for my liking." He glanced over the table. The vegetable terrines were already present with lids in place; the meat dish was the only thing they were waiting for. "You stay put, Katie. I'll go get it." *This will snap her out of it. There's no happier time for her than when her work in the kitchen is being enjoyed by the family.* He glanced up at the ceiling once more as he left the room. *Maybe I can go out with a torch after dinner and check on the roof then.*

Katie remained unresponsive as he left. The two youngsters kept throwing each other worried glances as their mother's lips continued to move.

"Mum?" Calum pleaded for a response, but none came.

"Here we go," Donald said, re-entering the dining room with a large porcelain platter. It was clear that he'd lit more candles and lanterns in the kitchen so he could see what he was doing, and now the dim glow followed him through the doorway. "I'll tell you what, Katie. You really know how to put on a spread."

He placed the plate down and the carving knife and fork glinted in the candlelight. He adjusted the large oval plate and pushed it into the centre of the table.

"Dad. Something's wrong with Mum," Alison said.

Donald had hoped his wife would have snapped out of her shock by now. He didn't handle things like this well. He grew up on this croft. He shadowed his father as Calum now shadowed him. The flock and the land were what he knew about. Feelings and fears were things that needed pushing deep down inside. "Katie. Katie," he said, trying to grab her attention, but still her eyes did not deviate. "Katie.

You're scaring the children." *You're scaring the crap out of me too.* He reached out, grabbing her hand, but withdrew his own just as quickly as he felt her icy fingers. But it got the desired effect. Katie's head turned towards him as if her neck were spring-loaded.

Her eyes were no longer distant; instead, they bored holes through him and Donald fell back into his chair in surprise.

"Mum?" Alison said as her mother slowly rose from her chair, knocking it over in the process. An eerie, unnatural smile bled onto Katie's face, gradually widening into a chilling grin.

"M-um?" Calum's voice quivered a little as his mother's face continued to morph.

"Oh, dear God!" It was their father's voice that alarmed them now. They turned to him as he trembled in horror. "Katie." He said her name in a whisper as her face became that of the malevolent old man who used to visit her in the night. The unshakeable presence in her bedroom that had lived with her ever since in the form of fear. There was no way Donald could know that for sure; he hadn't witnessed it, but he had heard her descriptions, he had seen the fear and horror in her eyes as she recounted her experiences and, in his heart, he knew it couldn't be anyone else.

It was real. It is real. Donald desperately tried to reason. *It's my mind playing tricks. It's the candlelight. It's ... it's....* There was no reasoning. *It's real.* He shrunk back further into his chair, throwing a glance towards his children. Until this point, he had been deaf to their fear-filled sobs as their mother's face transformed into this malignant vision that defied comprehension, defied reason.

"Mum. Stop it. Please," Alison cried with tears streaming down her face. She reached out, grasping her brother's hand as they both leaned back from the table.

Then, when it seemed that things couldn't become any more frightening, Calum lost control of his bladder as his mother with the face of the petrifying, deranged, evil-looking old man rose a little more. At first, it appeared as if she was standing on tiptoes, but then she carried on rising.

"Dad! DAAAD!" Calum screamed, daring to lean back and stare down into the shadows beneath the table. "What's happening, Dad?"

Donald was transfixed by the old man's gaze. His wife's arms were extended, creating a cruciform. The grin on her face was unnatural; he would have said impossible as it seemed almost elastic, stretching her lips to painful extremities. Then, in a heartbeat, it vanished, and Katie finally spoke. But they were not her words and it was not her voice. It was the voice of something menacing, something wicked. "You can't run away."

"NOOO! NOOO!" When Donald had originally heard his wife's stories of the nightly visits that prompted her lifelong fear of the dark, he had humoured her but ultimately put them down to girlish, airy-fairy nonsense. Now he understood. This horror that had visited her countless times in her bed, violating her mind with its forceful intrusion, was back. He tore his eyes away to glimpse his children crying, terrified, holding each other's hands like bairns.

"You can't run away. You can't run away. You can't run away."

Katie had said it was like a spell and it was. As much as Donald wanted to jump to his feet, grab Alison and Calum and charge out of the room, he couldn't. He was glued to his seat, unable to do anything but behold the blood-curdling spectacle. He could feel his breathing becoming more strained with each second that passed. *Got to do something. Got to do something.* He was the man of the house. As antiquated an idea as this was to some, it was how families like his had lived for generations. It was how they would continue to live for at least a generation more, judging by how Calum was turning out, and it was why he had to act, regardless of his own dread.

He climbed to his feet. "LEAVE HER ALONE, GOD DAMN YOU!" he boomed, the sound reverberating around the walls of the small dining room.

It worked. The voice fell quiet. A chilling silence hung in the air for a moment and then the ungodly veneer that had formed on Katie's face faded away to nothing, leaving behind her familiar features. Her skin was still ghostly pale, but as her body lowered, barely perceptible breaths of relief left the lips of her family.

Calum stretched again, risking another glance into the shadowy world beneath the dining table. He squeezed his sister's hand and pulled back, seeing that his mother's feet were planted firmly on the carpet.

Katie remained perfectly still with her arms outstretched as tears rolled down her face. "Wh-what was that, Dad? What's wrong with Mum?" Alison asked between sobs.

They were questions he wished he knew the answer to. "Katie? Katie?" he probed gently, hoping to prompt some kind of response.

His wife's eyes were distant as tears continued to pool in them. Her mouth was closed, for which he was eternally grateful. He wasn't sure he would ever be able to hear her speak again without hearing that infernal old man. "You can't run away. You can't run away," she suddenly whispered.

"Katie, stop that."

"You can't run away."

"Katie. That's enough," he said, more authoritatively, as he stepped towards her.

Again, her head swivelled with unnatural speed and her eyes transfixed him, stopping him in mid-step. "YOU CAN'T RUN AWAY! YOU CAN'T RUN AWAY!" she screamed, louder than any sound he had ever heard come out of her mouth. The children began to cry louder than before and Donald's mouth dropped open, desperate to reply but panic seizing him. "YOU CAN'T RUN AWAY!"

THE DEVIL'S FACE

Katie's hand reached out with cobra-like speed, grabbing one of the candles, snapping it from the waxy glue on the plate and plunging it into her husband's eye.

For a few seconds that seemed to last a lifetime, he remained upright. The wild, flaring flame had caught his forelock before disappearing into the chasm of his skull and now the orange dancing flicker spread to the rest of the black mop of hair that covered his head.

The children had stopped screaming and crying for a breath as the unimaginable had become real. They had both jumped to their feet as their mother's hand had extended with its fiery makeshift weapon. They clung to each other as if the other sibling was a life raft.

One.

Two.

Three.

Their father remained upright, his mouth still open with his final words forever frozen on his tongue, his head adorned with a hat of fire as his hair crackled and hissed. The protrusion from his eye dripped blood and hot wax onto the carpet; then his wife's hand finally withdrew.

Four.

Five.

Six.

Donald's body collapsed back like a felled tree. It thudded loudly on the carpeted floorboards and the only sound that could be heard was that of the crackling flames, which continued to burn his hair and scalp. Finally, the floodgates broke and Calum and Alison almost ruptured themselves with the sheer force of the screams that exploded from their mouths. They were cries of horror, true horror. Not those of children who had fallen backwards off a gate and cracked their skulls, not those of playmates reaching into their father's tool bag and slicing their hands open on rusty Stanley knife blades. These were the screams of the wretched, the screams of those who had glimpsed behind the red curtain and looked into Hell.

They continued to hold each other, too scared to do anything else, even though every fibre of their being was saying *RUN! RUN!* But then it dawned on them both instantaneously—*the spell*. "You can't run away. You can't run away." Their mother's words rattled around their heads as they stared across the table at her.

Katie's face was underlit now, giving it a devilish amber glow, and as her head twisted away from the body of her husband and towards her crying, screaming children, that impossible grin was back. Only, this time, it didn't belong to the thing that had commandeered her face before. It belonged to her. It stretched her lips as if they were giant pink rubber bands. The flames from the candles still on the table were mirrored in her eyes until it seemed like fire rippled in the sockets.

"M-um," Alison pleaded, hoping somehow she could get through to the woman she loved and snap her out of whatever this was.

"M-um." Katie mimicked her daughter before starting to laugh. Only it wasn't just her laugh. There were two distinct sounds. Hers and that of the old man who had visited them moments before. His demonic chuckle rose and fell in harmony with Katie's, sending the siblings into a new domain of horror.

Suddenly, with speed beyond anything they believed their mother capable of, Katie leapt, her left hand plucking the two-pronged fork from the joint, her right grabbing the carving knife. There was a loud bang as she landed on the other side of the table, colliding with a chair, which shot across the room and smashed against the wall.

The children wailed again. This wasn't their mother. They had no idea who or what it was, but it wasn't her. Katie's arms extended once more and her feet rose off the floor as her children, consumed by fear, began to back away.

"This can't be happening," Calum sobbed.

"This can't be happening," Katie cruelly echoed as she continued to levitate slowly. Her body came to a halt with her feet six inches off the carpet. Her vault over the table had knocked two more candles over, which had now set fire to the tablecloth.

The flames flickered and danced as her silhouette loomed over her offspring. She lunged, the fork thrusting through her son's left eye, the knife slicing across her daughter's throat. Their screams instantly fell silent and Katie's feet hit the floor like a marionette whose strings had been severed.

The elastic smile was back on her face as her head tilted, and first she watched Calum collapse in a heap; then her eyes angled towards Alison as her daughter held both hands up to her throat in a vain attempt to stop the bleeding. There was an expression on her face that shouted betrayal, that asked how could a mother do this to her own children. And even though she couldn't see Katie's broad grin on this side of the flames, Alison was able to spot the telltale jut of her mother's cheek telling her she was smiling. *She's smiling while she watches me die. I don't understand. I don't understand.*

Alison fell to her right, her body thumping against the floor as her lower half draped across her brother.

Katie remained in position for a few seconds as the flames behind her licked higher and higher; then she finally walked back around to her side of the table and picked up her chair, sitting down as her husband's body continued to burn near her feet. The grin remained on her face for a moment.

"You can't run away. You can't run away," and, finally, the last part of her memory from childhood came back to her. She'd heard it a hundred times before, probably even more, but her mind had blocked it out as some kind of defence mechanism. Tears began to roll down her face as the real Katie came to life. She had been present while the horror unfolded. She had been present and awake like a prisoner chained to a bed with her eyelids removed, forced to watch it but unable to change it. The fire began to rage around her, but the heat could not warm her blood. Nothing could take away the chill she was feeling as the old man's long-forgotten words forced their way into her mind. "You can't run away. You can't run away. You can't run away from your demons."

2

Nollie didn't have a clue what was happening. A few minutes had passed since the house had shaken. She had been taking a bath; in fact, she was still taking a bath. She had not dared to climb out of the cast iron tub, believing it would be the safest place for her if masonry started falling.

Could it have been an earthquake?

She knew they happened in Scotland, although she'd never experienced one, and from everything she'd read, they were nothing like as bad as the ones that occurred elsewhere in the world. They were little more than hiccups compared to the kind that seemed to take place on a relatively regular basis in places like Japan and Indonesia.

The light in the hallway had gone off at the same time, signalling a power outage. She snuffed out three of the candles she'd lit for her nice, long soak, realising that any chance of relaxing had well and truly passed and there was a good possibility she would need those candles if the power was going to be off for some time. There had been no …

what was the word for them? *Aftershocks. That's right.* So, she pulled herself up and reached for a towel.

She dried her arms and climbed out of the tub onto the waiting mat. She had just begun to dry the rest of her body when she heard a door open downstairs. Goosebumps rippled up and down her skin. She was alone in the house. Her parents were on holiday in Jamaica, one final romantic break before taking Nana out of the home and letting her live her final few months in familiar surroundings with the ones she loved.

Her parents had protested when Nollie had put her studies on pause to help. Her mother said it was silly and unnecessary to risk her education in such a manner. But her university had been more than reasonable and understanding. She was an exemplary student and her reasons for wanting to put her learning on hold were a testament to the person she was.

Leaving Manchester behind for the Highlands was a culture shock though. This house had been their holiday home growing up. It had taken Nollie completely by surprise when her parents had decided to retire here early, selling their semi-detached in South London where she had grown up and moving to this terminal doer-upper two and a half hours away from what anyone could call civilisation.

There were pros and cons to bringing her ageing gran to a place like this, but Nollie's mum was one of the NHS's finest. Nursing had been the only thing she'd wanted to do with her life and it seemed fitting that she should take on one more job before retiring properly. Nollie's dad had been a self-employed builder, never short of work, only short of time.

They had bought their house in Brixton when people like them could still afford a mortgage down there. The dilapidated shell that was once the property where Nollie was now standing was given in payment when the customer ran out of cash. Nollie's mother had gone mad with her husband at the time. It had been valued at eight thousand pounds, which was still less than the bill had come to, but her dad had seen the potential. It came with a little bit of land and he knew he could turn it into a swan rather than the ugly duckling that it was.

There was still lots wrong with it, but it was beautiful compared to what it had been like when they had first laid eyes on the place. Some of the windows wouldn't open properly. Her dad was going to get to those. Some of the steps creaked way too loudly, almost as if the board was going to snap. Her dad was going to get to those too and a thousand problems more, including the doors that seemingly swung open for no reason. "New mortice latches, Nollie. That's all they need. The doors and hinges are fine."

Her father's words came back to her as she started drying herself once more, convinced that the quake or whatever it had been had ruffled the building's feathers a little, causing one of the doors to fall open and the jolt of uncertainty to surge through her.

"Jesus, Nollie. You're not in Moss Side anymore. This is the bloody Highlands." She giggled a little, turning towards the candle so she could see the Egyptian cotton towel absorb the beads of water on her soft, espresso skin.

A wood-on-wood shriek like a heavy chair being pulled across floorboards made her jump and instinctively she pulled the white towel up to cover her breasts.

That wasn't a fucking door.

She reached for her jeans and T-shirt, quickly throwing them on, forgoing her drying ritual in favour of finding out what was happening.

Mum and Dad aren't due back for over a week.

She grabbed the candle, shielding it as she stepped out onto the landing. The cold air rushed to meet her, amplifying as it hit the still wet parts of her body. In truth, Nollie had been a little irked that her parents hadn't shelled out for a ticket to Jamaica for her. December had been freezing and January in the Highlands was never known as sunbathing weather.

She reached the top of the staircase and looked down into the darkness. She opened her mouth to call out, but the words stuck in her throat. She began the slow descent, one step at a time, still shielding the candle. Her pulse was racing. Their house was at least a quarter of a mile from the nearest neighbour, and it wasn't an easy quarter mile. It was a slog across a peat bog with scrub grass and reeds constantly whipping at your legs. She hadn't heard a car, so whoever had pulled out that chair had arrived on foot, which sent another shiver through her.

Then, as if things couldn't become any more confusing, the sound of a child giggling drifted towards her as she reached the bottom step. *What the hell is going on?*

She paused outside the slightly ajar kitchen door. This was the only room in the house with bare floorboards, the only room where a chair could make the kind of shriek she'd heard. The child's giggle rippled once more and Nollie looked towards the candle and noticed her hand shaking like a leaf. *Am I dreaming? None of this makes sense.*

She inhaled deeply and pushed the door open, not sure what would greet her on the other side. She paused in the doorway. A cold, blue January moon lit the room and Nollie searched the shadows beyond it for anything out of the ordinary, but the kitchen was in the same state she had left it in when she'd gone for her bath. The chairs were tucked neatly under the table; there was no giggling child, nothing.

Rather than putting her mind at ease, another shudder of fear jolted through her. *This can't be happening.*

Nollie was an intelligent, caring, loving and hardworking young woman. There was no hint of past trauma in the way she carried herself. But her family and those closest to her knew what she'd been through. At twelve years old, she had watched her friend drown. Despite warnings about not playing on the frozen pond in the park, they had gone anyway. What happened after resulted in Nollie having a complete mental breakdown. She had seen and heard things that weren't there, that weren't possible. Voices and visions plagued her day and night. The hospital and the care she'd received afterwards had helped, but that didn't stop her turning to drugs in her early teens.

She walked up to the window and looked out. Her eyes scoured the blackness beyond the enclosed garden. Everything looked as she would expect it to look. She placed the candle down on the draining board and reached under the sink for one of the battery-powered lanterns. Her dad had them all over the house. Power cuts were not uncommon in winter.

She switched it on and blew out the candle. Everything seemed less scary with the bright illumination.

It was just my imagination. The earthquake or whatever it was scared me and then my mind just went into overdrive. That's what happened. Nobody moved the chair. There are no giggling kids here. It was just my imagination.

She was about to turn around and head back out when her eyes were drawn to the sink. The washing-up water had frozen over. *Jesus. It's colder than I thought in here.*

A shiver of a different kind ran through her this time and she rubbed her arms. She'd only had time to throw on a T-shirt and jeans, but the adrenaline had masked the icy climate of the house. She hadn't bothered with the range or real fire since arriving at the property, preferring the convenience of the immersion heater and the electric radiators instead. She looked across to the antique Aga. *Maybe it's about time I fired you up.*

The problem with solid fuel was that it was so messy, but the prospect of the temperature dropping further and the power being off, for God only knew how long, was enough to sway her. She started across to the giant cast iron beast when the sound of gurgling water made her whip around. She held up the lantern and glared towards the sink as a shimmer of uneasiness ran through her once more.

Glug, glug, glug, glug.
It's the pipes underneath, you idiot.

"Why the hell am I so jumpy? Because I've just experienced an earthquake in the fucking Highlands. And now I'm talking to myself. Brilliant. Well done, Nollie, you're a picture of mental health."

Glug, glug, glug, glug.

"Yeah. Glug, glug, glug to you too. Where are the matches? Let's get some heat in this place."

She started across the kitchen but stopped dead as a child's playful giggle rang out behind her. Her whole frame began to shake as she slowly turned to see nothing there. A stifled sob left her lips. *It's happening again. It's happening again.*

This was her greatest fear. *It can't happen again. I won't let it.*

A single tear trickled down her face. She remained glued to the spot in the middle of the kitchen.

"Haha, hahahaha." The child's laughter was a little louder this time. Nollie broke her statuesque pose and swung around, keeping the lantern raised high.

Nothing.

CRACK!

She rushed back over to the sink believing it to be the sound of breaking ice, but the surface of the washing up water remained frozen over and in one smooth sheet.

What's happening to me?

She placed the lantern down on the draining board and stared at her bare skin. She couldn't remember ever having goosebumps the size of these. She swivelled her arms and her heart sank in shame to see the stubborn, years-old needle tracks that refused to disappear no matter how much time passed.

Glug, glug, glug, glug.

Somehow, in the lantern light, they looked redder than they had since they were first made.

"Hahahaha." The haunting, quiet laughter brought back a memory. The memory of the morning Jessica died. Now she thought about it, the laugh sounded like Jessica's, a playful little giggle that was always a prelude to mischief.

Mischief like stealing from Mistry's newsagents. Mischief like bunking off school to head to Leicester Square. Mischief like kissing practice. In truth, Nollie had enjoyed that more than she let on. "It's just practice, so we know what we're doing when we get boyfriends," Jessica had said. But it was more to Nollie. It awakened something inside her that she still hadn't reconciled within herself and certainly never spoke about with anyone else.

They both knew they shouldn't have been on the ice. They'd been warned, and yet the lure of it was too great, the danger too exciting, the thrill of skating across it with the icy breeze fizzing against their skin too exhilarating.

CRACK!

That had been the sound that changed the course of Nollie's life. That one frozen moment in time that, through years of therapy and self-care, she'd managed to learn to live with, if not come to terms with. She only heard it in her weakest moments, but this was something else. This wasn't a memory, this was a real sound, something that filled the kitchen. Something she could almost reach out and touch.

Her eyes were drawn back from the frozen water to the red pock marks on her arms. A few of them were bleeding now.

"Oh, God! What's happening. WHAT'S HAPPENING TO ME?" she screamed as her eyes fixed on the crimson holes. "Oh, God, NO. NO. NOOO!"

She was frozen again, staring in horror at the expanding red holes. Her body started to heave with sadness and fear. *What's happening to me?*

It was as if all her childhood torments were coming back to confront her at once. Tears streamed down her cheeks as seeds of insanity long forgotten came to fruition.

"Hahahaha."

"I'm sorry, Jessica. I'm sorry."

The real root of the madness, the addiction, the insecurity, everything bad that had happened to her was caught in those two words. *I'm sorry.*

I'm sorry for daring you to go further out. I'm sorry for just standing there when the ice broke. I'm sorry for not getting help. I'm sorry for ... everything.

The angry track marks vanished as quickly as they had appeared, leaving nothing but the vague insinuations of a problem past.

Nollie sucked in a desperate breath and glanced around the kitchen. She pricked up her ears to listen for foreign sounds. The kitchen was as it should be and the night was silent but for her sobs.

Doctor Trimble said if I ever had problems, I could phone, day or night. It had been years since she had last seen him, but she had him in her contacts. *I need my phone.*

She was about to grab the lantern and head out of the kitchen when—CRACK!

She stepped forward, glaring down at the frozen water in the sink, only it wasn't the morning's dishwater murk any longer. It was the spiderweb of cracks over the pond where she had seen Jessica vanish.

"NOLLIE! HELP ME! HELP MEEE!"

She stood there, her wide eyes staring down at the ice. The temperature in the kitchen must have been minus five. *Minus five.* That evening, when she had sat at home in front of the fire with blankets covering her, with her extended family around her, all taking it in turns to cuddle her, to comfort her, the TV news had washed on and off the screen, but she remembered the weather. She remembered seeing it was minus five. *Minus five.*

She couldn't drag her eyes away from the sink, but she was convinced that if she did, she would no longer be surrounded by the kitchen but the Brixton park where her childhood friend had died.

CRACK!

Bubbles appeared beneath the ice. They were the same bubbles that she saw under her feet on that fateful morning. They were the same bubbles that squashed against that frozen barrier as her friend's hands pushed it from below, hoping to break through. They were the same bubbles that carried Jessica's tortured, drowning pleas for help as her body drifted.

"I'm sorry. I'm sorry," Nollie cried as the memories, the smells, the feel of that morning attacked her senses. "I'm sorry."

Just as quickly as the wintery apparition had appeared, it vanished once more and Nollie was left staring down at the frozen washing-up water lying still in the sink.

I need to speak to Doctor Trimble. I need to speak to him now!

A sound. Not harsh. In fact, barely audible. A whisper.

Nollie held her breath, trying hard not to sob or even breathe. *What's it saying?*

She turned her head to look at the drain overflow in the sink and moved in closer. *It's coming from here.*

As insane as that sounded, it was true. The whisper echoed through the pipework, but still it was impossible to hear the words. She moved nearer, leaning right over the large, ceramic antique sink until her chin almost touched the frozen contents.

Finally, the hushed words became clearer. "You could have saved me. You could have saved me. You could have saved me, Nollie."

A breath caught in the back of Nollie's throat as she jolted up a little. Her eyes stared at the overflow, knowing what she was hearing, what she was experiencing was not possible. "This isn't real," she announced, desperately trying to convince herself.

Bony, grasping, claw-like hands suddenly burst through the ice, followed by the pallid face and upper body of her best friend from childhood. Jessica hooked her fingers into the back of Nollie's head, digging her nails in deep. All Nollie could do was stare wide-eyed, no matter how much she wanted to pull away.

"You could have saved me, Nollie." It wasn't her friend's voice who spoke this time. It was deep. Deep and slow, a man's voice played at half speed. No, not a man, something else.

It was clearly her friend's face, but it was grey, almost as if the universe's colour stopped when it reached her skin.

"This isn't happening. This can't be happening," Nollie sobbed.

"What's wrong?" It was Jessica's voice again, and now there was that old blue sparkle back in her eyes. "What's wrong, Nollie?"

"You're dead. This isn't happening."

Jessica's body had risen out of the sink up to her waist and now it was adorned with the familiar white blouse and striped purple tie of Smeaton Grammar. The colour had returned to her skin and the painful grip on the back of Nollie's head had eased.

"I thought you'd be happy to see me." Her voice was full of sadness and her eyes mirrored it.

"No. This isn't right."

Jessica withdrew one of her hands from the back of Nollie's head and suddenly ripped her blouse open. "How about now, Nol? You happy to see me now?" she asked as a menacing smile formed on her face. She grabbed Nollie's hand and placed it on her left breast. "Huh? You happy to see me now?"

When Jessica spoke again, two voices came out of her mouth at the same time, hers and the deep, threatening male voice from before. "Come on, Nol. Let's practice-kiss." Jessica reached around, grasping her friend's head in both hands once more, pulling her face towards her.

Nollie tried to struggle, but it was impossible. With each millimetre she was dragged, a little more colour drained away from Jessica's face until it became the same ghostly grey hue it had been on first appearance.

Jessica's mouth opened and a wave of decay and putridity assaulted Nollie's senses. She gagged a little as she continued to struggle, desperate to pull back. Then Jessica extended her tongue, pink, sensual, the only thing that broke the ghostly monochrome horror show playing out in slow motion. It lightly danced over her lips, hypnotising Nollie, pulling her attention away from the chilling grey eyes and pallid skin that had painted her friend's features.

In less than a heartbeat, the tongue turned black, extending forward like a thick, slimy worm. "Please, no," Nollie cried with fear-filled tears running rivers down her face.

"Please, yes." Not Jessica's voice. Not coming out of her mouth. The man's voice … or whatever it was. Deep. Menacing. Devilish. Followed by an echoing laugh that reverberated around the old kitchen.

Jessica's tongue continued to snake towards Nollie as their faces drew nearer. Nollie looked into her friend's eyes once more, but there was no trace of her childhood companion. The eerie grey orbs bore hateful black pinpricks in their centre, piercing whatever thin shield of sanity their victim tried to hold on to. A small hole suddenly appeared in Jessica's cheek, then another on the opposite side. Then another and another, and one by one, they gave birth to shining, thick ebony centipedes crawling out of the grey flesh and across Jessica's face.

"NOO—" Nollie's wail was cut short as the black, serpentine tongue entered her open mouth, slithering down her throat. Her eyes widened, threatening to pop out of her head as Jessica's malevolent gaze froze her. She couldn't breathe. She couldn't do anything other than feel—feel the blackness enter her body. The tongue was like ice, chilling every cell it touched as it wriggled down, down, down.

She wanted to cry. She wanted to scream. She wanted to run and run and run until she was a world away from this kitchen. Then, as she felt the centipedes touching her face and starting to burrow into her skin, she wanted to die. She wanted to die more than at any other time in her life to stop this suffering.

Jessica released her grip, but it didn't matter. Her tongue was inside Nollie, pulling her forever closer. Then

Jessica began to retreat back down into the sink, dragging Nollie with her. No matter how much her victim struggled, it was hopeless.

Nollie slapped her hands out, one on the draining board and one on the sturdy butcher block countertop, but it was no good. That did not stop her breathless descent as she continued to be pulled down. The fear, the pain of being explored by the hellish black thing probing her insides, the terror of the writhing insects drilling into her flesh, was like nothing she could ever have imagined. Her body fell forward, unable to battle any longer as the horror jolting through her every fibre exhausted her.

She didn't understand how she was still conscious. *Please, God, take me now.*

Almost as if her silent prayer had been heard, the menacing laughter echoed around the kitchen. Jessica's wild, hellish eyes submerged, her tongue continuing to pull her friend down with her. Then the icy water tore at Nollie's face, heightening the centipedes' enthusiastic burrowing.

She couldn't scream, but half a lungful of tortured air erupted from her nose as she felt one of the tubular insects begin to dig up through her right eye. Her entire body began to convulse. It wasn't the water that was drowning her but the blackness. Like the devil's ink, it spread through her body into her lungs, replacing her blood with its icy malevolence.

The laughter peeled once more before her ears disappeared beneath the surface of the water. Now the only sound she could hear was that of her own retching, gagging and suffering. The suffering. The suffering. The suffering.

Nollie fell still. So did the insects, so did the water. The tongue withdrew from her body and Jessica faded, sinking into depths that weren't there. The kitchen became silent, but it was too late. Nollie couldn't take a final breath, but a single thought flashed into her mind.

You can't run away from your demons.

3

Levon Stoll, Lev to most who knew him, lay on the floor out of breath. He'd pulled the plug out of the wall with such force, such speed, that he was amazed he hadn't dislocated his shoulder.

He'd thought the eight-millimetre video that arrived earlier in the day would be a nice trip down memory lane. It was certainly a trip, but not the kind he'd hoped for.

He'd dug out his old Sony camcorder; knowing full well the battery would have died a long time ago, he'd plugged it in, hooked it up to the TV and pressed play. The tape wasn't fully rewound, but he'd just have to be patient. The rewind button broke a long time ago, but when the tape reached the end, it would reverse back to the beginning and he'd be able to watch whatever he'd missed.

Expecting a journey back to the glory days, someone was always recording something in the studio, he'd headed over to the small corner bar where he kept a 1991 Teeling single malt for special occasions.

He looked across to the TV, expecting the tape to have started playing, but suddenly realised he hadn't selected the AV channel.

He hit the source button on the remote and started to pour when a wall of sound washed over him. Although familiar, it was not the one he'd expected or hoped. In fact, it was the last thing he ever wanted to hear.

The subsequent quake that rumbled told him exactly what this was and he had dropped his glass and almost flown across the room. He hoped that he'd managed to stop the tape before too much damage was done, but in his heart, he knew it was too late.

He looked at the end of the cord and suddenly realised that he hadn't pulled the plug out at all. In fact, he'd heaved the wires out of the plug. He flipped over onto his back and looked up at the ceiling light as a small moth circled it. It flickered once, twice before extinguishing and throwing the room into darkness but for the faint orange glow of a joss stick tip.

If I'd left it running, I'd have still had power. Nothing's surer.

The thought sounded both paranoid and a little insane as it formed in his head but he knew it to be true. He knew what this recording was, he knew what it represented. He knew what it did.

Lev sat up, feeling his way across the carpet until he reached his desk. His fingers followed the lip of the surface until he found the top drawer. He opened it and pulled out the matches. He struck one and gasped as a face, seemingly suspended in mid-air, stared back at him. It was pale, unnaturally so. Its eyes, dark, almost black, were sunk deep in the sockets of its head as it stared straight towards him.

He'd seen this face many times before. He knew it to be both real and imaginary. A face born of his darkest hours, his darkest fears, his deepest guilt, his deepest regrets.

It was a satanic depiction from a horror movie. It had haunted both dreams and waking hours for the longest time when he was younger. He'd snuck out with friends to see it against his parents' orders. His father was waiting for him outside the cinema when it finished. It was both humiliating and terrifying because Lev knew that strict punishment would follow. The car journey home was silent until the world-ending cacophony when a lorry ploughed into their vehicle. Lev was out of the hospital two days later. His father was dead on arrival and that eerie creation by a movie make-up artist became something very real for the longest time. It followed him around, making him believe that there was such a place as Hell and there were such things as demons, until, finally, he got the help he needed and the unholy apparition disappeared.

He'd seen it again, thirty-three years ago, over a period of a few days. Then it had vanished, until now, until this moment. And here it was in all its diabolical glory, a face of fiction staring at him in the orange glow of a match. The symbol of his guilt, his fear, his self-loathing. Real and not real at the same time. But….

It's real. He'd come to the conclusion long ago, no matter how much he reasoned, no matter how much therapy he received. But he'd found a way to beat it other than the hiccup—the unleashing.

The flame slowly eased its way up the matchstick as the shark smile on the figure's face became a gritted-toothed grimace then a snarl. There was no mistaking where this thing had come from. There was no mistaking its intent. There was no mistaking why it was here now.

"Fuck you!" Lev hissed, grabbing a candle and lighting it. Giving in to the fear wouldn't help him answer the questions bouncing around his head. When he was younger, the face had tried to wear him down, tried to take control, but somehow Lev had fought back. The love for his mother had kept him strong despite his fear.

This thing thrived on fear, fed on fear. But Lev had conquered it. For the longest time, he thought he was the only one who'd experienced such a thing, but when the unleashing came, he learned differently.

"Fuck you," he repeated, lighting another candle and flicking on a lantern. He didn't know how long the power would be out, but he knew it was pointless checking the fuse box. This outage had a very different cause, and this was the Highlands of Scotland, so it wasn't as if he didn't keep plenty of supplies on hand for such an event.

He clenched his eyes shut tight, and when he opened them, the face was gone, but a faint laugh that sounded like it came from the walls themselves rattled on for several seconds.

Lev slumped down into his chair and sat for a moment, staring at the candles.

He picked up the lantern and walked back across to the bar, snatching up the glass from the floor, pouring another drink, taking a swig then heading across to the desk. He sat down, his skin still bristling. He sheepishly glanced around the room, searching out every corner, looking for the face, but it was gone, for the time being anyway. He knew it would be back.

He turned to the camcorder then picked up the envelope the tape had arrived in. The return address in the top-left corner was scratched, faded and hard to make out. When the eight-millimetre cassette had fallen out, he had simply assumed it had been sent by Jodie or one of the gang from the Blazetrailer glory days. There were always a dozen cameras rolling in the studios and the very fact that this was a cassette told him it was from a different time.

Now he examined it all in closer detail, he reached into the thick padded envelope and found a Post-it note. It had probably been stuck to the actual tape but at some stage had become detached and stuck itself to the inside lining. It simply read, "She wanted you to have this."

He squinted at the return address once more and a flash of recognition sent a shiver down his back.

While Blazetrailer were on an extended hiatus and Lev was going through an expensive divorce, he had been desperate to work to get some extra cash. He had reached out to Jamie Garroway, the band's former guitarist, who left under a cloud, to see if he knew anyone who needed a sound engineer or even a session musician. Lev had recorded more than a few of Jamie's parts when the iconic guitarist had been too stoned to do so. Jamie had almost seemed giddy to hear from him. He knew of an opportunity and Lev was the perfect guy to help it get off the ground. The job was as a sound recordist for some cheesy ghost hunter documentary, but it was work and they had been through a lot together. Jamie was only too happy to help his old friend.

*

THEN

1991

"So, how are you enjoying your first day?" Anna, the director, asked in her warm Texas drawl. She'd done everything she could to make Lev feel like part of the team. She'd got the rundown of who he was and some of his many achievements. He'd also been honest about why he needed the work so desperately, citing his divorce and crippling legal bills as his driving force.

Lev smiled. "Work's work. Just happy to get the gig."

"FYI, I love Blazetrailer." She winked and a warm smile lit her face.

Lev nodded appreciatively. "They're a special band."

"Yes, they are. They've got a kick-ass sound guy too. And I find it hard to believe he couldn't get work in the industry rather than slumming it with us."

Lev smiled again. "I don't have a lot of friends in the biz. Pissed too many people off. I'm just lucky Jodie and the guys are in my corner."

"Jodie Starr is a pretty big name to have in your corner."

"She certainly is."

"She couldn't get you anything?"

"I didn't ask."

A puzzled expression crept onto Anna's face. "Sounds like there's a story there."

"Yep."

"I wonder how many drinks it's going to take to get that out of you."

Lev laughed as they came to a stop at the boundary of the property, which was due to be the location for the first episode of *The Haunted and the Hallowed*.

They'd left the rest of the production team back at the hotel. Work didn't officially start until the next day, but Anna and Lev were both keen to scout the location.

"Looks creepy as fuck," Lev muttered.

"Yeah. There was a reason Jamie wanted this place to be the star of the first show."

"What?"

"Jamie's been into this stuff for the longest time. Surely you knew that better than anyone."

"I didn't realise Jamie had anything to do with this. I know he helped me get the gig, but I thought he was just pulling in a favour."

Anna shook her head. "No. He's a major shareholder in Occulture Productions."

Lev raised an eyebrow. "I mean, I knew he was interested in this stuff … more than interested."

"Yeah. Didn't it lead to a bust-up in the band or something?"

Lev wasn't someone who dished dirt. He could tell a thousand stories, but he'd take them all to his grave. "It was always a complicated dynamic in Blazetrailer."

Anna laughed. "Oh, man. You have some gift for understatement. I don't care how tight-lipped you are right now; when we have the rap party for this series, I'm going to get something out of you one way or another." She winked playfully and unlatched the rusted chain link gate.

The expansive property had become known as the Demon House by some. It was a big white wooden building with forest to the sides and rear and a lake at the front. The dwelling itself was a mere shadow of what it once had been. Much of the paint had flaked away. Some of the windows had been broken on the dares of teenagers. But it was obvious why someone had wanted to build it.

"Pretty impressive setting," Lev said as he followed Anna through the gate. They'd had to leave the van at the bottom of the drive due to a fallen tree. It had been a long, long time since anyone had been here, and moving the remains of a giant redwood would not be a priority for anyone.

"It's beautiful," Anna said as they both looked across the lake. "Hard to believe the stuff that happened here."

"I read the notes. Being from the other side of the ocean, it never made the news over there, but I'm guessing it did over here."

"How fucking old do you think I am?" They both laughed. "The last time anyone lived in this place, I was a kid. I never used to watch the news, but when I started researching, it's like it's cursed or damned or something."

"You don't believe in stuff like that, do you?"

"No. I don't think."

"You don't think?"

She turned to look at him. "The more I read the more questions it raised."

"Like what?"

"The voices. The visions. I mean, sure, one person or even a couple of suggestible people hearing and seeing things can be written off. But…." She shook her head, a little afraid to give the wrong impression to her new sound man. She had a past that few people would understand. But it was the past and that's where she wanted it to stay.

"But what?"

"This place opened as a guest house in 1954. There were three accidental"—she gestured speech marks around the word—"deaths of the guests on the lake in the first two months."

"But that could be just co—"

"I spoke to a journalist who researched the story for a book he was writing. Of all the guests who stayed at the property, there were a statistically anomalous number of deaths. Suicides, car crashes, falls, electrocution, asphyxiation, the list goes on."

"Okay. That's a little odd."

"A little odd? Many of the people he interviewed spoke about experiencing strange feelings while they were here. They hadn't experienced the visions or heard the voices that others said they had, but nevertheless, they felt something wasn't right."

"Yeah, but didn't they find that the well where the place got its water from had dangerously high concentrations of mercury? I read it was something to do with an old pesticide factory that ended up getting closed down."

"Yeah. I read those notes too, and y'know, that may have accounted for some of it. It may have accounted for some of the visions and the voices and that kind of shit. Hell, it might even have accounted for Carlton Black murdering his entire family and the guest house staff. But eighteen years later, when the Church of Pure Enlightenment bought the place, the house was hooked up to the town's water supply. Nursette Chemicals had gone out of business seven years before and the lake had been cleaned up. So, that kind of blows that theory to hell with what happened next, don't you think?"

"Well...."

The two remained standing shoulder to shoulder almost, taking in the house and the view as they spoke like old friends. "Well, what?"

Lev exhaled. "The Church of Pure Enlightenment wasn't so much a church than a cult from what I read."

"And this makes a difference how?"

"They're already going to have been easily suggestible. I mean, people like that are looking to be led, are looking for someone to give them the answers. They're slightly damaged goods to start off with."

"And that accounts for what happened?"

"They wouldn't be the first end-of-the-world cult to commit mass suicide."

"No. I mean the six months leading up to it."

"I didn't see that in the notes."

"It's because it wasn't. That journalist I spoke to tracked down a girl, well, a woman. Lydia Branchette. Her parents owned the Branchette drugstore chain. Anyway, they had her kidnapped back from the Church of Pure Enlightenment and deprogrammed. Apparently, it took some doing, but it was worth it considering what happened to the rest of the members. They lasted six months there and she got out a few weeks before the end. She told the journalist of how a few of her friends had seen and heard things. She said the place felt evil. She said the head of the church, Ezekiel Wight, was convinced that the property was built above the gates of Hell and they were doing the Lord's work by stopping the occupants escaping."

"Uh-huh. You're not building a very strong case for your argument," Lev replied. "A bunch of nut jobs said they saw and heard things and the head nut job said the place was built above the gates of Hell."

"Not my argument," Anna replied, shrugging. "Just saying it makes a good story worth—"

"Putting a haunted house spin on to get viewers?"

Anna grinned. "Your pal seems to think it's worth exploring anyway."

Lev nodded slowly. "Jamie's always been a bit obsessed by this stuff. It's what caused…." He trailed off, realising he'd let his guard down.

Anna reached across and squeezed his arm. "See. I told you I'd weaken your defences. Come on, let's go check the place out." They began walking down the steps.

"This is private property," called out a voice from behind.

They both turned suddenly to see a sheriff standing there. She was about five feet six, with wavy, blonde, shoulder-length hair that had been tied back. She wore sunglasses and stood at the open gate with her thumbs hooked around her belt.

"We were given permission," Anna said, digging into her shoulder bag for a piece of paper as she and Lev retraced their steps. The sheriff remained unmoved for a moment, finally accepting the sheet that was handed to her.

"Son of a bitch," she hissed before spitting out a piece of gum and lowering her glasses to look over the top. "I wasn't told about this."

"I'm sorry," Anna said. "I wasn't involved in the process of getting permission. I assumed everyone who needed to be informed had been informed."

The sheriff shook her head. "You're making a big assumption there. You have no idea what a useless sack of shit our town mayor really is."

Anna chuckled, as did Lev. "Not a fan then?" Lev replied.

"You figured that out?" She let out a long sigh. "Well, you know what they say. You can't choose your relatives."

"You're related?"

"He's my brother."

"That must make conversation around the dinner table fun."

"I'd have taken my own life a long time ago if I had to share a dinner table with the son of a bitch. I'd probably have taken his, too, now I come to think of it." Her audience of two chuckled again.

"So, we're okay to be here?" Anna asked, reaching out to take the piece of paper back.

"You've got permission. Being okay to be here is something different."

"I don't follow you."

The sheriff looked towards the large white building and an involuntary shudder ran through her. "Look. You seem like nice folks. Come back to town with me. I'll buy you a coffee. Hell, I'll buy you breakfast. Just don't go in there."

"Is this part of the routine for tourists?" Lev asked with half a smile on his face.

The sheriff took her glasses off and stared him straight in the eyes. "Mister. Do I strike you as the kind of person who'd put a show on for tourists?"

He returned her look, surprised by the warmth of her eyes, surprised even more by the little tingling flutter he felt realising she looked a little like his first girlfriend. "I can live in hope," he replied and an embarrassed smile broke her steely gaze and she looked away.

She let out a long breath. "Listen to me. I'm not some inbred hick who wonders where the sun goes on a night. I don't think the world's four thousand years old and I don't believe Jesus is coming back to save us all. I believe there's a god. Growing up in a town like this, it's impossible not to." She gestured over her shoulder to the gate behind her. "But he stops back there. He's never set foot in here and that's my suggestion to you now. Leave this place and never set foot in here again."

"You don't think the story surrounding the house needs to be told?"

An uncomfortable laugh left the sheriff's lips. "Definitely not."

"Now you've got me intrigued," Lev said.

"Why?" the sheriff asked.

"Well, obviously you're an intelligent woman. You don't seem like the type of person who's easily scared. What happened to you here?"

She placed her glasses in her top pocket and put her hands on her hips. "I don't know is the truth."

"What does that mean?"

"It means teenagers do some dumb-ass things on dares."

"So, what happened?"

"I'll make you a deal. You forget about this project of yours," she said, pointing to the piece of paper still in Anna's hand, "and I'll tell you all about it."

"Um … Sheriff?" There was an inflexion in Anne's voice as if she wanted the other woman to finish her sentence.

"Tanner. Sheriff Tanner."

"As much as I'd love your story, I really can't do that. We've got a TV show to make."

The sheriff let out another long sigh and nodded sadly. She retrieved her glasses, flicking them open and putting them on in one smooth movement. "Well. I tried."

"You could come in with us if you're worried about our safety," Lev said.

The sheriff looked him up and down. "Let me tell you, hun. If it was Patrick Swayze heading into that place, there's still no way I'd go in."

"And now you've hurt my feelings."

The sheriff shrugged. "Don't get me wrong. You're cute. But not going in there cute." She turned and headed back through the gate, closing it behind her and keeping her fingers weaved through the chain links for a moment. "I'll sweep by tonight. If your vehicle's still here, I'll make sure it's towed back to town for you."

"We won't be here that long," Anna replied.

"Keep telling yourself that," Sheriff Tanner answered before turning to leave.

4

Lev and Anna stood with bewildered smiles on their faces for a moment as they watched the sheriff disappear out of sight. "Is that what they call Southern hospitality?" Lev asked.

Anna chuckled. "You could come with us if you're worried about our safety?" She laughed again. "Could you have flirted any harder?"

"FYI. That wasn't me flirting. When I'm flirting, you'll know about it."

"What was it then?"

"Getting someone else to help with this gear. It weighs a fucking tonne."

"I thought you Brits were meant to be tough and chivalrous."

"Yeah. I think you're mixing me up with a knight from the Middle Ages. I'm all for women's lib and it starts by not carrying all these fucking bags."

"Wow! And the mystery deepens as to how your wife let you get away."

"I know, right? I mean, what the hell was she thinking?"

"Pass one over here."

Lev flicked one of the bags from his shoulder and handed it across.

"Jesus! What's in this?"

"The batteries."

"For what, a submarine?"

He gently ran his fingers over another of the bags. "My baby."

"Your baby?"

"You'll see when we get in there."

The pair continued down, walking around the building to the front stoop. The steps up to the porch creaked a little underfoot and they both paused to take a look out across the lake.

"It's really something, isn't it?" Anna said.

"Hard to believe no one's bought this place and done it up."

"Are you serious? With everything that's happened here? Plus, it's not for sale. Ezekiel Wight's family sold it to the town after everything went down, and from what I understand, it's going to be left to rot like this until the end of time. Hence the chain link fence."

"Such a waste."

"Oh yeah. My thoughts exactly. So many people living on the streets in this country, why not free up a cursed demon house for them to hole up in?"

"Again with the curse."

Anna smiled. "Whatever went on here, it certainly had your blushing little sheriff rattled."

"She's not my sheriff."

"Uh-huh. The way she looked you up and down was priceless."

"Y'know, some women do find me attractive."

"I'm sure they do. Cute even," she replied, sniggering again.

"I wish I'd given you a heavier bag now."

"There are heavier ones than this?"

"Yeah. But I was being chivalrous and shit."

"Well, Sir Lancelot. Thank you for that. Shall we head in?"

The pair took one last look across the lake before entering. "They just leave it open? No key or anything?" Lev asked as Anna closed the door behind them.

"Who'd have thunk it?"

Despite the chipped white paint, and the dents and cracks where a hundred bottles and stones had been flung at the door by local teenagers, it had lost none of its integrity. It closed with an echoing clunk that reverberated around the small foyer. "Baffling how this place didn't win a Guesthouse of the Year award or something. It just screams home away from home."

They walked across to the mahogany reception desk and unshouldered all their kit. Lev unzipped one of the bags, pulling out a custom-built machine, which he carefully strapped over his neck and shoulder. "Looks like a small video recorder," Anna said.

"Yeah. I much prefer videotape for sound recording when I'm on location. So, I built this little baby," he said, plugging in the telescopic boom mike, another of his creations.

"On location? I thought you were a studio guy."

"When Blazetrailer recorded the *Sounds Like Hell* album, Jamie sent me all over the place to record interviews, rituals, even an active volcano. I'd hop straight off one plane and get on another. Sound trucks weren't an option and I wasn't happy with the portable machines that were on the market, so I built my own." Anna smiled. "What? What have I said?"

"I heard you were a bit of a savant when it came to this kind of stuff."

Lev shrugged, a little embarrassed. "I don't know about that. I just love what I do and I try to do it to the best of my ability."

Anna reached into her shoulder bag and withdrew a Sony CCD V800 camcorder. "This is my baby."

"Wow. They cost a few bob."

"A few what?"

Lev laughed. "Sorry. A few shillings. They're expensive."

"Yeah, well. I feel the same way about my work as you. I take Lily with me—"

"Wait, you named your camera?"

"Sure. Why not? I name everything that's precious."

Lev's eyebrows arched. "Suddenly, my mind's awash with questions."

Anna laughed and she shook her head. "I call my old VW camper Mrs Pettingrew."

"What?"

"It's a long story."

"I guess it would be."

"Anyway. That's for another time." She lifted the camcorder up and angled the viewfinder. "Whenever I'm checking out a location, I like to take this with me. I'll run a playback in my hotel room tonight and figure out the order of filming for us tomorrow."

Lev nodded. "I just wanted to take recordings in a few rooms. See where we're going to get the best acoustics for our star presenter." A smirk immediately curled the corner of his mouth.

"You have a problem with Fifi?"

The smirk broadened into a grin. "Not at all. I'm sure she's more than qualified."

"I sense a hint of sarcasm in your voice."

"Nope. I'm sure she got onto the shortlist on her own merits and completely aced the screen test."

"Just so you know, she'd already been chosen before I came on board."

Lev's brow creased a little. "I don't understand. I thought this was your baby."

"It is to an extent, but some of the choices had already been made before I was approached. Granted, two of them mysteriously dropped out when they heard where we were coming for the first episode."

"Dun, dun, duuuuun!" Lev emulated the dramatic horror movie music before another wide grin lit his face.

"And still you're making fun."

"Look. I've had some weird shit happen to me in the past. But a house is just a house is just a house. What people see or hear is down to them. Y'know, that's not to say it doesn't seem real or they're making it up. But at the end of the day"—he knocked on the sturdy wooden reception counter—"this is real." He pointed to his head. "And you can't always say the same about what comes from in here."

"Okay. Now you've got me fascinated."

"What can I tell you? I'm a fascinating guy."

"Well, Mr Fascinating. Shall we get to it?"

"Yeah, let me just strap on my lead weights and we'll be good to go." He picked up the battery pack, slinging it over his other shoulder and hooked it up to the recorder.

"Y'know, one day, they're going to have machines that can do that and they'll be no bigger than the palm of your hand."

"Yeah, right." They started up the staircase, each one creaking a little more than the last. "Okay. Actually, can we get this on tape? It'll be a good stock sound if we want some overdubs or creepy shit to throw in."

"Oh, okay. Good call," Anna replied, delighted at how quickly Lev had flipped into pro mode.

"Yeah. If we can just start back down at the bottom, I'll record you heading up to the first flight."

"Are you saying that I make the boards creak louder than you?"

"Not having a death wish, I would never say that to a lady."

Anna smiled as Lev raised the boom and pushed the record button. He nodded and Anna started up the staircase once more, raising her video camera.

Creak! Creak! Creak! She climbed step after step and the boom followed her as far as it could before she ascended to a level beyond its reach. She continued up to the first landing and stopped, turning around to see Lev with his headphones on and still monitoring the sound readout with another small custom monitor he'd built.

I like this guy. He's class.

Lev pressed pause, retracted the boom and started up the stairs after her. "There are twelve rooms in all up here," Anna announced.

"Well, you're the boss. I follow your lead."

They both walked up the second flight to the U-shaped landing. "Well. The front of the house faces west over the lake, and the sides and rear are surrounded by woodland, so, as far as natural light goes, we're probably better off filming in the west-facing rooms from late morning onwards. There's no electricity running to the place, and the only genny we could get hold of was a small one, so it's going to take Tim—"

"Tim?"

"Our DP, director of photography."

"Ah. The tall guy who looks about twelve?"

Anna smiled. "Actually, he's thirty-three and I've worked with him a dozen times before. He's a hell of a cameraman and I virtually had to beg him to come with me on this project. He read up on the place and he is beyond freaked out."

"Cameraman? I thought you said he was your DP."

"He is ... kind of. I had to offer him a pay bump, an assistant and a DP credit to get him to come."

"Shit. I should have held out for an assistant so I didn't have to lug all this shit around."

"Come on. Let's check out the main bedroom."

"Words every man wants to hear."

They walked around the landing, observing the chipped and peeled paint on the supporting spindles of the balustrade. "This place would have been quite something in its day."

"Absolutely. Come for the view, stay for the mercury poisoning. Act now and get two-for-one funerals when you lose your mind and butcher your family in their sleep."

"Wow. And the mystery deepens as to how such a caring guy hasn't been snapped up already."

"What can I tell you? There are lots of women out there with no sense of humour."

"Sure. I mean, what isn't there to find funny about a guy stabbing his children to death?"

"I know, right?"

Anna shook her head and opened the door. The hinges creaked loudly as it moved inwards. "You want that?" she asked, turning to Lev.

"You read my mind." She closed the door and stepped back out of the room while Lev put his headphones on, raised the boom and hit the pause button, resuming the recording.

Anna turned the handle once again and the door creaked inwards. She turned to look at him, but his eyes were cast down to the dial of his monitor. She stepped into the room, the heels of her boot clacking against the solid wood floor. When she reached the well-worn rug, she turned. "That okay?"

"Nice. Thanks." He followed her into the room.

"I like this view of the lake. This is going to be a good room to film so we can get the contrast between what's up here and what's in the basement."

"We haven't even seen the basement yet. It could be like a funfair down there for all we know."

"I've never been to the UK, but I think you and I might have different ideas about what a funfair should be."

The pair shared another smile. "Okay," Lev said. "If we're going to be recording in here, let's see what we've got." He raised the boom well above his head so it would be out of camera shot and hit the pause button once more.

"Err … what do you want me to say?"

"Whatever you want. I just want to check levels and make sure we're getting a clean, crisp sound."

"Okay. Um." She laughed uncomfortably. "Shit. What a time to be lost for words."

"Just say anything. Tell me how you got the gig."

"Okay. Well, I just finished working on a miniseries for ABC as an AD and I got a call from Tom Pennet, who I used to work with, wanting me to interview for this. I went down and met a couple of the other producers. They seemed to like me, and we got on, but I think what sold it for me was this thing that happened when I was younger. I used to suffer from the most horrific night terrors. I was actually part of a medical study. They happened from about the age of fifteen to seventeen and it was like the most terrifying thing that ever happened to me." That wasn't true. The true cause of the night terrors was the most frightening thing that had ever happened to her, but these were the residue that needed managing or they would plague her for the rest of her life. She liked Lev, but she wasn't prepared to share what had happened with him or anyone outside her family. Those events were buried, never to be dug up.

Lev lowered the boom and pressed pause on the recorder then slipped the phones off his head. "Now, you've got to tell me about that."

She gave a brief shake of her head. "I don't really like talking about it. I don't know what made me tell them. I suppose I wanted to sound a little more interesting than I was."

"So, now it's me wondering how many drinks I need to ply you with tonight."

She looked at him with no hint of a smile. "Seriously. I'm scared that talking about it might make it all start again. Trust me. I know what you must think of me for saying that, but I'd really prefer not to discuss it."

Lev knew only too well. He had confided his strange childhood experiences to just a handful of people, and each time, nerves had fluttered in his stomach, fearful of whether the admission would result in a reoccurrence of the horror he had suffered.

He reached out, placing a comforting hand on Anna's arm. "It's okay. I didn't mean to upset you. I was just pulling your leg a little."

"Sorry. You must think I'm a real weirdo now."

"Hey. We've all got things in our past that we don't like to think about."

"I suppose."

"Suppose nothing. Everyone has stuff that freaks them out, Anna."

"Thanks, Lev," she said, briefly placing a hand on top of his before shrugging it off. "How are the levels in here?" *Back to business.*

"We're good. We're here four days, so I'm going to construct a makeshift sound booth in my room back at the digs so we can do overdubs of anything we're not happy with."

Anna laughed. "You know, we will be taking all the material back to the studio for mastering. We can do any overdubs there."

"We're pretty much going to be on the road for the next month. It's easy to forget stuff. It's easy to mix memories. I'd like to get as much material as we can on an ongoing basis."

"Okay. But how are you going to build a makeshift sound booth, exactly?"

Lev smiled. "Do you know how many vocal tracks Jodie recorded in duvet forts?"

"What?"

"Before she came on board, the band wasn't really going anywhere. The record company gave them virtual pennies for the budget for the second album. When we came out of the recording sessions, about half the vocal tracks were unusable. Jodie was devastated. There wasn't any money for more studio time, so I built a small wooden frame, borrowed a load of duvets and hey presto. That was our sound booth."

"You're serious?"

"I'm serious."

"But her vocals on that album sound amazing."

"Necessity is the mother of invention."

"Evidently. But there's part of me that's just wondering if it's an excuse to get Fifi in a little duvet cave with you."

Lev laughed. "Really not my type."

"Come on. Let's check out the rest of the place."

They surveyed each of the first-floor rooms, checking the sound in just one other, but it was obvious that the main bedroom was the optimum location for the presentation of the upper floor of the dwelling. They headed back down the staircase.

"Where first?" Lev asked.

"Good question," Anna replied. She pulled out her notes and looked along the narrow hallway that ran parallel to the staircase. "That door leads to the quarters of the Black family. That's where…." Her words trailed off.

"That's where he hacked his family up into little pieces and then slit his own throat ear to ear?"

"Jesus, Lev. Don't you have any compassion? This was horrible. A young family being murdered like this by their own father."

Lev shrugged. "Stuff like this happens all the time. It's not that I don't feel sorry for the victims; it's just that it was decades ago and, y'know, what are you going to do?"

"How about showing a little more respect for the dead?"

"Well, sure … if you think that will help them."

"You're an ass."

Lev smiled. "So, it's through here, anyway?" He started walking down the corridor and Anna raised her camera, filming him, picturing Fifi taking the same steps, opening the same door.

He turned the handle, pulling the oaken slab from the jamb. "Did anything else happen here?" he asked. "Y'know, when the Church of Light and Bullshit moved in."

"The Church of Pure Enlightenment?"

"That's them."

"No. That all happened in the basement."

Anna followed him down the corridor and into the short hall beyond the entrance. They walked side by side, stopping at the first room, and she checked her notes again. She raised her camera and panned it around. "We're going to need footage of each of these rooms."

"Okay." One by one, Lev recorded Anna speaking, checking the levels and listening carefully through the headphones for anything that inhibited a clean sound.

After the final recording in the bedroom of Carlton Black and his wife, Martha, she lowered her video camera and looked out of the window to the woodland at the back.

"Such a beautiful setting. So much heartache."

"I don't want to sound insensitive," Lev began.

"Oh yeah, since when?"

He smiled before he continued. "But this isn't the place I thought it was going to be."

"What do you mean?"

He pulled the headphones off, letting them rest around his neck. "I mean, I stayed at a hotel in the Highlands that was meant to be one of the most haunted places in the UK. I didn't see anything. I didn't hear anything. But there was a vibe that was probably the source of what a lot of people manufactured in their own minds."

"What do you mean?"

"I mean there was an eeriness to the place. An electricity that made the hairs on your arm stand up in certain parts of the hotel."

"How can you be so certain that there wasn't a presence, that it wasn't haunted?"

"What was it the sheriff said? Because I'm not someone who wonders where the sun disappears to on a night. Everything's got an answer in science, whether it's chemicals in the brain creating an illusion, bad wiring behind a wall that screws up your nervous impulses, or air trapped in pipes making ghostly moaning sounds. There's always an answer if you look hard enough, but that doesn't stop a place from having a weird vibe.

"But I'm getting nothing here. This is just an old house that used to be beautiful but has become a little bit more dilapidated with each year that's passed. Some terrible and remarkably sad things happened here, but it all started with mercury poisoning, and whether that led to paranoid delusion and mass hysteria is something for the doctors and scientists to figure out. But this place is nothing more than wood and nails."

Anna stared at him for a moment. "Remind me not to have you in on the creative meetings when we're brainstorming for an ad to promo the series. Jeez. Way to sap the fun out of my job in twenty seconds."

"Sorry. I'm just saying, I'm not feeling anything."

"Yeah. Me neither," Anna replied sadly.

They both looked around the spacious master bedroom. "We could always splash some fake blood on the walls and say it appeared when we started filming."

"Y'know, the problem is I don't know if you're joking or not."

"Oh, I get it. You can't say outright for legal reasons. Okay, just shake your head and roll your eyes disapprovingly if you want me to sort it." She let out a long sigh and closed her eyes. "That'll do. Consider it done."

Anna started giggling. "You are such an ass. When they made me get rid of my usual sound guy to bring you on board, I wasn't too pleased, but—"

"Wait. What did you say?"

Anna's eyes widened. "Shit. I wasn't meant to say that. Please forget I said that."

"Jamie told me that he knew someone who was desperate for a sound guy and he put my name forward." Anna remained silent. "Come on. We've got on pretty well up 'til now. Please tell me what's going on."

"I'll tell you if you promise this doesn't go back to anyone. Please. It would cause a lot of problems for me. Do you know how long it takes for a woman to get to the position I'm at in this business? I've got good relationships with these people; if they thought I'd betrayed their trust, it would—"

"Okay, okay. I promise. I don't want to cause you any problems. But please tell me how this went down."

Anna perched on the long windowsill. Lev unhooked the mike, removed his cans and sat down beside her. "We were all set to roll. The original start date was two weeks ago. Then Jamie put a call into my boss and said you were going to be free and he wanted you, no matter what."

"Shit. I'm sorry. I didn't want to push someone else out of a job."

"Billy's good but young and he wouldn't be out with me on a scout like this. He'd be in a bar with the rest of the team drinking. He doesn't have a custom kit like you. He's solid, not innovative."

"Still. It's a tough industry. I don't like the fact—"

She put her hand up. "Jamie personally cut a cheque and he didn't have to do a thing for it. Billy's good. Better than good. It's spring break and he's chasing college girls somewhere."

"It's not nice getting bumped like that though."

"Look. All I know is that this project is seriously important to Jamie and the rest of Occulture Productions, and when he thought he could get you on this, he didn't hesitate. You could have probably named your fee."

"Now you fucking tell me."

"For what it's worth, I'm really glad they pushed for the change. It's nice to work with someone as professional as you."

"Flattery will get you everywhere."

"I'm serious. You're next level. Anyone can see that."

"Thanks. But I'd have preferred to get the gig without pushing someone else out."

"It's a tough business. And, as I say, Billy's regret will have lasted for about as long as it took for a drunk college student to shove her boobs in his face."

Lev shook his head sadly. "I missed out on so much growing up in the UK."

"Oh yeah. I forgot the vow of celibacy everybody takes when they enter the music biz."

"Exactly."

"So, shall we head down to the basement?"

"Yeah." He picked up his boom and placed the cans around his neck. "Thanks, Anna."

"No problem. I meant what I said. I'm glad it's you working on this project."

They headed out of what had once been the Blacks' private residence within the guesthouse, along the corridor and around the corner to the kitchen. "Anything ever happen in here?" Lev asked.

"I heard they used to make a pretty good breakfast."

"Not exactly what I had in mind."

Anna glanced at her notes. "No. But the basement door should be located at the side of the kitchen door leading out to the rear of the property."

Although a little shadowy, there was still plenty of light coming in from the high windows of the kitchen to allow them to see what was going on. "There's not much space in these aisles. Be careful not to damage your equipment," Anna said.

"Trust me. You never have to worry about my equipment. I keep it in tip-top condition."

"Does everything have to be steeped in innuendo with you Brits?"

"I grew up on a diet of Benny Hill."

"You make a fair point."

"This is it," Lev said, coming to a pause outside the basement door. "You ready?"

"No," Anna replied, digging in her shoulder bag. She handed Lev a battery-powered lantern with a strap extending from it. She kept one for herself and flicked on the camcorder light too as she started to record. "It's going to be dark down there without any power."

"Something tells me that even with a full lighting rig, it's going to be dark down there."

CHRISTOPHER ARTINIAN

5

Lev turned the lantern on, opened the door and began to head down the stairs with Anna following closely behind. They creaked like the main staircase until they didn't anymore. After four steps, they became stone, as did the mahogany panelling that decorated the wall. "Hmm," Lev said as goosebumps rippled up his arms.

"Anything to say now?"

"Yeah. I didn't expect the temperature change, but it's obviously as a direct result of the basement being constructed from bare stone rather than wood like the rest of the property."

"Wait a minute."

Lev paused on the sixth step and Anna joined him. For a moment, he didn't understand what was going on; then he watched her zoom the lens in on his goosepimpled arm. "Funny."

"I just want to get it for posterity. Y'know, when we're both lying dead in here and they find the footage, I want them to see that Mister Unflappable flapped for a few seconds at least."

"As I said, it's the temperature change."

"Uh-huh. Sure. It's the temperature change."

They continued down the staircase and gradually the temperature dropped further. When they finally reached the bottom step, they heard the door click shut, and both turned, lifting their lanterns to see nothing but darkness where there had been a crack of daylight before. "This place is so close to the shore, I bet there's subsidence and barely a straight floor in the house."

"Uh-huh." She angled the camera up to the door then back down and around. The basement had old furniture covered by dusty blankets stacked against one wall while the expansive floor, stretching out beneath the entirety of the property above, remained free of clutter.

Little detail could be seen in the spheres of light cast by the lanterns, so they both walked slowly across to the centre of the sprawling room. They paused as a fissure in the otherwise relatively smooth floor came into view. It was crooked, running at about six feet in length, and no more than ten inches at its widest point. Lev knelt down beside it, letting his hand hover above the gaping crack. "Well, here's the reason for the drop in temperature."

"I thought it was meant to be warmer the further down you went," Anna replied, crouching beside him and letting her fingers dance in the updraft of cold air.

"That depends what's down there, doesn't it? For all we know, there could be an underwater reservoir drained off from the lake or a stream or anything. The point is this is the source of the cold air; ergo, it's nothing supernatural; ergo, it's another explainable symptom of the sickness that's plagued this place."

"If I agree with you, will you stop saying ergo?"

Lev smiled. "I'm sorry. This house becomes less and less mysterious every minute we're in here. I don't think it's going to be the series launch you wanted."

She shrugged. "That's the great thing about TV. You can make something look like whatever you want it to."

"Are you suggesting skullduggery?"

Anna laughed. "What are you, a character out of *Oliver Twist*? Who the fuck says skullduggery anymore?"

"That's a yes then?"

"I'm not a storytelling purest. I want to create good TV that's going to creep people out."

"Shall I put a white sheet over my head and run around shouting boo?"

"You're just hilarious. Why didn't anyone warn me about your great sense of humour?" she said deadpan.

"Seriously. What's the plan?"

"Same plan. I'll probably add some stuff from the effects archive post-production. You've got to admit the story's pretty creepy if nothing else."

"Yeah. I'm sure Barbie Trixabelle or whatever her name is will do it total justice."

This time, Anna did laugh. "I'll have you know that Fifi came highly recommended."

"By who? Hugh Heffner?"

She laughed again. "Close. Jamie."

"Ha. Say no more then."

"Anyway, creepy or not, we'll be doing quite a bit of the filming down here, considering this is where the congregation took their lives, so you might want to—"

"On it," Lev replied, placing the lantern on the floor, slipping his over ears back on and raising the boom. He pressed pause and even in the glow of the lantern light, Anna could see a confused expression appear on his face as he looked down at his monitor.

"What is it?"

Lev shook his head. "It's weird. I'm getting interference of some kind."

"What do you mean?"

He angled the device towards her. It was the size of a small square alarm clock and the backlit display showed a semicircular dial with a small yellow section, a much larger green segment, which took up most of the face, then a narrow orange wedge and finally a red section about a quarter of the size of the green. The hand of the dial was currently flicking against the tiny raised plastic bollard of the red section that stopped it disappearing off screen.

"What do you hear?"

Lev shook his head. "Nothing. Zip." He slipped the headphones off and handed them across to her.

Anna put them on and shook her head. "I don't hear anything."

"Yeah. It's strange."

"Have you ever had that happen before?" she asked, taking them off again and handing them back across.

"Never."

"So, is your equipment broken or what?"

"I don't know," he replied, placing the phones back on, raising the boom and moving away from the giant crack in the foundation. "Whoa!"

"What?"

"The further I head over here the lower the readout." He walked across to the far wall and Anna followed, her camera raised, filming Lev and the monitor.

Sure enough, by the time he was at the other end of the room the hand on the dial was at zero. He paused for a few seconds then retraced his steps across to the fissure. With each one he took, the small white needle jumped further up the dial. He chuckled again.

"What's funny?"

"Nothing, really. It's just curious."

"Curious?"

"Well, it's obviously an anomaly."

"An anomaly?"

"You know what an anomaly is?" he asked with a smirk.

"Funny fucker aren't you? Yes, Lev. I know what an anomaly is, but what do you mean?"

THE DEVIL'S FACE

The smirk remained on Lev's face as he lowered the mike into the black, gaping crack. He regarded the small monitor on his belt to see the hand still slamming against the peak. The smirk was suddenly gone and his fists clenched around the boom. "Shit!" he hissed.

"What? What is it?" Anna asked, alarmed.

"I-I don't know. I … shit!"

His arms started shaking as he tried to withdraw the boom from the hole. "Lev, what's happening?"

"I don't know, Anna. I … I can't retract the mike."

"What do you mean you can't retract the mike?" Panic was rising in her voice.

"I don't know how many ways I can say it. The fucking thing won't budge. It's like something's got a grip on it."

"Something?" Her voice shook a little. "You're scaring me, Lev."

"Help me. Help me pull for Christ's sake."

Anna approached him, terror painting her face in the glow of the lantern light. "Wh-what do you want me to do?"

He shook his head. "Oh no. It's too late, Anna. We're too late," he cried.

"Too late. We're too late for what?" In the space of a moment, she'd gone from laughing and joking to being on the verge of tears.

Lev straightened up. "We're too late for the early bird special from the diner across the street from our digs." He backed up from the hole, chuckling to himself.

"You FUCKING PRICK!" She lunged forward, still with the camcorder strapped around one hand and punched him on the arm with the other. "That wasn't funny."

He continued laughing as he rubbed his arm. "I beg to differ."

"Seriously. It wasn't." She reached up to her left eye with the back of her hand and dabbed the corner.

"Shit. I didn't want to upset you. I just wanted to prank you."

"Yeah, well. I don't take kindly to pranks like that."

"I'm sorry, Anna." Any hint of a smile was gone from his face now.

She let out a long, shivering breath and shook her head, and when she spoke again, her voice had the timbre of a little girl who'd been picked on in the school playground. "It wasn't funny."

"Hey, look. I'm really sorry. I thought—" He reached out, trying to place his hand on her arm, but she flinched back, dragging it away.

"Don't. Let's just get what we need down here and head back to the hotel."

"Anna. I—"

"Let's just finish up, Lev."

"Okay. Sorry," he repeated and was about to reach for the recorder when she spoke again.

"So, that whole thing, the readout, everything, was just to play a trick on me?"

He shook his head and pulled his hand away from the small monitor. "No," he said, showing her. "It's still in the red, look."

She was tentative at first but then stepped forward and observed the dial as the boom hovered near the fissure. "Seriously, Lev. You're not doing anything to make that happen?"

"I swear on my children's life, Anna. I'm not doing anything to make this happen."

"So, what is it?"

"Like I said. It's just an anomaly. You'd need a Cozy Powell drum solo to make the dial read like this, and unless I'm going deaf, I don't hear anything."

Her eyes returned to the monitor and then angled up at Lev to gauge whether he was being truthful. "So how do we fix it?"

"That will require my years of expertise," he replied, pressing stop on the recorder, switching the monitor off and waiting a few seconds before pressing the record button and switching the monitor back on. This time, the needle remained static at zero. He waved the boom around a little then held it above Anna. "Say something."

"You're still a prick," she said with the start of a forgiving smile on her face. He stuck his bottom lip out. "I didn't know that about you."

"That I'm a prick? All you needed to do was ask around. It's a well-documented fact."

"No, you idiot. That you had children."

"Yeah. Freddie and Sal. They're … they're amazing."

"It must be tough in your line of work."

"Yeah. It was what caused all the problems. It's why I don't see them anything like how much I want to."

"I'm sorry."

Lev shrugged. "Nobody to blame but me. I chose this life. I chose to stay on the road rather than get a straight job."

"Still. It can't be easy."

He shrugged again and there was a sad expression on his face as he replied. "It is what it is. Come on. Let's do a few takes around this basement and then we'll head back to town and I'll buy you the most expensive cocktail I can find by way of an apology."

Anna sniggered. "It's a nice gesture, but I'd be surprised if the bar owners in this town know what a cocktail is."

The ice melted a little between them and they got to work. Ten minutes later, they had enough material for the purposes they wanted. Anna had an idea of where she wanted the lighting rig and how to frame the shots. Lev had found the perfect spot where the bare stone walls didn't result in too much echo.

"You happy with everything we've got?" he asked, pulling the cans down from his ears and letting the headband rest around his neck.

"I'm good," she said but continued to document everything with the camcorder.

Lev retracted the mechanism on the telescopic boom, checking that both the recorder and the attached monitor were switched off too.

"How about I buy you that drink?"

She smiled. "That's sweet, but I want to draw up a storyboard for tomorrow."

"Oh. Okay," he said, convinced his earlier apology had gone unheeded and that there was still some antagonism in the air.

"But I'll let you buy me two drinks after dinner tonight if you like."

"That's really nice of you."

"I thought so," she replied, laughing a little. "You really are a prick. I nearly wet myself earlier."

"Again, I'm sorry about that."

She shook her head. "In years to come, it's a story I'll be telling people, and it will be a hoot. Right now, it's a little raw, but I'll get over it." She turned off the camcorder, slipping it into her satchel. She'd got enough footage for what she needed.

They exchanged warmish smiles and Lev hitched the bags onto his shoulder, this time not expecting his companion to take one. "Well, let's get out of—" He stopped in mid-sentence.

"Just because I said I forgive you, it doesn't mean that gives you free rein to do it to me again," she said, seeing the look of concentration on his face.

"No," he said, putting his hand up. "Do you hear something?"

"I'm serious, Lev. Don't piss me off."

"No, Anna," he replied, reaching out and grabbing her wrist. They'd both got the lanterns strapped over their shoulders and the uplighting was a little shadowy, but she could see the earnest look on his face.

Been here before though. "I don't hear—" She stopped too. *Wait. What is that?* "Is that you? Have you got another machine on you with whispering voices to freak me out?"

He tightened his grip around her wrist. "It's not me, Anna."

And this time, she knew he was telling the truth. "What is it then?"

They both listened intently, finally turning their eyes down to the wide, elongated crack in the floor. The hairs on their arms and necks stood to attention as the sound continued. "It's coming from…." Lev's words trailed off. "That's ridiculous. It can't be." He reasoned with himself before vocalising the thought.

"It is." As impossible as it sounded, the whispering was coming from the crack. "Get this. Get this, Lev," Anna ordered.

He pushed down the fear rising from the pit of his stomach, connected the mike and pressed record, not bothering to extend the boom, instead crouching down by the side of the fissure. As soon as he did, the whispering stopped. The pair of them remained frozen, looking at each other for a moment until another sound, a strange, low-pitched vomit of unintelligible words blurted, followed by—

Silence.
One.
Two.
Three.
Four.
Five.
Blackness.

"Oh, Jesus Christ. Jesus Christ, Lev. Please say this is a joke. Please tell me this is a joke."

Lev rose, pulling the headphones down from his ears. "It's okay."

"AAAGGGHHH! Something touched me."

"It's alright. That's my hand," he said, taking hold of hers.

She reciprocated, gripping his tightly. "It's okay," he said, not believing it for a second. He tucked the boom beneath his arm and, with his free hand, clicked the power button on his lantern.

Nothing.

"Mine's dead too," she said, following his lead. The darkness was like nothing either of them had experienced and the tension in the air was palpable. A sob left her lips and Lev squeezed her hand a little tighter.

"Anna, you have to reach into your bag and get the camcorder. We need the light so we can find our way out." He heard another frightened, shivering breath leave her lips.

"D-don't let go of me."

He released her wrist and ran his hand up to her shoulder, gripping it firmly. "I'm not going anywhere." She started rifling through her bag while Lev stared through the pitch blackness towards the hole, towards where those unexplainable sounds had come from.

Anna sniffed. "I've got it." She hit the power button, turned on the camera light and exhaled a relieved breath.

They both stared down towards the giant crack for a few seconds, terrified of what they might hear or, worse still, see, but the room had fallen silent. "Come on," Lev said, releasing her shoulder and taking her hand once more. "Let's get out of here." In other circumstances, this would have seemed overly familiar, inappropriate even, but they both headed across the basement floor towards the staircase like two frightened children in a Grimm fairy tale.

They reached the bottom of the staircase and cast each other a solemn glance. "Wh-when the door closed, you don't think it l-locked too, do you?"

"You seriously don't need to worry about that. If I have to pull the thing from its hinges, we're getting out of here." They turned, searching the darkness beyond the glow of the camera light, before starting up the staircase, treading nervously on the last four wooden steps and finally coming to a tentative standstill at the top. Lev finally let go of Anna's hand and reached for the door handle, twisting it and pushing at the same time.

THE DEVIL'S FACE

They both let out huge sighs of relief as daylight cracked through. They stepped out and Lev slammed the door shut behind them. They both observed it for a moment, still trying to come to terms with what they'd experienced.

"I want to go back to the hotel."

"Yeah."

They headed down the corridor, not a word passing between them, but they both sensed the same thing. There was an electricity in the air. Goosebumps continued to ripple over their skin, and when Anna reached out to turn the handle of the front door, her lip quivered as it refused to budge. "Oh, God," she whispered.

Lev eased in next to her, nudging her hand out of the way and twisting the handle hard. The door budged with a loud wood-on-wood shriek. "It's just stiff, that's all." He opened it wide, letting her through first; then he followed, closing the oaken slab behind them. The pair stood on the porch for a moment, grateful to be back out in the open.

"Thanks, Lev," Anna whispered. She bowed her head and closed her eyes, still trying hard to come to terms with everything.

Lev rolled his neck before looking back towards the door. "I'm not really going to relax until we're driving away from this place," he began, turning to the serene lake in front of them. "How about…."

Anna opened her eyes and looked at him. "What? What is it?" He didn't say anything but glanced at his watch. "You're really scaring me, Lev."

He turned to her and then pointed up towards the sun. "It's not possible."

She didn't understand for a moment. She looked at her own watch. "This … this isn't right. This can't be. We were in there for half an hour, forty minutes max."

A long silence stood between them before Lev replied. "Apparently, we weren't. Apparently, we were in there for over five hours."

Anna looked back at the door. "What the hell's going on?"

"I don't know. But I really want to get out of here."

"Yeah. Me too."

6

Enola hated some parts of her life with a passion. School was one of those parts. At parents' evenings, it was always the same thing. "She's very bright, Sheriff Tanner, but she doesn't apply herself." *Sheriff Tanner. Never Miss Tanner or Beth, but Sheriff Tanner.* "She's a sweet girl, Sheriff Tanner, but she doesn't try to fit in." *They tell you to be yourself. They tell you to think for yourself, and then they want you to be a drone, a sheep, put up with fucking idiots for an easy life. They expect me to listen to Wilson Phillips, Color Me Badd and Boyz II Men just to fit in, just to have something to say to these empty-shell, Barbie doll wastes of skin. I mean, who the fuck listens to that shit without undergoing some kind of serious head trauma first?*

This was her favourite time of day. Home time. The bell had rung moments before and the hallways were jostling with hundreds of unfriendly faces. Enola held her book bag close to her chest as the usual scrummage to get to the lockers ensued. She finally made it to hers to see fresh Magic Marker graffiti.

Her heart sank a little, but she didn't let it show. It was a cartoon of two figures in capes. The larger one wore a badge. The smaller one had stink lines emanating from it. The inscription underneath read, "The dynamic duo, Sheriff Whore and Bastard Girl."

It wasn't easy being the daughter of the woman who broke up parties, arrested kids for shoplifting, told parents their children had been caught drinking or doing drugs or a hundred other things that would get them grounded for months. It wasn't easy having a father who ran out on her before she was born. In general, nothing about Enola's life was easy.

She opened her locker, withdrew her Walkman and placed the headband around her neck while she gathered the textbooks she needed to do her homework.

"Hey, No-no."

She closed the door quickly, turning the key and blocking the view of her locker from Bella, her older cousin and, arguably, the only real friend she had. She was everything Enola wasn't. She stood about eight inches taller, had blonde, flowing locks and sapphire-blue eyes. Everyone wanted to be her friend, especially the boys. This meant that no one in Bella's year messed with Enola either, and if any of them ever saw her getting picked on, they acted in order to curry favour with Bella. Bella was two when Enola was born and she couldn't actually pronounce her name, instead saying No-no, and it stuck as their personal joke.

"Hey," Enola replied, smiling, trying her hardest not to show the disappointment and humiliation she was feeling inside as the thought of the Magic Marker cartoon made her eyes sting.

"Miss Harlow's gone home sick. They've cancelled practice."

"Cool. I mean, not cool, but y'know. It'll be nice to walk home together."

A beaming smile lit Bella's face. She loved Enola like a sister. She was intelligent, funny, and caring but clumsy with her words, always doubting what she said. "Don't worry. I figured out what you meant."

"I'll just get my bag, and then we'll—" Her words cut off as she saw the tip of a black, shiny doodle behind Enola's head. "What's that?"

Dammit. Enola didn't have blonde-flowing locks. If she did, she'd have been able to block her cousin's view of the drawing. Her hair was jet black, like her father's, her eyes dark brown, like her father's. Although she'd never met him, she wore his features. Her skin was pale and the *Addams Family* movie that had come out earlier in the year had unleashed a library of jokes, comments and putdowns likening her to Wednesday Addams.

She tried to pretend it didn't bother her, but, in truth, most things bothered her. And when she had her long hair cut to shoulder length, everyone believed it was to end the comparisons. But it wasn't. It coincided with Jodie Starr revealing her new look. And if there was one person on this planet who was a role model to Enola, it was her.

Jodie Starr was everything Enola wanted to be. She was confident and didn't give a damn. She was exciting, bold, talented, and driven. Blazetrailer's music spoke to Enola like that of no other band. It was powerful and energetic and dark and menacing all at the same time. It made her feel alive, truly alive. Jodie was a pioneer. In a genre dominated by men, she led the charge for women and spawned a myriad of wannabes, but more than any of that, she was an artist. That's all Enola wanted to be, just a different kind of artist.

But, right now, she was not Jodie Starr. And she was not her cousin, and no matter how much she tried to cover it up, no matter how much she protested, Bella would see the drawing and go mental.

"It-it's nothing."

Bella gently pushed her cousin out of the way and stared at the cartoon. Anger welled in her eyes and she whipped around. She knew the type of people who did this only too well. She understood that they would be close by, desperate to feed on the sadness and hurt that they had caused. Her gaze locked on a group of five girls standing in a circle directly across from them. The tallest, the most confident, the ringleader with her long, straight, perfectly kept hair stared Bella straight in the eyes, almost as if admitting what she'd done before turning to her friends. A chorus of laughter erupted. Enola could see the fury notch up a level in her cousin. "What's her name?" she asked in a hushed tone. When Enola didn't answer, she asked again, more forcefully. "What is her name?"

"Lauren," Enola replied.

Bella reached into her bag and took out a small bottle of nail varnish remover, untwisting the cap and painting two lines over the top of the cartoon. The thick liquid barely dribbled, but the Magic Marker it came into contact with immediately became diluted.

She placed the bottle back and marched over to where the girls were standing, ripping the bag from Lauren's shoulder.

"What are you doing?" she screamed.

"Shut the fuck up, bitch!" Bella roared like a pissed-off lion. She had a reputation for being a psycho when the situation demanded it. She went out with a guy once who two-timed her. She'd found out but stayed quiet, seemingly as if nothing was wrong. They'd gone to a kegger, where she'd spiked his drinks. She took him up to a room where he thought he was going to get lucky, only for him to pass out. She then proceeded to strip him, shave his head, his eyebrows, and any hair she could find before writing, "I'm a two-timing little shithead," all over his body in indelible marker. If that wasn't enough, she set fire to his clothes on the front lawn of the party house before leaving. From that point on, few people had dared to mess with her.

"Stop me then," Bella replied as she rifled through Lauren's bag. Before the other girl could even say anything else, Bella's hand grasped a thick black Magic Marker.

"I ... I ... I don't know how that got in there." All the cocksureness was gone now.

Something approaching a snarl formed on Bella's face and her hand shot out, grabbing Lauren's thick, silky hair. The corridor was still packed and noisy, but it quickly fell silent but for the scream of pain as the girl was dragged across to where Enola was still standing. Bella proceeded to use the graffiti artist's wadded hair as a cleaning cloth while her pained, humiliated and frightened screams continued to siren, drawing the attention of everyone in earshot.

Several times, Lauren's head banged against the gun-metal-grey locker as Bella scrubbed at the image. Finally, she let go and Lauren fell to the floor, crying her eyes out like an infant. The cartoon was nothing more than black and grey smudges now, and much of the ink had leeched onto Lauren's hair.

"You listen to me, you little skank. You ever so much as look at my cousin the wrong way again, I will fucking end you." She straightened up, turning her stare towards the other four girls who had assembled around them in slack-jawed horror. "And the same applies to you. Leave her alone or I will bring down your fucking world." She turned to Enola. "Come on, cuz. Let's go home."

Enola struggled to believe what she'd seen. Part of her wanted to cheer. Part of her wanted to throw her arms around Bella, squeeze her and thank her. Part of her wanted to unleash a massive kick on Lauren while she was on the floor, but instead she joined Bella and the two strode side by side down the hall. This would not end the victimisation. It seemed to come from all angles, and much of it she kept to herself, but it was one little victory and it felt good.

When they were out of the building and off the grounds, Enola burst out laughing and finally Bella did too. "Oh my God! That was amazing!" Enola cried.

"Bitch got what she deserved."

"But … you could get into serious trouble for what you did."

Bella shook her head. "She won't say a word. She knows what'll happen if she does. That school is like a prison. There's a code. You don't snitch." An expression of sadness crept onto Enola's face. "What is it?"

"I'm going to miss you."

Bella placed her arm around Enola as the pair walked along. "I've told you. I'll be coming back all the time. Hell, you can come down and see me whenever you want. I'll be living off campus."

Enola nodded. "I suppose."

"Hey," Bella said, gesturing back to the school. "You're going to come across a lot of people like that in life. Don't let them get to you."

"Nobody ever tries that kind of stuff with you. It's like I'm a beacon for them."

A small laugh left Bella's mouth as she looked across at her cousin. "Fuck them. It's because you've got your own thing going on. So, you like metal, and you wear black, and you don't mix with those losers. So fucking what? All the great artists have their own style. All those fucking androids can do is copy other people in the hope that they'll fit in. Fuck them. You're Enola fucking Tanner. And you're perfect the way you are." Bella leaned in and kissed her on the top of the head. "I love you just the way you are."

A sad smile crept onto Enola's face. "I love you. You coming around tonight?"

"I can't. I'm meeting Ash and the guys at the diner. You can come along if you want."

It was Enola's turn to laugh now. "Oh yeah. They'd just love you bringing your geeky little cousin along."

"They like you."

"They like me because they like you."

Bella sighed and took hold of Enola's hand. "I'll call and cancel. We'll have a girls' night in, just you and me. We'll have a horrorthon."

"No. I don't want you to cancel."

"It's no biggie."

"No. Maybe we can do that tomorrow?"

"It's your birthday tomorrow."

Enola shrugged. "And you know how that usually goes."

"Your mom will want to—"

"Mom will probably get called out like she does every Friday night."

"Well. Whatever. I was definitely going to see you anyway, so we'll do whatever you want."

"Cool."

"Damn right it's cool. We'll have the best time. And I'll make sure I'm extra nice to Ash tonight."

"Um ... why?"

"He's got a pirate copy of *The People Under the Stairs*," she replied, winking.

Enola's eyes widened. "What, seriously?"

"Uh-huh! But don't tell your mom. She'll freak."

"I won't say a word."

Bella squeezed her cousin's hand before letting go. "Trust me. We'll have an awesome time."

*

The journey back to the hotel had been silent, but as they pulled up outside, Lev turned in his seat to look at Anna. "So, are we going to discuss this, or—"

"I just want to get back to my room."

"Anna, we—"

"I really think—JESUS!" The loud knock made her scream.

Tim was at the window staring in at them with a goofy expression on his face. She wound it down. "Hey! We've been wondering when you were coming back. You guys have a good time up there?" he asked with a laugh in his voice. The smell of booze washed over them.

"What do you want, Tim?" Anna replied.

"We were just about to head to the diner to get some dinner. We thought you might like to come so you could tell us all about it."

"No ... thank you. I'm going to go back to my room and I'm going to—"

"All work." He laughed and looked across to Lev. "We'll be at the diner if you want to join us, man." Tim turned and they watched as he staggered away.

"I was wrong to be sceptical. He seems top-notch," Lev said, but there was no response from his driver.

A few seconds passed and, finally, Anna turned towards him. "What did you say?"

"I said he seems top-notch."

"No. I mean after that."

Lev shook his head, a little confused. "I didn't say anything after that."

"You did. You whispered something."

"Anna. I didn't."

She broke eye contact and turned her gaze to the steering wheel. "I'm going to my room. I need a nap."

"A nap? Are you serious? We've just lost time, Anna, for Christ's sake. Something totally fucked up has happened to us and you're wanting to take a nap."

She put her hands up. "Please, Lev. I just want to go to my room and close my eyes. I promise, when I wake up, we'll talk about this, but right now, my head is in a spin. I can't think straight."

"Do you want me to come with you?"

"You don't let up, do you?"

"I don't mean anything like that. I mean if you're scared or something, I could, y'know, watch over you."

Anna let out a huff of a laugh. "So, now you're a knight wanting to watch over a fair maiden?" She let out a sigh. "I'm sorry. My head's not feeling great. It's sweet of you to offer, Lev, but I just want a couple of hours' sleep. I promise the moment I wake up, I'll come and find you and we'll talk about what happened."

"Okay," he replied, climbing out of the van and collecting his equipment.

Anna grabbed her camcorder and bag, locked the car, and they both started heading in when she stopped suddenly. "What?"

Lev looked confused again. "Anna. I didn't say anything."

Her brow furrowed a little. "I thought I heard you say something."

"I didn't say a word."

She shook her head. "Okay. Like I said, my head's all over the place. I need a nap."

"Are you sure you don't want me to come with you?"

"I'm sure. I'll see you later." Without pause, she disappeared through the entrance. Lev stayed on the step for a moment and turned around to take in the small town.

What the hell happened to us up there?

7

Beth leaned forward on the bar stool, placing her elbows on the freshly polished wooden surface. The place was quiet. A couple of muted conversations could be heard in the darkened corners. A few regulars were dotted around here and there, including at the bar itself, but it was rare that the place busied much so early on.

She took another drink from her Millers and placed it back down. It had been a long day. But nearly every day as the sheriff of New Scotland was a long one.

"You in here drinking on a Thursday before the sun's even gone down? Something tells me I'm going to need a drink too," Naomi, Beth's sister, said, reaching into the fridge under the counter and grabbing a bottle for herself.

Beth shook her head. "No. Nothing out of the ordinary. I just…. Forget it."

Naomi took a swig from her bottle and flicked the towel over her shoulder, placing her arms on the bar and leaning forward so she was at the same level as her sister.

"Come on, spill."

Beth took a long, deep breath and looked at her bottle. "It's just Enola."

"What about her?"

"She's always so down. I know she's not happy and I don't seem to be able to do anything about it." There was a sad resignation in Beth's words and her gaze.

"Have you thought about sending her back to Doctor Mullan?"

"I brought it up the other day and she nearly lost it with me. All she does is go to school and then lock herself away in her bedroom, listening to that god-awful music and painting. Unless Bella's around. Bella is the one person who seems to be able to put a genuine smile on her face. I think it's the prospect of her going to college next year that's got Enola in this latest funk."

Naomi straightened up and took a drink from her bottle. "You want me to have a word with her? You want me to see if she'll put her plans on hold for a few years?"

Beth laughed. "Would you? That'd be great."

"Oh, I forgot to tell you. Karen dropped off the cake today."

"Great. I should have ordered a muffin instead. Honestly. I've never known a kid go so far out of her way not to have friends."

"So, you couldn't change her mind about inviting people over?"

"There's going to be you, me and Bella. That's it."

"Shoot. That reminds me, I need to make sure Sam's okay to cover me with it being Friday night."

"Yeah. You do. Because if twenty-five percent of the attendees aren't there, then I'm pretty certain she's going to notice. And another thing—oh shit." Her eyes were drawn to a solitary figure as he walked through the entrance. It was the man who had been at Black's guesthouse earlier on in the day. He walked up to the bar and Naomi immediately went over to him.

"What can I get you?" she asked.

"Vodka and a Millers, please?"

"You're not from around here."

"No."

"Where are you staying?"

"The Inn Between."

"You like it?"

"Been in worse."

"You here for business or pleasure?"

Beth was watching and listening from the far end of the bar. He still hadn't seen her and now her sister had given him an opening; she knew he was going to start flirting.

"Work. I'm here for work."

Naomi put the opened beer down and he ignored it for a moment while he dipped into his jacket to pull out his wallet. "I can run you a tab if you like."

Lev paused, looking at the bottle, which was already sweating on the bar. Naomi placed the vodka down next to it and he picked the shot glass up straight away, knocking it back in one. "Yeah, actually. That would be good, thanks. Could I have another one of those as well, please?"

"Well, as you said please…." She reached back for the vodka and poured another. "Rough day?"

"Not at all. Time just flew by." There was no hint of a smile on his face. He picked his drinks up and was about to head over to a quiet, dark corner when he spotted Beth.

Don't come over here. Don't come over here. Don't come over here.

He simply raised his beer, nodded and carried on over to the corner.

"God, I love that accent," Naomi said, rejoining her sister.

"Stay well clear. I ran into him this morning."

"Stay well clear, I saw him first, or stay well clear, he's a jackass?"

"Well … neither really. I just got the impression he'd jump on anything that moves."

A smile cracked on Naomi's face. "You've still to say anything to put me off him."

Beth laughed. "Floozy."

Naomi shrugged. "Got to get my fun where I can. The pickings are pretty slim in this town."

Beth blew her cheeks out before another long breath escaped her mouth. "Ain't that the truth."

"So, anyway. Going back to more important matters. What have you got Enola for her birthday?"

"Oh, y'know, what every normal fifteen-year-old girl wants. A silver pentagram on a chain. That band she likes so much brought out a limited-edition live album that practically cost me a week's salary. Some new jeans … black, of course."

"If it's what she wants, it's what she wants."

"I know. But…."

"But what?"

"I'd just like to be able to do something special to really cheer her up, to let her know how much I love her."

"I'm pretty certain she knows."

"I just want her to be happy."

"Want who to be happy?" Bella said, appearing behind the bar.

"Enola," Beth replied.

A sad smile crept onto Bella's face. She loved her cousin. She loved spending time with her. She loved most things about her, but deep down inside, she knew she wasn't really happy. "Oh. Well, me too."

"Where have you been hiding, anyway?" Beth asked, changing the subject.

"I just came downstairs to say don't wait up," she replied, turning to her mother. When Naomi had taken the bar over, the accommodation upstairs had been run as a bed and breakfast. Now it was home to her and Bella.

Naomi laughed. "Nice try, sweetcakes. Where are you going?"

"Just going out with Ash and the gang."

THE DEVIL'S FACE

"Eleven o'clock."

"Mom! Come on."

"It's a school night. Most parents would be saying nine."

"And that's why I love you so much. You're nothing like a normal parent. Twelve?"

Naomi raised an eyebrow. "Eleven thirty."

"Deal." She kissed her mother on the cheek.

"Bye, Aunt Beth."

"Bye, sugar. Stay out of trouble."

"You know me, I always—" She stopped as her eyes were drawn to the man in the corner with a shot and a Millers sitting on the table in front of him.

"He's way too old for you, kitten," Naomi joked. Her daughter's brow furrowed a little. "Bell? What is it?"

Without a word, Bella turned and disappeared back out of the bar. "What the hell was that all about?" Beth asked as she and Naomi both turned towards Lev, who was still sitting in the corner, oblivious to everything that was going on around him.

"You don't think he could have … y'know … seen her around town and tried to make a move or something?"

"If he has, I'm going to find an eight ball of coke on the son of a bitch during a routine traffic stop." Her sister laughed. "You think I'm kidding? You need to go after her and find out what's going on."

Naomi put her bottle down. "Do you think?"

"Hell yeah, I think. Bella's not the kind of kid to get freaked by seeing someone like that."

They both looked across at Lev, who continued to remain detached from his surroundings. Naomi was about to make her way out of the bar area to look for her daughter when Bella came running back in with a CD in her hands.

"I knew it. I knew it," she said excitedly.

"You knew what?" Beth asked, standing up from her bar stool as Bella took out the CD inlay. Naomi crowded around, too, as her daughter flicked open the pages.

It was a Blazetrailer CD that Enola had insisted she borrowed. There were several photo collages on the last few pages and Bella pointed to one after another after another, showing her mother and Beth. "He's not a member of the band, but he's like the sound guy or something."

There was a shot where he was at a mixing desk. Another where he was sitting shoulder to shoulder with Jodie Starr and they were both in fits of laughter. Another where he was on his hands and knees setting up a drum mike and Jodie had plonked herself down on his back as if he were a stool.

"Are you sure it's him?" Naomi asked.

"Yes. I'm sure." She handed the inlay across to Beth. "You should speak to him. Maybe he can get their autographs or something for No-no."

"Err...."

"Can you imagine what that would mean to her?"

Just the thought of having to walk up to a virtual stranger and ask for something made Beth's skin crawl. She was vehemently independent, but this was for her daughter, the light of her life. She would walk over hot coals or through Hell for her. She let out a long sigh. "Give me that," she said, gesturing to the CD. She drained her bottle and turned to Naomi. "Let me have two more Millers. I'm about to sell my soul."

*

Fear had accompanied many of the formative years in Anna's life. But she had defeated it, or at the very least buried it so far down deep inside her that she was able to get on with her day-to-day routines without it affecting her. Occasionally, something would bubble to the surface, ratcheting up her anxiety levels and making her retreat deep within herself.

It's happening again.

Losing time. Hearing voices. These were markers on a path she didn't want to tread but nonetheless was being forced to take.

THE DEVIL'S FACE

Why the hell did I take this job? You were headhunted, sought out. It made you feel good, fed you some worth. Idiot. Idiot, Anna. Idiot.

She hadn't gone straight to bed after returning to her room. She had intended to go back through the tape in order to at least try to find some rational answers amid all the craziness, but as it rewound, the battery warning light had flicked on and she realised she'd left the charger in the van. She decided to take it as a sign that she should get some rest and go back to it with a clearer head.

"There's no escape."

The whispered voice was clear this time. It made her freeze.

She had been tossing and turning on the bed, knowing that sleep wouldn't come despite her best efforts, but now goosebumps rippled up and down her arms once more. She'd closed the curtains, blocking out the last hours of the day before trying to get some rest and now she wished she hadn't. It wasn't fully dark outside yet and she wanted light. She wanted light to put her mind at ease.

"It's not real. It's all in my head." Her voice shook as she said the words.

"You're mine. All mine."

"It's not real." This time, tears welled in her eyes. She tried to reach for the bedside lamp but couldn't and another pang of fear shuddered through her. This was how it used to happen. He'd come to her, inject her with something. She'd see, feel and experience everything but couldn't do anything to stop it. She could talk. She could plead. She could cry. But her body was like clay.

Six months. Six months she lived in that hell as a teenager. Hoping, praying all the time that this would be the day they found her. This would be the day that the police stormed in, saved her and returned her to her parents.

This isn't real.

She felt a sudden cold breeze prickle the small of her back.

I'm naked. How can I be naked?

She desperately tried to mentally retrace her steps.

I walked into the room, dumped my gear in the corner, tried to rewind the camcorder, gave it up as a bad job, closed the curtains and flopped down on the bed. I didn't undress. I didn't. I know I didn't.

Then came the sound that made her realise this wasn't a dream, that he was real. It was happening again. They never found him. Had he found her on today of all days? *How can that be?*

Ever since her teenage years, the noise of cellophane being unfurled from a roll sent violent shockwaves through Anna, so much so that once she even lost control of her bladder when her aunt was wrapping some leftovers for the refrigerator. It was one of the things he did. One of the things to remind her that—"There's no escape."

A whimper left her mouth as she felt her lower legs being lifted and cling film wrapped around them. *He was strong. He was always strong.*

"Please. No." Her words were hushed. The times she'd screamed had always ended badly. When she'd screamed, he used to beat her and slap her. Slapping was the worst. Cocooned in cellophane, the pain of a slap remained fresh for minutes sometimes. And it wouldn't be just one. There'd be many. Calves, thighs, buttocks, stomach. No. Screaming wasn't good. Pleading. He liked pleading. Sometimes, he'd fall asleep to the sound of her pleading and he'd have to go when he woke up.

"Round and round and round we go," he whispered as he continued to wrap her.

Another shuddering breath left her lips. "This can't be happening."

He lifted and stretched until her entire body was covered. She had never forgotten that sensation—superheating beneath the tightly wound cling film. But that wasn't the worst of it. The worst was still to come.

"Mine. You're all mine," he whispered in her ear before walking over to the far end of the room.

THE DEVIL'S FACE

Strike!

A single match, a single candle, and just enough light to see the tall, terrifying figure that changed her life forever. His naked body, hairless but for brows and lashes. His skin greasepainted red from toe to head. His eyes almost black in the dim glow of the flame.

Waiting. Waiting. Waiting for the perfect moment to unleash that smile. That terrifying yellow-toothed grin that made the blood freeze in her veins.

"No. Please," she sobbed.

Finally, his lips curled upwards and she wanted to close her eyes more than ever, but closing her eyes was punishable too. Not by beating, not by slapping, but by….

Oh God. He brought them.

In the glow of the candlelight, she could see the small container next to his neatly folded clothes on the chair. She listened carefully and now she could hear them too. Hundreds of cockroaches clambering over one another, jostling for position in a plastic box with no position to jostle for. If she was bad, really bad, then they would be emptied into a carrier bag, which would be placed over her head and tied around her neck. The bag was meticulously perforated with tiny holes to make sure she could breathe while the roaches crawled over her head, tangled in her hair, tried to force their way up her nostrils. The first time, she had screamed and screamed and screamed, but screaming was bad. Screaming allowed them to get in her mouth. Screaming unleashed the slaps and punches. So, she learnt to breathe through gritted teeth. She could feel them on her lips, tapping at her incisors and canines as they explored. *Not the roaches. Please, not the roaches.*

She learnt how each indiscretion was punished only by committing it. She also learnt how to be good. Being good was the safest option. Being good meant the least amount of pain. But that too came with a price.

Anna remained on her side, watching, not screaming, not wriggling or trying to escape, as ludicrous as that would be. The seconds ran on to a minute, then two, then more and he just stood gazing at her with that grin. He reached out and gently caressed the plastic box, reminding her of the power he had, of what he could do if he so wished.

Finally, he started towards the bed, disappearing from view as he circumnavigated the foot. She felt the mattress shift as his weight bore down on it, her skin almost sizzling beneath the tightly bound wrap. Then she squirmed as he pressed up against her, draping first his leg over then his right arm. She didn't move or recoil. Moving was another crime.

"All mine," he whispered.

The first few times this had happened, she was convinced it was a prelude to some violent, unspeakable act that would take away her innocence forever. But it wasn't like that. Even though she could feel the contours of his naked frame as it pressed against her, even though sometimes his hand would inadvertently run across her breasts, stomach or thighs, there was never anything overtly sexual. She wasn't a psychiatrist; she didn't know the motivation behind what he was doing, but after the first few times, she never felt threatened in that way. This was about ownership. He wanted to own her. He did own her. She couldn't escape. She couldn't disobey the rules. She couldn't do anything he didn't want her to do without incurring punishment. To all intents and purposes, she was his belonging, and his body draping over hers was the climax of this act of ownership.

She was his, all wrapped up in cellophane like produce plucked straight from the supermarket shelf.

"There's no escape. You're mine. You'll always be mine."

She had escaped though. One day, he hadn't seemed himself. He was distant, nervous. Almost as if the net was closing in. He had dropped off her dinner plate and disappeared back out of the cellar, not watching her eat as he usually did. She wasn't allowed utensils, only her hands.

He didn't like mess. Mess made him angry. Mess was punishable. So, at meal times, he let her feed at a small table in the corner. He allowed her a damp cloth to wipe her hands, wipe the table and wipe the plate clean. It was one of the few times he expected her to be somewhere other than the bed.

On this particular night, pork chops were on the menu. She had to eat them. There was always punishment if she left anything on the plate. As she stretched the L-shaped bone to gnaw the last fibrous strands of undercooked flesh, it snapped, leaving her with a cigar-sized, dagger-shaped bone clutched in her fist.

The candle was at the other end of the room, but as she held her hand up with the remains of the chop still in it, the silhouette sent a wave of certainty running through her. She would either remain in this cellar until she died, merely a thing, an object for this monster to do with as he pleased, or she could seize this moment. She could take this one chance and try for freedom.

When he had returned to collect the plate, it was as if someone else had taken over her body. She thrust the sharpened bone through the side of his neck. He had staggered back, wheezing, spluttering, before finally falling on the floor, and Anna had run. She had run through that open door, slamming it shut behind her, sliding one of the many bolts across. She had torn up the stairs, barging through another entrance into the darkened kitchen. The curtains were all closed. She had tried the heavy door only to find it locked with no key.

Finally, she'd found a light switch and the hallway leading to the front door. No key again. She'd run into the living room, sweeping the closed curtains open. Streetlights. She'd seen streetlights. The window had been locked, but she'd picked up the portable TV in the corner and flung it through. The glass had exploded and her naked body was lacerated in several places as she'd climbed through, but she hadn't cared.

She had run out onto the street screaming for help, and eventually several bewildered neighbours emerged. The police had come. Then her parents. The nightmare had ended, only it hadn't.

The Red Man wasn't in the cellar when the police entered the house. There was plenty of blood but no sign of him. The cellar door was open. And even though Anna had sworn that she had bolted it from the outside, the police were convinced she had got confused. She knew though. She knew she'd bolted it.

They never found him, and on occasion, in her weakest moments, she would glimpse his smiling face in a crowd or in the mirror or somewhere. She knew he hadn't died. To this day, she was convinced he was still … somewhere. And now he was here again, with her, draping himself over her, taking ownership.

This was why she'd taken the job. Worth. She needed to feel like she owned her life, that she was in charge, and that she was not taking order after order, which, in reality, was just an extension of being owned by someone. This was a major step up for her. This and the promises that came with it. But now all her plans, all her hopes meant nothing.

How did he find me?

Her body went even more rigid beneath the thick layers of cellophane as he pressed against her harder. He inhaled deeply, sniffing her hair like a starving man would sniff a plate of hot food. She felt him exhale against the back of her neck and felt his nose gently push against the prickling hairs.

She felt sick. But she couldn't be sick. Sickness led to punishment. She would need to push down all her feelings of revulsion unless she wanted to endure whatever twisted pain the Red Man decided to unleash.

"You're all mine. There's no escape. You can't run away. Not this time. You're all mine, Anna." The whispered words lashed at her like whips and a wave of fresh tears stung her eyes.

Ever since her imprisonment she had experienced episodes of lost time. *Why didn't I just pack up and get the hell out when I arrived back at the hotel? Too coincidental. It was bound to be him. It had to be him.*

"Please," she whimpered.

He ran his hand over her shoulder, down her arm, over her hip, down the side of her thigh. "All mine," he whispered again. He only ever whispered. But whispers could be the most menacing, chilling sounds in the world if they came out of the wrong mouth.

"I'll be good," she cried through another shivering breath.

"Yes. Yes, you will. You wouldn't want me to punish you. Not today."

She felt her whole body shaking despite the restrictive wrap of cellophane around her.

"No. I'll be good." Another pang of sickness. How quickly she had reverted to the scared teenager. She looked towards the door. She knew the rest of the crew were out, probably getting wasted. There might be other guests. There might be the owner or auxiliary staff just out there in the corridor. One shout, one scream could save her. But it could also end everything. One shout if there was nobody there would be bad. So, so bad. Her body stopped trembling and for the first time since all this had started, her head relaxed on the pillow. She had been here so many times before. There was nothing to do. *It's all over.* The thing she had sworn would not define her life had come back to take away her freedom, to shatter her goals, hopes and dreams. *It's all over.*

Darkness.

KNOCK! KNOCK! KNOCK! KNOCK!

"Miss Polson. There's a telephone call for you downstairs."

Anna's eyes stretched wide. *This is it. This is my chance.* She was about to scream when suddenly she felt cool air surround her entire frame. It prickled her skin, causing all her hairs to stand on end. She was no longer bound, and she reached up, running her fingers over her naked flesh. She stretched, turning the bedside lamp on and spinning around in a single fluid movement, but it was clear she was alone in the room.

Her head shook involuntarily. *It can't have been a dream. It was so real.*

"Miss Polson?" The voice came again, followed by another four knocks.

"Y-yes. I'm coming."

She threw on her jeans and top, slipped her feet into her waiting trainers and rushed to the door, flinging it open and letting the hallway lights wash over her like some soothing balm.

"Are you alright?" the hotel owner asked.

Anna looked back into the empty room. "Yes," she replied unconvincingly.

The woman opened her mouth to say something else but stopped herself. Eventually, she broke the silence. "You can take it at the front desk."

Anna followed the woman along the corridor and down the stairs. Twice the hotel owner looked back at her with a slightly confused look and twice Anna wiped her cheeks, sure that the silver streaks had given her away. The more distance she put between herself and the room the more relaxed she became. *It was a dream. A weird, terrifying fucking dream, but a dream, all the same.*

She had felt everything, though, just as if it was happening. A shuddering breath left her lips once more. She was still raw. Dreams and nightmares could do that sometimes. You could wake from them, and even though they were conjuring tricks of the mind, they felt as real as day. *How the hell did I end up naked though? Must have been sleep-walking or sleep undressing or something. Jesus. It felt so real.*

She thought back to the house where she had spent much of the day. It was obvious that had something to do with it. That had brought on this traumatic sleep terror. She had suffered with them for so long and it was obvious now that's what this had been. Half a sob left her lips again as they entered the lobby and the hotel owner looked over her shoulder with concern.

"Are you sure you're okay, Miss Polson?"

Anna nodded. "Yeah. I just…." She paused for a second then laughed a little and shook her head. "Before you knocked on the door, I was having the worst nightmare. It was so real."

"You were up at the house on the lake today, weren't you? The Demon House? The sheriff dropped by, told me she'd seen you."

"Well, yes. We're making a documentary about it."

The hotel owner nodded. "That place has been the cause of many nightmares, Miss Polson," she replied, gesturing to the phone and returning to the pile of bills she'd been sorting through before leaving to fetch her guest.

Anna looked at her for a moment, but the other woman did not return her gaze. She merely continued with her paperwork.

"Hello," Anna finally said, picking up the receiver.

"Anna, Anna, bobanna."

Her brow furrowed for a second until she heard the raucous laughter in the background and put two and two together. "Tim?"

"Yeah. Hey, look, we're all down here having a great time. Why don't you close your notebook for an hour and just come and hang with us mere mortals?"

His words slurred a little and the last thing she wanted to do was head to a bar, but there was something reassuring about hearing his voice. She looked across at the hotel owner once more to see she was staring at her, only for her eyes to immediately return to her paperwork as the glance was returned.

"Um. Maybe a little later. Where are you?"

"We're at a place called Toto's. They do great food too. Their tacos are addictive."

Just the mention of food made Anna's stomach growl a little, and as more laughter rang out from somewhere in the background and a jukebox began to play, she suddenly realised that maybe seeing a familiar face and spending the evening in a packed bar was exactly what she needed. "Tacos, you say?"

"Addictive. Trust me."

"Okay. You've sold it to me. Where is this place?"

"Just down the street from the hotel. Head in the direction of the church and you can't miss it."

"Okay. I'll be there in ten. Order me a serving with a side of fries ... and a beer."

The hotel owner looked across at her and smiled politely before disappearing into the back.

"Okay. See you soon."

She put the phone down and started walking away when it rang again. She paused, looking towards the door the hotel owner had gone through moments before, but now there was no sign of her. *Could it be Tim asking me to bring something? Realising he gave me the wrong directions or the wrong bar name?* She waited a moment longer then picked up the receiver.

"Hello?"

The line crackled loudly and she winced a little to try to hear if there was any conversation from the other end. She was about to place the handset down when a voice whispered, "You're all mine, Anna."

The line went dead, but Anna remained there, frozen with her ear to the phone. The hotel owner re-emerged from the back. The polite smile vanished in an instant as she saw Anna's drained face.

"Are you okay, Miss Polson?"

For a moment, Anna couldn't say or do anything as her mind tried to make sense of everything. *That didn't just happen. It's all in my head. That used to be a thing. In the first months after it happened, after the abduction, I used to see and hear lots of things that weren't there. That was my imagination. I had a sleep terror in my room and this is the aftermath. The phone didn't really ring. I didn't just hear the Red Man. It's all in my head.*

"D-did you hear the phone ring?"

"Well, sure. That's why I came to get you."

"No. I mean just now. Just a few seconds ago."

The hotel owner's brow furrowed. "No, Miss Polson. I went into my back office there. I heard you bring your conversation to a close and that's when I came back out. Are you sure you're okay?"

Anna shook her head. "It's just been a really weird day."

The other woman nodded sympathetically. "I couldn't help but overhear. Maybe some food and a drink is just what you need."

The start of a smile bled onto Anna's face. "Yeah. I think it might be." She started walking away again.

"Oh, and Miss Polson."

"Yeah?" she replied, turning around.

"I'm sure you were going to fix yourself in the mirror before heading out, but just in case." She gestured towards her cheek. "I think you might have had a little mishap with your lipstick earlier."

Anna pressed her fingers up to her face. She withdrew them once more, but there was nothing there. *What the hell's she talking about?* "Thanks for the warning," she said, heading out of the lobby and ascending the staircase.

She opened the door of her room and turned on the light, casting a glance towards the bed before sitting down at the dressing table. She looked in the mirror to see three red streaks on her cheek. At first glance, someone might have mistaken them for lipstick marks, but on a closer inspection, the centre one was elongated. They were finger marks. Red finger marks.

A shivering breath left Anna's lips. *It was real. It happened. As impossible as any of this is, it happened.*

She saw something in the corner of the mirror and spun around on the small stool, convinced the Red Man would be waiting there and her ordeal would continue, but there was nothing.

No. No. This can't be happening. It's that house. This place. This goddam place.

She jumped to her feet and ran across to her sports bag, stuffing in her few unpacked belongings before running back to the dresser and grabbing the van keys.

"I won't let this happen again. I'm not going to let this happen again," she sobbed, flinging the door open and almost sprinting down the corridor. She charged through the lobby, not stopping as the owner called after her.

Tim had walked up from the bar to collect her, but she ran past him too.

"Anna! Anna!" he cried as she charged through the doors.

She paused as she placed the keys in the van door. "I can't do this. I can't do this, not again. It's all happening again. It's all happening again," she cried, almost diving into the van and throwing her bag into the passenger footwell.

Tim just stood there, open mouthed and confused, as he watched his friend start the engine. The tyres screeched and the wheels spun until, finally, they gained traction and the vehicle sped out of the car park. There was another rubber on tarmac squeal as the van took a corner, but then she was on Main Street. She pressed down hard on the gas, gaining more and more speed.

The buildings became more sporadic, giving way to the road out of town, the road back home. *Home.* That was where she would be safe. *Home.*

8

Beth walked over to the table where Lev was sitting and plonked herself down on the stool opposite him. She pushed a bottle across and kept one for herself.

He observed her for a few seconds, still a little lost in his own thoughts. Finally, it was she who spoke the first words. "Tough day?"

"Could say that."

"Wanna talk about it?"

Lev observed her for a moment. In jeans, boots, jacket and a T-shirt, she seemed like a different woman to the one he'd met in the morning, far more approachable. But he still hadn't really come to terms with the events of the day and the last thing he wanted to do was give the impression of being some kind of kook. "Definitely not," he eventually replied.

Beth smiled a warm smile and took a drink. "I get that. I have those kinds of days, sometimes."

"So, Sheriff," he said, raising the bottle. "Do you buy drinks for all out-of-towners or am I a special case?"

"Beth."

"Hmm?"

"My name. It's Beth."

"Oh. Okay. I'm—"

"Levon Stoll."

A crooked smile started on his face. "Is there a wanted poster hanging up for me somewhere?"

Beth laughed. "That wouldn't surprise me for a second. But that's not the reason I came over."

"It's Lev, by the way."

"What is?"

"Lev. That's what my friends call me."

"So, I'm your friend?"

"You bought me a beer. You're already ranking higher than a lot of my family."

Beth chuckled again. "Good to know."

"So, how do you know my name exactly?"

"My niece. She showed me a CD."

"Aha!"

"So, what's a high-flyer like you doing here?"

"A high-flyer?"

"Compared to the people who usually come through here."

"I'm hardly a high-flyer. I love what I do, and the pay's okay, but when someone like me isn't in the studio or manning the desk at a gig, then I'm not earning money. And when you're in the middle of a divorce, and your ex won't be content until she bankrupts you and shows your kids what an unreliable, monumental, deadbeat screw-up you really are, then suddenly you're counting every penny."

Beth looked at him long and hard. "Wow!"

"Wow, what?"

"Wow, that was honest. I mean, it wasn't what I expected from you."

It was Lev who laughed now. "Thanks."

"I'm sorry," she said, shaking her head, suddenly realising how that sounded. "It's just that after meeting you this morning, I thought you'd have bigged your job up to impress me."

Lev took another drink of his beer. "Well, Sheriff Beth, you've caught me on a weird day. Go on. Ask me something else. All I've got for sale this evening is the truth."

"If I took a blood sample, what would the narcotics lab find in it?"

Lev laughed again. "Zip. I don't do drugs."

"Now I know you're lying. Someone in your industry not doing drugs."

"Seriously. I don't do them. Booze? Absolutely. I can handle my booze. But nothing else. I know plenty who do, but the music's always been my buzz. That's enough for me."

Her eyes narrowed. "You're serious, aren't you?"

"I told you. I'm all out of bullshit today. What else do you want to know? Ooh, I've got a good one. The flirting and innuendo are just masks to shield my insecurity and lack of self-worth. If ever someone actually took me up on anything, I'd turn into a nervous gibbering wreck and they'd be running for the door before I even got to buy them dinner."

Beth took another drink and tilted her head. "Seriously. What the hell happened to you today?"

Lev shook his head. "Don't want to talk about it." He paused for a moment. "Look. I'm sorry. The last thing you want is to come over here to find me in the middle of some existential crisis."

"Actually, you've pleasantly surprised me. I thought I was going to come over here and find that you were an even bigger jackass than I thought you were, but actually you're kind of sweet."

"Ahh! The words that prelude most of the car-crash relationships I've been involved in. So, anyway, why did you come over here if you thought I was such a jackass, as you put it?"

Beth looked around the bar. It was still quiet. The odd local kept rubbernecking, trying to understand what she was doing buying this stranger a drink.

"I don't usually do this," she began. "In fact, I've never done this." She pulled out a small wallet and retrieved a photo. "This is my daughter."

"She's beautiful. Adopted, I'm guessing?"

"Prick," Beth said, giggling a little and taking the photo back.

"She's going through a bad time. I mean a really bad time. I know for a fact that having her mom as the sheriff doesn't play well for her at school. And she's a little different to start off with. She doesn't really see the world like most people see it."

"Different's good."

"It's not good when you're a parent and she's going through all kinds of shit and there's nothing you can do about it."

"I'm sorry. I know what that's like."

"Well, this is crazy, but she is obsessed with Blazetrailer." Lev smiled and took another drink of beer. "If she even knew I was talking to you now, she'd be here in a beat and you'd still be answering her questions when my sister opened this place back up tomorrow."

Lev looked across to the bar. "That's your sister?"

"Uh-huh. And before you go there, I know she's the pretty one."

He shrugged. "I'd say you're on a par."

"That's my fucking sister."

"I was being serious and I was trying to pay you a compliment."

"Oh. Okay then. Thanks, I guess. Anyway. It's my daughter's birthday tomorrow, and I realise this is a long shot, but no longer a shot than someone who knows the band actually showing up in this town. But—"

"Are you okay? You're kind of talking like you're about to have an embolism or something."

"That's exactly what it feels like whenever I have to ask anyone for a favour. But here goes. Have you got something, like a piece of memorabilia, something unique that you can't buy in the shops or from the fan club, because trust me, she's got it all? Have you got something, even if it's just a small thing from the band that might just put a tiny smile on her face?"

"You came over here in the hope that somehow I could help pull your daughter out of the rut she's in with a discarded piece of Jodie Starr's chewing gum or something?"

Beth sighed deeply and shook her head. "When you say it like that, it does make me sound pretty desperate, doesn't it? I'm sorry. It was stupid. You've had a lousy day and the last thing you need is some crazy woman demanding—"

"You're not crazy. You're a good mum. Sorry, mom. I sometimes forget how much you yanks have bastardised the language."

Beth laughed. "Ass. But thank you. It's nice to be called a good mom, even if it's not really true."

"It is. I can't imagine how much self-respect you had to swallow to come across here and ask me for a favour."

"You have no idea."

They both laughed before Lev continued. "I don't really carry around much in the way of priceless Blazetrailer memorabilia in the hope of impressing someone who might be geeky enough to recognise me."

"No. I don't suppose you would. Like I said. It was a stupid idea."

"But how about this." Lev paused for a moment, the trials of his day temporarily forgotten. "Are you having a party for your daughter or something?"

"Enola. Her name's Enola."

"Okay. Are you having a party for Enola?"

"Well, it's hardly a party. Me, my sister and my niece."

"That's it?"

"I told you. She's struggling at the moment."

"Okay. When is this?"

"Tomorrow evening."

"And what are you doing? You going out or—"

"We're ordering pizza, eating a cake that serves about twenty people and watching a movie."

"What if I got Jodie to call her?"

Beth's eyebrows arched. "If you're joking right now, it's really not funny."

Lev shook his head. "I'm not joking. I might be speaking a bit prematurely. I'd have to phone her and make sure she could do it, but do you want me to see if I can set it up?"

"Jesus, yes!"

"There's a price."

The happiness that was threatening to light Beth's face suddenly dissipated. "What price?"

"You let me buy the next round."

Beth flashed a wide grin. "Deal."

"Is there a phone in here I can use?"

"You're calling now?"

"Yeah. I want to make sure we can do this, otherwise we'll need a plan b."

Beth stood up. "Come on. I'll take you into the back."

She led him behind the bar, winking at her sister, and into the hallway behind the small kitchen. She stood there watching him as he picked up the phone. "Um … I might be a little while," he said.

"Oh, God. Sorry. What am I thinking?" I'll leave you to it."

He watched as she retraced her steps then stared at the receiver for a moment. It had been a few weeks since he'd last spoken to her. He knew a conversation was overdue, and this was certainly not the best time for it, but the sheriff's pleading had reminded him of the hopelessness he felt. His children were an ocean away. He'd do anything to see smiles on their faces and there was something inside him that was saying if he could make this girl smile, if he could make her happy, if he could give this desperate mother some sense of worth, then maybe there was hope for his kids, and him.

He dialled the number and waited. The housekeeper picked up the phone.

"Hello?"

He smiled. You'd think one of the biggest rock stars on the circuit would have someone more professional answering the phone, but in fairness, it was probably a pretty good way to weed out stalking fans. Few would expect this greeting. "Hi Greta, it's Lev. Is Jodie there, please?"

"I will see if she's available, Mr Lev."

He stood there a little nervously. He hadn't told her about this job or, more importantly, who had got it for him. He knew that there was nothing she wouldn't do for him, but he didn't want favours. He didn't want preferential treatment. As old-fashioned a concept as it was, he wanted to pay his own way.

"Fucker. Where the hell have you been?" finally came the response from the other end of the phone. "I've been trying to get a hold of you for over a week."

"Hi to you, too."

"Screw that. Where are you?"

"I took a job."

"You took a job? You took a fucking job? You've got a job."

"When you're working, when you're gigging, I've got a job. When you're taking time off, I'm unemployed. And right now, I need to keep money coming in."

"Who are you working with? Which studio?"

"I'm not working with a band. I'm the sound guy for a TV crew."

There was a pause. "You're what?"

"It is what it is. It's not like I've got an abundance of friends in the industry. It's work and it's helping to pay my blood-sucking lawyers, so it's all good."

"You could have just come to me."

"I know I could."

"Then why didn't you?"

"Because I don't want you bailing me out."

There was a pause. *Shit. I know what's coming.*

"How did you get the gig?"

Another pause. "Jamie knew a guy who knew a guy." It was only a white lie. She didn't need to know that Jamie had a vested interest in the production company.

"I fucking knew it. You'd take help from him, but you won't take help from me."

"The difference is your help would come in the way of a cheque. I need to earn my own living, Jo."

"Listen to me. You earn your living a hundred times over. You basically produced that last album while that hack the record company lined up spent most of his time snorting blow off a hooker's tits. Hell, I'm pretty certain that's your guitar solo on *Frozen Lake*. So don't start with—"

"I got paid to do a job and I did it. End of story. I'm getting paid to do another job now, but the second you guys are ready to go back in the studio, I'll be there."

"You make me want to hurt you sometimes."

"Thanks."

"So, where are you?"

"A little town called New Scotland in Tennessee. You'd love it. Not."

"So, I'm guessing you don't have access to the British tabloids there."

"I think the local newspaper runs a haystack of the week competition, so it's not as if we're without modern culture here."

"Uh-huh. Make jokes all you want, prick. They published the photo yesterday and Cassie thinks their affiliates will be running them over here tomorrow."

"Well. We knew it would happen."

"How can you be so matter-of-fact about it?"

"Because we knew it was going to happen. Are you okay?"

"I got off lightly. Showing some skin will probably boost sales by twenty points. You're the one whose life fucking imploded as a result of the whole thing."

"Hey, look. Whatever problems me and Lottie had were there long before her lawyer hired that investigator."

"But I could have made all this right."

"This is how it had to play out."

"But—"

"But nothing."

"But it's not right. None of it's right. This is the second time you've bailed me out like this. I should—"

"Stop it. Listen to me. There are like three people in this world who I will kill or die for. You're one of them. Whatever happens happens, but it stops for you with that photo."

There was a long pause. "It's not fair."

"Life isn't fair."

Another pause. "So, what's this thing you're working on?"

"It's a series of forty-minute documentaries."

"About what?"

"Haunted houses and shit."

Another pause. "And it just so happened that it was Jamie who was somehow involved in this."

"Yeah."

"I've warned you about him. I've warned you and warned you. You don't want to get mixed up in the shit he's mixed up in, Lev."

"I'm not getting mixed up in anything. I'm the sound guy for this series and we're in this cosy little town to record an episode at this place that used to be the Church of Pure Enlightenment or some shit. You'd love it. You always struck me as a God-fearing girl."

"Dick."

They both laughed. "It's just a job, that's all."

"There's never a 'that's all' with Jamie."

"I can look after myself."

"Just be careful."

His mind flashed back to the Black house. *I think that boat's sailed.* "I will."

"There's something you're not saying."

Shit! She really does know me too well. "It's nothing."

"Tell me."

"It's—"

"Tell me, Lev."

He let out a long sigh. "Something really weird happened today, that's all. It creeped me out a bit. We went to this house and…. Look, it doesn't matter. I was on the road for the best part of twenty-four hours before I arrived here, so I'm overtired."

"What happened?"

"It doesn't matter. Look, that's not the reason I'm calling."

"Well, if you weren't calling to tell me what you're doing, and you haven't called about the photos, what are you calling about?"

"I've got a favour to ask."

"Okay, shoot."

"There's this kid who is like your biggest fan. She's going through a shit time, and it's her birthday tomorrow, and I said to her mum that I'd see if I could get you to call her."

"Tomorrow?"

"Yeah."

"What time?"

"I'd guess it would be about eight here, so it would probably be about six where you are."

"Six? Sure. I'll probably just be getting up around about then."

"I mean six in the evening."

"I know what you mean." They both laughed. "So, I'm guessing she's got a hot mum who you're trying to impress."

"She's actually a sheriff."

"Women in uniform. I can dig that. When can I meet her?"

"You do understand what under the radar means, don't you, Jo?"

"I was joking, arsehole. If anybody knows how to live a lie, it's me."

"Don't say it like that."

"It is what it is. It's not like I'm the first, the last or the only."

"At least that photo will help a little."

"That's not funny. If I could go back in time and make everything right, you know I would."

"You're sweet. Nobody would believe it if I told them."

"Fuck you."

"That's my girl."

"Always."

"So, you'll do it?"

"Course I'll do it. Get me the details and I'll phone her dead on six."

"Okay."

"If I'm not around, just leave the number with Greta. And leave the number of where you're staying too. I've got the contract meeting tomorrow. I want to tell you how it goes."

"I doubt you'll know anything tomorrow."

"I know. But I miss talking to you."

"I miss talking to you too."

"Promise me you'll be careful, Lev."

"I'm just a sound recordist on a TV show. I'm not on a candidate list for blood sacrifices or anything."

"Yeah. Well, knowing Jamie the way I do, I'd read the small print in your contract."

"I know you don't like the guy, but he's always been cool with me."

"There's only one person he's interested in. No, I tell a lie. There are two. Does Satan count as a person?"

"Exaggerate much?"

"He's into some weird, sick shit is all I'm saying."

"I promise you. I'll be fine."

"Okay. You know best. You always know best."

"Don't get huffy."

"If Jodie fucking Starr wants to get huffy, Jodie fucking Starr will get huffy."

"Did you really just refer to yourself in the third person?"

They both burst out laughing again. "Remember to let me have those numbers."

"I will."

"Hope it helps get you laid." She started laughing again.

"That's not why I'm doing this."

"Whatever."

"Thanks, Jodie."

"Anything for you. You know that."

"Yeah. Love you."

"Love you too."

Lev placed the receiver down and turned to see Beth there. "I'm really sorry. I just came back here to make sure you were able to get through and everything. I didn't mean to earwig."

"Listen. Jodie's like a little sister to me. I love her to bits, but there's nothing like that."

"It's none of my business."

"I'm telling you. Jodie's my best friend. I wouldn't do anything to screw that up. I need all the friends I can get."

"Okay." There was an unconvinced smile on her face as she said the word.

"I need your phone number. Jodie's going to call the house at eight o'clock tomorrow."

Beth's eyes widened to the size of golf balls. "You're serious?"

"I'm serious."

An expression of joy that Lev hadn't witnessed on anyone's face in the longest time swept over Beth's. She threw her arms around him. "Thank you. Thank you." Then she suddenly pulled back, putting her hands up apologetically. "God. I'm so sorry. I don't usually do that. It's just that this will make her so happy. You've really no idea."

"Glad I could help."

"Thank you. Seriously. Thank you."

"You've said that already."

"But this is huge. You don't even know me. You don't know her. This is so nice of you."

"How about that drink?"

"Hell, yeah!"

She led him back out and as they emerged, her sister was standing there waiting. "Well?"

"She's calling her at eight tomorrow."

"Holy shit. This is going to put a smile on her face that will stretch from here to the Pacific."

"I know."

"You're not paying for any drinks tonight," Naomi said, turning to look at Lev. "You've done an amazing thing for my family."

"Honestly. It's—"

"Enough. Same again?"

"Well—"

"Same again," she said, uncapping two more Millers before reaching for a couple of shot glasses. "This is worthy of a celebration."

The doors suddenly burst inwards and all eyes shot towards them. "Tim?" Lev said, more than a little bemused by the dramatic entrance.

"Anna's gone," he said, rushing up to the bar.

"What do you mean she's gone?"

"I mean she's taken the van. She's taken all her stuff. She's just packed up and left."

"I don't understand. We start filming tomorrow."

"Not without our gear, we don't."

"Well, did she leave a message or anything?"

"She said she wasn't going to let it happen again." From the smell of his breath, it was obvious that he'd been drinking, but the shock seemed to be sobering him up fast. "She was coming down to have a drink with us and I decided to walk up to the hotel and meet her, but when I got there, she had her stuff and she almost dived into the van."

Lev's hopes of a quiet drink with Beth were in tatters now. "Um. I don't know what to say."

"You were with her all day. Did anything happen between the two of you? Did you have an argument or something?"

Lev shook his head. "No, nothing like that."

"You were gone a hell of a long time, man. I mean did something else happen? Did you touch her or something, you son of a bitch?"

"What? No."

"Well, I've worked with her plenty and she's never done anything like this before, so something freaked her out. You were the one who spent the day with her." He took a step closer to Lev and it was clear that the booze in his system was stirring up again.

"You need to calm down, mister," Beth said, immediately stepping up.

"Calm down? This son of a bitch spent the day with her, and when they arrived back, she didn't want to talk about it. Now she's run off. That doesn't sound at all suspicious to you?"

"I said calm down." She sniffed deeply. "It's clear you're upset, but it's also clear that there's probably a fifty-fifty split of booze and blood in your veins at the moment too. Don't make me put you in the drunk tank."

THE DEVIL'S FACE

"What do you mean?"

"This is the sheriff, Tim," said Lev.

"The sheriff? Well, good. Put out an APB on Anna or something. And then when she confirms what happened, you can put this bastard in cuffs."

Beth reached out, placing a hand on Tim's chest and pushing him back a little. "I'm not going to tell you again." The doors opened and the rest of the production team walked in. "You need to get your friend back to the hotel and sobered up."

"I'm telling you," Tim said, pointing aggressively towards Lev. "He's got something to do with this."

Beth looked at the others. "He's got about thirty seconds before I slap a pair of cuffs on him." In truth, she didn't have any cuffs on her, but she'd strong-armed plenty of men and women alike, much bigger than her, down the street to spend a night in lockup.

"Come on, Tim." It was Fifi who took hold of his arm and guided him back to the exit.

"This isn't over, you son of a bitch. I'm going to get to the bottom of this."

The doors crashed once more as the group departed. Beth's eyes remained on them for a moment before turning to look at Lev. "So, are you going to tell me what that was about?"

"I honestly don't have a clue."

"Well, he seems pretty sure."

"He doesn't know what he's talking about."

"You were with her all day."

"Pretty much."

"I see."

"No, you don't."

"Look. You two seemed pretty cosy when I saw the pair of you. Maybe you—"

"It was nothing like that."

Beth folded her arms. "Well, how about telling me what it was like?"

"Look. Can't you put an alert out for the car or something?"

"Is it stolen?"

"No."

"Do you think this woman poses a risk to herself or others?"

Lev shrugged. "Probably not."

"It's not like she's a missing person. It's not like someone abducted her. She got in the vehicle of her own volition and drove off. Not telling anyone where she was going might be inconsiderate, but it's not a crime. It's not something I can do anything about. But it is curious, I'll give you that. And it's even more curious that you spent the whole day with her and you say nothing happened."

Lev sighed deeply. "I didn't say nothing happened. I said I didn't do anything."

Beth's head tilted a little, like a curious dog trying to understand something. "Right now, this is none of my business, so if you don't want to tell me, that's fine. But if somehow this becomes my business, I'm going to be pissed that you stayed silent."

"Come and sit with me," Lev replied, picking up his drinks.

"What?"

"Come and sit with me and I'll tell you what happened."

9

The more distance Anna put between herself and New Scotland the better she felt. She knew what she was doing was impetuous, that it would require a lot of explanation, that it would probably torpedo any chance of her getting another job with Occulture or might even screw her chances in the industry. *Pros don't act like this.*

But that was the least of her concerns. Those things had happened. As much as she wanted them to be figments of her imagination, they weren't. The Red Man had been in her room. He had cocooned her. He had draped himself over her, inhaling her, touching her. She didn't know how it was possible. In fact, now she thought about it, it was impossible, but that's what made it all the more frightening.

It was impossible that he had lived all those years ago when she had stabbed him in the neck with that bone dagger. It was impossible that he had escaped the bolted room. But he had. And somehow, he had shown up today.

He had shown up and disappeared again just as quickly. It was impossible, but the fact that it had happened meant it wasn't impossible. And if it wasn't impossible, then that meant that anything was possible, and that's why she needed to get the hell away from that town and that house.

She looked down at the speedometer then checked her mirrors. She was doing over eighty. *The last thing I need is for the cops to stop me.* She eased her foot off the gas a little.

There was a long stretch of straight road in front of her. Although the nearest car was probably over a mile ahead, it gave her some small modicum of relief and made her feel like she wasn't quite alone while all the time putting more and more distance between her and that godforsaken town.

It's something to do with the Demon House. It was way too coincidental. Real or not. Impossible or not. Everything was fine until she and Lev had shown up there in the morning.

Now she wished more than ever that she had taken him up on his invitation to talk. She wanted to talk it through, find out if they'd both experienced the same thing.

When he went back to his room, did he have something weird happen to him the way it happened to me? Maybe I can call him tomorrow.

*

Lev knocked back the vodka in one slug and took a drink from his bottle. "So, that's the story. And I don't blame you if you think I'm bullshitting you because I was there and I still can't believe it."

Beth let out a sigh and took a drink too. "I warned you. I stood there and I warned you. But you two knew best. I could tell what you were thinking. I could tell you thought I was just some hick sheriff from a backward, tumbleweed town."

"That's not true."

"Bullshit. But I can't blame you. I suppose I came on a little strong."

"So, you believe me?"

"Hell, yes, I believe you."

"That's a relief, anyway."

"Oh, sure. You lose hours of time, not having a clue what happened to either of you, but it's a relief that I believe you. My mind would be completely at ease if I were you."

Lev chuckled. "Yeah. I'd be lying if I said it wasn't what I was dwelling on before you came over to talk to me."

"The truth is you'll never know."

"What do you mean?"

"I mean logic stops when it comes to that house. I've lived in this town all my life, Lev, and I've seen things and heard stories that would turn your hair white. If you think you're the first people to go there and have no recollection of what happened next, you're mistaken."

"It happened to you?"

"Hell, no. The closest I ever got was with my friends as a teenager. We thought it would be cool to have a Halloween party in the grounds of the place. But…."

"But what?"

"From the moment we arrived there, we all started feeling the same thing. I mean, we were sixteen. We'd grown up hearing stories about this place, but we'd never ventured to the other side of the lake to see it for ourselves. If we had, our parents would probably have torn us all a new one. But when we got there, we kind of understood. Nobody said it out loud, but we got it. We got why that place had such a reputation. There was this feeling, this aura, this … I don't know. I've never been that great with words, but it was like it was marked."

"Marked?"

"Cursed."

"You believe in curses?"

"I didn't. Not really. I still don't, I suppose, but there's definitely something wrong with the place."

"That's it. That's your story. Because you all had a Halloween party in the garden and got a weird feeling? No offence, but that's pretty lame."

"Well, plus the fact one of the couples thought it would be fun to check out the insides of the place. Nobody noticed for a few hours or so. Finally, when we did, we cut the music and started a search, thinking they'd gone into the woods for some quiet time. Y'see, we'd had an agreement before we went that nobody, and I mean nobody, was to go in the house, but they thought they knew better."

"What happened?"

"We heard frantic banging and muffled screams. Damian, my boyfriend at the time, dared to step onto the porch and open the door. Alicia almost flew into his arms, crying her eyes out. Her and Dean, her date, had gone down into the basement and the door had slammed behind him. No matter how they'd both tried to open it, they couldn't. She said it had only just happened, but when she'd gotten outside and seen that the moon was high in the sky, she got really scared. They'd ventured in there at just after seven-thirty. It was near to eleven when Damian had opened the front door. We were all deciding what to do about Dean when he came strolling out as if he was on his way to church."

"Was he okay?"

"He was distant. I mean, normally you couldn't shut this kid up, but it was almost as if he was half asleep."

"You didn't think that was strange?"

"Hell, yes, I thought it was strange. It completely freaked me out, especially as Alicia was such a total mess. Needless to say, the party broke up soon after that. The idea of being there at midnight didn't just freak the girls out and Dean started to act way strange."

"Way strange how?"

"He started whispering."

"Whispering?"

"To start with, everyone thought he was just doing it to creep us all out; y'know, with it being Halloween and all. I mean, we were all in fancy dress and he'd gone as a zombie. He'd put all this make-up on and he looked plenty scary.

But then, when Damian got pissed with him and told him to stop, he just stared, but it wasn't his stare. We all saw it. We all felt it. There was something malevolent in it. Then he smiled and it was the most chilling smile I've ever seen in my life. Oh, Jesus." She shuddered and took a drink.

"You okay?"

"Sorry. It's still there, y'know," she said, tapping the side of her head.

"You don't have to go on."

"I've got this far, so I may as well tell you the rest of it. Anyway, the party was officially over. We packed everything away and any effects of the little bit of booze we'd sneaked were well and truly gone by this time. We drove back into town and went home. It was weird."

"Weird how?"

"Well, this was kind of a rite of passage for us. Halloween's a big thing over here and this was the first time some of us had licences so that we could actually get out of town and not be under the watchful gaze of our parents, and yet we were heading back into our houses and going to bed before our little brothers had even finished watching the late-night Halloween special."

"Understandable, considering what had happened."

Beth took another swig from her bottle. "I suppose. That night, we all had dreams, bad dreams. It was as if we'd witnessed something terrible, experienced some big trauma, y'know; but in actual fact, we'd just been drinking and partying while Dean and Alicia had been locked in that place. We'd witnessed nothing but the aftermath. But all the same, none of us slept well. The next day, we met up at school before lessons like we usually did, except there was no Dean and Alicia was like some flaked-out crackhead. She looked like she'd been crying most of the night."

"So, where was Dean?"

Beth shook her head. "Gone."

"Gone? What do you mean gone?"

"I mean gone."

"He never made it home?"

"He made it home okay. His parents and his little brother were watching TV. He walked straight past them and went up to his room. He'd had a big lecture from his father earlier in the day, and it got heated, so they just assumed it was as a result of that that he'd ignored them. When they finally went to bed, his little brother Petey went in to see him and tell him about his haul from all the trick-or-treating, but he couldn't wake him up. He said he was still in his costume, lying on top of the bed but passed out. He'd seen his dad passed-out drunk enough times, and he'd known what Dean was doing and where he was going that night, so he wasn't about to tell on him. He figured he'd let him sleep it off and show him his haul the next day. But there was no next day."

"He disappeared in the middle of the night?"

Beth nodded. "Vanished."

"So, he ran away?"

"If he did, he ran away without packing any clothes, without the money he'd saved from his weekend job, without even changing out of his costume. He was gone."

"What happened?"

"The biggest search in the town's history is what happened. Even the state police got involved. But there was nothing. Obviously, our secret party didn't stay a secret, and we all got hell for going up to the house, but none of us were too worried about getting grounded. Our friend had disappeared. I mean, even the bloodhounds couldn't pick up a trail. It was like he'd gone to sleep in his room and just evaporated. Needless to say, Alicia freaked out even more. She ended up having to go away."

"Go away?"

"To a psychiatric hospital. She came back a few months later, but she was never the same again. Her parents moved away from the area shortly after. I don't think anyone's heard from them since."

"Jesus."

"Yeah."

"So, did anything else happen to you as a result of being there that night?"

Beth shook her head. "No. I only vowed never to go in that house. And to this day, I've kept that promise."

"You think everybody who heads in there gets the curse, the mark as you call it?"

She stared at him long and hard. "No. In truth."

"But you won't go in there?"

"No. I won't. Listen, there are people who live in the hills around here. A lot of the locals think they're just crazies. But I was up there one time searching for a pair of hikers who'd got lost. This woman, Martha Dupree, her name was, she recognised me from the group photo that was on the front cover of the local paper when Dean went missing. She obviously had a pretty keen eye because that was twelve years before, by this time. She invited me into her cabin, which is probably the kindest way I can describe it. There was no electricity in the place, but this was the afternoon and there was plenty of daylight.

"I asked her about the hikers; she hadn't seen them, and then we got on to Dean's disappearance. What she didn't know about the Black House was nobody's business. She took me into this room. She called it her den and the walls were just full of newspaper clippings and articles about the place as well as obituaries and any strange events that had happened around the town."

"So, she was a kook?"

"That's what I thought at first. But the more I talked to her the more I believed it was like she had some otherworldly knowledge about the place. Apparently, her mother before her was like that too. She'd passed on everything she knew and believed."

"Believed?"

"Yeah. She said that the house was a kind of gateway. She said there was great evil present there and it affected different people in different ways. Some were completely closed off to the place. Most could feel that there was something not right about the house, but other than that, they would remain largely untouched. A few could see, hear and experience things. Others could become conduits for the evil within, doing the work of the devil."

"The devil?" Lev asked with a smirk on his face.

"I know how it sounds, but I kind of believed her. It made sense. I mean, I know people who've been in that place and been fine. I know most people in town avoid the place like the plague and—"

"Surely that could just be because of its reputation."

"Well, sure. Maybe. But I saw with my own eyes what happened to Alicia and Dean. And what happened to the occupants of the guesthouse and the Church of Enlightenment was well documented. And maybe it's not the devil as he's spoken about in the Bible. Maybe it's the devil in a broader sense. Y'know, evil. What if that's what she was talking about?

"I mean, whatever happened today it's certainly freaked your friend out enough for her to grab her keys and get the hell out of town. What do you think would make a person do that?"

"I really don't have a clue. She seemed to have it all together."

"Well. There is the other possibility."

"What's that?"

"A day working with you made her lose all hope for the project and she just got out of here the moment your back was turned." A self-satisfied smile lit Beth's face as she took another drink from her bottle.

"You've been dying to say that, haven't you?"

"You have no idea."

"Feel better now?"

"Much. Thanks."

Lev smiled before exhaling deeply. "I suppose this leaves me up the proverbial creek without a paddle."

"What do you mean?"

THE DEVIL'S FACE

"I mean no director, no documentary, no job."

"But surely you've got a contract?"

"Kind of."

"What do you mean?"

"We all work on the basis of finished hours of production and a small back-end royalty. Effectively, we were entering into this as a production company who were going to sell the end product to our customer, Occulture."

"Is that standard?"

"I was told it was. This was my first TV job."

"So, what are you going to do?"

"Honestly, I don't know."

"I mean, how broke are you?"

Lev pulled his wallet out and placed just short of two hundred dollars on the table. "That broke."

"That's it? That's everything you've got?"

"Pretty much."

"Do you have to pay the hotel out of that too?"

"No, thank fuck. We were due to stay there for four nights, but I'm guessing, with Anna gone, the plug will be well and truly pulled."

"So, you'll probably be getting on the bus tomorrow." There was a hint of sadness in Beth's eyes. For the first time in a long time, she was talking to a man and it was easy. It flowed.

"No."

"I'm confused. So what are you going to do?"

"Stay as long as two hundred dollars will allow me to stay and try to figure out what the hell happened up there today."

"You're going back?"

"Listen. There are several hours of my time I can't account for. That's bad enough, but then someone who seemed perfectly rational, and pleasant, and intelligent, and decent completely freaked out today. Now she's taken the van with most of the equipment and just gone AWOL. That's not normal."

"And I've told you about that place. I've told you what it does to people."

"I know. But I can't leave it there, Beth. I just can't."

It was Beth's turn to exhale a long breath now. "Stay here," she said, standing and heading over to the bar.

"Why?"

"Just stay here a minute."

*

I love you weren't just words for Jodie. She really meant them where Lev was concerned. She loved him just about as much as she'd ever loved anyone, but it wasn't how the press was trying to portray it.

Jodie Starr was a megastar. A crazily talented singer and songwriter who had become the lead vocalist with Blazetrailer and helped catapult them to stardom. They were on a hiatus, but that didn't mean that the public stopped devouring stories about one of the most iconic women in rock. Jodie's real name was Jodie Weller. She grew up in Lewisham, London. There was nothing amazing about her teenage years other than a devotion to music. She loved it. She absorbed it like a sponge. Rock, classical, soul, jazz, country, anything and everything she could get her hands on. She got to grade eight on the piano but taught herself guitar as well as a whole host of other instruments.

When most kids were out partying, she was in her room with the lights off and headphones on. She had a happy life but didn't really start to live until she formed her first band. The moment she did, the intelligent, quiet, reserved Jodie Weller was gone and Jodie Starr was born.

Things had happened quickly. She was still only twenty-seven, but she'd accomplished more than most people who'd spent a life in the business. She'd had a string of high-profile boyfriends—none of them serious. She'd appeared in every music, entertainment and gossip mag on both sides of the Atlantic. But Jodie Starr wasn't real.

Jodie Starr was a character. Underneath, she was insecure and self-doubting and ... gay. It was a very small circle who were privy to this information. The record company was concerned that if it came out, it would shatter the image, the persona. It would kill Jodie Starr as the idol she had become to millions around the world.

Jodie loved music. She loved Blazetrailer. She loved her life, but she hated living a lie. She continued to be photographed in public on the arms of handsome movie stars and celebrities, but it tore her up inside. Then she found a kindred spirit. Madison California was the guitarist with an up-and-coming outfit who'd secured the support slot on Blazetrailer's headline arena tour. They'd had a hit album and, after the tour, were heading into the studio to record another. Madison was on the up and somehow she knew who Jodie was behind the mask. She saw herself and a covert romance blossomed.

The only person Jodie confided in as to what was going on was Lev. He became her fixer, pretending to have a thing with Madison when needed so he could sneak off with her and secretly deliver her to Jodie. His room was always opposite or next door to hers, and while most people spent life on the road out of their skulls on booze or drugs, Lev did his best to hold things together. Things weren't going well for him at home and he knew his choice of work would probably end up costing him his marriage and his family, but he continued anyway.

During a five-night run at the Hollywood Bowl, Jodie woke up after passing out drunk to find Madison naked next to her on the king-sized bed. Her skin was almost white, and to this day, she could still remember the sound of the scream she'd made when she realised her lover was dead.

She'd run across the hall to Lev's room. He was always her first port of call whenever she was in trouble. It took him about ten seconds to figure out she'd OD'd. Jodie was so upset that she hadn't noticed the syringe on top of the quilt or the blood spot that had dripped from between Madison's big and second toes.

"You fell asleep in my room," he'd said.

"What are you talking about?" Jodie had replied.

"You passed out drunk in my room; Madison and I came in here. I fell asleep and I woke up to find her like this."

"No. No, you can't."

He hadn't accepted no for an answer. He'd bundled her into his room and immediately phoned Nine-One-One. He was taken away by the police but released without charge when the initial results came back from the hospital. This was LA and the doctors knew an overdose when they saw one. The tour manager and the record company arranged a different support act in a heartbeat; Lev was second-stringed to being an assistant guitar tech for the remaining leg of the tour, having to sleep on one of the tour buses rather than in a hotel.

More often than not, though, he would end up spending the night in Jodie's room, holding her while she fell asleep in his arms. Madison's death had been well-publicised, as were the rock-and-roll circumstances surrounding it. The story was the final nail in the coffin for Lev's marriage, but he never spoke a word about the real circumstances.

It was just one of the many reasons why when Jodie said she loved him, it was true from the bottom of her heart. A smile lit her face as she pulled a cigarette from the packet with her teeth. For him to ask her to call this girl to wish her happy birthday there must be something special about the mother. *I hope so. If anybody deserves to find happiness, it's him.*

The smile faded as her mind drifted to the rest of the conversation. She flicked her lighter on and sucked deeply until she heard the comforting crackle of the tobacco catching.

She reached into the drawer of the small table next to her couch and pulled out an address book. She followed the lines until she reached one that simply read Taleen.

Taleen had come into Jodie's life during the recording of Blazetrailer's *Sounds Like Hell* album. It was their third but Jodie's second with the band. Taleen was someone unique, someone indescribable. The thought of her alone confused and amazed Jodie in equal measure. She'd heard of her before then. Who hadn't heard of Taleen Zakarian, the world-famous artist whose works had become among the most sought-after for any modern art collector? But it was not to do with art that Taleen had reached out to Jodie. It was to do with Jamie. She had seen Jodie's innocence behind the façade and felt the urge to warn her.

Now hearing her best friend, her family for all intents and purposes, was working with or for him again troubled Jodie and she needed guidance.

"Hi. Can I speak to Taleen?"

"Who is this, please?"

"Jodie."

There was a pause of a minute or so before Taleen picked up the phone. "I was just thinking about you the other day, darling."

"Oh? Is that a good or a bad thing?"

Jodie could hear the smile in Taleen's deep, mysterious voice as she replied. "Always good where you're concerned. Now, what can I do for you? Are you finally going to pose nude for me?"

"Um. No."

"Oh. Too bad."

"It's about Jamie."

"Oh. That's never good. I was hoping it would be a long time before I heard that name again."

"Yeah, well, you and me both."

"What do you need, darling?"

"Taleen, do any alarm bells sound when I mention the Church of Pure Enlightenment to you?" Silence. "Taleen?"

"What business have you got with the Church of Pure Enlightenment?"

"Not me."

"Who then?"

"Lev."

"Ah. Your soul mate."

"He's not my soul mate."

"You say this, but all evidence suggests otherwise. Okay. What's his business with the Church of Pure Enlightenment?"

"Jamie's got him a gig with a TV crew doing a series of documentaries. This is the first one on the list."

"And the last."

"What do you mean?"

"The Carlton Black Guesthouse is not a place to be trifled with. It's not somewhere to be filmed, written about or visited."

"What are you talking about? What's the Carlton Black Guesthouse got to do with anything? I said—"

"It's the same place. Whatever they choose to call it, whatever purpose the building serves, what lies beneath is where the true purpose can be found."

"Okay. You're creeping me out a little, Taleen. But I suppose that's nothing new. What do you mean by the true purpose?"

"Your friend needs to quit this job. He needs to get out of town before setting foot in that place."

"I—"

"Is it too late? Has he already been there?"

"I think so."

Taleen let out a long, heavy breath. "What are you doing now?"

"Not much. I was heading to the Troubadour tonight, but—"

"Forget the Troubadour. If you care about your friend you'll come over here now."

A sudden shiver ran down Jodie's back. "Okay. Okay, I'll be over in twenty minutes."

10

Anna's intention had been to drive through the night, get a few hours' sleep at a motel, and then continue until she got back to LA. But she had changed her mind. LA was where she had lived these last few years, but it was not home in the real sense.

She wanted to see her parents. She wanted to see her sister and her nephew and nieces. She wanted to go back home, the real home, Pilot Point, near Dallas. That's where she'd grown up. That's where her happiest memories were made. That was the womb she needed to feel safe and secure again. She wanted to be with her family. She wanted the security that gave her. It might be for a day, a week or a month.

Maybe I could get a job with the Pilot Point Post. The alliterative title had always been a source of amusement for those visiting the area. To the natives, it was simply called the *Post*.

I used to do a lot of writing when I was younger. Maybe I wouldn't get the buzz that I get from directing, but I'd make a healthy profit on the apartment. I could get somewhere bigger in Pilot Point, maybe settle down and start a family.

A thousand thoughts a minute were flashing through her head. All of them had been nothing more than fleeting up until this journey. Until today, her career had been her focus. But there were things far more important than a career. *Sanity, for one.*

Now she was on the road, at least fifty miles away from New Scotland and that hellish house, it all started to seem far less plausible again. *There's no way any of that could have happened.*

Stress. Overwork. That could account for it. She'd heard of people in the industry getting totally burned out. Hallucinations, hearing things, extreme paranoia. It all fit with what was going on.

The phone call and the whispered words. *Wait a minute. The hotel owner had only been in the next room and she hadn't heard a thing. That could have been in my head too.*

Suddenly, she started to feel a little better about herself. Yeah. *It's overwork. I'm having some freaky episode because the last few months have been relentless and—*

The three red marks on my face. How the hell can I explain those away?

Her left eye twitched. She looked at the clock on the dashboard then at the gauge. She had the best part of three-quarters of a tank. She'd probably need to fill up again, but all being well, she could be having breakfast with her family.

The three red marks. Her mind drifted back to them again. The hotel owner had mentioned lipstick. Was there any way she could have drawn them on her own face while asleep? When she'd suffered those horrific night terrors in her teens, it had obviously been as a direct result of the abduction. But had her fear come true, or half-true at least? Had the night terrors come back because she'd predicted that very occurrence with Lev earlier in the day? Had she somehow drawn those lines on her own face? Had her subconscious created this whole thing?

When she'd interviewed for the job, she'd spoken about the night terrors, but she couldn't bring herself to speak of the thing, the event that set them in motion. That was something that stayed between herself and her family. Sure, someone with a long memory might remember the news. *Hell, I was plastered all over it for days.* But news gives way to news, gives way to news, and, suddenly, the most horrific, awful, chilling thing that's reported fades to something else and something else and something else. There had been thousands of news cycles in between the event and now, and why would she possibly have brought something like that up?

Dwelling on it had brought no end of panic attacks and bouts of depression. She had learned to deal with it, learned to cope with it, and part of that coping mechanism was not talking about it with strangers. That's what they were. They weren't relatives, they weren't friends, they were just … investors. Yes. They had invested in her for this project, but they didn't own her. She'd confided about the night terrors. That's more than she needed to, and to be honest, even now, she didn't quite understand why.

The interview had felt a little bit like a show and tell and it was true when she'd said to Lev that she wanted to sound a little more interesting than she actually was. Because work had become her entire focus. It had given her something to throw herself into and occupy her mind.

Focus, Anna. Her thoughts were still running at a thousand miles an hour.

Lipstick.

She reached across into her handbag and pulled it out, turning on the internal light and flicking off the cap with her right hand while keeping her left firmly gripped around the steering wheel. She stared at the waxy, oily crimson stick that protruded from the casing. *Yes. Yes, that could be it. It wouldn't be the strangest thing that I'd done in a dream.*

She remembered back to the time she'd woken her parents by digging a hole in the back garden. Somehow, they'd guided her back to bed and it was only the next morning, when she discovered muddy smudges on her hands and arms, that they confided what had happened. She had no recollection of it. And maybe the same thing had happened now.

She retrieved the cap from the passenger seat, skilfully replaced it, and then put the stick back in her purse. She carried on driving for a moment, her brain working overtime as she desperately tried to piece together the sequence of events to make sense of them.

"Okay. Let's get this straight," she said, checking the mirrors and slowing down a little as if a reduction in speed would help her mind begin to process things more methodically. "Okay," she said again. "Let's figure this out, Anna."

Forget the Black house for the moment and what happened there. Let's pick up where I came back to my room.

I closed the curtains, flopped down on the bed. She wracked her brain to recall any other details, no matter how small. *Nothing else happened and I drifted off. When I woke up again, it was all happening. Only, I didn't wake up, did I? I didn't wake up until the hotel owner knocked on the door.*

A smile lit Anna's face and tears welled in her eyes. "I didn't wake up. I didn't fucking wake up." *It was a night terror. And even after it, I was still only in a semi-lucid state. When I thought I heard the phone ring after my conversation with Tim, it was my subconscious again. It was a kind of waking dream. My mind hadn't fully woken up.*

In one way, this was a disturbing revelation because it had been years since she'd suffered from events like these, but the alternative was far more worrying.

When I get to Pilot Point, the first thing I'm going to do is make an appointment with Doctor Moore. We can nip this thing in the bud. It was the house. The house freaked me out, whatever it was that happened there, and the rest was a fait accompli.

The smile broadened into a grin. *Thank you, God.*

*

THE DEVIL'S FACE

Beth returned to the table in the corner with two more drinks. She gave one to Lev and kept the other for herself. "We'll finish these then I've got something to show you."

"Okay, but you don't need to get me drunk for that. You're an attractive woman."

Beth laughed. "You're an ass."

"It's been said before. I dare say it will be said again."

"Yeah, I dare say," Beth replied, taking a drink.

"So, what are you going to show me?"

"First of all, I just want to repeat that I think this is a terrible idea. Going back to that place is just opening up a can of worms you really should be running the hell away from. But you're a grown adult and I can't force you. My jackass of a brother gave you permission, so—"

"Your brother."

"What about him?"

"You said that Enola's birthday celebrations were just you, your sister, and her daughter. What about your brother?"

"We don't have that kind of relationship. It's strained I think is the kindest way I can put it."

"Okay. I won't pry."

"There's nothing to pry into. There's no scandal, no mystery; we've just never got on and Naomi and me are too old to bother pretending anymore."

"Fair enough. Anyway, sorry I interrupted you."

Beth thought back to try to pick up her thread but then shrugged. "I'd kind of finished what I was saying. I just think it's a bad idea is all."

"And what is it you're going to show me?"

Beth took a deep breath. "This isn't something I do on a regular basis, okay?"

"Now I am intrigued."

"Steady your horses, there, bud. It's nothing like that. There's a little apartment out back. When we bought this place, the upstairs rooms were being rented out and the apartment was accommodation for the owners. Naomi didn't want to bring Bella up with a bunch of strangers living in the place, so we remodelled, and they live upstairs, and the apartment kind of became a bit of a storage facility. It's nothing fancy, but it's clean and it's free. You can stay there as long as you need to."

"You're serious?"

"Sure. Like I said, it's just sitting there."

"But ... you've only just met me. You don't have to do this."

She locked eyes with him, and when she spoke, he knew she was being sincere. "What you did for Enola tonight is just about the nicest thing anyone's ever done for her or me. You could have made a thousand excuses, but you didn't hesitate. You're one of the good guys, Lev. I can tell them a mile off."

Lev looked embarrassed and stared at his bottle. "Nah. You just don't know me well enough yet."

A smile lit her face once again. "I'm a pretty good judge of character."

"I don't know what to say. Thank you."

"That's enough."

"I mean it. When I get working again, I'll pay you back for this."

"You've already paid me."

"I don't like being a charity case."

"It's no big deal. I mean, if you insist on heading back to that house, the chances are you'll disappear or be dead by next week, so it's not as if you're going to inconvenience us that long."

Lev sniggered. "Well, there is that, I suppose."

"Seriously. Are you sure I can't talk you out of this?"

"I don't like things being taken from me."

"What do you mean?"

"I mean my time was stolen. I don't have a clue what happened in that place. I don't know what happened to me and I don't know what happened to Anna. What I do know is that it freaked her out enough to do a runner with all our gear. I need to get to the bottom of it, Beth."

"All I'm saying is that it's a dangerous path you're travelling down."

"I really appreciate your concern. It means a lot."

"Don't get me wrong. My concern is for me. Do you have any idea of the amount of paperwork that's involved with a dead body or a missing person?"

Lev laughed. "I like you."

"You don't know me well enough yet."

He shrugged. "I'm a pretty good judge of character."

They both smiled and took another drink. "I was thinking."

"What?"

"Assuming you're still alive tomorrow, would you like to come to Enola's little party?"

"Don't you want to keep it to just the family?"

"That's what it is pretty much every year. Provided you don't mind a thousand questions about Blazetrailer and Jodie Starr, you'd be more than welcome to come. Enola would love it."

"Mm."

"Mm? What does that mean?"

"I'm just thinking how strange life is sometimes."

"What are you talking about?"

"I mean when I met you this morning, I didn't think for a second that by the end of the day, you'd be asking me out on a date."

Beth laughed. "Jackass. In no way, shape or form is this a date."

"Uh-huh. Bit spineless using your daughter's birthday party as a cover, but I guess you've been off the scene for a while, so your confidence might be a bit shaky and you need a plausible out if you get rejected."

Beth laughed again. "You've seen right through me. I'm always falling for out-of-work men in the middle of sticky divorces with egos the size of Texas."

"Shit. You really do know me, don't you?"

"Told you. So, will you come?"

"You said there'd be cake?"

"More than four people could hope to eat in a night."

"Okay. Sold."

They both smiled. "Come on. Let's finish these drinks and then I'll show you to your new luxury condo."

"Thanks for this, Beth."

She shrugged. "It's no big thing."

"It is. It's a long time since I've had to rely on the kindness of a stranger."

"Who are you, Blanche Dubois? It's what happens in small towns. We look out for one another."

"Well, thanks anyway."

*

Jodie liked Taleen, but she was scared of her too. Taleen was into all kinds of weird stuff. It wasn't just because she was an artist, although she'd found most artists to be a little eccentric. This was something else.

Taleen had referred to herself a few times as a guardian of light. It was a title that had unnerved Jodie a little. There was no humour in the remark and it had always come after discussing dark topics, usually the occult and Jamie in particular. There was part of Taleen that was very open with Jodie, but there was another part that was completely closed off.

Taleen was openly gay, but her fan demographic wasn't bothered by such things, unlike Jodie's, whose record company had told her that if ten million slavering young men suddenly found out they didn't stand a chance, her sheen would soon wear off.

It was insulting and sickening in equal measure. Jodie felt sure the music would speak for itself, but her agent had put as much pressure on her as the execs and so she was forced to live a lie. Nobody would ever dare tell Taleen how to live her life. If for no other reason than she probably scared them as much as she scared Jodie.

Jodie's car had dropped her off fifteen minutes before and one of Taleen's staff had provided her with a drink and taken her through to the spacious sitting room. Few people kept Jodie waiting these days, but Taleen kept everybody waiting.

"Darling," she said, appearing in the doorway. She wore skin-tight black jeans and a black vest with splashes of red, blue and orange paint. There were a few small splashes on her face too. Her dyed raven hair was tied back and there was a sparkle in her eyes. For a woman of nearly sixty, she barely looked forty.

"I'm sorry I kept you. After putting the phone down to you, I was suddenly inspired. I'd been waiting to feel a soupçon of genuine, heartfelt contempt to finish the piece I was working on."

"I made you feel contempt?" Jodie asked nervously.

Taleen laughed as she swept into the room like a Gothic wraith. "Oh, my darling, Jodie. Never you," she said, reaching out and gently brushing the younger woman's cheek with the back of her hand. "No. I hadn't thought about Jamie for some time until you called. The mention of his name was just the spur I needed."

"Glad I could help."

Taleen smiled and looked to the doorway to see one of her staff by the door. "Champagne," she said to the woman waiting patiently for her order. "Cristal. We're celebrating."

"Can I see it?"

Taleen stared long and hard at Jodie. "Yes. Yes, I think you can." She started heading out of the room once again, leaving Jodie just sitting on the sofa. She disappeared out of the door for a few seconds before popping her head back around the corner. "Well, come on then, darling."

Jodie finished her vodka and ice then jumped to her feet and followed her. It was more of a Gothic mansion than a house. The broad spiralling staircase was covered with dark red carpet. The walls were grey stone punctuated by some of Taleen's own creations. They finally reached the landing and continued down a long hallway to the studio.

"I really love this place," Jodie said.

"By all means, make me an offer," Taleen said, glancing back at the younger woman with a mischievous grin on her face.

"If I sold everything I had, I don't think I'd be able to afford it."

"There are things more valuable than money."

A small shiver ran down Jodie's spine. *What is it with this woman? Nobody creeps me out like her, but she's kind of addictive at the same time.*

They entered the studio and in the centre of the expansive room was a mini-van-sized canvas of the Armenian flag waving in the wind. In the central blue section, there was a silhouette of a figure burning on a cross with a splatter of red paint running through it.

"Whoa. That's powerful. It's gut-wrenching too." In one of their previous conversations, Taleen had told Jodie how her grandfather had been crucified and then set on fire during the genocide. It was easy to see that this was a depiction of that event. Jodie gulped, and she couldn't help it, but a tear appeared in the corner of her eye. "This is your grandad," she said, her voice quivering a little.

"It is."

"It's beautiful and horrible and magical and heart-breaking all at the same time."

Taleen reached out and squeezed Jodie's wrist. "Thank you, darling. I think that's the loveliest review I've ever had."

"What are you calling it?"

"Ottoman Cunts."

Jodie's mouth fell open a little. For a second, she thought her friend was joking, but as she side glimpsed her face, she realised she was completely serious. "Oh. Fitting."

"Yes. I thought so." She clapped her hands together. "Anyway, let us get to the purpose of your visit. Come."

They retraced their steps down the long hallway and stairs then down another flight to a basement that spread the full length and width of the property.

"Jesus! This place is huge. You could hold gigs down here."

One wall was covered with tall, black oak bookcases. Each shelf was packed. The wall opposite was uncluttered and painted white. Various display cases were dotted around, featuring a host of religious and irreligious artefacts.

"Welcome to my lair."

"What is this place?"

Taleen turned around and gone were the affectations now. The basement was quite dark, but an up-lit display case just a few feet away from them cast enough illumination for Jodie to see that her companion's face was earnest.

"You and I are friends."

It was a statement, but there was a questioning element to it as well. "Yes."

"I'm about to bring you inside, Jodie."

"What do you mean?"

"Remember the first time we met?"

"Course I do. You warned me about Jamie."

"Yes."

"Everything you said was true. He was into some dangerous shit. Those people he had hanging around the studio were…."

"Predatory."

"Yeah. Then, after, there was that gig at the Garden when he wanted the whole band to take part in that ritual thing. You told me it would happen. You warned me. I was young and naïve at the time, and if it wasn't for you, I'd have probably been sucked in. That black magic stuff was okay for a cool album cover, but—"

"There's a lot more to it than that. A lot more."

"Your drinks, Miss Zakarian," said the woman who had taken her order for champagne earlier.

"Thank you. Put them over there, will you?"

The woman placed down a silver tray with two full glasses and the remainder of the bottle. "Will there be anything else?"

"No. Have a nice evening, Lucia."

"Thank you, Miss Zakarian. You too."

Taleen waited until she was gone before turning back to Jodie. She took hold of her hand. "Come and sit with me." She led her over to the table where the tray had been put down and gave a glass to her friend before taking the other for herself. She drank it as if it were water and poured herself another.

"Are you okay? You seem a little nervous."

Taleen smiled. "I suppose I am."

This made Jodie nervous. In all the time she'd known this woman, she'd exuded only confidence and this change of state made her wonder what was coming next.

Shit! She's got rid of the help. We're down here in this basement alone. Is she going to make a pass at me or something? She really liked her but not in that way.

Taleen took another drink from her glass.

"You're starting to scare me a bit. I don't think I've ever seen you so on edge before."

"Jodie."

"Yeah."

"Have you ever known me to lie or exaggerate to you?"

"No."

"Have I ever given you the impression that I'm weak-minded or easily scared?"

"Never. The opposite, in fact. You're one of the most intelligent, strong, formidable people I've ever met."

A small laugh left the other woman's lips. "Formidable. That's code for bitch."

"No. I just meant—"

Taleen raised her hand. "I'm toying with you." She took another drink before continuing. "The reason I'm asking you these things is because what I'm about to tell you will be hard to wrap your head around. If it came from a stranger, you'd probably be calling the psychiatric hospital to get them admitted. But you came to me because you want to help your friend, and that's all I want too, and to do that, I'm going to have to bring you inside. Are you ready to be brought inside, Jodie?"

It was Jodie's turn to take a drink now. Her heart was racing. She had no idea where this conversation was going and there was a part of her that didn't want to know. There was a part of her that dreaded what was coming next. "I don't know what inside is."

"Inside is knowledge that maybe a handful of people on the planet truly possess. Don't get me wrong; there are many more who have fragments of information, but to help your friend I need to bring you fully inside and I need to make sure that this stays between us. I need to make sure that I can trust you to keep this knowledge safe. In truth, there was a part of me that never thought I'd have to share it, but now I see it all happened for a reason."

"I don't understand, Taleen. What happened for a reason? What are you talking about?"

"Me coming to you to warn you about Jamie. Only now for you to come back to me to help your friend because Jamie's back on the scene. I think it was more than altruism that made me want to reach out to that young girl a few years ago. I think it was destiny. I think it was because I saw myself in you."

"You've really lost me."

Taleen leaned forward and squeezed Jodie's knee before retreating back into the comfort of her chair. "I'm sorry. I'm sorry for what I'm about to impart to you. I'm sorry to give you this knowledge, but I can tell you love this man, this Lev. And I'd never forgive myself if I allowed you to lose your soul mate."

"I told you. He's not—"

Taleen put her hand up to stop her. "I'll come back to the Black house in a moment, but first I need to give you a little background. Good and evil do exist. They aren't just abstract concepts. They are real things that are acting on us every day. They are all around us. In most cases, we have free will and we can decide to take an action or not. In most cases."

"In most cases? You're talking about people who are insane, whose minds aren't working properly."

"There are those who have a diminished capacity for thought, who make poor judgements, who commit evil acts, but let us stay with those who have all their faculties for the moment." She gestured to the staircase. "The painting I just showed you. The men who crucified my grandfather then set him alight. The power of good and evil was within them and they chose the latter. They could have decided to set him free. They could have decided not to barricade the doors of his church and set it ablaze with his friends and some of his family inside. They could have decided not to make him watch it all while he was up on that cross. They could have decided not to set him on fire when the last screams of the suffering fell silent. At any stage, they could have made a decision not to compound their evil doing. That capacity for good, for doing the right thing lies within all rational human beings."

"Okay," Jodie said, still not sure where the conversation was heading, never mind what it had to do with Lev.

"Evil is far more prevalent than we would like it to be."

"I don't understand why you're telling me this."

"Because it's important that you comprehend that the evil that led to my grandfather being tortured and murdered in that way is present in every human. It's uncomfortable to think like that, but it's true. There is nothing physically stopping me from doing the same to you right now. I could strip you, beat you to within a few inches of your life, nail you to a cross and set you on fire."

Jodie stared into Taleen's wild brown eyes. "Um...."

"But you're my friend, and I love you, and I have no motivation to do that. Nevertheless, there's nothing stopping me from doing it either."

"Well. You'd get arrested and—"

"I'm on about natural laws. There's nothing in nature preventing me from doing it if I chose to."

"I suppose not. But I still don't get why you're telling me this."

"I'm telling you this, darling, because there are places on this planet that can make people do those kinds of things whether they choose to or not."

There was a long pause before Jodie finally replied, "What?"

"And I believe Lev has just walked right into one."

CHRISTOPHER ARTINIAN

11

The relief running through Anna was like Valium. She didn't realise it at the time, but her whole body had been physically tense ever since climbing into the van. Now she was relaxed. She'd figured out the mystery. The only thing she hadn't worked out yet was the house.

Something strange definitely happened there. Both she and Lev experienced it, and it wasn't like he'd been abducted by the Red Man when he was a teenager, so whatever happened was completely unrelated, which now she thought about it was another good thing. It was one further step removed from it all being tied in and her experience earlier on in the evening being anything other than a night terror.

What the hell happened though? That was the big question. But there were a lot of other questions bouncing around her head, like how the hell was she going to explain leaving a bunch of people stranded in a small town and absconding with all their equipment?

"Shit!"

When she'd got into the van, the only thing she'd thought about was escaping the nightmare that had engulfed her. Now that she'd had time to reason everything out, her actions seemed rash beyond belief.

Why didn't I go for a drink with Lev and discuss it all? Why didn't I just get out of the hotel and mix with a bunch of people? Because you were scared out of your wits, and it wasn't like you were in a rational state of mind, and it wasn't like there was no precedent already set for being open to that kind of crap in the past.

She let out a long, tired breath. Reason and honesty were her friends. The sooner she acknowledged what was happening the sooner she could figure out how to deal with it.

Fact. I'm done with Occulture.
Fact. My rep will be trashed.
Fact. I thought I was over all this stuff, but obviously I'm not.
Fact. I'm long overdue to be with my family.

In truth, she'd been missing them for months. She'd had to cancel going home for Thanksgiving, then Christmas. The once-a-week phone calls had become once a fortnight, then once a month.

She loved her family. She loved being with them and when she had to cancel those two things they all looked forward to all year, phoning them had just been a cruel reminder of how much she missed them, so she'd stopped doing that with the regularity she once did.

But she was heading to them now. *I can't wait to see Mom's face when I walk through the door.* Her family was the reason she'd survived her childhood trauma. Her family was a lifeline.

Was that it? Was today a trick played by my mind, feeding off my weariness and overwork, telling me that I wasn't happy, guiding me towards the thing that always made me happy? Was it one last night terror to push me in the right direction?

She could drive herself mad thinking about it. *Clear your mind, Anna. Concentrate on the road. Tomorrow morning, you'll be back home. You'll be in the loving embrace of your mom and pop and you can book an appointment with Doctor Moore and figure all this out.*

*

"The lock can be a bit sticky sometimes," Beth said as she jingled the key before finally pushing the door open. "Watch yourself on the bikes in the hallway." She turned the light on to illuminate four bicycles lining the already narrow hall. "I told you it was used as a bit of a dumping ground."

They walked through to an open-plan area with a couch and a portable TV in a corner. There was a small dining table with four chairs and a breakfast bar separating that from the kitchen.

"It's perfect," Lev said.

"I really wouldn't go that far." Boxes were piled against one of the walls, leaving even less space, but it was clean and light and it didn't smell of dampness or staleness as he had first feared when he'd been told that it had remained unused so long. "Come on. I'll show you the bedroom."

"And my luck just keeps getting better and better."

"Funny fucker, aren't you?" she replied, smiling.

She led him through the only other internal door and into a short hallway. There was a box room just big enough for a single bed but currently packed floor to ceiling with crates, a bathroom with bath and shower and finally the bedroom. "Seriously, Beth. It's perfect. Thank you."

"Like I said, it's not used. So it's yours as long as you want it." She handed him the key. "Check out of the hotel tomorrow and move your things in whenever you want."

"Again. Thank you."

"Enough already with the thank yous. You've done me a favour; I've done you a favour. That's how it works."

"Bit of a difference. I made a phone call. You're letting me live rent-free in this place."

Beth leaned back against the wall. "You could see it like that."

"How else is there to see it?"

"I let you live rent-free here for a little while. But what you've done is going to make my daughter happier than she's been in years. Jodie Starr could read a grocery list to her over the phone and it wouldn't matter. Hell, I'd give you this place if it could make her half as happy as she used to be."

"I should have held out longer."

Beth smiled before she became more serious again. "I meant what I said. What you're doing means the world to me and it will mean more than that to my girl."

Lev nodded. "Like I said, I know what it's like when your kids are down and there's nothing you can do to help them. It's my pleasure, Beth."

She stared at him longer than she intended to and shook her head before straightening up. "Come on. Let's head back to the bar."

"What? What were you going to say?"

"Nothing," she replied as they retraced their steps.

"You were going to say something."

"No, I wasn't."

They walked back out into the night air. "You were definitely going to say something. Probably along the lines of I'm not as big of a jackass as you first thought."

"Nope." She was a little embarrassed. She knew the stare had lasted too long and that was pretty much exactly what she was going to say. In fact, she liked Lev and it had been a long time since that had happened with any man.

"So, are you going to give me your number?" he asked as they stepped outside.

"My number?"

"So I can give it to Jodie."

An embarrassed smile flashed on her face. *Get a grip, Beth.* "Sure. Sorry. It's been a long day."

"Yeah. I get it. I'm going to head back to the hotel and see if I can get in touch with my employers before turning in for the night."

THE DEVIL'S FACE

"Your employers?"

He shrugged. "Without Anna and all the equipment, I'm pretty sure this project is dead in the water, but it's worth a call."

She handed him a piece of paper. "Well. Good luck."

"So, I'll see you tomorrow then."

They both shared a smile. "Sure. See you tomorrow."

*

Jodie looked uncomfortable. "I…." She wasn't quite sure how to continue without offending her host and that was the last thing she wanted to do.

"You don't believe in things like that," Taleen replied with a smile.

"I'm an atheist. I don't—"

"Oh, we're all atheists, darling."

"I think there are a lot of people who'd disagree with you."

Taleen shrugged. "There have been over eighteen thousand gods since the dawn of mankind. Who still believes in Zeus or Ra or Odin? Being an atheist these days means you believe in just one less god than most other people. But I'm not talking about God or the devil; I'm talking about something else."

"I'm not sure I really understand then."

"People talk about Hell and demons quite casually. They picture Hell as this vast cavern dripping in lava and a horned monster prodding at them with a trident. They see demons as his little havoc-wreaking helpers, but what if the thing people believe to be Hell isn't that at all? What if demons aren't what people believe to be demons? What if it's all something different?"

"Like what?"

"I, and others, believe there are portals on this planet."

"Portals? Portals to what?"

"To somewhere else. To something else. We can't go through them, but whatever is on the other side can manifest in some of us. Most of the time it's transient. Sometimes, it can continue longer. When most people come across these places, they might feel a chill at the most. Sometimes nothing at all. But then there are others."

Jodie was sceptical about all of this, but Taleen was compelling. "Others?"

"We've all had experiences in life. Things that we weren't sure whether they were something else. It could be as momentary as a reflection in the bathroom mirror when you turn on the light and for a split second you believe that it's not you staring back. That for just a tiny broken shard of a moment there is something in that image that doesn't belong. Or it could be a feeling. Like when you step outside on a night and sense a presence or feel eyes watching you. The hairs bristle on your arms and you can't explain why. You can call out asking if anyone is there, but you know you won't get a response.

"It could be something as seemingly benign as reading a book in your bed to try to drift off. You're lost in your own little world, burrowing ever deeper into the author's mind, and suddenly you feel compelled to look up. You raise your head above your paperback parapet because you can feel something there in the room with you. As crazy as it sounds, you know it to be true. It's something you can't put your finger on. The hairs stand up on the back of your neck and everything becomes exaggerated. Every sound becomes something else. The gentle rustle of clothing is a hushed whisper. The hiss of the refrigerator in the kitchen makes you turn towards the door and the cold darkness beyond the crack now hides a hundred possible faces staring back at you, waiting until you fall asleep, but you know that sleep won't come for a long time. Your mind is playing a thousand tricks, and when you do finally drift off, let's face it, probably with the light on, you're going to have nightmares. The kind of nightmares you had when you were a child. The kind of nightmares that made you scream through the darkness for your mother. But no matter how loud you scream or how long, nobody will come to help you. You'll be by yourself.

"You'll try your hardest to shrug it all off. You'll stare through that crack in the door, tense and with ice running through your veins, but you won't see anything. You'll listen intently beyond the sound of the refrigerator, trying your hardest to hear anything else. But you won't. You'll look back to the corner of the room to where you'd first lifted your eyes from the page and it will be empty. You'll go back to your book telling yourself it's all in your imagination but knowing it isn't.

"These things are all around us. And they can't touch us even though we can sometimes sense them or even glimpse them. Even though they can unnerve us and chill us. We might put them down to figments of our imagination, but they live among us, by us, with us. They're like the air we breathe, the rain that falls on our skin. Out here, we might sense them, but they can't do us any harm."

By now, Jodie's skin had drained of colour a little. Her fingers clawed into the soft fabric of the armchair as Taleen spoke. "Jesus, Taleen. I don't think I'm ever going to sleep again."

A smile flashed on the other woman's face, but it was gone again just as quickly. "But the portals are a different matter. The portals occasionally let them take possession of a host in one way or another and step into this world, albeit, usually, just for a short time."

"What do you mean in one way or another?"

"I'm coming to that. Do you know, darling, almost one in five of us has had an actual paranormal experience? And those are just the people willing to admit it. One in five. That's one in five who've probably brushed with these things out here in this world. I'm not talking about those who've stumbled across the portals. I dare say that ratio would fly up."

Jodie reached for her drink and gulped it back. "You're not really helping to put my mind at ease."

"And with good cause. There are thousands of so-called haunted houses in America and those are just the reported ones. Not every haunted house is a portal, however. In fact, there are probably only a handful of portals on the planet. But I, and others, believe one may exist near or around the Carlton Black house. The circle that possesses such knowledge is very small and the stories surrounding the place are hokey enough to make people believe it's no different to any other so-called ghost house." She stood up. "Come with me, darling."

"Where are we going?" Jodie asked nervously.

"Just over there."

They walked across to two waiting armchairs and Taleen reached across to a waiting projector on a small table between them. She flicked it on and an image of the house appeared on the wall. During the next few minutes, she proceeded to give Jodie a potted account of the strange happenings at the house as well as a known tally of the deaths surrounding it.

"Jesus!" Jodie hissed when the lights were finally turned back on.

"I don't think he's had much to do with the place."

"So what are you telling me, Taleen, that Lev's in danger?"

"Where Jamie is concerned, I'd say that's an understatement."

"What do you mean?"

"Jamie isn't the man he used to be."

"What, you mean a devil-worshipping psychopath who wanted to have blood sacrifices in the studio while we recorded?"

"Well, yes. He was part of a cult and he was also heavily into drugs, you know that."

"Other than the drugs, I've heard that nothing's changed."

"That's not quite true, darling. He left the Temple of the Dark Harvest, but—"

Jodie burst out laughing. "Is that seriously what they called themselves?"

Taleen smiled too. "They were amateurs. What would you expect? They thought those stupid rituals would bring about the rebirth of a biblical bogeyman who never existed in the first place. They were sad and pathetic and they suited Jamie to the ground."

"But you warned me about them."

"No. I warned you about him. I saw strength in you. I saw the woman you were going to become, and if he'd been left to marshal Blazetrailer and continued to do things his way, it would have had a tragic ending. I saw a kindred spirit in you, darling, and I didn't want you to get hurt."

"Thank you."

"No thanks necessary."

Jodie pointed to the projector. "I get that you think this place is dangerous, but if Jamie's no longer a part of that temple, what's his interest in it? Why would he be sending Lev down there? And why do you think he could be in danger?"

"I told you that I'm a part of a very select group who possess this knowledge. As was my father, and his father and his father before him. It's a sacred duty."

Jodie tensed again. There was a part of her that believed what Taleen was saying, but there was another part that thought she was out of her mind. "A duty?"

"You think I'd choose to know all this?"

"You? Yes."

Taleen's head lolled back as she let out a deep and loud laugh. "Well, yes. You're probably right. But that's not to say that it isn't an onerous responsibility. I and the others who possess this knowledge take our stewardship seriously, and I hope you will too."

Jodie put her hands up. "I'm not going to say anything to anyone, but I'm here because you think Lev might be in danger and that's where my interest ends."

"Fair enough."

"I get that bad stuff's happened here, and I'm going to—"

"Has Lev ever confided anything in you?"

"What do you mean? We talk a lot. He's like my—"

"Soul mate?" she asked with a smile.

"Brother. My best friend. We've confided in each other."

"There's a reason Jamie would have wanted him specifically."

"I don't understand."

"Has he ever told you about anything that's happened in his past, maybe something that goes beyond the realms of possibility?"

Jodie's brow creased a little. "This is all starting to sound a little—"

"Crazy?"

"I love you, Taleen, but—"

"Think. We've all had things happen. We've all shared with people in moments of weakness or tenderness. Did he ever share anything with you?"

Jodie shook her head. "No. Nothing like that."

Taleen sat back in her chair with a confused expression on her face. When she spoke again, it was more to herself than anyone else. "Then why the hell did he choose him?"

"Because he was getting a bargain. Lev is a magician and he was going to work, probably for peanuts, on a Mickey Mouse documentary. It's pretty simple."

"Hmmm," Taleen replied, unconvinced.

12

Lev took a breath before re-entering the hotel. There was a part of him that wondered if Tim would be waiting there for a drunken rematch, but as he walked through the doors, all was quiet. There wasn't even anyone at the reception desk. He looked down the hallway to the bar and heard the clink of glasses.

It had been a long day and it wasn't over yet. He needed to make at least one phone call, probably more, but he wanted to speak to someone from the production team who wasn't after his blood to get a little more perspective on what was going on.

He headed down the short corridor and as he stepped into the bar area, he caught sight of a couple of guests at one of the tables and Fifi sitting by herself in a corner looking positively dejected.

"You mind if I sit down?"

She shook her head. "It's a free country."

He pointed to the almost empty glass in front of her. "What are you drinking?"

"It's the house white. White what, though, I'm not quite sure."

Lev smiled. "Let me get you another." He returned a moment later with a beer for himself and another glass of wine for Fifi.

"Thanks."

"Are you okay?"

"Oh, I'm just great. I get to go back home and tell my Mom she was right all along. Her daughter's a failure."

"How do you figure?"

"I spent four years bussing tables and going for every bit part I could. Every call home was, 'When are you going to get a proper job? We can't support you all your life, you know.'" She took a drink. "I was supporting myself, but I wasn't paying back any of the money I'd borrowed."

Lev was a bit taken aback. It was as if he'd walked in right in the middle of a whole thing. "Um. It's a tough industry."

"You've got that right. And then this came along. This was going to be it. I know it's not much, but I was going to wow. I was going to give it my everything and make anyone who watched it sit up and notice me."

Lev's eyes were suddenly drawn to the open neck of her blouse, but he quickly brought them under control and took another drink. "They would have done."

"Thank you," she replied sincerely then took a sip of her wine. "But now it's all over."

"So, have we had word? Has the plug officially been pulled?"

Fifi shook her head. "Tim, Kelly, and Sam have all made calls, but they can't get through to anyone. They left messages, but no one came back."

They won't have Jamie's home number. I'll call him when I'm done and confirm what I probably already know. Lev sat back in his seat. So much had happened today. He was still a million miles away from reconciling it, but the evening's events had been a welcome distraction.

He looked up at the small TV just above the bar. The news was on, but no one was paying attention and the volume was turned down anyway. "Listen to me," he said, causing his companion to raise her eyes from the gently swilling liquid in her glass. "This might be just a hiccup. Anna might come back. The company might send another director down here. A hundred things could happen. But if this gig doesn't work out, there will be others."

"You make it sound easy."

He shook his head. "I know it's a hard industry. But y'know what, I bet there were a tonne of people who applied for this job and you got it off your own merits, Fifi. You did it. Not your mum or your dad. You. You got this gig because they saw something in you, and you'll get others."

Fifi raised her head a little more. "You're right."

"I know I'm right. You're talented, you're young, and if this is what you really want to do, don't let anyone tell you that you can't."

For the first time since he'd entered the bar, a smile lit Fifi's face. "Yeah. Screw them."

"We only get one crack at this life and it's too short for us not to do what we love."

The smile became a wide grin. "Yeah. Yeah, thanks, Lev." She took another drink and was about to say something else when her eyes were drawn to the TV and the smile vanished in an instant.

*

It was still quiet in the bar. There was a tournament going on at the pool hall down the street, and when that was over, things would liven up. But for the moment, it was a welcome lull as Naomi and Beth got to spend a little time talking between customers.

"So," Naomi said. "I haven't seen that little twinkle in your eye for a long, long time."

"Uh-huh. Screw you. The guy's doing me a favour, so it seemed only decent that I help him out."

"Sure. The two things are so comparable; asking his friend to put a call in to your daughter and free accommodation for as long as he wants. Tit for tat, right?"

"I repeat my previous position. Screw you."

"Hey. I'm not judging. My hat goes off to you. It's a perfect set-up."

"What are you talking about?"

"Well, you can't access the place except through here. Nobody will be able to see you come and go. So if you're in the mood for some afternoon loving, you can just sneak in and people will believe you're here to see your sister. They won't think anything of it. Your own private gigolo. It's brilliant, really." Naomi burst out laughing and Beth raised the middle finger on her left hand while taking another drink. She placed the empty bottle down on the bar.

"You got that tail light fixed yet or am I going to have to write you up?"

"Don't be sore. You know I'm only kidding."

Beth's face turned a little red, and when she spoke again, it was in a more hushed tone. "He doesn't seem like other guys. He's honest and a little vulnerable."

The grin was gone from Naomi's face. "So, you do like him?"

Beth shrugged. "Jesus. I only met him today."

"But—"

"Sure. He seems nice."

"Nice is a good start," she replied, putting another beer down in front of her sister.

"I should be getting back home."

"It's only early. And you deserve a couple of drinks. You've lined up the best birthday present your daughter could ever get and you've met a guy who can put a little smile on your face. That's a good day."

"I suppose." They both shared a smile before Beth raised her eyes to the TV screen. In an instant, the smile vanished as the censored image of a naked Jodie Starr being held by a fully clothed man flashed onto the screen. The photo had been taken by a paparazzo. They were in front of a window in a high-rise hotel. The man was Lev. He was kissing her bowed head as she had her arms wrapped around him.

Naomi turned to see what had sucked away the levity from her sister's demeanour. It took her just a split second. "Shit."

*

Lev looked to see what had mesmerised Fifi. *Shit*. This was the night Madison California had OD'd. They'd known about the picture for some time and the record company execs had done their best to acquire it, but they'd been unsuccessful. A thousand stories would be born from the publication of this image. A thousand speculations. Lev was of little consequence in the photo. It was a naked Jodie in the arms of the man who had just discovered Madison California dead.

Was it more than just an overdose? Were there kinky sex games involved? Why was Jodie naked and the man dressed?

It was a split second. What the photo didn't show was Jodie was distraught and in tears. What it didn't tell was the woman lying dead out of shot was someone who Jodie loved with the heat of a hundred suns. What it did show was exactly what the photographer, the papers and the networks wanted it to show. Celebrity skin and intrigue. More than that, Jodie was a household name. This photo was gold.

Like Jodie said earlier in the evening, she'd got off lightly. This wouldn't do anything to harm sales. The story would keep going for a few days and radio plays would probably go through the roof as every pundit would want to talk about the photo and what better way than to segue to or from a hit record?

It would harm Lev though. It would give his wife plenty more ammunition for an already acrimonious divorce, but worse than that, it would hurt his kids. He peeked at his watch. *It'll be the middle of the night in the UK.* All he wanted to do was talk to them, tell them it wasn't what it looked like, tell them that he loved them. *FUUUCCCKKK!*

He turned back around towards his companion, who was still entranced by the image on the small screen. She finally broke her gaze and looked towards him.

"Um."

"It's not what it looks like," was all he could offer.

"No. It's none of anyone's business anyway."

He glanced at the three-quarters full bottle still on the table and decided the day had gone on long enough. "I'm going to see if I can get through to anyone and then I'll probably call it a night."

"Err ... yeah. Okay."

"Goodnight," he said, climbing to his feet.

"Night."

Before he left the bar area, he turned to see her transfixed by the screen. *Today just keeps getting better and better.*

The inside of his head was like a squash court with a thousand games all being played at the same time. There was so much to think about that it was hard to pick out one single ball to hit. The events earlier in the day had rattled him to the core and he still needed a quiet moment to wrap his head around them, but that would come later.

He walked up to the payphone on the wall of the lobby and picked it up. He glanced over to the reception desk to see there was now someone in attendance. The man gave him a suspicious sideways look before returning to shuffling the paperwork in front of him. *Has he seen the news? Is that the kind of stare I can expect for the next few days?*

He pulled out a pocketful of coins and observed them in his hand for a moment. These and the notes in his wallet were the sum value of his worth. It was more than a little kind of Beth to let him crash in the apartment for a while, but it wasn't a long-term thing. It would be some time before Blazetrailer went back into the studio and longer than that before they went on the road. If he had, as he suspected and feared, lost his current job as the sound guy on a shoestring-budget haunted house series, then he wasn't quite sure what he was going to do.

Finally, he fed some coins into the slot and dialled. The phone rang and rang. This was Jamie's private number. It wasn't an office. The answering machine clicked in.

"Jamie, it's Lev. No doubt you've heard that Anna's taken off. She didn't say a word to anyone, just disappeared with the van. Nobody knows what's going on here, man. It would be good if someone could let us know if the gig's still on or not." He waited, listening to the hiss on the other end, hoping that his friend might be screening calls and that he might pick up. When he realised there was no hope of that, he hung up the phone.

He let out a long sigh and started up the staircase. When he reached his floor, he could hear televisions playing and muted conversations going on in the rooms around his. *I wonder how many of those are going to be about me.*

He walked back into his room, flicked on the TV and flopped down on the bed, slipping his shoes off and weaving his fingers behind his head. Barring the few minutes he'd spent in here after returning with Anna, it was the first time he'd had to himself all day.

He thought back to the house and the inexplicable passage of time between entering the basement and leaving it. He'd experienced things in his life that he couldn't explain at first. His mind drifted to the fateful night of the car crash that ended his father's life. *That face. The devil's face.*

Over time, he'd convinced himself that it was the trauma, the stress of the situation that had made him see it so clearly. He was sure it was a figment of his imagination even though he'd glimpsed it many times since. He was still sure it wasn't real. That's all it could have been; the devastation short-circuiting his brain, making the whole thing light up like a giant telephone exchange, occasionally reappearing to remind him of that night.

Think! Think!

He prided himself in his logic. But on the surface, there seemed to be no logic for the missing time that both he and Anna had experienced. *The smell.*

When they'd entered the cellar there had been a noticeable odour. *Could it have been something toxic? Is it possible that the mercury problem was never properly rectified and the happenings in the house have been a result of harmful vapour bleeding up through that fissure?*

He wracked his brain. *What do I know about mercury?* Several seconds passed before he answered himself. *Not fucking much, obviously. Can inhaling the vapour cause hallucinations, cause people to have funny episodes? There are funny episodes and then there's what we experienced. Two people, exactly the same thing.*

He shook his head. It didn't make sense, but tomorrow, while he was waiting to hear back from Jamie or someone else at Occulture, he'd maybe seek out a doctor or something. Try to get answers.

He flicked channels to see another broadcast showing the paparazzo shot.

"Christ." He let out a long breath and changed channels again. One of the *Pink Panther* films was on. He'd seen them all a dozen times before and they seemed to meld into one, but after the day he'd had, he needed something light. He needed something he could switch off to while his head weighed up options and reasons.

A few minutes passed and gradually his eyes started to get heavier. A few more minutes went by and Lev fell asleep. The station switched as he rolled over onto the remote. There was a horror film showing. It was the same horror film Lev had sneaked out to see all those years ago. It was the last film he'd ever watched before the death of his father.

Lev was asleep, but his eyelids began to flicker as snippets of dialogue rang out through the small TV speaker.

The face. The terrifying, menacing, demonic face that jerked everyone in the theatre when it had seemingly appeared out of nowhere flashed on the screen. Gasps and cries had sounded all around. Hands had gone up to hearts. Others had seized their dates in vice-like grips. That pallid face, the make-up artist's interpretation of the face of the devil, now exploded onto the small screen. But it didn't vanish this time.

It lingered. Its eyes seeing everything. Its dark lips taut, revealing foul yellow teeth at the start of a wicked grin. The TV image fuzzed, returned to the face, and then fuzzed again. Seconds passed by, then a minute, until finally a screen test card and the familiar high-pitched tone to accompany it made the small TV vibrate.

Lev jerked awake, sucking in a deep breath as if being awoken from a nightmare. He stared at the TV and realised it must have been the sound that had woken him up. He blinked once, twice, three times then reached for the remote. It was still relatively early, but he was tired, and sleep might help his brain figure out what had happened in the house.

He switched the TV off then turned over and slowly drifted off to sleep once more.

*

"There was this one thing," Jodie said, trying to appease Taleen, who seemed a little affronted that there were no forthcoming snippets of information to back up her theory as to why Lev might have been chosen for the job. She went on to tell her about the night of the car crash. Jodie had only been the second person Lev had told the full story to. At the time, he'd admitted Jamie was the only other one.

Taleen nodded. "And I bet if you checked the names of the other people in the crew, they would all have experienced some sort of inexplicable event in their lives."

"We can't know that."

Taleen shrugged. "We can't. But it would tie in with my reasoning."

"Which is?"

"All that shit that Jamie was involved in, do you know what he and that crazy cult were trying to do?"

"No, in truth. And I didn't want to know. I mean, *Sounds Like Hell* was a good album, and we had tracks on there that were featured in the two biggest-grossing horror movies that year, so that vibe was fine as far as it went. But then, when we started writing the next one, and he wanted to have his culty friends hang out in the studio and chant and shit, I was all over it in a heartbeat. It's one thing to play a part for the cameras; it's another to think that shit's real."

"He did think it was real, and so did his culty friends, as you put it. The Temple of the Dark Harvest was nothing more than a punchline to a bad joke. They intended to raise the devil, which is a little akin to trying to raise Santa Claus or the Easter Bunny. You can't raise what doesn't exist. But then Jamie met someone. Someone who had acquired some of the knowledge that I'm privy to. Someone who believed in the portals and what lay beyond them. Musab Kazem—a wealthy Iraqi. If the stories are true, he could have made the Marquis de Sade blush with what he got up to. He befriended Jamie and imparted him with what shards of knowledge he himself possessed.

"Kazem was convinced that if a live host could be captured, and an unholy sacrament read, then the Azelophet could be seized, possessed, controlled, like some sort of all-powerful genie."

Jodie's face contorted into an expression of confusion. "Wait, the what? The Azelophet?"

"It's what we've been talking about. It's the thing that passes through the portal. It is one. It is all. But up until this point, despite all their research and numerous fishing trips, they haven't really come close to identifying a portal. It's not like there's an official encyclopaedia of them. We're not sure where they all lie. But we're trying to identify them one by one and acquire them."

"Acquire them?"

"Or the land they reside on."

Jodie shook her head. "I don't understand any of this, Taleen."

"Come with me." The pair stood and walked across to the wall that was basically one giant book case. Several pedestals with encased texts and parchments stood in front of them. "Sumerian. Akkadian. Egyptian. Persian," she said, reverently touching each of the glass cases as they walked along.

"These must have cost a fortune."

"Oh, I don't own them, darling. I'm just their keeper." She stopped and turned. "Since records first began, thousands of years before any of the Abrahamic religions, thousands of years before the concepts of Heaven and Hell, the Azelophet was referred to or at least intimated."

"But what is it?"

"In terms that you or anyone in the modern world might comprehend it is the devil and all demons. It is one, and it is all."

"So, it's like a hoofed monster with horns and a tail or something?"

"It is most certainly not. The Azelophet has no defined physical form. It steps into this world through the body of hosts. It preys on them, making them see or making them experience the things they fear the most, or even just become the thing they fear most, the thing that lives down deep inside them that they try to repress, try to deny. The Azelophet is literally the embodiment of your worst fears. When it takes possession of someone, it often forces the host to commit acts upon themselves or others with fatal consequences."

"But why? To what end?"

"There is no why. There just is. Think of it in these terms. This is something that lives in a different dimension to us, and for this, we should be grateful. Usually, its presence in this world is fleeting. When its host dies, it's gone. The Azelophet is chaos, it's anarchy; it is evil."

"But I don't understand."

"We're not meant to understand. Knowing what the Azelophet is is the most we can hope for. Trying to minimise interaction with the portals is the best we can do."

"And the Carlton Black house. You said you believe it might be a portal?"

"I said we believe it might be on or around a portal." They returned to their seats and Taleen took a drink from her glass. "Like I said, there is no exact science to this. Some in my group even believe the portals themselves may be transient and that they might open and close in different locations over time.

"No one knows exactly who will be affected in what way. I think the people in Jamie's little TV crew will have been selected for events that have occurred in their past that make them more susceptible to the Azelophet. They are receivers, if you will, metaphorical canaries."

"But you can't say for sure that the Carlton Black place is one of these portals."

"No. There was a history of mental illness in Carlton Black's family. As there was in Ezekiel Wight's. There was also a pesticide factory in the area that was responsible for mercury bleeding into groundwater, wells and the lake."

"What's that got to do with anything?"

"Exposure to mercury can cause all sorts of illnesses, both physical and mental."

"So, all this could be coincidence?"

"It could. But tell me honestly, does it feel like coincidence to you? And knowing what I've told you about Jamie, do you think it sounds like coincidence to him? I think this TV series is a subterfuge. I think they've selected a team of people who have had inexplicable events occur in the past that may or may not have been previous brushes with the Azelophet. I think Kazem and Jamie believe that if these people come into contact with a portal, they will show signs of possession as a result, and that will give them the knowledge they've been looking for to put their insane plan into action. That will give them a gateway."

THE DEVIL'S FACE

"I really don't like this. I don't like Lev being down there."

"I don't like it either."

"Hypothetically, Taleen, if Jamie and his little cult did what they set out to do, what do you think might happen?"

"I have absolutely no idea. Nobody has any idea. The provenance of this unholy sacrament I spoke of is unknown to anyone in my group. In all likelihood, it's a fake, something manufactured by a savvy conman who saw a sucker in Kazem."

"But if it isn't. If they manage to trap the Azelophet?"

"What we know about the Azelophet has been pieced together by ancient texts and supposition. But what do you think will happen if, somehow, the most powerful, destructive, malevolent entity you could imagine is suddenly dragged from its own dimension into our plain of existence? Do you honestly think it would do the bidding of those who summoned it? Or do you think it would take the opportunity to wield the kind of devastation it's never had the freedom to before?"

"What does that mean?"

"In terms a modern theologian would understand, Armageddon. But just so you understand." She turned back to the projector, opened the drawer of the small stand it was on, and placed in another slide.

It revealed what looked like hieroglyphs of some kind, but the figures were all in the throes of the most debased, violent and terrifying acts imaginable. Dozens, hundreds of pictures displaying violation, suicide, murder, self-mutilation—destruction of mind-bending proportions. Blood dripping, bodies ablaze, mutilated, scarified. Cannibalism—children, babies being boiled in pots, torn asunder, eaten raw. Eyes gouged, entrails unfurling, limbs amputated, heads scalped, torsos scattered on the ground, all while a crimson lake formed at the foot of the unholy collage.

"Holy fucking shit! What is this?"

"This was found on the wall of a cave in what is today Siberia. It's estimated to be around six and a half thousand years old. I told you before that the concepts of good and evil were around long before the popular religions of today. All over the world, there are similar drawings foretelling similar events. You asked me what this is. You asked me what would happen if the Azelophet was summoned to our world as an entity in itself and not as a guest in someone else's body? This is it, darling. In terms that most people would understand, we would have Hell on Earth."

13

Jodie usually went out of her way to talk to her driver, but tonight was different. She'd spent longer at Taleen's than she'd expected and got way more information than she wanted.

She was very protective of Lev. Lev was loyal. He was decent. He was also pretty naïve in many ways. He rarely saw the bad in people and put up with way more shit than he should. He saw Jamie as a friend, but the truth was that Jamie didn't have friends. He just had people he used. Any acts of kindness he committed, or any shows of affection or camaraderie, were only tools to open magic boxes of compliance that he needed for his own purposes, his own ends. After all this time, Lev still didn't see that, but Jodie did. When she had joined the band, Jamie had been the driving force, but she had been the key to the massive commercial success they enjoyed and there was no Blazetrailer without her.

When Jamie had left, it had been chalked up to the old chestnut of "artistic differences", but the truth was he scared Jodie. What the rest of the band saw as theatre and an act she knew was real.

That dick was always into some dark shit and now he might have Lev stuck in the middle of it too.

Might.

That was the question rendering her silent and deep in thought as the still bustling streets blurred by. Taleen had been a protective force, a guiding light where Jamie had been concerned. She had known some of the execs at the record company. Jodie owed her a lot. But the story she'd told was ... crazy.

Portals? The Azelophet? Hell on Earth?

Now she was out of that basement, a hundred questions and even more doubts were rattling around in her head.

Sure, lots of plenty weird stuff went on at the Carlton Black house, but ... there were reasons. Mercury. A history of mental illness. The vibe of the place.

The latter reason had not been discussed, but it's something that needed considering. Places had vibes. *You walk into the Troubador and it's got a vibe. You walk into Taleen's place; it's got a vibe. If all that scary stuff happened at the Black house as a result of the mercury and the whackjob factor, then that would give off a pretty weird vibe too, which might have caused even more mental stuff to happen.*

Surely, all that was more plausible than the Azelophet. And the other thing not to rule out. *It might actually be haunted.*

Jodie wasn't one for believing in ghosts hovering around the house in white sheets, but there was a part of her that didn't rule out residual energy. Maybe she'd lived in LA too long, but she'd heard lots of stories about stuff happening, some more convincing than others, and although she wasn't a fully paid-up subscriber to the idea that ghosts did definitively exist, there was a part of her that couldn't one hundred percent rule it out either. And certainly after being confronted with all the facts about the Black house, there was that possibility to throw into the mix.

"Do you want to stop off anywhere before we head back, Miss Starr?" There was no response as Brian, her driver, posed the question. "Miss Starr?"

"Hmm. Oh, shit. Sorry, no. I'm good."

"Is everything okay, Miss Starr?"

She shook her head. "Just got a lot to think about. That's all."

"Of course. The big contract negotiation."

Jodie had virtually forgotten about that. "Oh, shit. Y'know, I'm so sorry. I've got you driving me home at stupid o'clock and you're going to be picking me up again in a few hours. Apologise to Judy for me."

"You know there will never be a need to apologise, Miss Starr. Judy will always be as grateful as I am for what you've done for us."

Brian's life had come crashing down around him when his youngest child had been diagnosed with leukaemia. Back then, he owned a small fleet of limos. The business had crumbled as his world slowly fell apart. Jodie, who had been his biggest customer, came to the rescue. The business was unsalvageable, but she hired him as her driver, let his family live almost rent-free in an investment property she'd bought the year before, and bailed him out with the medical bills his less than reputable insurance company refused to honour. When Jodie met someone decent, she always tried her hardest to look after them. Loyalty was the single most important thing to her and Brian had seen plenty that he could make a quick buck off when he'd been driving Jodie around in the early days, but he was solid. He was gold, and she rewarded loyalty with loyalty.

"We look after each other. That's what we do."

"Well. Needless to say, I'll be with you at eight a.m. tomorrow and I'll be wearing my four-leaf clover cufflinks for luck."

Jodie laughed. "You think I'll need them for the negotiation?"

"You're an amazing talent; you've got a crack team of lawyers and an agent who could put the fear of God into Dracula, but a bit of good old-fashioned Irish luck can never harm, Miss Starr."

She laughed again. "I suppose you're right."

They paused at the gates. Within seconds, a man appeared from a small cabin. He opened them up and nodded at the vehicle as it passed through. The limo carried on for a moment until it pulled up in front of the imposing white mansion.

"I'll see you bright and early, Miss Starr."

"Thanks, Brian. See you."

She got out of the car and the front door was opened for her by Greta before she could even reach for the handle. This life was a universe away from the one she grew up with. There were a number of messages waiting for her, but none of them were from Lev, and for the time being, he was the only person she was interested in hearing from.

I really hope he's okay down there. I hope I'm wrong about Jamie. I hope this was an old friend helping another friend out. As she ascended the staircase, she reflected on what she'd seen and heard. Part of her still believed it was all impossible. Another part believed every word Taleen had spoken.

All she wanted to do was see Lev, get him the hell out of that godforsaken place.

The meeting.

It was too important to blow off. She'd be letting more than herself down if she didn't go. Too many people were relying on her now. Blazetrailer had become a huge lumbering train with a vast crew and she was the driver. She paused on the landing.

I'll be speaking to him again tomorrow. She looked at her watch. *Well, today now. I'll tell him to get the hell out of there. I'll convince him never to have anything to do with Jamie again. Hell, I'll go down there and drag him out of that town by his hair if I have to.*

She entered her room, slipped out of her clothes and fell into bed. Sleep would not be forthcoming for some time, though, and when it did arrive, it was troubled.

*

It wouldn't be too long before the sun rose, but for the time being, it was still dark. Anna had pulled into a gas station. She'd left it for as long as she could, putting as much distance as possible between her and that place, but now the dial was hovering dangerously close to E.

There was another car and a truck at the pumps. Adjoining the small store was a twenty-four-hour café where three people were stooped over their coffees seemingly pondering the mysteries of life.

Half a smile appeared on Anna's face as the fuel began to flow. After spending the night alone, it was good to see people again. It felt normal. Normal was what she wanted more than anything.

She let out a long, deep sigh.

"You're way too pretty a lady to be sighing so deeply at this time of morning."

She was taken by surprise and jumped a little as the driver of the truck spoke to her. She'd not noticed as he'd exited the café with a lidded coffee in hand.

"It's been a long night."

"They always are when you're travelling alone. You got far to go?"

"Still some way."

"You should get yourself a cup of Joe. If you've been on the road so long, it's easy for tiredness to creep up on you near dawn. I've spent my life on the road and I can't tell you how many accidents I've seen at dawn and dusk. You ask me, they're the two most dangerous times to drive."

Anna nodded. "That's good advice."

The trucker tipped his baseball cap. "Drive safe now, missy."

He climbed back into his vehicle and she watched as he drove away. *Missy.* It had been a long time since anyone had called her that. She finished filling the tank, paid, and then, as the trucker had suggested, went and bought a coffee.

She climbed back into the van and took a couple of sips before setting off. Thoughts of home started to fill her mind again, aided by the brief but friendly conversation she'd had. *That guy definitely came from a small town.* That's how things were in a small town. Strangers being friendly, looking out for others. Moving to LA had been a huge culture shock. Friendliness was often viewed with suspicion.

If someone was being friendly to you in a big city then there was usually an ulterior motive. She'd covered hundreds of miles since she'd first set off and most of that time, she'd been thinking about her home and family. Sometimes it took a long, lonely journey to admit truths about yourself.

I was never really that happy in LA. I never found a relationship there that I thought would last. Even my friendships were superficial. It was flattering getting the call from Occulture, and in many ways, it felt like validation, but it wasn't the path to happiness.

Happiness wasn't a path at all. Happiness was at the end of this road, this journey. That's what the events of the previous day had been telling her. The night terror was her mind giving her a wake-up call. She needed to be with the people who had helped her through those traumatic teenage years, the people who had got her back on her feet after the—BANG!

Anna smashed on the brakes, bringing the van to a skidding stop. She hadn't seen another car since leaving the gas station and this stretch of road was the absolute worst place for something to happen. Dense forest lined the tarmac on either side and, for the time being, the moon was hiding behind a thin layer of cloud.

The engine was still purring, but loud bangs were never good. She remained frozen in the driver's seat for a moment, her fingers clenched tightly around the wheel.

Did I hit something? Has something fallen off the van?

THE DEVIL'S FACE

She looked to the trees to her left then her right. Shadows upon shadows upon shadows stretched out of sight. Finally, she released the steering wheel and opened the door.

She sucked in a nervous breath as the cold air hit her and she walked around the van, inspecting it as well as she could in the periphery of the illumination provided by the headlights. She crouched down and squeezed each of the tyres.

They're okay.

Suddenly, she heard rustling in the bushes and froze.

What the fuck?

Her heartbeat started to race once more and a dozen stories of carjackings instantly flashed in her brain. She tensed as branches of a large, overgrown shrub began to sway and took one step towards the open door of the van before a doe stepped out onto the road.

She relaxed again, letting out a nervous laugh. The moon came back out from behind the cloud and the pair surveyed each other for a moment before the graceful creature continued across the road. Anna watched it, still smiling, chastising herself a little for being so paranoid.

She was about to head around to the front of the vehicle and check it once more when her eyes were drawn to something reflecting in the moonlight. It was about fifteen feet back from the van, and when she reached it and picked it up, she identified it as a pry bar. It was only twelve inches long but heavy and thin. If this had been left at the side of the road, it would have been easy not to notice it, easy for her front tyre to go over it, causing it to ricochet off the underside of the vehicle and make the bang that had scared her.

She kept it in hand as she walked back to the van. She got down onto her hands and knees, looking underneath the vehicle to see if there were any hanging or dripping silhouettes that shouldn't be there. When she was satisfied she had carried out as good an inspection as she could without a torch, she got up, climbed back in and slammed the door shut.

Hopefully, that's going to be the last little piece of drama on this trip. She slowly moved away, listening to the sound of the engine, making sure everything was as it should be before relaxing back into the driver's seat.

This really has been some twenty-four hours. She reached across and turned on the radio, adjusting the dial until it settled on a rock station. Blazetrailer's *Demon Child* was in full swing and she started to sing along. She'd been travelling for hours, lost in her thoughts. Why had it only just dawned on her to turn on the radio? She smiled as she sang, thinking back to Lev. *This is some coincidence.*

The song came to an end and the DJ announced that they were heading across to Travis Hank in the newsroom for a roundup of the day's stories. The bouncy five-note fanfare announcing the start of the news came to an end and Anna looked towards the radio as silence followed. A few seconds passed but there was no news presenter.

"Someone's going to get their ass kicked for this," Anna said with a smirk forming on her face as the silence dragged on. Finally, it was interrupted by a whisper. Then another. "You've got your mike on, jackass." She started giggling at the ineptitude of the presenter and the early morning production staff.

"Someone's going to get their ass kicked for this." The whisper through the speakers made her pause for a second as a voice echoed her very words; then she started laughing even louder.

"At least someone knows what's going on there."

"You've got your mike on, jackass." The whispered voice repeated her words again and the laugh froze in her throat. Anna's brow creased as she dragged her eyes away from the road and glanced towards the radio.

Silence lingered for a few seconds until more words whispered through the speakers. "At least someone knows what's going on there."

THE DEVIL'S FACE

Her blood turned to ice. "No. No," she said, not understanding what was going on but knowing that something was amiss, strange, unnatural, impossible.

"No. No," her words repeated again, but this time, they did not come from the speakers. This time, they came from behind her.

She turned her head, looking into the back of the van. The only illumination came from the dashboard lights and all she could see were silhouettes of the equipment cases.

She turned back to the road, her fingers digging into the steering wheel harder than ever. *It's my mind playing tricks. It's my mind playing tricks. It's my mind playing tricks.*

She reached out, changing the station. After a hefty dollop of static, Blazetrailer's *Demon Child* roared through the speakers.

This time, she did not sing. This time, tears filled her eyes as reality skewed and twisted, seeming further and further out of reach for her by the second.

"What the fuck's going on?" she asked through her sobs, inadvertently pressing down harder on the gas as her subconscious urged her forever faster towards her home.

"Okay. That was *Demon Child* by Blazetrailer. And now we're heading over to Travis Hank in the newsroom for a roundup of the day's stories."

Anna's vision blurred further as rivers of tears poured down her cheeks. The radio fell silent once more and she was about to switch stations again to find a sound, any sound that proved she wasn't going mad, when she heard another whisper from behind.

"Mine. You're all mine."

Her body started to shake and she pushed down even harder on the accelerator, too afraid to turn around.

"This isn't happening. This isn't happening."

Silence.

Seconds passed as she waited to hear another whisper, but none came. Then something far worse. The shriek of cling film as it unfurled from a roll reverberated.

"You can't run away," the hushed voice sang out. "Not this time."

"NOOO! NOOO! NOOO!" She screamed at the top of her voice, twisting in her seat, and in the momentary flash of moonlight that shone down between the arc of branches hanging over the road, she saw him. His naked red outline crouched on the periphery of the white semicircle of light. In his hands, he held a taut length of cellophane. "NOOO! NOOO!"

As the terrified cries rose from deep down within, she couldn't hear herself; she could only hear the girl she once was. The petrified child who was locked in that basement for six months, knowing only that pain and torture would visit her before the day was through. "NOOO!" There weren't any other words to use. *No. No. No. No,* branded the inside of her mind. She could feel the searing pain, she could smell the charred flesh, all of it tipping her further and further towards the horror she knew was coming.

CLACK! CLACK! CLACK! CLACK! The wheel shook in her hands and she was forced to turn back around, but it was too late. The van veered, smashing over the curb, causing her to squeal in fear as a different terror approached.

She smashed on the brakes too late, only then realising that she'd never put her seatbelt back on after inspecting the van. A deafening crash filled her world for a split second before....

Darkness.

14

It was after nine a.m. when Lev made it downstairs. He was about to head through to the dining room for coffee when a call from behind stopped him. He turned to see Fifi with her coat on and a bag over her shoulder.

"Hi," he said, a little confused as to why she was heading out so soon.

"We're leaving," she replied, a little uncomfortably.

"We?"

"Me, Tim and the others. We're returning the rental and there's a bus that will take us to the airport."

"Um…."

"I'm sorry. I didn't think it would be a good idea for you to travel with us. Tim is still kind of…." Her words drifted into nothingness.

"I don't understand. Did you manage to speak to someone at Occulture?"

"My agent did. He only spoke to a secretary, but her brief was to tell him that the project was on hold until further notice. Apparently, they got all our answer machine messages and had a meeting but didn't bother to tell us anything." She shook her head. "I should have known it was all too good to be true."

"Hey. Remember what I said to you last night."

She nodded but couldn't help looking a little forlorn. "Anyway, we're all heading back home. I don't know if this thing will go ahead or not, but there's not much of a project without Anna, so if it does, it will be a while." She looked over her shoulder. "I'd better be getting a move on. I'm sorry we can't give you a lift, but—"

Lev put his hand up. "It's fine. I was planning on sticking around here for a few days anyway."

"Well, if it's any consolation, the rooms are paid up until the day after tomorrow. You may as well take advantage of that."

"Actually, I've got something else sorted for a few days at least."

Fifi looked a little surprised. "Whatever. Hope things work out for you anyway." It was obvious that she was referring to the news article that broke while they were having a drink together the previous evening, but Lev didn't really want to get into it.

"Thanks."

"Take care, Lev."

"You too." He watched her head down the hallway and out of the entrance. A crooked smile crept onto his face as he thought about Tim and the others. He wondered how many rumours must already be circulating about him then shrugged it off and headed into the dining room.

He felt the eyes of several guests watching him as he poured himself a coffee. He had no idea how many times that photo had been shown since the previous evening, and he wondered how long it would stay in the news cycle, but for the time being, at least, he had other things on his mind.

Since waking, he had been thinking about the Black house. He had been thinking about the lost time. He didn't know how long he was going to spend in New Scotland trying to figure out what had happened, but in the absence of work, he didn't have anything better to do for the time being, and a small town was probably the best place to ride out the media storm around the photograph.

He grabbed a piece of dry toast and took a bite before heading back out of the dining room. He caught a woman's gaze who immediately looked down at her plate, embarrassed. Again, he smiled to himself. Whatever hardships this would cause him, it was worth it. He'd do anything for Jodie and he knew the same was true for her.

The door clicked shut behind him as he re-entered his room. In the corner, on the chair, was his custom recorder. The boom and the rest of the equipment were in the back of the van, but that didn't matter anyway. He had no intention of doing any more recording while he was here.

His T-shirt and underwear from the previous day were neatly folded on the dressing table and it took him about ten seconds to bundle them into his sports bag along with a packet of mints, his toiletries and a notebook.

There were few pleasantries exchanged as he checked out. The rest of the production team had spent most of the previous day drinking and were far louder than most guests. The owner was happy to see the back of them, especially as the funds for their stay had already cleared.

Lev stepped onto the street and took a deep breath. A shallow wave of sadness hit him. Even though this job had only been temporary, it was a job. Now he had nothing. He'd spend a few days here then he'd be heading back home, but he had no idea what he'd do then.

Blazetrailer weren't due back into the studio for several months. There were no tours planned. They were taking a well-earned and much-needed hiatus, but Lev would need to find something; otherwise, declaring bankruptcy was a real possibility. He didn't even have healthcare at the moment. It was never something he had to think about while he lived in the UK.

Maybe I go back. Maybe I go back to the UK and.... His thoughts trailed off. He wouldn't even be able to do that without borrowing money for the flight. All his cards were maxed out. *Fuck!*

He started down the road, his recorder and battery pack over his shoulder, his sports bag in his other hand. It was just after nine and even though New Scotland was only a small town, people were rushing to their work. They filed past him in both directions. Occasionally, he caught the gaze of one. Occasionally, their eyes lingered on him a little longer than usual, suggesting there was some paused cog in the back of their mind trying to remember from where they might recognise his face.

Finally, he reached the Bellanola Bar. The thick wooden doors to the entrance were locked and he stepped back, looking above the cloudy grey obscure glass to the thin clear panes above. There was too much reflection from outside to see if there was a light on and he wondered if he was going to have to find a café or diner until it opened.

He knocked gently on the door and waited. He shrugged the recorder and weighty battery pack a little further onto his shoulder and started to walk away.

He'd only gone a few feet when the sound of a heavy lock disengaging stopped him. He turned to see Naomi popping her head out. "Jesus, man. You're going to have to give me more time than that."

"Sorry. I thought maybe you weren't up yet."

"Ha! You've not worked in a bar, have you? The work never stops. Plus, I always make sure I'm up to see Bella off to school." She paused, waiting for him to move. When he didn't, she gestured with her head for him to enter. "So, are you going to stand there all day or are you actually going to come inside?"

"Course. Thanks." He slid past her and entered the bar he'd visited the previous evening. When he'd left, there had been hardly any occupants, but as he walked inside, the smell of beer and cigarettes hit him like a tidal wave. His eyes flicked from table to table to see full ashtrays and sticky rings on the wood. Multiple glasses lay half empty. "Jesus!"

"Yeah. It got crazy after you left."

"I don't envy your cleaning staff."

"The cleaning staff would be me."

"You serious?" he asked as the doors clunked shut.

She nodded. "Bella normally helps before school, but she was going around to Beth's place early to surprise Enola with her present." Beth cast her eyes over the bar. "So, the fun is all mine."

Lev walked across to a corner table, which had already been cleared and cleaned. He put his bags down and slid off his coat. "Okay. Give me a cloth and a bucket."

Naomi laughed. "Yeah. Sure."

"I'm serious."

She shook her head. "I can't ask you to—"

"You're not asking me. I'm offering. In fact, I'm not even offering; I'm just doing it. I'm getting free accommodation, so this is the absolute least I can do."

"You're going to make Enola's year with what you're doing, so it's hardly free."

"You know what I mean. Please. It will make me feel better about this. When I was a teenager, I used to make extra money on a weekend as a cleaner at a local social club. I can provide references if you need them."

They shared a smile. "Okay. Thank you. If truth be told, I was kind of dreading this. I'll go get the gear."

Memories of mopping the floors and cleaning toilets came flooding back to Lev as he got to work emptying the ashtrays and wiping the tables. The radio played in the background, and as unpleasant a job as it would seem to most people, contentment swept over him.

The exchanges he had with Naomi while they laboured together were friendly and humorous. They worked well as a team, and as Lev wiped the final bar mirror clean, Naomi emerged from the back with two steaming mugs of coffee.

"If ever you get bored of the music thing, you've got a job here."

"That's good to know. Thanks," he replied, taking one of the mugs. They sat down side by side on a section of cushioned seating set against the rear wall. The place was gleaming and the lemon-fresh cleaning fluid had finally conquered the smell of tobacco and booze.

"Seriously. Thank you. I don't know how long this would have taken me, but opening time would probably have been delayed."

"It was my pleasure."

"Somehow, I doubt that."

"No. Seriously. It helped me clear my head a little."

"Oh. Yeah. I guess having that guy after you who was in here last night can't be much fun." Lev laughed. "What?"

"I wasn't even talking about that."

"Sorry." She took a sip of her drink. "You mean the job? You were thinking about what you do next?"

"Actually, not that either."

"Now I am intrigued," she replied, swivelling in her seat a little to face him.

He shook his head. "I don't want to burden you. I talked off your sister's ear yesterday. It's just something I need to figure out."

"Oh, come on. You can't leave me guessing like that."

He shook his head again, letting out a long sigh. "Something weird happened to us up at the Black house and I'm guessing that's what freaked Anna out enough to leave town."

"Ah. And there the mystery ends. I thought it was going to be something mildly scandalous or at least gossipworthy."

"What do you mean the mystery ends?"

"I mean weird and the Black house go together like peaches and cream. You could knock on the door of any house in town and they'd all have at least one tale to tell."

"Have you got one to tell?"

Naomi smiled. "No. I'm a fraidy cat. But I've heard enough never to want to go up there. I've seen the pale, drawn faces of people telling me stories. I think there's a tonne of crap to deal with in this world without going looking for it."

"So, you think there's something about the place; there's something wrong with it?"

She shrugged. "There's plenty wrong with it. What that might be is no business of mine."

"Beth said she experienced something there."

"I know."

"But you don't want to say what?"

"I wasn't there."

"But you must have seen her afterwards. You must have talked to her."

"Like I said, I've heard enough from other people never to want to go myself. Sounds to me like you experienced it firsthand yesterday, and if I were you, I'd use that as a learning moment."

Lev laughed and took a sip of coffee. "You may be right. I just don't like unfinished puzzles."

"Be careful what you wish for. But I can't help wondering if this is about something else."

"What do you mean?"

"I mean I spoke to Beth last night after you left."

"Sounds ominous."

"It's none of my business, but that's never stopped me sticking my nose into someone else's before."

Lev laughed again. "Feel free to stick your nose in. We're just talking here."

Naomi looked at the drinks in front of them. "What do you say we Irish these up to celebrate a job well done?" She gestured to the gleaming bar.

"Sure. I never say no to free booze."

She climbed to her feet and returned a moment later with a bottle, pouring healthy measures into both coffees before taking her seat. "You're away from your kids and Beth told me she could see that was hurting you. You're going through a nasty divorce. All of a sudden, you're out of work too. And then that photo shows up to bite you in the ass."

"So, you saw it?"

"Sweetie. I'm guessing most of America has seen it by now. My point is this tornado of crap is twirling around you, and you feel out of control, and you want it all to be right. You want everything to go back to normal and you're focusing on this one thing that happened in the hope you can figure out all the rest of it if you find the answer."

"Are you a bar owner or a psychiatrist?"

"Sometimes it amounts to the same thing. I hear everyone's sad stories in here."

Lev thought for a moment. "Shit."

"Shit what?"

"There's a part of that which may be true."

"Just a part?"

"What happened to me and Anna yesterday didn't make sense. It doesn't make sense."

"And no matter how much digging you do, I can guarantee you won't find anything out that helps you. In fact, if you go back there, I think you'll just be opening up a whole new world of pain for yourself."

"Naomi. I lost time. There are several hours that I can't account for. You're saying I should just leave it at that?"

"Listen, Lev. I like you. You offered to do something amazing for my niece when there was nothing in it for you when you were going through this world of trouble yourself. That tells me you're a good guy. You and this Anna were the only people up there yesterday. You're saying you lost time. I believe you. But there are only two people in this world who know what happened yesterday—you and her, and—"

"But that's the point. I don't know what happened."

"And that's my point. If you don't know, nobody will, and no amount of snooping around will help you. But it could cause you a lot more problems. All the time I've lived in this town, nobody has ever told me a warm, fuzzy story about that place. Do you really want to add that shit into the mix?"

"You're serious, aren't you?"

"I've never been big on church. I think ninety-nine-point-nine percent of all the bad stuff that happens in this world happens because of us. But I think there's shit that we don't understand too. And that house is just one giant ball of shit that we don't understand." She took another drink. "Stay here a few days. Hell, stay as long as you want. See what life's like living in a small town. But don't go back to that place. Don't look for answers that you'll never find. Like I said, you're a good guy. I don't want to see something happening to you."

He was about to reply when Beth walked through the door from behind the bar area. "Oh. I'd just come to see if our guest was settling in." Her eyes focused on the bottle that was still on the table between the two coffee mugs.

"Lev helped me clean up. It got crazy last night after you left. I think the pool hall must have emptied in the space of five minutes and everyone came here."

"You helped?" she asked Lev, looking around the place with her hands on her hips.

"Seemed like the least I could do."

"I thought you'd have been busy."

"Doing what?"

"I don't know. Cradling some naked women in your room. Is that actually a job or is it just a perk? I don't know much about the music industry."

"I'm guessing you saw the photo then."

"What photo? The one they showed on TV last night or the one that they're showing this morning? Or the one that's on the front covers of the papers?" There wasn't a hint of a smile on her face as she spoke the words.

"I don't suppose it would help if I said that it's not what it looks like."

Now a smile did creep onto the sheriff's face. "Oh, man. Those were the exact same words that came out of my husband's mouth when I found him with his tongue stuck down another woman's throat."

"Beth—"

"You don't need to explain yourself. It's none of my business."

"But—"

"I just wanted to make sure that everything's set up for tonight."

"I need to phone Jodie later with the details, but she said she'd do it and she's never let me down before."

"Oh, I'm sure. I've seen the photographic proof, remember."

Naomi sniggered. "I'm going to go check the dishwasher."

"Beth—"

"Like I said. It's none of my business."

"I told you last night. I swear on my kids' lives that Jodie and I don't have that kind of relationship."

"And last night, I believed you. Then I saw the photo." She shrugged. "Anyway. It doesn't matter. Like I said, it's none of my business. I just wanted to make sure you were settled in and everything is still on."

"Yeah." He paused for a few seconds. "Y'know, I don't have to come to the party. Jodie will be phoning bang on eight. I don't need to be there."

"You do need to be there. It will blow Enola's mind to have someone so close to the band there."

"Okay. Good. I'd be happy to come."

Some of the iciness left Beth's eyes. "So, what's your plan for the rest of the day?"

"Well, I'm not sure at the moment."

"I thought you were going to try to figure out what happened to you yesterday."

"Your sister psycho-analysed me. I'm weighing up my options."

Beth looked in the direction of the kitchen. "She's pretty good at that. She's psycho-analysed me plenty in the past. Beats paying a therapist."

"Yeah. On the subject of paying for a therapist, do you know any doctors or anything in town who'd be willing to give me five minutes of their time without charging?"

Beth laughed. "Oh, man. You're a real catch, aren't you? Relying on free accommodation and now free healthcare."

"Thanks for reminding me."

"Sorry. That was cruel."

"I deserved it."

"No. You didn't. I'm sorry. What's wrong? Are you not feeling well?"

"Nothing like that. I was just wanting some expertise."

"About what?"

"About mercury, actually."

"What, like the planet?"

"No. The chemical element."

Beth looked at her watch. "At eleven-thirty every day, my old science teacher goes to the diner down the street. What he can't tell you about every chemical on the periodic table isn't worth knowing."

"What isn't worth knowing?" Naomi asked, appearing back from around the bar to join them.

"Mister Poots, our old science teacher. Lev was asking who he could quiz about mercury."

"The planet?"

"No. The element."

"Sure. He'd tell you everything you'd want to know. Why?"

"I think I'm going to take your advice," Lev replied. "I think what you said was absolutely spot on, but I just want one question answering before I draw a line underneath this thing, and then I'm never going to think about the Black house again."

"Okay. Good."

"Well, I'm going to get back to work," Beth said.

"Okay. I'll see you tonight," Naomi replied.

"Don't forget the cake."

"As if I'm going to."

Beth turned to Lev. "Don't forget to phone your friend with the details."

"I will."

"Good then."

They both watched her go before Naomi sat down once more. She took the top off the bottle and poured a little more whisky into each of their mugs. "Thought you could probably use a drop more after that."

Lev laughed. "She's pretty direct, isn't she?"

"Ha! You've no idea."

15

Jodie didn't feel like being a rock star today. She didn't feel like playing a part. The long conversations she'd had with Taleen the previous evening had shaken her and all she wanted to do was phone Lev and coax him down off the ledge, tell him to get the hell out of New Scotland and away from that house. But she knew him too well. He was stubborn and, more to the point, he was broke and wouldn't take charity. Hopefully, this contract negotiation would help him a little too.

Limos on the streets of LA, especially in this part of town, were nothing unusual. Today, though, the occupant of this particular vehicle was not wearing a tux or a designer gown. She was wearing Ray-Bans, 501s, a low-cut black vest and a leather jacket. In all likelihood, there would be paparazzi waiting for her when she got to the record company offices. Hopefully, there'd be security to usher her through as well.

Her agent had contacted her first thing, sounding almost gleeful about the publication of the photograph. Their phone had been ringing off the hook ever since, and while Jodie considered it a huge invasion of privacy, her agent saw a definite upside. She'd even had a call from a casting director wanting Jodie to audition for a new movie.

She reached for the sawn-in-half brick that was the car phone and dialled. She wanted advice from Taleen. Everything had been a whirlwind the previous evening; there had been too much to take in, but now her head was filled with questions.

She still wasn't sure what all of this was, but if Jamie and his people were involved, it wouldn't be good for Lev. Jodie wanted to know what she could do to stop them.

The phone rang and rang until Lucia finally picked it up. "Hi. Can I speak to Taleen?"

"Miss Zakarian is not here."

Jodie paused. Taleen had told her on multiple occasions that she was a night owl, rarely getting up until late morning, and this was a long way from late morning.

"When will she be back?"

"Um. I don't know. Miss Zakarian left this morning, saying that she would be gone for a few days. She said she would call in for her messages."

Another pause. "Lucia, it's me. It's Jodie. I was there last night. Do you know where she went?"

"No. Only that her driver took her to the airport."

Jodie let out a long breath. "When she gets in touch, will you tell her that I need to speak to her?"

"Yes."

"Thanks, Lucia." Jodie hung up the phone and slumped back into her seat. "Shit!"

*

Lev left the bar just before opening time. He'd tried to get in touch with Jamie again, leaving another message, this time alluding to some of the events at the house that might have scared Anna away, but to no avail. He'd

THE DEVIL'S FACE

contacted the Occulture Productions number and, again, all he'd gotten was an answering machine.

His head was still a jumble as he walked into the diner. An older man was sitting in a booth. He had a menu in front of him and a cup of coffee was steaming by his side.

"Mr Poots?" Lev asked.

A confused smile crept onto the old teacher's face. "Yes?" he asked in a soft, inquiring tone, pulling his round spectacles down and looking over the top of them at the out-of-place younger man.

"I'm really sorry to bother you. Beth and Naomi said I should seek you out."

"You're English?"

"Yes, sir." Lev almost laughed. It had been longest time since he'd called anyone sir, but the reverence with which the two women had spoken of this man and the fact that everything about him said he was an educator made it seem natural.

"Please, take a seat," Mr Poots said, gesturing to the opposite side of the table. "I can't imagine why they would recommend you seek me out."

"I'm sorry to interrupt your routine, sir. My name's Lev and I just need a little information."

The old teacher smiled. "When you get to my age, you relish every interruption to the routine. Now, what can I do for you, Lev?"

"Mercury, sir."

"I hope you're not going to ask me whether it's in retrograde or not because—"

"No, Mr Poots. The element mercury."

"Ah. I see. Go on."

"What effect can it have on a person?"

Mr Poots took a sip of his coffee. "Well, that would depend on the context. How much, proximity, etcetera."

"What I'm asking is could it affect someone's mental state? Could they lose their grasp of reality? Could they forget things, lose track of time?"

The old teacher sat back in the cushioned seat just as a waitress came up to the table. "Could I get you a menu, sir?" she asked.

"No. I'm okay, thanks. I won't be stopping long."

"A drink then, maybe?"

"Water would be good, thanks."

"Big spender."

"Sorry, I—"

"Just joshing you, sugar. Are you ready to order yet, Lionel?"

"Not just yet, Bernie. Give me a few minutes."

The waitress was about to walk away when she stopped in her tracks. "Wait one minute. You're that guy in the photo? The one holdin' that singer and her fake boobs."

A look of confusion swept across Mr Poots' face and Lev shrunk a little in his chair. "Um, yeah. It's me. But they're not fake. There's nothing fake about Jodie."

The waitress shrugged. "Well, you'd know, honey." She started walking away again, but as she went behind the counter, a whispered, "You'll never guess who's talkin' to Lionel," rippled across the diner to meet them before she disappeared into the back.

"I'm sure that made sense to both of you, but I'm not one for watching television."

Lev shook his head. "Oh, don't worry. It's in all the papers too. You can't miss it."

Half a smile lit the old man's face. "You sound like you're having a day."

"Oh, I've had a string of them all sewn together. They kind of blur after a while."

"Don't worry, son. We all go through tough times."

"I suppose we do."

"Getting back to your question. It sounds like what you're talking about is erethism, or Mad Hatter's disease."

"Mad Hatter's disease?"

"So called because they used to use mercury in the making of hats and prolonged exposure to low levels caused all sorts of maladies from irritability to depression to changes in personality to delirium. In extreme cases, far worse symptoms were recorded."

Lev slumped back in his chair a little. "So, that all happens over time? It's not something that can cause, say, someone to lose time or—"

"Lose time?"

Lev let out a long, deep breath. "What the hell. You're probably going to think I'm mad anyway, so I may as well give you the whole story." He was about to continue when the waitress returned with the glass of water and put it down in front of him.

"There you go, shug."

"Thanks." She winked as she left the table and Lev reminded himself that this notoriety would only be a thousand times worse in a city. He went on to tell Mr Poots what had happened and the old man listened intently. When he was done, Mr Poots considered his response for a few moments before replying.

"I think you're a very intelligent young man."

"It's a long time since anyone's called me young."

"Well, comparatively speaking, you're young. Everyone has leapt to conclusions about the old Black place and I've always remained adamant that the problem with it remains an environmental factor rather than a supernatural one. The clean-up, in inverted commas, happened at a time when the regulatory body that made the decisions was nothing more than a couple of easily paid-off officials who sent water samples to a lab and put a rubber stamp on a piece of paper. Those samples could have come from anywhere. Oh, don't get me wrong, I think the lake was cleaned up; otherwise there'd be a furore. But wells and groundwater, I mean, finding all those sources and purifying them would take vast amounts of time and money I can't even comprehend.

"Now, the story goes that the well at the Black place was cleaned up, but it coincided with a new property development half a mile further up the road and the roll-out of mains water to that part of town. So, I'm fairly certain the Black house got hooked up to the town supply. Subsequently, if the water was tested, it would be fine. But from what you're saying, you discovered a fissure in the basement and noticed a significant temperature reduction as well?"

"That's right, yes."

"Of course, without investigation, I could only theorise."

"Beth and Naomi were kind of in awe of you. So it's your theories I want."

A fond smile lit Poots' face. "They were both good girls. Headstrong, decent, honest. They weren't the best students I ever had, but they were among my favourites."

"I've only known them for a day, but they seem like salt of the earth types."

"They are that and more besides." He took another drink of coffee and drew a long breath. "Well, if it's theories you want, here's one. I think you and your friend probably experienced mercury poisoning. I think that fissure in the basement floor is probably directly above a reservoir of groundwater for the well, which in all likelihood occurred due to subsidence."

"So, you think the vapours rose up through the crack and—"

"It's not quite as simple as that. Mercury vapour is denser than air. I think what probably happened is that when the fissure occurred, there was a sudden and violent displacement. The floor and foundation dropped and the vapour erupted, settling on the basement floor. Obviously, it's invisible, but imagine it as a low-hanging mist of smoke for a moment. When you and your colleague entered the basement, you disturbed the mist and started breathing in the vapour. Now, without further study, there's no possible way to tell how much there is down there, but by the sound of it, you had a lucky escape. In extreme cases, it can kill."

"So, are you actually telling me that breathing in that stuff could have caused us to have some kind of episode, which resulted in us losing time?"

"From what you've told me, I think that's highly likely, and, as I say, I think you're both lucky. It can cause all sorts of illnesses. But I think what probably happened is by disturbing the vapour, there was some kind of overload to your nervous systems that, in effect, put you into a kind of waking coma, if you like."

"Have you ever heard of anything like that happening before?"

"Not that specifically, but I've heard of all sorts of adverse effects on the neurological system. I've heard of people losing their minds. I've heard of violent outbursts as well as kidney diseases, lung diseases and, ultimately, death resulting from exposure to mercury and mercury vapour. And let's face it; my hypothesis is far more plausible than ghosties and ghoulies taking possession of you, isn't it?"

Lev laughed. "Yeah. I suppose it is." He remained seated for a moment, processing everything the retired teacher had told him; then he nodded to himself, convinced that was what had happened. "And all the other stuff that's happened over the years?"

"Well, remember, all the incidents in the early days were due to actually having contaminated water running out of the taps. And who's to say other cracks might not have occurred in the garden or elsewhere on the property? But as far as the legend of the place goes, I think a lot of that comes down to small town hysteria. A rumour, a thought, a spoken word can gain traction like a snowball rolling down the side of a mountain in a town like this. That factor should never be underestimated."

"I really can't thank you enough for your time, Mr Poots," Lev said, extending his hand.

The other man extended his and they shook. "It's my pleasure. As I said, any break from the routine is welcomed when you get to my age."

Lev rose from his seat and looked across to the counter where the waitress was leaning into one of the punters, whispering something, in all likelihood about Lev. He smiled to himself and made his exit.

*

Beth was at her desk signing overtime sheets when Doug, one of her deputies, walked in. Beth had an office of her own, but she rarely spent any time in there, preferring instead to sit in the open plan area with the rest of the staff.

Lucille, the receptionist, and Carl, another of the deputies, were in conversation when they noticed the slightly troubled look on Doug's face.

"You okay, hun?" asked Lucille.

Beth looked up, registering the mild concern in the other woman's voice.

"Just writ someone up for speeding," he said. "Weirdest goddam people I ever did come across."

"Weird how?" Carl asked.

"All dressed in black and just ... weird."

"Maybe they was headin' to a funeral or somethin'."

"Well, I don't know of any funerals today, do you?"

"It ain't against the law to wear black, hun," Lucille said, fluffing her coal blouse.

"I know that. I just mean there was somethin' strange about the way they looked is all."

"Strange how?" Beth asked, putting her pen down.

"Um ... intense, I suppose."

"Intense?"

"Like they was starin' holes through me."

"They were threatening?"

"Well ... I can't say they was. I can't say they even meant to be. They just seemed ... weird."

"Where did they go?"

"They went to the Heston."

Beth raised her eyebrows. The Heston was a small but beautiful hotel outside of town that was prohibitively expensive for most people. Subsequently, they rarely got

THE DEVIL'S FACE

guests other than business customers, and when they did, they tended to be high rollers.

"Well, weird or not, they've obviously got some coin to spend."

"Well, yeah. They had a real nice car. German or something. Rental from the airport. It'll have cost a pretty penny. But like I say, there's just something not right about them."

Beth shrugged. "You've usually got good instincts, Doug. Keep an eye on them."

"If it's all the same, I'd rather not put my eyes on them again. They gave me the creeps and then some."

In the time she'd been sheriff, she'd learned not to show frustration on her face. She'd learned not to let her shoulders droop, not to come out with insults and not to let things like this make her die a little inside. "Yeah, well, unfortunately, it's our job to protect this town and we can't limit that protection to only those people who don't creep us out." She pushed her chair out and stood up.

"Where are you going?"

"I'm just going to have a little drive out to the Heston. See if they're still having problems with kids screwing in the bay behind the kitchen."

"They told me that hadn't happened since they put that fake camera up."

"Yeah, but they didn't tell me, did they?"

"I don't get it. I just told you now."

Beth exhaled deeply. That was one of the calming exercises she'd learned from that self-help cassette. "Yeah, but y'see, this gives me an excuse to go over there and talk to them while at the same time getting a look at our new visitors, all without creating suspicion."

"Oh! That's smart."

"Thanks, Doug. That means a lot coming from you."

"Well, I guess that's why you're in charge here."

Beth clenched her teeth together tightly and headed for the door. "See you all in a while. I'll be sure to call for backup if things get too weird." As the door closed behind her, she knew that last little snippet of sarcasm would go above all their heads, but it made her feel better, and if this job had taught her one thing, it was to get little pleasures wherever she could find them.

*

Enola didn't look behind her as she delved into her locker. There was a part of her that didn't think Lauren and her friends would dare do anything after Bella humiliated her so badly. There was another part that wondered if it would lead to brutal retribution, but while she was only looking into her locker, she was in a wonderful kind of Schrödinger's cat territory kind of denial. Both could be true, even though, deep down in her heart, she believed that Lauren's venom would finally tip the balance against her good sense.

When she felt a tap on her shoulder, her eyes fell shut for a beat. All the air left her lungs and her shoulders sagged. *Today's my birthday. Can't I have just a single day where other people don't go out of their way to make me feel like crap?*

She turned, bracing herself for whatever came next.

"Ash?" He and Bella weren't officially boyfriend and girlfriend, but they were there or thereabouts. He was someone who most girls drooled over—good-looking, funny, a member of the football team.

"Hi."

"Hi." Although he said hello to her when passing her in a corridor, he'd never walked up to her like this before. "Is everything okay?"

"Yeah," he said with a smile, pulling something out of his backpack at the same time. "I was going to give this to you a couple of weeks ago, but Bella told me to hold on to it until your birthday." He handed her a small box bound in decorative wrapping paper.

"What is it?"

"Well, the idea is that you open it and find out." An excited smile flashed on Enola's face as she tore the paper off, revealing a cigarette box. "I'm sorry. That was the only thing I could find that it would fit in."

Enola flipped it open and pulled out a metal belt buckle. The Blazetrailer logo was emblazoned across it. "Oh, my God!"

"I made it in shop. It's not perfect, but—"

"Oh, my God," she repeated, opening her eyes wide, trying her hardest not to cry. "I love it," she said, flinging her arms around Ash and kissing him on the cheek before remembering herself. "I'm sorry. It's just nobody's ever done anything like this for me before."

"Don't say sorry. If I knew I was going to get kissed when I brought you a present, I'd have started a long time ago."

Enola giggled, covering her mouth. "Sorry. I love it."

"Like I say, it's not perfect. I had a bit of difficulty with the Z."

"It's perfect to me."

"I'm glad you like it. Bella told me a few weeks ago that you were going through a bit of a tough time, and I know you're a huge fan of the band, so I thought I'd have a go at the logo for you."

"You've no idea what this means to me. I'm going to be smiling for the rest of the day."

"That's good. You've got too nice a smile not to use it more often."

Enola blushed. "Thank you again for this."

The bell rang and Ash hoisted his backpack onto his shoulder. "Well, I suppose we'd better get to lessons. Happy birthday, Enola," he said, leaning in and pecking her on the cheek before disappearing into the crowd.

She could feel eyes on her as she stood in front of her still-open locker. She could hear the whispers starting, but for once, they weren't because she was the butt of anyone's jokes. Ash Colton had just given her a birthday present and then kissed her on the cheek. For once in her life, Enola was the envy of nearly every girl in that corridor.

She put the belt buckle into her bag, closed her locker and headed to class with a beaming smile on her face. There was a first time for everything, after all.

16

Lev stepped through the doors of the Bellanola and already the smell of lemons had dissipated a little. "Hi."

"Hey," Naomi replied, polishing a glass and placing it with the others behind the bar. There were a few people in, but most were quietly cradling drinks. "You find Mr Poots?"

"I did. And he was everything you said and more."

"So he helped you with what you needed?"

"Yeah. He's a clever man."

"You can say that again. Most of what he used to say to me went completely over my head. I was always more of an art than a science girl. I'm glad he was able to help you, anyway."

Lev looked at his watch. "Do you think I could use your phone? I need to give the details to Jodie for tonight."

"Of course. You know where it is. Oh, and before I forget, here's a key."

"What's this for?"

"The front door. In case you ever want to get in or out and I'm not around."

"Seriously?"

"Sure."

"Thanks, Naomi." He pulled up the bar flap and headed into the back. He knew Jodie's number by heart and it was only a few seconds before the phone was answered. "Greta, it's Lev. Is Jodie there?"

"Yes, Mr Lev. Please wait."

"I'm so glad you called," Jodie said as she answered. "I've got a load to tell you."

"Well, I'm on someone else's phone so make it quick if you can."

"Give me the number, I'll call back." He did as she asked and a few seconds later the phone rang. "Okay, listen. First things first. I actually found myself in two meetings."

"Two?"

"Yeah."

"What was the second one?"

"Mortensen and the label want me to record a solo album."

"That's brilliant news."

"Yeah. It was even more brilliant when I told him I already had at least a dozen songs for it."

"What do you mean?"

"Those tracks you and I worked on that got voted down by the rest of the band. I had a demo cassette in the car. Mortensen heard three and he loved them. I don't think I've ever seen him so excited. He got two other execs in to listen."

"That's brilliant, Jo. I'm really happy for you."

"Happy for us. Us. Co-writing credits, Lev. That's proper money. And it means that you'll be getting a royalty, not just getting paid when we're on tour or in the studio. And the other thing is you're going to be producing it, too. But that's not even the best part." A bewildered smile lit Lev's face as Jodie continued excitedly. "I said in the group meeting that I wanted you to produce the next Blazetrailer album and the rest of the band stood with me. Davey said what I've been saying all along; that it was a joke you were only credited as the sound engineer on the last album. He actually used the words cokehead piece of shit to describe Garret and he said you were the reason the album sounded as good as it did. He also said that if they insisted on Garret producing again there wouldn't be an album. The rest of the band stood shoulder to shoulder with us for once, insisting that it was you."

"And Mortensen agreed to that?"

"Too fucking right he agreed."

"That's amazing news. Thanks, Jo. I really don't know what to say."

"You know you never have to thank me. But there's something else, Lev."

He instantly recognised the change in her tone. "What?"

"I called Taleen last night." Silence. "I know you don't like her, but—"

"That's not true. What I said is she scared the hell out of me."

"Yeah, well, you and me both, and what I'm about to tell you isn't going to change your mind about her."

"What do you mean?"

"Okay. Before I continue, I want you to promise that you're not going to get pissed off with me and I need you to know that I was only doing this because I love you and I'm looking out for you."

"Go on."

"When you told me Jamie was involved, my twatdar immediately went into overdrive and I wanted to know if any alarm bells rang for Taleen with this place. Anyway—"

"You don't have to worry."

"What do you mean?"

"I mean I'm not going any further with it. I'm pretty certain I know what happened. I'm pretty certain I know why all the weird things have happened in that house, and since Jamie and his company seem to have left us all high and dry down here, I don't really have any interest in continuing employment with him even if he got another director and wanted to continue the series."

"Oh. Good. I mean that's good. But I got a lecture on the place last night and it completely freaked me out. What changed your mind?"

"I met with Beth's old science teacher and he had an explanation for the goings-on there. Mercury poisoning."

"Mercury poisoning?"

"Yeah. It's a long story. There was a pesticide factory that closed down but not before a shit load of mercury seeped into the lake, land and groundwater. Apparently, mercury can cause all kinds of weird shit to happen including hallucinations, blackouts, you name it. He reckons pretty much everything that happened at the Black house can be traced back to mercury poisoning and hysteria."

There was silence on the other end of the phone for a moment before Jodie spoke again. "Taleen was pretty sure it was something else."

"No offence, but Taleen could find the devil in a bag of marshmallows. I mean have you seen her work?"

"I can't argue with that."

"So, anyway. You don't need to worry. I'm going to stick around here a couple of days and then get on a Greyhound and—"

"A couple of days. Why are you staying a couple of days? I've just told you we've got work to do. I've also had papers drawn up to give you an advance. And an advance isn't charity, an advance is I need you working with me on these songs and you can reimburse me at the back end."

"I think this is a good place to ride out the current media frenzy."

"I thought you said stuff like that didn't matter to you and nobody—wait a minute." A smile started in Jodie's voice. "This is about your sheriff, isn't it?"

"That would be crazy. I mean, where the hell would the future be in that? I live in LA. She lives in a backward little town in Tennessee, and besides, she doesn't even like me. I thought she was going to pull her gun this morning after she saw that picture."

"Oh, man. You do like her, don't you?"

"Look. I'm going to go to her kid's party. Stay on here for a couple of days while this photo gets dropped from the news cycle, and then I'll be back with you and you can take the piss out of me all you like."

"Cool."

The rest of the conversation covered some of the more boring aspects of the meeting as well as Lev giving Jodie the phone number and telling her the little about Enola that he actually knew.

"So, eight o'clock."

"Eight o'clock."

"Jodie."

"Yeah."

"Thanks for everything."

"I told you. You don't need to thank me. I'll never be able to repay you for what you've done."

"And I told you that there's no need to repay me. You're like my little sister. I'd do anything for you."

"Love you."

"Love you too."

He hung up the phone and turned to see Naomi standing there looking like she'd just walked in on something she shouldn't have. "For fuck's sake," Lev said, starting to laugh.

"It's none of my business."

"I'll tell you what I told your sister. Jodie is family to me. There's nothing like that, and I know that photo that's in circulation suggests something different, but it's not the whole story."

"Like I said, it's none of my business. I didn't realise you'd still be on the phone."

"Is everything okay?"

"No, actually. I've screwed up."

"What's wrong?"

"I arranged extra cover for tonight, because obviously I'm going to be at my sister's. But I moved the person's shift without getting cover for this afternoon, and Friday afternoon is always busy. I mean we do sandwiches and snacks. Things get really chaotic and then stay busy the rest of the day. I feel shitty asking this, but could you help?"

Lev smiled. "Course I can. It'll be a laugh."

"You won't be saying that when you've been working with me for twenty minutes."

"Come on," Lev said. "Let's get to work."

The hours flew by and, as Naomi had foretold, the Bellanola got busy as people began to wind down for the weekend. Another member of staff came in to work behind the bar and she and Naomi were rushed off their feet while Lev worked in the back throwing together sandwiches and loading the dishwasher. Occasionally, he would step out from behind the bar and collect glasses, but the rest of the time, he worked up a sweat in the kitchen.

At five-thirty, another two members of staff arrived, and at six, Sam showed up, who was the assistant manager and the one who would make everything run smoothly in Naomi's absence.

"That's you and me done," Naomi said, reaching out and grabbing hold of Lev's arm as he was about to collect another tray full of glasses.

"Too bad. I was having fun."

"Uh-huh."

"I wasn't being sarcastic. I genuinely had fun."

"Making sandwiches and washing glasses?"

"You wouldn't understand."

"Try me," she said as they walked into the back away from the increasing hubbub in the bar.

He shrugged. "I grew up in a poor household. If I wanted money as a teenager, I used to have to work for it. I cleaned, I washed glasses; I did all sorts. I told myself that when I left school, I would do something I love. And I do. I do something I really love. And after speaking to Jodie today, I got some news that's going to make things even better."

"That's great, but I don't understand why that made today fun for you."

"Because it reminded me how lucky I am to be doing something that gives my life meaning. There are always going to be ups and downs, but if you follow your dreams, no matter how rocky the road can be sometimes, then it's a life worth living, isn't it?"

"Wow! I never had you pegged as a philosopher."

"Funny girl."

Naomi smiled. "Make sure to give me your clothes when you change. I'll get them washed for you. Trust me. You don't want the stink of cigarettes and booze rubbing against the rest of your things."

"Thanks."

"Right. Beth gave you a map to the house?"

"Yeah."

"And you're going to be there at seven forty-five?"

"You sound a lot like your sister."

"You take that back."

"I'm sorry. I'm just kidding."

"Good then. We won't have a problem." She smiled too. "Thank you for this. All of it. Enola is such a special kid and she doesn't have the easiest life with her mom as the sheriff. Tonight is going to blow her mind."

"It's my pleasure. It's the least I can do."

They parted with more smiles and Lev went back to the small apartment. He stripped off his clothes and winced a little as he smelt them. The odour of cigarettes, booze and sweat had slowly bled onto them without him noticing, but now he was out of the bar environment, they were pungent.

He climbed into the shower and stood there for a moment, basking in the hot, cleansing water. The broadest smile he'd managed in a long time lit his face as he thought about the day. For all the tumult, confusion and insecurity since arriving in this small town, things had taken a real turn now. *Producer. I'm officially going to be Blazetrailer's producer.* It was a really big deal for someone like Lev. A huge deal. He reached for the shampoo and washed his hair then scrubbed himself with the soap.

When he climbed out of the shower, he felt like a new man. He towelled himself down, only then noticing his custom-built sound recorder in the corner of the room. He'd charged the battery pack up the previous evening, not really knowing why. It was unlikely to be used again for some time. *Who knows, Jodie might want some nature sounds for her solo disc.* He smiled again. She was going to use his songs and it was a certainty that her album would be huge. She hadn't really put a foot wrong since entering the music arena and the fans couldn't get enough. *I'm going to be absolutely rolling in it.*

He turned on the TV and watched the news for a little while before digging the map out of his wallet. He picked up the card he'd bought and the little present he'd managed to find in the bottom of his sports bag. It was only a token and he'd be sure to send her something more substantial when he got back home, but at least he wasn't going empty-handed.

Beth's place was on a quiet street at the edge of town. The lawn was well kept, the house freshly painted. As he walked up the garden path, he could hear laughter from inside, and although he'd been invited, he couldn't help feeling like a bit of an interloper.

That sensation disappeared as soon as the door was answered, however.

"No. Fucking. Way!" The girl who greeted him wore her jet-black hair just the same way as Jodie. Her eyes bore the same thick liner; she wore skin-tight jeans with a Blazetrailer belt buckle and a band T-shirt. "No. Fucking. Way!" she repeated. In between her two exclamations, her mouth had gaped in disbelief and now it fell into this position once again.

"I'm guessing you're Enola," Lev replied.

Three figures had crept into the hall to see the teenager's reaction and the trio had started to giggle gleefully.

"You're Lev Stoll."

"Guilty as charged."

"But … but…." She turned around to look at her mother and a blinding flash lit the narrow hallway as Bella caught the moment on camera.

"Lev was in town for work. It was Bella who recognised him. I was actually looking for reasons to throw him into a cell, truth be told," Beth said.

"I'm sure you'll get your chance," Lev replied.

"So, are you going to make him stand on the step all evening or are you going to invite him in?"

Enola shook her head a little, still trying to come to terms with what was going on. Then she reached out and grabbed Lev's arm, dragging him into the house. "I believe a happy birthday is in order," he said, reaching inside his jacket and pulling out a card and a small gift.

"What's this?"

"When I set off from home, I had no idea I'd be coming to a party, so I had to scrabble around for something to give you. But I promise, when I get back to LA, I'll send you something a little better."

Enola carefully tore open the paper revealing a backstage pass on a lanyard. The artwork was of the last Blazetrailer album with a superimposed photo of the band in front of it. That had been the tour poster design. It was the exact same poster Enola had hanging on her wall among all the other band memorabilia.

"No way!"

"That was the one Jodie wore."

Enola looked up at him wide-eyed. "Jodie Starr wore this backstage pass?"

"Yeah. It's actually the one you see on the Madison Square Garden video."

Enola stood gawping at it for a moment before turning around to her mother again. "Can I take Lev upstairs to see my room?"

"Sure, sweetie. What mother wouldn't want their fifteen-year-old daughter taking an unemployed heavy metal roadie at the centre of a huge sex scandal up to their room? They're the words I've been wanting to hear all my life."

"Thanks," Enola replied, grabbing hold of Lev's arm again and pulling him towards the staircase.

"Remember. I've got a gun," Beth said as Lev was dragged past the still laughing trio. Despite the waspish nature of Beth's words, this had been exactly the reaction she was hoping Lev's visit would garner. Enola was behaving like the excited, life-loving little girl she had once been and it brought genuine joy to her mother's heart.

Lev laughed too as he was hauled up the stairs.

"I really can't believe this. It's like … unbelievable," Enola muttered as they hit the landing. They continued along, finally entering the far bedroom.

"Holy shit!" Lev said. It was like a shrine to Jodie and the band. Posters, magazine cuttings and album artwork decorated two of the walls and on the third were drawings and paintings of the band, but primarily Jodie.

"Do you like it?" Enola asked excitedly.

Lev walked up to the wall with original artwork on it. "Did you do these?"

"Yeah."

"Jesus, Enola. These are amazing."

She shook her head. "You don't have to say that."

"No. I'm serious. These are seriously good." He continued to survey them then let out a laugh.

"What's funny?" she asked nervously.

He pointed to an ink sketch of Jodie on stage at the final Madison Square Garden show with the lanyard around her neck. "What are the chances?"

"That was a real nightmare. Our video will only pause for like five minutes before it starts playing again, so I was continually having to rewind."

"You've got some serious talent here, kid. You've kind of captured the essence of the show in one black-and-white drawing. I'm well impressed."

Enola beamed. "Thank you."

"Jodie would love this bedroom," he said, looking around the rest of the room. "But she would be absolutely blown away by this wall, and this drawing in particular."

"Really?"

"I'm not kidding you, Enola. She would love it."

Enola went into her wardrobe and pulled out a poster tube then walked to the wall and unpinned the ink drawing before carefully rolling it and pushing it into the cardboard cylinder. "Would you give it to her?"

"Are you serious?"

"Yeah."

"But it's brilliant. Don't you want it on your wall?"

"Given a choice of having it on my wall or Jodie seeing it, I'd take the latter any day of the week."

"Course I'll give it to her. And y'know what; I bet you anything she puts this up in her home studio."

"Sure," Enola said, giggling but hoping it was true at the same time.

"I'm serious. She's got a wall in there that she calls her feel-good wall. I can almost guarantee that this will be going up on it."

Enola's eyes widened. "I'm sure I'm going to wake up in a minute and find out this whole thing was a dream."

Lev smiled. "Hey look. You're the first person I'm officially informing about this news, but Jodie's going to be recording a solo album." Another expression of unbridled excitement lit the teenager's face. "I'm going to be producing it and working on the songs with her. How about I send you a couple of photos from the studio and I'll bet you good money that you'll see this drawing up on the wall."

Enola opened her mouth, but she didn't know what to say. She handed him the tube. "I—"

"Everything good in here?" Beth asked from the doorway.

"No, Mom. We were just about to have sex. Can you give us a few more minutes?"

Beth shook her head. "Teenagers. Too young to throw out. Too old and ugly to put up for adoption."

"Lev's giving one of my drawings to Jodie. He said that she'd probably put it up in her studio, and he said that he's producing her next album and he'd be working with her in the studio and—" The phone suddenly started ringing downstairs and she stopped in mid-sentence.

"That's probably going to be your Aunt Maisie wishing you a happy birthday. She said she was going to phone."

Enola's shoulders sagged. "Mom, please." She gestured to Lev. "We've got guests. Not just a normal guest either. I mean, how many times in my life am I going to have someone who's practically a member of Blazetrailer here? I mean, Aunt Maisie will sap half an hour out of my life telling me about her feet and—"

"Don't be ungrateful. You weren't complaining when you opened that envelope with twenty dollars in. Anyway, dinner's nearly ready, so if it's dragging on, I'll just cut her short and say we have to go."

"ENOLA! IT'S FOR YOU!" Bella shouted from downstairs.

The teenager let out an exaggerated sigh and exited the room. "She's a really sweet kid," Lev said as Beth leaned against the doorway and looked at the gap on the wall where the drawing used to be.

"Between the two of us, will Jodie really get to see that picture?"

"Too right she will. No word of a lie. This will end up on her studio wall. I know she'll love it. Your girl is seriously talented. I mean it."

THE DEVIL'S FACE

"NO FUCKING WAY!" Enola's cry of excitement raced up the stairs to greet them and they both laughed.

"I guess it's not Aunt Maisie," Lev said.

"I guess not. Thank you again for organising this."

"Honestly. Not a problem. It's not a problem for Jo either. She actually loves talking to fans. The bigger she gets the less she can do it, but trust me; she'll get as much of a buzz out of the conversation as Enola."

"Somehow, I doubt that. Anyway, I'd actually come up here to—"

"Give me a hard time?"

Beth smiled. "No. To see whether you wanted red or white."

"Wine? Very cultured."

"Let me guess. You thought we'd be drinking moonshine and finishing the evening with a banjo duel."

Lev laughed. "Not that you have any preconceived ideas about me or anything."

"Oh, sweetie. We don't have time for me to go into all the preconceived ideas I've got about you. So I'm working purely on a need-to-know basis. Red or white?"

"White. Please."

"You can follow me down if you like. Unless you'd prefer to stay in my teenage daughter's bedroom all by yourself for a little while."

"It's good to know that photo didn't sway your opinion about me in any way."

"You know what they say. A picture speaks a thousand words and I can think of a few straight off the bat."

"A glass of wine sounds great round about now. Please lead the way."

Despite the fact that her shields were obviously up and she didn't hold him in very high regard, Lev couldn't help liking Beth even more after their brief exchange. She was funny. Very funny. She was smart, clearly didn't suffer fools or bullshit, and he wondered just how much of a dick her ex must have been to make her this way. They walked down the stairs and passed Enola in the hallway who was standing in slack-jawed awe as her idol spoke on the other end of the phone.

Bella and Naomi were back in the living room as they continued to the kitchen. Beth opened the fridge, plucking out a bottle of Chardonnay and pouring two glasses. A bellowing laugh from the hall made them both smile.

"Thank you for this," Beth said, raising her glass and clinking it against Lev's.

"You've thanked me like fifty times, and I told you, it's no big deal."

"It is to Enola. It is to me. You've helped make this special. So, thank you."

"You're welcome," he said, taking a drink. "Nice."

"I got a taste for Chardonnay when I spent a week in France."

"You've been to France?"

"He asked condescendingly."

"No. I asked with surprise. That's not a cheap ticket from here."

"I worked my way through Europe for five weeks before college. I saved every penny I made through babysitting, serving at the market on weekends, picking fruit in summer. From about the age of twelve, I dreamed of visiting Europe."

"So, where else did you go?"

Beth flashed a happy grin as she reminisced. "Belgium, Germany, Austria, Spain, Italy. God I loved Italy. I think I put on about ten pounds in Italy."

"Oh, man. I love Italy too. Where did you go?"

"Rome, Florence, Venice. I mainly stayed at hostels, but in Florence I treated myself to a hotel." She sighed deeply and took another drink. "Who knows, when I retire, maybe I'll treat myself and go again."

"You're only young, Beth. That's a hell of a long time to wait."

She shrugged. "It's not cheap bringing up baby. And when the deadbeat you married disappears, leaving you without child support, it gets a little harder."

"Disappears?"

"He ran off with some college student before Enola was even born. I heard from his parents that they'd got postcards from Canada, then Mexico, and that was it."

"But you're doing okay, aren't you? I mean you're partners in the bar with Naomi."

"The bar's doing okay, but we had to get a big loan on the place and we had to sink all our savings into it too. The profit we've made we've ploughed into Bella's college fund. We should just about have enough for her to finish by the end of her first year and then we need to start saving for Enola."

"Wow!"

"Wow what?"

"That's impressive the way you look after each other like that."

"We're sisters. We've always been close."

"NO WAY!" Enola's exclamation travelled in another excited wave to join them in the kitchen and they both laughed again.

"I heard you went to see Mr Poots."

"Yeah. He helped me out, big time."

"Oh?"

"He gave me a perfectly plausible scientific explanation for what happened to me and Anna."

"Too bad you couldn't tell her before she fled town frightened for her life."

"If I can ever get through to the production company, I'll try to get her number and tell her what he told me."

"Well. You can science it up all you want, but I've told you what I think about the place and what I experienced."

"Yeah. And what he said was—"

"Mom! MOM!" Beth walked out into the hall to find her daughter extending the phone towards her. "Jodie says that we can visit her in the studio."

Oh, for the love of Christ. She expects us to travel all the way to California to go see her for a day. "Um. That's terrific, honey."

"She wants to speak to you."

"She wants to speak to me?" *Oh, God. How do I get out of this without breaking Enola's heart? I don't have the vacation days. I don't have the money. I don't have—* "Hello," she said tentatively, taking the phone.

"This is Beth?" Beth watched as Enola ran into the living room and heard her practically screech the news to Naomi and Bella. It had been the longest time since she'd seen her like this and it warmed her inside, despite having to negotiate the practicalities of the situation.

"Yeah. I just want to say thank you for taking the time to speak to Enola. You've kind of made her decade."

"My pleasure. Listen, I hope I didn't speak out of turn by inviting you guys down to the studio."

"Err ... well ... I—"

"Look. It's an open invitation. No time limit."

"That's very kind. Thank you. I know Enola would love it." Jodie cleared her throat on the other end and there was a momentary pause in the conversation. "Hello? Are you still there?"

"Yeah. Beth. That photo that's everywhere at the moment. It isn't what it looks like."

"That's really none of my business."

There was another long pause. "Lev is like a brother to me."

"Like I said, it's none of my business, I'm just incredibly grateful you took the time to—"

"There are only a small handful of people who know what I'm about to tell you, but Lev likes you, and he's a really good judge of character, and he's without question the most decent and honourable guy I've met, and I love him, and I'm pretty certain I've already cost him his marriage, and my agent and record company would go insane if they knew I was telling you this, and I'm just going to have to trust you and hope you—" *She stopped herself. Jesus, Jodie, you sound like a crazy woman.*

"Hello?" Beth said again, wondering if the line had in fact gone dead this time.

"Beth. I'm not into guys."

There was another pause. "Um. I don't understand."

"I like women, not men. That photo isn't what it looks like. That photo is of a guy who is holding a confused, heartbroken, naked, drunk young woman. The photo doesn't show the tears running down my cheeks. It doesn't show much other than what the piece of shit who took it wanted it to show."

"I see."

"It's up to you what you do with this information. If you want to go to the papers, I wouldn't blame you. Hell. It would probably beat all this running around pretending to be something I'm not. But I wanted you to know because my best friend's down there, waiting for this all to blow over, and all everyone sees is this picture for what they think it is. But in truth, it's just a photo of a really decent guy looking after a really broken girl."

"I don't know what to say. Thank you for being so honest. And don't worry. I'd never betray a confidence."

"Y'see, that's what I mean. Lev is a really good judge of character. And whether he's there for just a couple of days or not; whether there's nothing more to this than a cup of coffee and a friendly chat or not, it doesn't matter. Life is made up of moments. People come into our small spheres and some leave an impression and some don't. I'm guessing Lev will have made an impression. And I don't want your impression of him to be tainted by something he hasn't done."

"Well, thank you."

"And you guys really should come down. We'll have a blast. We'll spend a couple of hours in the studio then you, me and Enola can go out shopping while we leave Lev with the nightmare of making everything sound good."

Beth laughed. "That sounds like fun."

"Yeah. Like I said, it's an open invitation."

"Well, thank you."

"And Beth."

"Yes."

"You've got a really special kid there. You've obviously done a great job raising her."

"It's easy to say that when you don't have to see her on a daily basis."

Jodie laughed now. "Lev said you were funny."

"Who's joking?"

"Anyway. It was good talking to you both."

"It's been nice talking to you. Do you want to speak to Lev?"

"Fuck no. I'm going to be working with him twenty-four-seven, soon. I need all the break I can get."

Beth giggled. "Sounds reasonable."

"Enjoy the rest of the party."

"Thanks. You too." *You too? What the hell am I talking about?* "I mean evening. Enjoy the rest of your evening."

"I always do." And with that, she was gone.

Beth stood for a moment just looking at the phone before finally placing it in the cradle. She could hear Enola in the living room still recounting the conversation to the others. Beth retraced her path to the kitchen to find Lev perched on one of the stools.

"Does Jo want to talk to me?" he asked, climbing to his feet.

"No. She hung up."

"What, seriously?"

"Uh-huh."

"Oh. Okay."

Laughter rose from the living room and a wide grin lit Beth's face. She leaned in and pecked Lev on the cheek. "Come on. Let's go join the party."

The hours zipped by. Lev answered question after question from not just Enola but the others too. It was a different world he lived in and although many of the stories were toned down for a younger audience, they were all captivated and enthralled by them.

At one o'clock, Naomi dragged herself and Bella away, knowing it would only be a few hours before she would have to start her daily routine. Another half hour past and, reluctantly, Enola made her way to bed but not before hugging Lev like a koala, telling him it was the best birthday she'd ever had and finishing by saying that she couldn't wait to see him when they got to LA.

"And then there were two," Beth said as they walked into the kitchen.

"Yeah. I suppose I should be getting off."

Beth held a bottle up. "I'm guessing there are two glasses left in here. What do you say we finish it?"

"Okay." She poured the contents of the bottle into the waiting glasses and handed one to Lev. "Thanks."

They remained in the kitchen and sat down on the two stools by the breakfast bar. "So, now I'm going to have to figure out a way to get time off to get to LA."

"Yeah. That's the thing with Jo. She's lived in her world so long she's forgotten what it's like to live in the real one. I mean she'd probably organise a hotel for you. She's very generous, but if she didn't, you could both bunk at my place. I mean, it's only a one-bedroom apartment, but it's got a double bed and you and Enola could take that. I could sleep on the fold-out couch."

"That's sweet of you."

"I feel responsible. Like I kind of got you into this mess."

Beth giggled. "I suppose it's a nice mess to be in. This whole thing will have done so much for her confidence, her self-esteem. It's like she'd been drifting further and further into herself and away from me for so long, and tonight, it all came back. I got my little girl back."

"I'm glad."

"Oh shit. I'm so insensitive. I'm sorry. I'm talking about getting my little girl back and you're in the middle of a battle with your ex and are thousands of miles away from your kids. I'm sorry."

"Hey. The two things are completely unrelated. I'm just really pleased I could help out. Enola's an amazing kid. I hope she—"

Beth leaned across to kiss him. "WAAH!" The stools were old, the cushioned stuffing uneven, and instead of kissing him, she disappeared from view, crashing to the kitchen floor.

Lev just sat there looking down for a second, not sure what the hell just happened. "Um. Are you okay?"

"Oh sure. I always try to get a good ten or fifteen minutes on the kitchen floor every day. Little help."

"Sorry. Of course." Lev slid off his stool and reached down, helping her to her feet. "What happened?"

She straightened up. "In case you can't tell, I don't do this often."

"Do what?" He had been oblivious to her attempted kiss as he was speaking, so the confusion continued for a moment until Beth reached around the back of his head and she gently pulled him towards her.

"This." Their lips met. The chill from the white wine dissipated in seconds as the electricity they both felt warmed them. Their tongues gently brushed together and when their mouths finally parted, there were knowing smiles on both their faces.

"That's too bad. You're good at it and my mum always said you should do what you're good at."

Beth let out a girlish giggle and then they kissed again to make sure it wasn't a fluke. The same energy flowed through them both once more, and this time, their fingers weaved together. When the kiss was over, their hands remained clenched for a few seconds before they finally let go. Beth returned to her stool and Lev stood there for a moment before he did the same. An awkward silence hung in the air.

That was stupid. Why the hell did I do that? In truth, there were lots of reasons. She was lonely. It had been forever since she'd last had any kind of intimacy, no matter how clumsy and short-lived. More than anything, though, she liked Lev. She liked him, even when she was pissed with him. That was another thing. *Why the hell was I so pissed about that photo? I barely know this guy.* "I'm sorry."

"What for?"

She shook her head. "Because you're leaving here soon and it's not like there's any possible future for us, even in the short term, and it was stupid and selfish of me. There's nobody in this town I have the remotest interest in and you're someone who just—"

He took her hand, silencing her. "You've just done a whole thing in your head without even talking to me."

"What's the point?" she asked, shuffling her hand free.

"When I first started with the band, it was like the most exciting thing in the world. Young women practically threw themselves at me in order to get a backstage pass or whatever. I was pretty inexperienced at the time, and the whole thing blew my mind. But then I realised it was crap. They weren't interested in me. There was no emotional connection and the whole thing really screwed me up.

"I thought I'd struck gold when I met Lottie, but I fucked that up, monumentally, and other than Jo, I haven't really had a connection with anyone since then.

"Now, I've known you all of what, two days? And I'm not saying this is love at first sight, or I think we were made for each other or any crap like that, just so you'll let your guard down after a few glasses of wine and invite me upstairs with you. But I like you. I like your sense of humour. I like your outlook. I like how much you sacrifice for the people you love. I like how generous you are and I'm pretty certain we click."

She let out a long sigh. "Okay. Saying all of that is true. What's your point?"

"My point is that I'm done with throwaway relationships."

"Me too. Which is why—"

"What if I stayed around for a week or so?"

"What do you mean?"

"Maybe we go for lunch together tomorrow or dinner. Maybe we go for a long walk. Maybe we just spend a little bit of time getting to know each other. And if there really is something there, then maybe we build on it. If there isn't, then what have we lost?"

She took a drink. "But my point is there's no future in it and I'm not getting any younger, Lev. I don't want to put—"

"My point is, if we decide we really like each other, then the future's whatever we choose to make it. I'm not getting any younger either. This job I have, yeah, it's pretty intense when we're recording or on the road, but there's a hell of a lot of down time in between. I could come back on a regular basis. There are a thousand ways to make something like this work and there are a thousand more to make it fail. But surely it's worth finding out if there's even a possibility before throwing in the towel, isn't it?"

Beth finished off her wine in one go and turned to look at him. "It's time for you to go home and it's time for me to get some sleep."

Lev's head drooped a little. "Okay."

"I'm taking the money pit shopping tomorrow morning. She's spending the rest of the day with Bella. I'll swing by the bar at about twelve. We'll go for a picnic on the lake. Just you and me."

Lev's face lit up. "I'd like that."

"Yeah," she replied, finally admitting defeat. "I would too. Now get your jacket and go before I do something stupid and impulsive and screw up any chance of us getting to know each other properly."

They both smiled before she walked him back to the door. He grabbed his jacket from the rack and slid it on. He was about to step out into the cool morning air when he stopped. He leaned in and gently kissed her again. This time, it was nothing more than a short goodnight kiss, but again, their faces lit.

"Night, Beth."
"Night, Lev."

CHRISTOPHER ARTINIAN

17

It was a sad indictment of how used to drink Beth had become, but she woke without a hangover, just a mildly groggy feeling and a mouth that felt like carpet. A clatter from downstairs had stirred her. *Teenagers. No inclination that there are other people in the house.*

Thud, thud, thud, thud.

For a girl who weighs about eighty pounds soaking wet, she sure makes a lot of noise.

"Wakey, wakey, rise and shine," Enola said, entering her mother's bedroom with a tray.

"What's all this?" Beth asked.

"I made you eggs and coffee."

"And we've still got a kitchen?"

"Yeah. And everything I used is in the dishwasher."

"I'm still dreaming. I'm obviously still dreaming." She reached for the coffee and took a drink. "What's the occasion?"

"Hmm. Let me think. Is it because that was the most fucking awesome night ever?"

Beth smiled. "You got away with cursing yesterday because it was your birthday."

"Sorry. It was though." Her eyes widened excitedly and there was a smile on her face that plucked at Beth's heartstrings.

"I'm glad you enjoyed it, baby."

Enola flung her arms around her mother, nearly knocking the tray over. "I love you, Mom. I really, really love you."

"I really love you too."

"I'm going to get showered while you eat your breakfast."

"Okay. We're going to have to swing by the office before we go into town."

"You said you weren't working today," Enola replied as a frown formed.

"I'm not. I left my credit cards on my desk. Of course, we could always use your money to go shopping if you don't want me to go there."

"No. I'm good with heading to the office," she replied with a grin then disappeared back out of the door.

Beth looked at the gap where she had been and another smile charged her face. *It's like she's a different kid.* There had been times during the past few months when she had lain awake at night trying to figure out how she could change things for Enola. There had been conversations with her sister that had dragged on past midnight and into the early hours forming plans of what to do, how to get back the girl she once was. Beth had even thought about standing down as the sheriff, but they were dependent on the security of that income for the bar loan, for the college fund, for everything.

But all the worrying, all that heartache now seemed to be over.

*

"Okay," Naomi said as she and Bella walked into the bar, "I think you need to forget about this whole music thing and come and work here."

Lev smiled as he wiped the last table clean. "I woke early. Had a lot going through my head, so I thought I'd give you a head start."

"Woke early? Did you go to bed at all?"

"I've only done the tables and ashtrays."

"The tables and ashtrays are huge. That's saved us hours."

He shrugged. "Like I said, I woke early. I hope you don't mind. I made some coffee. It should still be hot."

"Mind? You're a godsend. Literally. You are an angel that's been sent down from Heaven."

"Mom. You're embarrassing him," Bella said.

"I'm not."

"Well, you're embarrassing me then."

"When am I not?"

"I don't know. When you're sleeping, maybe."

Naomi put her arm around her daughter. "Sometimes, you just want to squeeze them and squeeze them until their face turns blue and they're taking you away in handcuffs."

"Your sister's the sheriff. I'm sure she'd be an expert at making something like that look like an accident."

Bella and Naomi laughed. "Because you did all this and made coffee, I won't tell her you said that."

"Thanks."

"Bella, you can go fetch me a drink before we start work."

"Can I really? Gee, thanks, Mom."

Naomi leaned in and kissed her daughter on the head. "Don't mention it. Actually, you can make some toast too." She turned to Lev. "You want some?"

"I'm good, thanks."

"Enough for just the two of us then."

"What did your last slave die of?"

"A whoopin' because she kept answering back." She slapped her daughter on the rear as she walked away.

"Ow! God, college can't come soon enough."

"Oh, man. What have I told you about reading my diary?"

"Nice way to make your daughter feel wanted, Mom. Why did you ever bother having me?"

"Shit. You have been reading my diary."

"Bitch," Bella shouted with a laugh in her voice from the other room.

"It's great that you can joke like that," Lev said.

"Who's joking?" Naomi replied. "So, what are your plans today?"

"Well, I'll finish helping you guys down here and then—"

"No way. You helped me yesterday. You've already given us a massive head start on the day's work. You're not doing anything else."

"I'd argue, but I know what it's like trying to argue with your family."

"Good then."

"Um. I'm actually meeting up with Beth later. We're going for a picnic."

"My sister going for a picnic? Man! You must have made an impression."

Lev coloured up and shrugged. "I doubt that somehow. Anyway, I'll go get a shower if you're sure you're—"

"Go. Go, and thank you again."

*

"We didn't expect to see you this morning," Lucille said as Beth and Enola walked through the doors.

"I'm not here," Beth replied. "I've literally come in for my credit cards then I'm out again."

"You make sure she uses those cards to get you something nice, Enola," Lucille said, smiling warmly at the teenager. "You enjoyed your birthday yesterday?"

THE DEVIL'S FACE

"It was amazing, thanks," Enola replied and Lucille's eyebrows arched upwards. There was an enthusiasm and spark in the teenager's voice that she hadn't heard in all the years she'd known her.

"Amazing?"

"Yeah. Y'see, Mom…." She started telling the story of the party as Beth headed into the back.

Doug was on duty, if you could call it that. He had one of the Saturday papers and was relaxing back in an office chair with his feet up on the desk. Saturdays were always quiet until the evening when the bars got busy.

"Make sure you don't work too hard, Doug. I wouldn't want you taking time off due to stress," Beth said, playfully knocking his feet off the desk as she walked by.

"I'm just bracin' myself for the rush when all those weirdos start causing trouble."

"I went to check them out," she said, stopping in her tracks for the moment. "You were right. Whoever they are, they've got some serious money, but I spoke to Rita and she doesn't seem too worried by them. Sure, they're a little eccentric, but polite and good tippers."

"Yeah, well, maybe they are, and maybe they ain't, but we got some new ones in town. Well, when I say in town, I mean over at the RV park. Showed up in the middle of the night too."

"New ones?"

"Didn't take a census or nothin', but I reckon there's at least a dozen. Came in three top-of-the-range Winnebagos. Serious money again, but weird lookin' just like the others."

"Do me a favour, will you, Doug? You and Lucille phone around the neighbouring towns to see if there's something going on that we've missed. A music festival or film festival or arts festival or something."

"Sure. We can do that," he said, folding his paper.

"Thanks. I mean, it's probably nothing. Probably just a weird coincidence, but it's curious."

"That's what I was thinkin' too."

"You said no work," Enola said as she walked up to join them.

Beth put her hands up. "We're going. We're going. I'm just getting my cards."

*

Lev left the bar and headed out back to the apartment. It was true; he hadn't been able to sleep long. His head was buzzing. The events with Beth the previous evening had shifted his mind into overdrive. He knew it was crazy to start thinking about a long-distance relationship with someone he barely knew, but there had been a spark that he hadn't felt in a long time, and that was worth exploring at least.

He flicked on the TV and flopped onto the couch as the news came on. He didn't take in any of the features until the entertainment section of the programme flashed a photo of Jodie. It mentioned the new contract and intimated the notorious picture had played a part in such a lucrative deal. The newscasters in the studio all sat with knowing smiles on their faces, which said as much too. Lev started to wonder if Jodie's agent had, in fact, orchestrated the thing. *It's not a huge stretch, I suppose.*

He flicked off the TV again and climbed to his feet. He was about to head to the bathroom to get a shower when he looked at the recorder in the corner of the room and something dawned on him. Even though he was now convinced the events were exactly as Poots had surmised, there were several hours unaccounted for as a result, and at least a couple of hours or so of those would be memorialised on tape. *I wonder if we spoke to each other or said anything.*

He had time to kill and the thought suddenly intrigued him. Even though he'd designed it as a portable unit, it could be hooked up to a mains supply, too, and he set it up on the small coffee table in the corner, connecting a single speaker. If there was anything worth listening to, he could always plug in the cans, but this would mean he could get on with other stuff.

He hit the rewind button and went into the bedroom to lay out his clothes. He decided it was time for another coffee and Naomi had been good enough to provide him with a jar of instant and a kettle. By the time he'd made it, the tape had just clicked back to the start. He pressed play and stood back for a moment, watching it. Seconds passed before the sound of creaking steps came through the speakers followed by Anna's voice.

I really am going to have to get her number and tell her what Poots said. To do what she did, there must have been some underlying problems she didn't tell me about. I mean, taking flight with a van full of hired gear was extreme.

Lev crouched down by the side of the machine and hit the fast-forward button, stopping occasionally to see where the tape was.

Memories of the conversation started coming back to him in snippets at first as he continued to advance through the tape.

"Do you hear something?"

"I'm serious, Lev. Don't piss me off."

"No, Anna."

The whispers. He'd almost forgotten about the whispers, believing they were a part of the effects of the … what was it? Poisoning. *I don't suppose there's any other word.*

He stopped the tape once more.

"Get this. Get this, Lev," Anna had demanded and the moment came back to him clearly.

He remembered crouching down by the side of the fissure, and that's when—He pressed play and here it was. The garbled noises that sent shivers running through both of them.

"FUUUCK!" There were no mercury vapours now as he listened to the tape. He rewound it and played it again. "Voices. Dozens of voices. Hundreds of voices. But … there's something wrong. There's something not quite right about them." He reversed the tape and played it again. "Are they backwards? Are they fucking talking backwards?"

Lev had gone way past the point of goosebumps now. This was marrow-freezing listening. This was impossible, and the contentment and surety he'd felt after his conversation with Poots seemed a million miles away.

I need better equipment. I need to transfer this to my reel-to-reel at home and play it back in reverse. He looked at his hands to see they had started shaking a little. *Why the hell wouldn't they? This happened. It's on tape. It happened.*

The sound came to an abrupt end, followed by silence. Then—"JESUS FUCKING CHRIST!" Lev covered his ears and fell to the floor as a thousand, ten thousand, a hundred thousand voices screamed and wailed, pleading and crying.

The room suddenly began to shake, but it took Lev a moment to notice as the hellish cries continued at a deafening volume. He felt like his brain was about to explode. He finally clawed his way back to his knees as spears of noise continued to skewer his senses. It was then that he noticed the floor shaking beneath him.

Something caught his eye and he turned to see the face he'd seen all those years before. The face from the horror film that had led to the events that changed his life forever.

The noise carried on and he wanted nothing more than to shut it off, but he was transfixed as this terrifying image floated towards him.

The devil's face.

That's what he had believed it to be. After that fateful night when he had seen the life bleed out of his father's body, he'd seen that face staring at him through the darkness while he struggled with his own injuries. Those were the words that flashed into his head.

It was the frightening construction of a make-up artist, but it was real too. It was real because he saw it then and he was seeing it now. And then the epiphany struck him.

THE DEVIL'S FACE

Fear is always real. It doesn't matter what form it takes. It's always real.

The lips of the apparition curled into a menacing smile then grinned, flashing its yellow-brown teeth. The head floated there all the time the tumult continued and, as painful as it was to endure, Lev had no option. He was frozen for the time being.

The devil's face began to rise, and as it did, a body formed, cloaked in a black habit. Pallid hands with long, bony, grabbing fingers extended from the loose cuffs as the thing that he'd locked away for so long in the dungeon of his mind towered over him.

There had been occasions when he'd been sure he'd seen it but then simply put it down to his mind working overtime. He'd look up from a library book to catch a momentary glimpse of this face staring at him from behind a shelf. He'd blink and it would be gone.

He'd be driving back from a gig alone and he'd see those eyes glaring at him from the back seat. He'd swivel, only to find the car was empty.

Over the years, he'd seen it, felt it dozens of times, but always written it off as an illusion. Now he knew. It had always been with him, ever since that fateful night.

His dad had died in that car crash. But Lev always knew that was only part of the story. It was this thing that had ripped his father from him. It had wanted him that night too. He felt it. And even though he was injured, he had been too strong. If he was gone, there would be no one to look after his mother, and Lev wouldn't allow that. As scared as he was then, he had refused to give up, and as scared as he was now with this horrifying giant standing over him, seemingly powered by the tormented cries blasting through the speaker, he would refuse to give up again.

Sally. Freddie. Jodie.

He had other people relying on him now. Other people whose worlds would be changed forever if he left them, like his had been all those years before.

An image of Beth and Enola appeared in front of him, almost as if this thing was threatening to take them away, too, as it had done his father. They were in what looked like an office, grasping on to each other.

"FUCK YOU!" he screamed, reaching out and tugging the plug from the wall.

The figure's demonic eyes widened in anger and horror as his would-be victim again defied his attempts to conquer. The cacophonous sound halted and Lev was alone in the room once more. Everything around him continued to shake for a few more seconds then fell silent.

He remained there, kneeling on the floor in shock, just staring at the player.

"It all happened. Mercury poisoning bollocks. It all happened."

18

Beth held Enola tightly. When the quake had begun, she'd grabbed her daughter and pulled her into the doorway of her office. Doug had dived under his desk, and Lucille had just stayed in her chair, a little too overweight and slow-moving to do anything quickly.

The occasional scream had left her mouth as the rumble continued, but now it was over.

"Is everybody okay?" Beth asked. It had been years since they'd experienced a quake, and as scary as it was, this just seemed like a small one, and, barring any aftershocks, it was finished.

"I think I might need a new pair of shorts," Doug said, emerging from underneath the desk, "but otherwise, I'm alright."

"Oh, my goodness," Lucille cried, holding her hand up to her chest. "Oh, my," she said again for good measure.

"You okay, baby?" Beth asked, pulling back to look at her daughter's face.

Enola still had her arms wrapped tightly around her mother, but she nodded. "I'm okay, Mom."

The lights had gone off, but that was no surprise under the circumstances. Despite this, the sun shone in through the windows, which meant they had no difficulty seeing. "Have we still got the phones?" Beth asked.

Lucille picked up the receiver and pressed for an outside line. "Y-yes. The phones seem fine."

"Well, get ready. I'm guessing they're going to light up any minute." She turned to Enola. "Baby, I might have to stick around here for a little while."

"That's okay, Mom," her daughter replied, still clearly shaken.

"You want me to call Carl and Eddie in?" Lucille asked.

Beth looked at her watch then looked around the office. Despite it being frightening while it was happening, there had been no damage. There weren't even any skewed pictures. "Not for the moment. We'll see what calls we get."

The entrance doors suddenly opened inwards and all eyes turned towards them. Rusty Adelman, a man in his seventies, an Auschwitz survivor, the beloved founder of Adelman's Ice Cream Parlour, which to this day was still operated by his son, stepped inside.

"Rusty. Is everything alright, hun?" Lucille asked, seeing his long, drawn face. His normally warm eyes looked wild and frightened.

"You bastards. You BASTARDS!" he cried.

"Rusty. Hun. What's going on?" She slowly started to rise from her chair.

Beth and Doug exchanged confused glances before returning their gaze towards one of the town's favourite figures.

"I won't let it happen again. You took my parents. I won't let you take any more of my family. You bastards."

Lucille started towards him but stopped and let out a chilling shriek as Rusty withdrew a gun from his coat.

"Rusty," she whispered. "What—"

He fired and Lucille's arms windmilled as she staggered back before falling heavily on the floor. A crimson pool formed instantly.

"You came for us in forty-one. Well, I won't let you come for anyone else."

Doug was in a state of shock, struggling to process what was going on. He reached for his weapon but too late. Another deafening crack reverberated off the walls as the old man walked forward. Hatred lit his face as Doug dropped to the floor too.

"Baby, get down," Beth screamed, pushing Enola into the office.

Crack! Crack! Crack!

Beth dived towards where Doug had fallen. She was off duty. She didn't have her own gun, but she scrambled across the floor while glass shattered, papers flew, and hate-filled shouts from Rusty fought against the gunshots to be heard.

"We should have done this in thirty-eight. We could see what was happening. It was obvious what was happening. Well, never again. You hear me? Never again."

Beth reached Doug in time for his head to loll to the side, his face eternally locked in an expression of confusion. She grabbed his gun as wood splintered above her head. It didn't matter whether Rusty had gone mad. If she didn't do something, she would die, and without question, her daughter would too.

"RUSTY, DROP THE WEAPON. THIS IS YOUR ONLY WARNING."

Crack! Crack!

A bullet exploded from the drawer of the desk, winging her. Blood immediately started to pulse from her wound, dripping onto her jeans and the floor. She couldn't feel the pain though. Adrenaline was coursing through her body and her only concern was protecting her daughter.

Crack! Crack!

She could hear the echoing footsteps in between the gun reports.

She took a breath then twisted around, rising to one knee and taking aim all at the same time. She fired, deliberately targeting the left of the clavicle. It wasn't a kill shot, but it would put someone down, especially a man in his seventies, whose health wasn't that great to start off with, but no. He continued shooting and Beth had to duck down quickly as more wood and papers exploded above her.

She stayed down for just a second then dived out into the aisle, firing one, two, three times. Rusty remained upright for a few seconds, but the gun fell from his hand.

"Beth. Beth, my love. I've saved some mint choc chip just for you." He shook his head. "Don't tell the others." He winked and smiled the smile he'd flashed to her ten thousand times before. "Don't tell the others," he wheezed this time before collapsing back like a felled tree.

Beth was open-jawed. Tears stung her eyes. This man was one of the kindest, sweetest people she'd ever met, and now his memory would forever be sullied by this final insanity. She took a breath and leaned up on her elbow, staring beyond his fallen body to Lucille. She twisted to look at Doug. She'd known both of them all her life and now they were gone.

"Enola? Enola, stay there, baby. I don't want you to see this." Silence. "Enola?" A shiver of fear jolted through Beth and she quickly climbed to her knees and then her feet. "Enola? Baby?" Her heart began to race as she saw that the sound of breaking glass had been the windows to her office, and as she looked now, there were holes in the paper-thin walls too. "Enola? Enola?" She ran to the doorway. "ENOLA!" Her daughter was propped up against a wall. Her hands were covering her stomach, but as the blood flowed between her fingers, it was obvious what had happened.

"Mom?" was all she managed to say before slumping on her side.

THE DEVIL'S FACE

*

Julia had been hanging washing in the garden when the quake hit. She'd quickly snatched Larry, Lawrence Boyd Junior to his grandparents, out of the pushchair and knelt down, holding him tight, coddling him in her arms.

It didn't last long, and although she was shaken and Larry was crying his eyes out, no damage was done. Not a shingle had been shaken loose, and once the terrifying sounds had abated, it was as if nothing had happened.

Somewhere towards town, she could hear what sounded like gunshots, but that was nothing unusual. There were plenty of yahoos around here who would get drunk and decide to do target practice at empty beer cans. Yes, the day was only just beginning, but the likes of Manny Sales and Thom Catcher were fixed to stay up drinking all night before finally collapsing mid-morning.

Wastes of skin, both men.

She waited a while to see if there were any aftershocks before placing Larry back in the pushchair and wheeling him inside. If anything else came, she'd simply whip him up and go stand under the cover of a door frame. It had been a shallow quake, though, and she guessed that would be the one and only rumble.

Today would be a busy day and she didn't have time to waste waiting for things that might never come. She'd agreed to make a few batches of chocolate chip cookies for the church bake sale and she just hoped Larry wouldn't act up. He'd been doing that a lot recently.

She lifted him out of the pushchair and placed him in front of his little activity centre. He loved this toy. Her parents said he would. Mirrors, buttons, spinning cubes that rattled. He'd spent the best part of an hour playing with it yesterday.

She looked across to the cellar door and noticed it was slightly ajar.

Strange. The quake must have jolted it open. She went to close it, but it clicked open again just as quickly.

"Well, darlin'. We'll just have to get your daddy to take a look at that when he gets home, now, won't we?"

Larry gazed up at her for a moment and giggled before returning to his toy. Julia headed back to the kitchen table. She'd laid all the ingredients out before dealing with the washing, but now she dusted the floury pages of her recipe book and pulled the scales close.

"EEEE!"

She looked up suddenly and stared at her son as the echo of the high-pitched squeak reverberated in her head. *Did he make that sound?*

"Was that you, sugar pie?"

Larry looked up at her open-mouthed and let out another little giggle before returning to his activity centre. She carried on watching him for a moment before turning back to her book. Her finger traced its way down the page to the quantities.

"Okay, then. It says here that we need six ounces of choc—"

"EEEE!"

Her head shot up again, and this time, her heart fluttered a little. *Nope. No way is that what it sounds like.* When she was six, her brother had locked her in an old shed on their property. All sorts of strange sounds used to come out of it and he swore that it was haunted. She screamed and screamed and screamed to be let out, fearing she'd see ghosts or demons or whatever else it was that made the place so scary, not just to her but to any of their friends who came to visit.

The truth was much more frightening for Julia though. The floorboards were rotting, as was much of the shed, and as she ran up and down, banging on the walls, making as much noise as she possibly could, in the hope that her parents would hear and release her from this terrifying imprisonment, her foot went through one of the narrow planks, and a loud, pained squeal rose up as her pump landed on the snake-like tail of a giant rat.

Suddenly, dozens of them were climbing her leg using it as a flesh and bone ladder to gain access to the shed. The smell of rodent faeces, rot and decay from below was overpowering.

"EEEE! EEEE! EEEE! EEEE!"

The sound rang out a dozen times, a hundred times, and a hundred times more as the frenzied creatures, their razor-sharp claws puncturing her skin, fled their underground prison.

"MUUUM! MUUUM! DAAAD!"

Some bit her, latching on to her fleshy calves. She could smell copper as blood flowed down her leg. She finally managed to withdraw it from the hole, but still the things hung on. Eventually, her father heard her cries. It was he who had unlocked the door, letting in a broad triangle of sunlight. The rats burst out into the open, fanning out as they did, and even her dad let out a fear-filled cry as they scurried over and between his feet.

Ever since that day, nightmarish images of the creatures had appeared in her mind during waking and sleeping hours. Her husband had been a childhood friend. He understood. He had made their house almost rodent-proof, which was no mean task when one lived in the country. He had made it a virtual safe haven for her, but—

"EEEE!"

A shivering breath left her lips and she took a step towards the open kitchen door, ready to grab Larry and flee to a neighbour's house if she caught sight of—*No. It can't be. It's got to be in my mind.*

But what if the quake opened a crack in the wall or something? What if—

"EEEE!"

She turned to the rotary washing line in the garden and another squeak sounded as it tipped ever so slightly during its rotation. Her eyes remained glued on it for a moment as it happened again and she let out a relieved laugh. A single tear had run down her cheek. She'd not realised it at the time, but the fear had taken a proper hold as it had on so many occasions before. No matter how she'd tried, she'd never been able to conquer it. She'd been on sleeping tablets for years, pausing while getting pregnant but resuming again quickly. Those nine months had been the hardest of her life. She'd woken up screaming on more occasions than she could remember, convinced there were rats in the bed, rats crawling over her, rats in the corner of the room waiting to pounce.

A bone-chilling shriek made Julia spin on her heels and, just like that morning in the shed all those many years ago, the dam burst and urine soaked her jeans. Rats were swarming over her baby. Already, there was no part of him visible. It was as if he was wearing a vast, moving shroud of filth as the giant army of rodents vied for position.

Julia's mouth fell open in horrified disbelief. The biggest part of her wanted to run out of the door and not look back. But this was her child. She'd kill for him. She'd die for him if she had to, and as these things of utter terror for Julia continued to pile out of the cellar and over her son, she knew there was only one option.

"WAAAGGGHHH!" Larry's cry was like nothing she'd heard before.

Julia grabbed the rolling pin and the short vegetable knife she always used to open bags and packets and charged towards the growing mountain of writhing bodies that was massing over her darling.

"GET OFF HIM! GET OFF HIM! GET OFF MY BABY!" She swished and struck; one of the rats flew through the air like a baseball, smashing against the kitchen wall before dropping to the floor. It quickly gathered itself, but rather than re-entering the fray, it fled towards the open kitchen door.

Juila struck again and again. More creatures detached from the foul scrum of wriggling bodies.

"MAAHAAHAA!" Her heart broke again each time she heard her child's desperate wails.

THE DEVIL'S FACE

One of the rats lunged at her, using the others as a springboard. With ninja-like prowess, she brought the knife around, skewering it. It let out a shriek of its own but did not die. It fell from the shiny blade onto the linoleum and ran back towards the cellar, leaving a bloody trail in its wake.

"GET OFF HIM! GET OFF MY BABY BOY!" Her yawp almost made the walls shake. Her fear was matched only by her fury as these things that had been the bane of her existence for so long now threatened the one thing most precious to her. The pyramid of writhing, dark-haired creatures came up to over her waist as they continued their assault on the toddler.

"GET OFF HIM! GET OFF HIM! GET OFF HIM!"

Tears were now flowing in torrents down her face as she continued to smash and swipe and beat the Hell-sent beasts back. Some went flying to where she didn't care; others dislodged, disappearing out of the kitchen door or back down into the cellar.

THUD! WHUMPH! SMASH! HACK!

There were cuts on her hands and arms as some of the vile things leapt at her, clawing, biting, but she continued, disregarding her own horror for the moment as her child continued to howl.

Images of what torn, bloody fragment of a body Larry might be reduced to if she couldn't beat them back strobed in her mind like a gory flip book.

My baby!

Her whole body was shaking. Her heart was pounding just about as fast as it ever had.

"Julia?"

It was her husband's voice. *Thank God.* She wouldn't have to face this alone anymore. "Don't just stand there. Help me!" she cried.

"Julia. What the hell have you done?"

She looked up at him, not understanding why he wasn't rushing to her side. Not understanding why his voice sounded so incredulous. It was clear to anyone what was going on. She turned back to the pulsating mountain of bodies and was about to raise the rolling pin again when a breath caught in her throat.

She staggered back, dropping the two makeshift weapons simultaneously.

"What have you done?" Her husband's voice shook this time. There was panic and fear and confusion and horror in his words. "What have you done?" He began to sob.

Julia stared down at what was left of her baby boy, a bulbous, bloody sack of broken bones. There was not a single rat in sight. She looked at her hands and arms, both covered in blood, but not hers. There were no bite marks, no claw marks. She looked at the trail on the floor where the bleeding rat had fled, but all she saw was arterial spray from her own child.

She collapsed to her knees, scooping her baby up in her arms. "NOOO! LARRY! MY BABY! NOOO!" It was the howl of a wounded animal that came out of her mouth. It was the sound of desperation, sorrow and confusion. It was also the last sound Julia would ever make.

19

It was Kazem's people who had come up with a shortlist of possible gateways, but it had been Jamie's idea to establish Occulture productions. It was going to be a long-term project and, in truth, neither man saw it bearing fruit for some time. The initial five-episode series of *The Haunted and the Hallowed* was a trial run in order to get all the pieces into position, make sure they had the right people for the job.

It had been fortuitous that Levon Stoll had called Jamie looking for work when he did. Hands down he was a better candidate than the original sound recordist for so many reasons. Not least of which was Jamie could vouch for his experience. Lev had told him about his episode as he remained trapped in the car with his dying father. He had told him how that face had lingered in the dark in front of him, how he could sense its malevolent presence.

Jamie had also done his research with regard to Anna. More than done his research, in fact. He had paid a hefty sum to get hold of her medical records. She had been famous for more than fifteen minutes when she was younger. The abducted girl who spent six months imprisoned in a cellar, finally escaping only for her abductor never to be found.

A documentary had been filmed about her, and twelve months after the event, she had been interviewed briefly with her parents present. She had spoken of the night terrors that still plagued her and how she was in an experimental programme for treatment.

When he had learned that she was working in TV and had ambitions, the concept for Occulture Productions came to him in a flash. She was the one and only director to be interviewed for the job. They only briefly talked about her career to date. They were more interested in what she had experienced. Of course, they couldn't overtly come out and explain their intentions, but their questions were geared in a way that suggested they had a keen interest in her, in developing her, in having her on board as an integral part of Occulture Productions moving forward.

In the end, she had jumped at the opportunity, and then they had gone about the task of assembling the remainder of the team. Nearly all of the small production team involved, to some extent, had an inexplicable event that had taken place in their lives. The need to establish this had been explained as Occulture wanting people who genuinely believed in what they were doing, who believed there was more than just the world around them.

In reality, it was something else. As far as Jamie, Kazem and their small cult were concerned, night terrors, not nightmares, but full-on night terrors, waking up powerless, waking up in places the victim had no recollection of, were a sign of possible contact with an Azelophet. Visions, seeing things that had no right to be in this world, were another. Hearing voices. The amount of people who were in institutions for hearing voices in their heads was astronomical. Jamie and Kazem firmly believed that the vast amount of these were not mentally ill at first. The voices may have driven them insane, but they too were a symptom of contact with an Azelophet—*The* Azelophet, for it was one, and it was all. But these brushes were rarely fatal. In these situations, the Azelophet's power was fairly limited.

When Jamie had first met Kazem, he had no knowledge of such things, but in Jamie, Kazem had found a kindred spirit, someone who was looking for a key to power beyond the physical plane.

Jamie's involvement with Satanism had been woefully misguided but nonetheless alerted Kazem to what was essentially a mutual interest. He had taken Jamie under his wing and educated him. He had shown him ancient texts and ancient glyphs explaining the Azelophet and how it occasionally showed its face, albeit briefly. It was empowered by human misery, frailty and fear. It somehow materialised in this world when people were at their emotional weakest. He explained about the gateways and how they allowed the Azelophet to materialise in a stronger incarnation and for longer, albeit not permanently. In these stronger incarnations, the Azelophet caused chaos, some of its more susceptible victims often becoming either murderous or suicidal.

But unlike the outside world, the gateways meant the Azelophet was not dependent on finding a victim at their weakest or most fearful, merely that their victim was open, that they were receivers.

Not all people in the world were. In fact, receivers probably accounted for only ten to fifteen percent of the population, if that. And not all receivers could become conduits, and it was a conduit they needed now.

Kazem had shown Jamie a Mayan wall painting, the only one of its kind across all the ancient civilisations who had encountered this thing, who had believed in this thing.

The painting suggested the Azelophet could be trapped and its power commanded by those who caught it.

For years, Kazem had corresponded with the unholiest of scholars, dredging texts and paintings to find a clue as to what sort of incantation could gift him this most prized of magics. With money as no object, they had constructed what they believed to be the method, the means and the words.

Occulture Productions had been established with a long-term plan. Not for a moment did Jamie or Kazem imagine that they would have hit first time lucky.

A series of answerphone messages from Tim and others had alerted them to Anna's erratic state of mind after returning from the Black house, and they'd gone on to say how she had fled in the van with all the equipment. Then further messages from Lev, and one in particular where he'd briefly spoken of some of the strange events he'd experienced at the house convinced Jamie that they'd found what they were looking for.

They'd immediately mobilised, jetting in from all over the country, greeting each other in near jubilation. With the kind of money Kazem had, anything was possible, and three giant Winnebagos had been waiting for the motley dozen on their arrival. Eleven of the group knew exactly what was happening. One, Kazem's brother, someone whose limbs were prone to wild spasms, who had been a victim of endless teasing and bullying, who had suffered with mental illness all his life, and someone who Kazem knew to be a receiver at least, but in all likelihood a conduit, travelled with them.

He spoke with difficulty, and often his symptoms were mistaken for those of someone with cerebral palsy, but Kazem could always understand Navid, although others struggled. Despite everything that he suffered and everything that had happened to him, he was a sweet and gentle soul. His only real vice was smoking. And although normally Kazem couldn't abide the habit and did not allow cigarettes to be lit anywhere near him, today was the exception.

There was a part of Kazem that felt guilty for using his brother in this way. There was another part that believed it was a means to give his brother's life meaning and maybe even cure him once they had established the boundaries of how the Azelophet's power could be used to meet their own ends.

Navid's hand steadied for long enough to bring the cigarette up to his lips and he sucked deeply before his head began to shake a little once more.

"You okay, Brother?" Kazem asked. Having been sent away to boarding schools in the UK and then to Oxford, Kazem spoke with virtually no trace of his Iranian roots.

"Y-y-yes," Navid managed to say before shuddering a little due to the effort.

"I can drive if you want," Jamie said, appearing from the back. They were in the lead vehicle of the short convoy and it was plain for anyone to see that the driver was driving way too fast. The buildings quickly gave way to trees reminding them all this was a universe away from city driving.

"I'm good," he replied, coughing a little and waving at the air to fan away some of the blue smoke.

They'd spent the night in an RV park and the journey to the house wasn't a long one, but everyone wanted to get there in one piece. If all went to plan, today would be the most important day of any of their lives.

"I think we travel on this road for a couple of miles and then—"

The entire world around them suddenly began to shake and, despite his best efforts, the steering wheel slipped through Kazem's fingers as the motorhome careered.

Navid started screaming, his left hand shaking violently. Jamie clamped his hands around the headrest of the driver's seat as the tyres of their vehicle and the two following screeched loudly. There was a deafening crunch against the undercarriage and the Winnebago veered dramatically.

"FUUUCK!" Jamie's scream tore through all the other sounds but fell silent as the luxury motorhome ploughed into a giant redwood. A cupboard door flew open, cracking him on his temple, and he collapsed to the floor, bleeding.

Kazem hadn't been wearing his seatbelt as the collision occurred and all Navid could do was watch as his older brother catapulted forward, his head bursting as it smashed against the windscreen.

The rumble continued, but another thunderous crunch overshadowed it as the second vehicle ploughed into the back of them, quickly followed by the third.

Navid remained in his seat for a moment. The rumble came to an end as screams and cries of pain filtered in through the open windows and from further back in the vehicle. Navid twisted to see the other passenger lying in the aisle, her face bloodied, her left arm twisted at a cringeworthy angle.

"Help ME!" she screamed.

Navid liked Emily. He had only met her a few times, but she had always been nice to him, unlike many of the others on this trip. "Em-Em-Emily."

"Navid. My arm's broken. And ... I can't move my leg. I need help."

Navid's shaking hand lifted to his mouth and he sucked on the cigarette again before stubbing it. He tried to reach for the seatbelt release, but he was shaking too wildly. "I-I-I'll t-try." His eyes shifted briefly towards the red explosion on the windscreen before turning his head back to the seatbelt clasp.

"Thank you, darling," she said through pained gasps. "I think. I think something might have fallen on—" She stopped as she suddenly felt a presence. Twisting, she looked up to see Navid standing there. "You did it. You did it. Well done, Navid. I was just saying I think something might have—" Her words cut off as she looked more closely at the figure looming over her.

His hands and face were not in spasm as they often were. His expression was not one of pain and bewilderment. It was wide-eyed, fear-filled, panicked, what she deemed to be a reflection of her own face at that time.

It must be shock or something. It must have frozen his symptoms and—

"He's coming," Navid said in a whisper before sniffing the air like a wild animal. There was no stutter. The words weren't laboured as they usually were. "He's coming. We need to make sure we're clean before he gets here. We must all be clean."

Confusion gripped Emily. She wasn't sure what was more disconcerting, the fact that Navid was talking in a way she hadn't heard in the years she'd known him or what was coming out of his mouth. *The pain. I'm not thinking straight. I'm not hearing right.*

She tilted her head again, but now there was no sign of him. "Navid? Navid?" She heard footsteps from behind somewhere, but it was too painful to see. "What do you mean, Navid? Who's coming?"

"He's coming," he said again, kneeling down by her side and taking her by surprise. The shouts for help and screams of agony could still be heard from the other vehicles, but they were becoming of less consequence by the second as Navid's strange behaviour became her focus. Navid sniffed at the air once more before covering Emily in a blanket.

"I don't need covering, Navid. I need you to help me get up. I need—"

She broke off as he opened a bottle of vodka and poured some into a cloth before rubbing it against the side of her face. "Need to get clean before he comes. Need to get all of us clean, otherwise…." His words trailed off as he vigorously rubbed the wet cloth over her neck and even her hair.

He's in shock. He's just watched his brother die in front of him. He's in shock. "Navid. I need you to go outside and see if you can get someone from one of the other vehicles to help."

He paused, looking to the rear of their own Winnebago. It had been stoved in where the second motorhome had ploughed into it. Miraculously, the rear curtain remained drawn across, blocking the view, but the cries of its occupants could still be heard.

"No. They need cleaning too, but you first. You've always been the nicest. You first. Then me. Then them."

He jumped to his feet and ran over to the door.

Jumping? Running? I thought his condition meant he couldn't do any of those things.

Navid opened it and breathed in deeply. When he returned to Emily's side, there was something resembling a smile on his face, which creeped her out way more than everything else up to this point.

"Please get help, Navid," she said, almost sobbing as another surge of pain jolted through her.

"Somebody's been kind to us." She twisted again to look at Navid's face. It was set with the giddiness of a child on Christmas morning. It was barely recognisable from the one of terminal suffering that she was used to.

"I don't … understand." Tears stung her eyes now.

"Don't worry," Navid said, tucking the blanket in beneath her, causing another spasm of pain. "Don't worry, Emily."

"Please, Navid."

"Don't worry," he said again. "I'm going to clean you first. I'll clean you good as well, so he can't hurt you. You've always been nice to me. I'll clean you good." He stroked her head as if she were a pet then disappeared again.

She twisted, trying to see what was going on but, due to her injuries and the fact that she was almost cocooned in the thick woollen blanket he'd wrapped around her, she couldn't see what was happening.

Suddenly, she froze, and an expression of disgust painted her face. *Is he pissing on me? Is he fucking pissing on me?*

She could hear the sound of a stream of water splashing against the coarse wool. She could feel the light ripple of movement as it ran up and down her back.

"Navid," she cried. "What are you doing?"

"Don't worry. You'll be clean before any of the others. He won't be able to touch you."

Revulsion continued to well within her until the sound finally stopped. She froze, concentrating on the next sound, trying to figure out what it was that followed the faint squeak. Then she realised.

That's a bottle top. He wasn't pissing on me. He was pouring something on me. What the hell is he—

Strike! WHOOSH!

For a moment, she couldn't feel the flames. The blanket was too thick. But then it was as if all the suffering she'd felt in her life was suddenly shrouded over her.

"AAAGGGHHH! NOOO! NAVID, NOOO!"

"It's the great cleanser. They call it that for a reason. He can't hurt you now. You're clean."

"NA-HO. NA-HO. ARRGGHH! NOOO!"

"Wha-What's going on?" Jamie croaked as the shrieks roused him from unconsciousness.

"PLEASE! NOOO! NAVID! AAAGGGHHH!"

Navid walked past Jamie as he continued to come around slowly. He leaned over the back of the driver's seat and pulled the keys from the ignition as Emily's screams and pleas continued to fill the air. Then he exited the vehicle, locking the door behind him.

It felt like the fires of Hell were licking her body. She could hear the wool crackle as it fused with her skin. She was still partially bound despite this and unable to roll, but as her flowing locks started to catch, she knew it was too late anyway.

Her targeted pleas for help ended and just a single, garbled, eternal shriek sirened from her mouth as Jamie finally scrambled to his knees. His vision was blurred, blood poured from his head wound, and he still wasn't in full possession of his senses as Emily finally fell silent and still. All he could do was stare for a moment and try to figure out what was going on.

A knowing smile of accomplishment warmed Navid as he walked away from the door. He'd done what he set out to do. He'd cleansed Emily. She was his favourite anyway and it was essential he took care of her first, and now he had.

He could see the flames inside begin to take hold of the rest of the Winnebago, and Navid felt sure that his work would be done before *He* got here.

When the luxury motorhome had veered, its undercarriage had crashed over a deeply set rock by the side of the road, puncturing the gas tank and causing its contents to pool. Navid stamped his feet like a child playing in a puddle as he marched into the middle of the fuel slick. It had spread out and along, disappearing beneath the wheels of the second and third vehicles in the convoy too.

Shouts for help still rose from the other motorhomes and Navid breathed in deeply, inhaling a lungful of fuel vapour as if it were melted chocolate. A smile lit his face. "Don't worry. I'll help," he called out. "I'll help all of us."

The door of the third vehicle burst open and out staggered a bleeding figure. "Navid?" asked Glen, one of Jamie's friends, as he continued to try to figure out what was happening.

"He's almost here."

"Who? What are you talking about?"

"Don't worry. He won't be able to hurt us." Navid struck another match and dropped it to the ground.

"NO!" Glen cried, too late. The inferno spread in one massive, expanding plume. He dropped to the ground, writhing in agony, rolling in more fuel. The fire licked against the other vehicles, climbing up through the open door like a living thing, whipping at the veneered oak effect of the built-in kitchen cabinet as more flames spread beneath the Winnebago.

Navid just stood there. He turned from one vehicle to the other until his eyes finally came to rest on his own. His clothes were burning. He could smell his own skin charring as he stood in the lake of fire, but no cries of pain left his lips. He just smiled. Navid had cleansed them all before *He* had arrived. *He* who had been the source of all the terror and fear in his life, all the pain and torment. But Navid had finally won. Navid had beaten him.

He let out a short laugh. But it died in his mouth as the echo continued from within. It wasn't his laugh. It wasn't his voice. It was that thing. His punisher. His torturer. Jamie started beating against the window of the first motorhome and Navid's eyes were drawn towards him for the briefest moment, but then he fell to the ground, his fingers curling, becoming spastic once more as the laughter continued to reverberate around him.

He was here all along.

The pain. The agonising pain as all trace of foreign actors left his body. He had been possessed for a short time, allowed to feel normal for the purposes of Azelophet's game, but now he would suffer his last few moments on this planet more than he'd suffered at any time in his sad, tormented life.

He was inside me all along. He was watching everything, hearing everything.

"N-Nooo!" His speech reverted, too, to the unintelligible garble that only those closest to him could understand. "Mu-Mu-Musab." He tried to scream the word like he had screamed it a million times before when he had been scared, when he had needed help, when he had just wanted to feel the embrace of his beloved brother. But all that could leave his mouth was a hoarse, grating whisper as the flames scorched his throat.

He glanced towards Jamie and then his eyelids finally welded shut. The laughter continued to echo around him until his eardrums exploded.

20

When the first gunshots had sounded, somehow Lev knew that it would involve Beth one way or another. He tore into the bar, barely even hearing Naomi's words as a flurry of questions blurted from her mouth.

"Can you call your sister?" he asked.

Naomi didn't answer for a moment, finally shaking her head, snapping out of the shocked daze the quake had caused. "I spoke to her a little while ago. She was heading to the sheriff's office to get her credit cards then going shop—"

Lev didn't wait for Naomi to finish. The devil's face, whatever it was, whatever it represented, was telling him they were on his list. He was going to rip Beth from Lev as he had done his father. He'd passed the sheriff's office the day before, never thinking for a second he would end up inside, but now he realised it was the place he needed to be more than any other.

Lev charged through the entrance doors and onto the street. His eyes were immediately drawn to the upper floor of the municipal building across the way. A woman was dangling from one of the windows with wire cord around her neck. Three people were gathered below, staring up in shock.

A man stumbled by, his clothes dyed red with his own blood. He continued up the street, seemingly oblivious to the woman hanging out of the window, oblivious to the gunshots that continued to ring out from elsewhere in town, oblivious to the screams and shouts and the electricity pulsing through the air.

On any other day, Lev would have helped. "What the hell's going on?" Naomi cried as she and Bella emerged onto the street behind him.

"Something's really fucked up. Help people if you can. But be careful too," he replied before charging down the street in the direction of the sheriff's office.

*

Beth ran to her daughter, her own pain, the blood pouring from her wound, unimportant.

"Baby. Baby!" she cried, dropping to her knees. Blood continued to flow from her daughter's stomach as more shots rang outside. Screeching tyres could be heard further afield. She had no idea what was going on and it didn't matter for the time being. This was her world, everything in this room.

She reached up to her daughter's neck and felt a faint pulse. *She's not dead. She's not dead.*

"Beth? BETH?" It was Lev's voice.

"Lev. In here. In my office."

Two seconds later, he was standing in the doorway. "Her pulse is weak," Beth said, cradling her daughter. She started to cry, shock and fear overriding good sense.

"We need to get her to the hospital," he said, bending down and scooping Enola up.

Beth remained on the floor for the moment, still lagging behind the events, still not comprehending what was going on. "We were going shopping," she said weakly.

"Beth. Stand up. You need to take a breath and we need to get Enola to the hospital now."

"What's going on?"

"I don't know. All hell's breaking loose out there. But that's not important right now. We need to get your girl to hospital before it's too late."

These were the words that shook her from her daze. *Before it's too late.* She nodded and followed Lev, swooping down and picking up the gun she'd dropped. Something told her that, before this day was over, she'd need it again.

*

Barry Wilkins had always been a good-for-nothing drunk. Naomi had come close to barring him from the Bellanola a few times but had never actually gone through with it. Thankfully, he had started frequenting one of the other bars in town, but she knew one day he'd come walking back into her life.

"Shit. Get inside, Bella," she cried as she saw him charging down the opposite street towards them. "Get inside, now."

At first, Bella didn't see what her mother had seen; then she caught sight of the kitchen knife in Wilkins' hand as he sprinted towards them. He was still a good distance away but was shouting at the top of his voice like a madman. "You've always tried to control me. You and that bitch sister of yours. Always telling me what to do. Well, now it's my turn. It all stops today. Nobody controls Barry Wilkins no more."

Naomi pushed the heavy door shut behind them, turned the key and slid the bolt across; then the pair backed away. They held their breath for a moment, but both let out terrified screams as the thick wooden barricade juddered.

"What's going on, Mom?"

She wished she knew. It seemed like bedlam was unfolding in New Scotland. None of it made sense, but right this second, the only thing that was important was looking after Bella.

"I don't know." Another crash sounded against the door.

"Little pigs. Little pigs. Let me come in. I've got something for you. I've got something for the pair of you." A maniacal laugh started from the depths of Wilkins' lungs. It sent a shiver through them both.

*

For so long, Jamie had believed in Hell. Kazem had shown him the light, proving the concept of a fire-filled cavern with flowing rivers of lava and a horned beast marshalling its captives with a trident was just a manmade construct. But as he looked around the blazing cocoon he was trapped in, as he battered on the windows while his lungs filled with smoke, as flames danced around his feet, threatening to climb his jeans, to consume him, he wondered if he had been wrong. He wondered if Hell was real and he wondered if he was in it.

More questions still plagued his mind, but he feared they would go unanswered. The motorhome pinged and crackled as metal expanded, wood burned and plastic melted.

He stared through the window one last time towards Navid's burning corpse. It didn't make sense. When he had slowly been coming around, he was sure he had seen him standing normally, his body not in spasm as it often was. He was sure he'd heard him speaking just like anyone else. Usually, there was a great effort in everything he said, but he had almost sounded like his brother.

The burning husk he observed now, though, was almost foetal, wrists and fingers crooked, deformed. Had it all been an illusion or—Jamie collapsed to his knees then to the floor.

His eyes stung, his lungs burned, and as he looked across towards the frazzled corpse of Emily, he understood that it would only be moments before he shared the same fate.

We came so close. So close to unlocking unimaginable power.

He started coughing again, but this time, he couldn't stop. The cough reached down deep inside, scraping his lungs, running its nails through the inside of his chest cavity.

The heat. THE HEAT.

His body felt damp all over as the fire surrounded him, roasting the interior of the motorhome like a giant oven.

Sizzle.

"SHIT!" He kicked his leg hard as if doing so would extinguish the flames that had caught the bottom of his jeans.

Coughing again. Coughing more as he ruffled and flapped the material, trying to fend off the orange pain. The cuffs of his jacket caught, all while still coughing, all while still simmering in his own juices. He started to flap his arms around wildly.

"FUCK! FUUUCK!"

More coughing. More sizzling.

He started rolling in the narrow aisle, floundering like a beached fish on burning sand. "ARRRGGGHHH!" It was a primal, guttural sound that burst from his mouth as the fire raced up his frame, melting the denim and his skin alike.

He descended into another coughing fit, his body spasming all over as the heat of what felt like a thousand suns crackled over him as if he was nothing more than a piece of kindling. He cried, shrieked, and screamed again and again as he was fully consumed by the fire.

Pop! Pop!

He heard his own eyeballs burst. He'd read about it once but didn't think it was possible. Didn't think that level of pain was possible. It was as if God himself was keeping him alive to suffer.

Is this Hell? Is this what eternity in Hell will be like?

He could feel his skin crisping, his dyed black hair frizzling. He could feel every cell in his body reaching boiling point. He began to convulse, almost as if he was drowning in fire, until, finally, he fell still. Coiled up as if trapped inside the womb of a demon, in heights of pain even the darkest of ancient texts could never have prepared him for. A loud, rattling breath ravaged the back of his throat and blackness surrounded him.

*

Four loud bangs hammered against Taleen's door. She and her companions had arrived in town the previous day. Her conversation with Jodie had convinced her that Jamie had stepped up his efforts; in fact, not just stepped up his efforts but entered a whole new league.

"Something's happening," Viktor blurted. He was around six feet four, formerly Russian mafia, wider than the average beer barrel, but all of it pure muscle. He was her bodyguard. Over the years, Taleen had received countless death threats. Whether it was her outspoken views on the church, the Turkish government, the US government or because she was such a strong supporter of gay rights, it didn't matter. She had come under fire for them all, but with Viktor by her side, trouble rarely came knocking. That did not mean he lost any of his preparedness should it happen.

He was not fully aware of what this small group of protectors, as Taleen called them, did, but he didn't need to know. His only job was to keep her safe, and it was something he took as seriously as life itself.

"Well, thank you for letting me know, darling. I've been listening to gunfire for the past five minutes; if you hadn't come along to share that revelation, I wouldn't have had a clue."

The doors to the neighbouring rooms opened and her two other companions on this trip, Xavier and Delane, joined them. "Maybe we've arrived too late," Delane said. "Maybe this is it. Maybe we underestimated Jamie and Kazem and now the toothpaste's out of the tube."

Taleen ran her fingers through her long black hair. "If this happens, it will be more than a few distant gunshots that we have to worry about. But something has definitely occurred and we need to find out what it is."

"Easier said than done."

"Get ready. We're all leaving here in five minutes." Xavier and Delane disappeared back into their rooms. "You," she said, turning towards Viktor. "Rambo up, or whatever it is you do. I have the feeling this is going to get rocky."

An excited smile lit his face. This was what he lived for. "Yes, Miss Zakarian."

She headed back into her room, closing the door behind her. Her window was open a crack, and in between the sound of shots, she could hear screams. She picked up the phone and dialled.

Before the woman on the other end even had the chance to say anything, Taleen jumped in. "Greta, get me, Jodie—now."

"Yes, Miss Zakarian." Taleen had an unmistakable voice and always left an impression on the people she spoke to and met, one that suggested that under no circumstances should she not be taken seriously.

A moment later, a groggy-sounding Jodie answered. "Taleen?"

"I'm in New Scotland. Give me the details of where Lev is staying."

"You're what? You're in—"

"There's no time to explain. Something's happening here, something big, and I need to find Lev now."

"Um. Um." Rustling came from the other end as Jodie frantically started looking through pieces of paper by the side of her phone. "He's stopping at somewhere called—FUCK! Is that gunfire? Can I hear gunfire, Taleen?"

"Where? Where is he?" Jodie had never heard Taleen flustered in all the time she'd known her, but there was definitely panic present in her voice.

"He's staying somewhere called the Bellanola Bar. It's on Main Street. Do you want the number?"

"No point. No time. We saw the place on the way in. We're on our way."

"Taleen, what the hell's going on?"

The line went dead and all Jodie could do for a moment was stare in anguish at the receiver in her hand. *Those were gunshots. It sounds like the world's coming to an end down there, and Lev's right in the middle of it all.*

*

"Look out, Lev!" Beth screamed from the back seat as she continued to hold her daughter.

It was like the pickup had been waiting for them. It launched out of the alleyway and, even though Lev smashed on the brakes to the police cruiser, he couldn't avoid it in time. There was an almighty crunch and they mounted the pavement and smashed into a newspaper vending machine.

"Be gone. Be gone, demons," the minister who climbed out of the truck demanded. He held up a cross in one hand. In his other, there was a shotgun. "I command thee, in the name of GOD ALMIGHTY, to go back to the place from whence you came."

"GET DOWN, BETH!" Lev shouted as a boom erupted, quickly followed by another. The shot broke the windows, shattered the screen and disappeared into the panelling of the car, but when Lev re-emerged from his ducked position, he was still in one piece.

"I knew this day would come. It's the day I've been preparing for all my life," the minister called out as he broke the shotgun and prepared to load two more shells.

Lev opened the door and was about to rush him when another man ran up the street screaming. The minister's attention was suddenly drawn to him. "Help. Help me, please!" the man cried.

"Demons! Demons everywhere." There was another booming explosion as he squeezed the trigger and the man flew back, landing heavily and lifeless on the road.

Shit! Lev had no idea what was going on. Maybe Hell had arrived on Earth; maybe he was going mad and this was a prelude to him being carried away in a straightjacket. But whatever it was, he knew he had to deal with the cross-and-shotgun-wielding maniac before he ended up dead. He dived before the minister had the chance to turn and another thunderous crack erupted as he tackled the madman.

The shotgun fell to the ground and a pocketful of shells spilt from the crazed minister's jacket. "Demon! I command you—"

Lev started punching and didn't let up. He'd been in more fights than he could possibly remember. In the early days, when the band were on the road, it seemed like there was at least one in every town and the single most important thing he'd learned was when you start punching, you don't stop until you're sure the other guy can't punch you back. Thump! Whumph! Whumph! Crack! "Fucker!" He exhaled deeply as his victim stopped moving. He glimpsed his still balled fist to see blood dripping from his fingers.

"Lev!" He turned to see Beth looking at him pleadingly from the rear of the car, still holding Enola in her arms. He looked at the front end as a pillar of steam rose from the engine and then he looked towards the pickup. There barely seemed to be any damage. He grabbed the shotgun and the shells, ran around to the open driver door and restarted the engine. He dived back out, ran to the car and helped Beth carry Enola to their new vehicle.

Noise continued to resonate all around them. Windows broke, shouts and screams soared, but for the moment, there were no threats approaching them. "It's okay," he said, reaching across and squeezing Beth's arm. "She's going to be okay."

Tears were streaming down her face as she clutched her daughter and the vehicle began to reverse.

"What the hell's going on, Lev?"

"I really don't know. But when I've got you to the hospital, I'm going to find out."

*

Lauren was still shaking from the earthquake. The sound of the gunfire did nothing to alleviate her fears, but there was something else, far more concerning, occupying her thoughts for the moment.

She'd been in the diners' toilet, applying her make-up, when the quake struck. She was still there now. It seemed like the safest place for the time being as gunshots and screams rang outside. The sturdy door was locked, the high windows were open, and even though the power had gone out, she could see what was going on. It wasn't like the toilet in the cinema or the one at Adelman's Ice Cream Parlour. They didn't have windows. If the lights went off there, she'd have been in the dark, and the dark was one of her deepest fears … one of them.

She moved closer to the mirror, focusing on what appeared to be a small mound to the left of her nose.

"Is it a zit?" She had a strict skincare regimen, using industrial quantities of balms and remedies if one so much as hinted that it might appear.

It's certainly red.

A panicked cry in the alleyway outside made her glance towards the open window above, but immediately her eyes were drawn back to the mirror. She prided herself on her looks. Most boys in her year fawned over her. Her looks were worth the effort, and it was a lot of effort.

Thankfully, her mother didn't mind if she used some of her make-up and products. She wasn't sure her father would have been so understanding if he knew how much they cost, but what he didn't know couldn't hurt him.

"Ow." The throbbing became more noticeable. She squinted. *It's got a head. I should burst it before it gets out of hand and then put some concealer on.*

She expertly lined up her two index fingers at either side of the little white dot and was about to squeeze when it suddenly moved.

She sucked in a deep, fearful breath, backing away from the mirror. *No. No, it can't be. No.*

Her breathing became erratic, the breaths shivering in her throat before leaving her mouth.

"It can't be." She could feel tears welling, ready to erupt, as she moved closer to the mirror. Her eyes focused on the little white dot and stayed focused. "It's just a zit. It's just a zit. It's just a zit," she said. "No." It moved again and she jolted away from the mirror once more.

Yes, dark was one of her fears. The other, even bigger one, was worms. Not the kind of worms that you see in the soil, although they did send the odd shiver running through her when she thought about them too long. No. It was the kind of worms that could find a home in a human host. The kind of worms that could move under your skin. Tapeworms, hookworms, pinworms, roundworms.

The type of worms that laid eggs that formed bulbous mounds beneath the epidermis before exploding through the surface like some monstrous, taunting parasite.

She was almost hyperventilating by the time she closed in again. *It's a worm.* "It's a worm," she sobbed.

She reached into her make-up bag for her tweezers. Its head had protruded a little further now. There was part of Lauren that wanted to throw up. There was another part that wanted to run home, screaming, but something was happening in New Scotland today, something bad, and right now, she was trapped in this toilet.

It looked like a thick piece of wriggling cream-coloured cotton as she clamped it between the tweezers. She sniffed deeply, trying her hardest to hold back tears as she gently pulled the vile parasite out.

"Nooo!" she cried as the writhing thing snapped like a rubber band. Half of it continued to dance, stuck between the jaws of the tweezers, and the other half disappeared back underneath her skin.

Oh, God, no. No. No.

She relaxed the steel jaws and watched the half worm drop into the sink, wriggling, wriggling, wriggling, just like its other half, wriggling beneath her skin.

She moved right up to the mirror with even more tears streaming down her face. She peered towards the small hole where the half-worm had disappeared, but all she could see was a tiny blood spot. She put down the tweezers, drew up her index fingers once more and squeezed. A little more blood appeared, but no worm.

She continued to sob as the certainty that this thing was twisting and flexing beneath her skin seized her in a vice-like grip. Panic simmered deep in the pit of her stomach. *No. I can't have this thing moving around inside me. I can't.*

She reached in the make-up bag for her nail scissors, taking the point of one of the blades and pressing it against her flesh. It was extreme. It would probably leave a small scar, but it could be covered up with concealer, and it definitely beat the alternative.

She pressed harder, then harder still, until a thin red line formed beneath the shiny metal point. The pain was irrelevant. All that mattered was getting this thing out of her.

There.

She saw it flailing in the rivulet of blood and immediately dropped the scissors, picking up the tweezers again and grabbing it. She pulled, and now she let out a grunt of pain as it seemed to drag a bloody trail with it.

She held it a few inches away from her face, gazing at it in horror for a moment before disgustedly dropping it into the sink. She looked back up to her face to see the gash was wider than she had expected. She retrieved a cotton wool pad from her bag and dabbed at it.

All the breath left her lungs as she felt something pulsing on the other side of her face.

No.

This time, it was in the centre of her cheek. There was no head, just a small red mound, and as she observed it more closely, she could see a thin shape beneath, spiralling round and around.

Without a second thought, she grabbed the scissors once more, stabbing into her flesh at the centre of the mound. Almost as if a snake charmer's flute was playing accompaniment, rather than the screams and shots that were still echoing outside, a small head appeared through the crimson well of blood and Lauren swapped for the tweezers again, carefully tugging at the stomach-churning parasite.

Again, she released it into the sink. She looked down to see the two halves of the first worm still squirming while the second twitched between them. She looked up towards the mirror. The two bloody holes in her face were a small price to pay to be free of those things.

A sudden sharp pain drew her attention to her hand and an audible shriek left her lips. She had seen pictures of this. Hookworms were long. They lingered just beneath the skin, dark red in colour; they moved and twisted vigorously.

"What's happening to me?" she cried, grabbing the scissors and cutting into the back of her hand. A small red-purple head rose out of the pooling blood, and again Lauren swapped one instrument for the other, pulling this third invader out of her body. No sooner had she dropped it in the sink than her eyes turned to the mirror once more; a new level of fear spasmed through her as she saw a much longer pinworm seemingly circling her right eye. Instinctively, she cut herself open again, ejecting the burrowing creature before it could do any more damage.

They might all have laid eggs. I could be infested. There could be hundreds ... or thousands.

No sooner had the thought entered her head than every inch of her skin seemed to start bulging and rippling. She stabbed and hacked, digging deeper, and each time she did, heads of more worms reared from the craters.

She started screaming and screaming and screaming, and even when Nancy Puggs, the woman who owned the diner, was hammering at the door, she didn't stop. She didn't stop hacking at her face and arms and stomach. She stripped off all her clothes, and to her horror, it wasn't just the upper half of her body that was riddled with these things. They were everywhere.

She carried on screaming, drowning out Nancy, drowning out anything that was happening outside. She screamed and hacked and screamed and hacked. Thighs, hips, breasts. She could feel them everywhere. She could feel them inside her, swimming in her stomach, her intestines, her colon. She could feel them in her ears, beneath her scalp. She could feel them in her veins. She turned her right arm over and saw dozens of them swimming up. She dug in the scissor blade and cut a deep, thick line. Blood began to gush, but so did the worms out onto the tiled floor.

She carried on screaming as she did the same with her other arm. She screamed, and she screamed, and she screamed as she dropped down onto her knees, crying and pleading to a god who wasn't listening. She screamed and screamed until she didn't scream anymore.

The door burst open and Nancy rushed in, immediately losing her footing on the vast slick of blood. She fell, smashing her head on the sink and collapsing to the floor. Before she lost consciousness, she looked across at Lauren. There was virtually no skin left on the teenager's face. Rivers of blood ran over her naked body as large chunks of flesh had been gouged in no specific pattern. Crimson fountains still gushed from her arms, but with each second, their force diminished a little more. The smell of copper in the air was overpowering, and that was the last thing that passed through Nancy's mind before she followed Lauren into death.

21

The frantic hammering finally came to an end, but that did nothing to ease Naomi or Bella. They continued their vigil of the door wondering if Wilkins had given up or whether he was trying to figure out another way into the bar.

The deafening and sudden crash as the long obscured-glass window shattered into a hundred pieces told them soon enough. They both let out terrified cries as Wilkins crawled through, cutting himself in multiple places on some of the jagged shards but not noticing himself. Red lines streaked his jeans and arms and an eerie smile bled onto his face as he straightened up. He faced the two women with the kitchen knife still clenched firmly in his hand.

"Look. You haven't done anything that can't be undone yet," Naomi said, pushing Bella behind her. "How about I just open up the door for you and you can leave, and then, when you sober up—"

"Oh, I'm sober. I'm plenty sober. And that's a good thing. I want to be sober for what comes next."

Naomi and Bella began to back away once more, their eyes flitting from Wilkins' face to the knife and back again. He lunged forward, stabbing the air with his blade and making a grabbing motion with his hand.

"I'm warning you. If you so much as—"

"You're warning me? Ha! Well, isn't that just like you? You're warning me. You and that cunt sister of yours have always been so high and mighty. We should have guessed she'd end up as a pig sheriff. You were always more like one of us, though, until you got this place and, all of a sudden, you became too good."

"My mom was always too good for you and the other deadbeats," Bella shouted defiantly.

Wilkins laughed. "Like mother. Like daughter. As I said, I'm going to enjoy this." He took a step towards them before suddenly becoming airborne as a chair knocked his feet from beneath him. Bella and Naomi both screamed, not sure what was going on, and as their eyes came to focus on the giant who had unbeknownst to all of them climbed in through the window and thrown the heavy chair as if it was made from balsa wood, they screamed again.

Naomi held on to her daughter tightly, unsure if he was going to turn his attention to them next.

"What the fuck? What the fuck?" Wilkins demanded, scrambling to his feet. He charged at the hulking figure with the kitchen knife outstretched, but the giant in the black suit remained steadfast until a second before the blade entered his body. He grabbed Wilkins' wrist and extended his leg, knocking his feet out from under him and throwing him to the floor. Then, while Wilkins tried to gather himself, the big man laid one knee down on his chest and began to pummel Wilkins' face. After three hits, he was unconscious, but the beating didn't stop straight away.

The man eventually rose and looked at the two women. "Don't you dare come near us. My sister's the sheriff. She'll—" Naomi's words cut off as the man turned, walked back to the door and opened it.

A flood of panic burst into the bar and riding the sound were Taleen and her two companions. She glanced at the bleeding, unconscious man on the floor then towards her bodyguard, who was wiping his hand clean.

"I'm guessing you're the proprietor," she said, turning her gaze to Naomi.

"Who are you? What's going on?"

"The latter is something we're wanting to find out. I believe you have Lev Stoll staying here."

"Lev?"

"Am I mistaken?"

Another loud cry echoed outside and all heads turned to the opening where the window had once been before the noise disappeared into the distance. "Lev went to the sheriff's office to find my sister."

"The sheriff's office?"

"You go down the street for a couple of blocks. You can't miss it."

"If somehow he makes it back here before we find him, tell him to stay put."

"Do you know what's going on? Ever since the earthquake, it's like everyone's gone ma—"

"Earthquake?" Taleen looked towards her companions and they all shared the same blank expression. "Earthquake?" she asked again.

"Yeah. The earthquake. More or less, as soon as it died down, everything went to hell."

"Be sure to tell Lev to stay here if you see him. You might want to arm yourselves as well, just in case." She turned to her bodyguard. "Viktor. Immobilise him, just in case."

The huge Russian pulled a zip tie from his inside pocket, flipped Wilkins onto his front and bound his wrists. Then he retrieved more ties and did the same with his ankles before dragging him to the door, opening it and throwing him outside. He marched back up to Naomi and Bella then drew a flick knife from his pocket. The blade sprung out and both women flinched a little, still overwhelmed by everything that was going on.

"Someone come at you, stick this in their stomach, just below the ribs and twist, yes? They won't come at you no more." He flipped the knife, catching the blade and offering it to Naomi, who, still wide-eyed, took it.

"Thank you," she replied weakly.

"It must be love," Taleen said. "He doesn't usually give women lethal weapons until the second date. Remember what I said. Keep Lev here if he comes back."

*

The hospital was on the outskirts of town and as the tyres of the pickup screeched around the corner and Lev floored the gas towards the emergency intake, it appeared just like any other Saturday morning.

A single nurse stood outside enjoying the morning sun while sucking on a cigarette. The smile on her face soon changed as she saw the sky-blue vehicle tearing towards her. She could just make out Beth in the passenger seat and a figure slumped in her arms.

She ran to the open entrance.

"CODE BLUE. WE'VE GOT A CODE BLUE!"

The tyres screeched once more as Lev jammed on the brakes. By the time the truck came to a stop, a gurney was already being wheeled out. Doctor Tulip Benson, one of Beth's oldest friends, rushed out behind them.

"She's been shot," Beth announced, climbing out of the vehicle, her hands covered in blood where she'd tried to apply pressure to her daughter's wound.

"You have too," Benson said, looking at the blood streaming from her friend's arm.

"It's just a flesh wound. My baby's been shot," Beth blurted as tears started to roll down her face. Two male nurses climbed into the pickup, carefully lifting Enola out and placing her on the gurney.

Benson turned to another of the nurses who had emerged from inside. "Prep her for surgery now. Call Doctor Thorpe. His plans to go fishing today are well and truly screwed." She turned back to Beth as Enola was wheeled through the doors. "What happened?"

Beth shook her head. "Rusty Adelman came into the office and just opened fire. He killed Doug and Lucille."

The doctor's eyes narrowed. Like Beth, she'd known Adelman all her life. "Rusty?"

"Yeah."

All the time they were talking, they followed the gurney down the hallway as another doctor examined Enola. "That doesn't make sense."

"Nothing makes sense. After the earthquake hit, everything just—"

"Earthquake?"

"Yeah."

The doctor looked around at the other staff as they all regarded her with equal confusion. "What earthquake?"

"Surely you felt it?"

"No."

"How's that even possible?" She looked to Lev.

"It wasn't a huge one, but you're not far out of town here," he said. "You must have felt something."

"We didn't feel a thing," Benson replied.

"I'm going to head to the bar. I'll get Naomi and Bella and come back. Then I'll try to figure out what's happening." He knew whatever it was had something to do with the tape, had something to do with the Black house.

"This is as far as you can go, Beth," Benson said as Enola's gurney disappeared through two doors.

The normally stoic sheriff whimpered and another trickle of tears ran down her face while the second doctor could still be heard shouting frantic orders. An older admittance nurse appeared with a clipboard and placed a gentle hand on Beth's back. "We're going to need some details, sweetheart."

"Help. We need help here. Someone attacked my wife!" The pleading shout travelled up the long corridor towards them. It was followed by a blaring car horn as another vehicle pulled up.

"Oh, Jesus Christ," Benson said. "That's Lewis Ritter, our old English teacher." Without another word, she started running down the hall towards him.

"What blood type is Enola?" the admittance nurse asked.

"Huh?" Beth was in shock. It was as if her whole world was crumbling around her.

"Sweetheart, what blood type is Enola?"

"O positive," she said, her eyes distant as she stared down the corridor.

"Okay, that's a start. O positive," the nurse shouted to another nurse waiting in the doorway.

"State police," Beth muttered. "I need to call the state police and Carl and Eddie. I need to—" She felt a firm hand on her arm and turned to see Lev still standing there.

"Listen to me. Don't worry about any of that. The only thing you need to think about is Enola and getting your arm patched up. I'll call the state police. I'll call whoever the hell I have to. I'll get Naomi and Bella here." He turned to the admittance nurse. "Look after her."

He set off at a run down the corridor. More cars were pulling up as he reached the entrance. It was pandemonium. There was no one at the reception desk as every available hand was helping the injured into wheelchairs or onto gurneys. "You can't use that phone," a nurse shouted, glaring at Lev as he picked it up.

"I'm doing it on the sheriff's orders. In case you hadn't noticed, everything's gone to fuck here. Now, how do I get an outside line?"

The nurse looked flustered for a moment, but as the sound of another engine roaring towards the emergency department raced towards her, she understood what the stranger said was true. "Nine. It's nine for an outside line."

THE DEVIL'S FACE

Lev dialled nine and then nine-one-one. At first, the operator thought it was a prank call, but overhearing Lev's pleas to be taken seriously, Doctor Benson grabbed the phone from him and explained how it was a full-scale emergency. By the time she put the receiver down the operator was under no illusions as to how serious the situation was.

"Thanks," Lev said.

"It's not like I was telling a lie," she replied, looking back to the entrance as even more people piled through the door. "What's going on?"

"When I've figured it out, I'll be sure to let you know." Lev leapfrogged the reception desk and sprinted out to the waiting pickup.

*

"It looks like there was trouble here," Viktor said, leading the quartet into the sheriff's office.

"And what would lead you to that conclusion, darling?" Taleen asked. "The three dead bodies or the broken glass, bullet holes and streaks of blood on the walls?"

A sudden clatter made them all turn. "The sheriff. Where's the sheriff?" a frightened-looking young woman screamed. "My ex is coming after me. He said he'd kill me one day and—Oh God! He's coming. You've got to help me." She ran inside, and a moment later, a tall, lanky figure with a shotgun appeared in the doorway.

"This him, Colette? This the sumbitch you left me for?" he said, raising the weapon. "Ma always said you thought you was too good for me. She always said it, but I never listened. You broke me. You broke me good. Guess finishin' you and him together is kind o' poetic." It was almost as if he didn't see Taleen, Delane and Xavier standing there.

"Robbie. These is strangers. I don't know—"

Three explosions cracked in quick succession and Robbie lowered his shotgun before staggering back and falling to the floor. They all turned to see Viktor with his Makarov pistol extended. He immediately returned it to the holster beneath his jacket.

Colette stared at him with a combination of fear and awe on her face. "What's happenin'? It's like the whole town's gone crazy. Nowhere's safe."

Viktor reached down to his ankle and pulled out another knife, flicking it open. "Someone comes at you, you stick them with this, just below rib cage then twist. They not come at you no more." He handed her the weapon then turned back to Taleen.

"Did Costco have some kind of deal on those?"

He ignored her question and gestured to the bodies. "Any of these the one we are looking for?"

"A rotund, middle-aged receptionist, an extra from *The Dukes of Hazzard* or Methuselah's older brother? No darling. I've only met Lev a handful of times, but I can safely say none of these fit his description."

"Then we will go to hospital."

"The hospital?"

Viktor pointed to the blood on the wall. "Owner of that blood is not here. Hospital is where we'll find them."

Taleen's eyebrows arched. "Not just a pretty face, are you?"

"Where is hospital?" he demanded, turning to Colette.

"Huh?"

"Hospital. Where is it?"

"Um. You head down Main Street, take a right at the end. Carry on for about a mile then take a left, then a right. You'll see signs as soon as you're out of town," she replied, looking at the knife in her hand once more before returning her gaze to Viktor.

"Good then. Remember"—he pointed to the area just below his ribs—"here, then twist." With that, he marched back out with Taleen and the others following closely behind.

22

A steady line of traffic was moving in the direction of the hospital as Lev headed back into town. Panic and trauma painted every face he looked at. He put his foot down on the accelerator. He wasn't quite sure why. He had no idea what he was going to do or if there was anything he could do, but without a doubt, he was responsible, in part, if not wholly, for the cataclysmic events that had struck the town.

The earthquake. How is it possible that they didn't feel the earthquake at the hospital? In fact, fuck the earthquake. How is any of this possible?

A black Mercedes suddenly swerved onto his side of the carriageway, blaring its horn and flashing its lights. Lev jammed on the brakes, bringing the old pickup to a skidding stop. He reached for the shotgun ready for whatever this was and jumped out of the vehicle, temper flaring like a forest fire as he approached the Merc. A figure in a black suit stepped out.

"Fuck me!" Lev said under his breath as he took in the height and girth of the man. *A shotgun won't stop this bastard. I'd need a cannon.*

"Lev!" a call came as one of the rear doors opened.

"Taleen?"

"Lev, whatever is going on, it's got something to do with that house. And I've got a horrible suspicion that your friend Jamie is in town and it's got something to do with him too."

Lev stood there open-mouthed. All this was too strange. "Taleen?" he said again.

"Yes, yes," she replied, walking up to him and grabbing him by the arm. "Me Taleen. You Lev. Did you hear what I said?"

He shook his head, squinting his eyes shut at the same time, and then took a breath. Several vehicles passed them on the other side of the road as the seconds dragged on.

"Um. I'm not sure this had anything to do with Jamie."

"What do you mean?"

A loud horn hooted behind them, followed by the blaring siren of an ambulance. They turned to see the driver gesturing towards the skewed pickup. At that moment, there was a break in the traffic the other way and it spun its wheels, veering around the parked vehicle. "You need to clear the road. There'll be more emergency vehicles heading this way," the driver shouted before accelerating away.

"Look. I'm stopping at a place called—"

"The Bellanola, yes. We've already been there."

"Okay. Let's get back there and I can explain—"

"No. Viktor, follow us in that," she said, pointing to the truck. "You're my new driver. Now hurry."

From the few times Lev had encountered Taleen, he knew she was not someone to be messed with. He also knew that she was spectacularly strange and into all kinds of shit he didn't even understand. From the point he got behind the wheel, it took her less than a minute to demonstrate that she understood more about Jamie's venture and the Black house than he could learn in a decade.

When she was done, it was his turn to recount as much as he could remember in as short a time as possible. The journey back to the bar was not without event and they had to swerve two crazed drivers. But as Lev pulled on the handbrake behind the rear of the building and looked in the mirror to see Viktor pulling up behind them, they were more or less up to date.

"You're saying the moment your tape reached the part that should have been whispers, screaming erupted and this mysterious localised earthquake ensued, followed by utter chaos?" She gestured with her hands just as another gunshot cracked a couple of streets away.

"I know it sounds crazy, Taleen."

"And you saw this face. This face that first came to you as a boy at the moment of your father's passing?"

"Like I said, I know it sounds crazy."

"Well, darling, crazy is the new normal and we're buying it by the truckload today. And I know what you said about the recording, but I have a feeling in my blood that Jamie and his little cult aren't far away from here either."

They climbed out of the car and walked around to the front of the building with Viktor leading the way. Although everything was far from normal, things seemed quieter than when they were last here. Lev pulled out the key he'd been given by Naomi and unlocked the front door. "Oh shit," he cried as he saw the gaping hole where the window once was. "Naomi? Bella?" he called out, running inside.

"Don't worry. We were here to take care of the miscreant responsible for this. Well, I say we; Viktor did whatever Viktor does to people to silence them."

"LEV!" Naomi cried, running towards him as he entered with the others. "I was trying the sheriff's office. I couldn't get—"

"Listen. Something happened."

"What happened?"

"Err...."

"What happened, Lev?" she asked with growing panic in her voice as she noticed the bloodstains on his clothes.

"Enola got shot." His voice quivered and it even took him by surprise. In such a short time, he'd grown attached to the girl and her mother. "She's in a bad way, Naomi."

"Mom!" Bella cried, taking her mother's hand. "We've got to go."

"Beth got hit, too, but it's just a flesh wound."

"Oh, Jesus. Oh, Christ, Lev." She turned to her daughter. "Go get my keys."

"Listen to me. It's bad out there. Things are bad; they're mental. It's dangerous. The hospital was in danger of being overwhelmed by the time we left."

"That's my sister and my niece. Nothing else matters."

"All I'm saying is be careful. Whatever this is, it's not over."

"Here," Viktor said, reaching into his jacket and retrieving a compact pistol. "Is small but does the job. This is safety, yes? You flick this off and it goes bang when you squeeze the trigger."

"Take it," Taleen said. "You'll only hurt his feelings if you don't. It's a Russian gesture of friendship."

"Really?" Naomi replied, taking the pistol.

"How the fuck should I know? But he seems to be carrying around more weaponry than a platoon of marines, so just take the thing, darling, and hope you don't have to use it."

Bella arrived with her mother's purse and keys. Naomi placed the pistol inside the purse and turned back to Lev. "Are you coming?"

"He's not," Taleen responded for him.

"What are you going to do?"

"We're going to try to stop this nightmare, darling. And then we're going to try to prevent it from ever happening again."

*

Despite the personal strife Beth was going through; despite the fact that she was injured, her department was in tatters, her daughter was on the operating table and only time would tell if she'd pull through or not; despite all of that, she did not get a free ride at the hospital. There were no free rides today.

She was in the process of having her arm bandaged when Millie White, who'd been brought in unconscious after she'd tried to kill one of her children and her husband had knocked her out, suddenly woke. Millie had immediately reached for a bottle of surgical spirit being used to help clean the leg wound of a patient on the next bed. She smashed it, holding the jagged glass that was remaining like a makeshift dagger, and lunged towards her husband, screaming at the top of her voice.

They'd been married twelve years, and although Millie was not exactly well-liked, she never gave the impression she was a raving psychopath. She'd driven the glass dagger through her husband's neck, shouting, "Leave my family alone," at the top of her voice, then lunged for the nurse who was treating the neighbouring patient.

The emergency room was already full, so a ward was being used to treat people, and Beth had been on the bed opposite when the events had unfolded at high speed. Now she was in the thick of it again. She'd leapt across, knocking Millie off balance and sending her crashing to the floor.

She pulled her gun but didn't want to use it. It was obvious the woman as well as a good portion of the rest of the town had somehow lost their minds. Millie's children were howling at the top of their voices as their father bled out a few feet away.

Shit. If I don't do something, we're going to have half a dozen more dead bodies to deal with.

"Millie, put the glass down," Beth ordered, raising her weapon.

The bandage that had been half wrapped around her arm had already unravelled and her own blood was dripping onto the floor. "You can't either," Millie hissed, jumping back to her feet and staying low like some wounded animal. She slowly circled Beth, clutching the piece of glass so tightly that a crimson stream began to flow from her fingers.

"I can't what, Millie?" Beth asked.

"You can't take away my family."

"Nobody wants to take away your family."

Millie's eyes were wild, crazed. They were barely recognisable as belonging to her. "Fucking bitch. You and him. How long was it going on?"

"Me and who? How long was what going on? What the hell are you talking about?"

Her eyes shifted from Beth to her three children cowering over in the corner. "When I'm finished with her, you're next, you little fuckers. Weaselling your way in. WHAT HAVE YOU DONE WITH MY BABIES?"

"Mom," cried the youngest girl. "Mommie."

"Fuck you, you little parasite." She turned back to Beth. "Give me back my family."

Beth raised one of her hands placatingly while keeping the gun firmly pointed at Millie. "No one's done anything with your family but you. Look, Millie." She pointed to her husband lying still as a red lake formed under him. "You did that. Please don't put your kids through any more trauma. Drop the weapon and—"

"BITCH!" Mille screamed, diving towards Beth with the glass dagger raised.

Beth's finger was poised on the trigger, ready to squeeze, but the sound of the crying children behind stopped her. She jumped back, parrying Millie's strike with her free arm as she overstretched and fell off balance. Beth brought the butt of her gun down with lightning speed, smashing her assailant on the back of the head. There was a crack as Millie hit the floor and the bloodied glass triangle spilt from her hand.

Beth was on top of her before there was any chance of her reaching for it again, but Millie was dazed now, her words and speech muddled as she tried to gather herself. Beth reached for her cuffs only to remember she wasn't on duty and didn't have them. "Get me something to tie her hands," she ordered as the sound of the children's cries at seeing their father dead and their mother semi-conscious but utterly insane reached a new crescendo.

"Here," one of the nurses said, handing Beth a roll of adhesive wound dressing. The sheriff proceeded to wrap it around one wrist several times, then moved across to the other, then bound the both together tightly. By this time, Millie had come around a little bit more and was starting to struggle again, so Beth ordered one of the security guards to pin down her prisoner's legs while she bound her ankles too.

"We're going to need a holding room or something. There are kids here, not just hers. She's freaking me out, so God knows what she must be doing to them."

"There's the maintenance cupboard," the security guard replied. "There's no windows or nothin' and it can be locked."

"Perfect. Get her in there. Secure her to something so she can't hurt herself then get back here. It's going to be a long day."

"What on earth is going on?" asked the nurse who had been bandaging Beth's arm.

"I really have no idea. But I don't think we've seen the worst of it yet."

*

Jodie hadn't been able to go back to sleep after receiving the call from Taleen. Like a fretful father waiting for the birth of a child, she had paced up and down, occasionally looking towards the phone, willing it to ring.

She turned on the TV and continued her pacing with the remote in hand, flicking from channel to channel until she stopped on one with a breaking news banner at the bottom of the screen. She immediately turned the volume up to hear what the presenter was saying.

"—although we've had no official confirmation from authorities. We'll keep you posted on this story, but very concerning news there from New Scotland, Tennessee."

She flicked the TV off. She didn't need to hear anymore. In her gut, she knew something was wrong. She knew Taleen wouldn't just go down there on the off chance. Whatever Jamie had been planning was bad, and now this was confirmation.

She picked up the receiver and dialled. It was only a few seconds before she got an answer. "Brian. I'm really sorry to do this to you, but I need to get to the airport. I need to get there now."

23

They all stared at the custom-built recording device. "Do you want me to press play?" Lev asked tentatively.

"To hear the sound that caused a localised earthquake and a good portion of this town to become possessed? Yes. Absolutely. I'd love to hear what generated such chaos. I know; why don't we hook it up to an amp so they can hear it two towns over?" Taleen replied.

"Well ... I just thought you had a plan for containing this shit or something."

Taleen's shoulders sagged and she let out a long breath. "We've got a plan, but it's a million miles away from a sure thing." It really was. All this had been last minute. She'd had experience with the Azelophet before. She hoped she would be okay this time too. Viktor wouldn't be anywhere near the action, so he wasn't of concern, but she hoped Delane and Xavier could hold their own. They were prominent members of her group, very knowledgeable, and had shown a lot of strength, but they were untested in a situation like this. *What are you worried about, Taleen? It's only the fate of all humankind that hangs in the balance.*

"When you say a million miles away, what do you mean?"

It was Delane who replied. She had white, closely cropped hair and, like Taleen, was probably in her late fifties but didn't look her years. She spoke with a European accent, but Lev couldn't put his finger on where he'd heard it before and it wasn't exactly important given the circumstances. "Kazem and Jamie tracked down what they believed to be a spell to trap the Azelophet from a single text. A questionable one at that, but when haven't cults been happy to jump on the coattails of questionable texts in pursuit of their goals?"

"Okay. What does that have to do with how we stop this thing?"

"We believe that we may have found a containment ritual. But I must point out the ritual was simply to close one of the gateways, not stop whatever is going on in this town."

"Does anybody know what's going on in this town?"

"I have a theory," Xavier replied. He was tall with pointed features and looked like a stiff breeze would knock him over but he had an intense stare that hid behind a pair of round prescription sunglasses, only to be witnessed occasionally as he peeked over the top at his addressee. "I think what happens around the portals is usually like osmosis. No, not osmosis, maybe like a very, very fine, lingering mist. I think whatever comes through to this world tends to be slow, ebbing away at its victim. Certainly, that would explain how some people managed to live in the property for extended periods of time before succumbing."

"What about what happened to Anna and me? That wasn't that slow. We lost time."

"Yes, but nothing actually happened to you, did it? And you were obviously selected by Kazem and Garroway because you were probable receivers. When all this is over,

I'd like to interview you with regard to any experiences you've had in the past. It might give us a better understanding of how the portals work."

"That sounds like a real blast. But, for now, indulge me. What happened here?"

"Well, if we use my analogy about the fine, lingering mist to consider how people slowly become consumed by what lurks on the other side, I believe what you did by taking a recording from the portal and playing it back was a little like throwing a grenade into a small pond. I think you created an otherworldly sonic blast of sorts. It was powerful enough to effectively open a gateway within a radius of this machine and an amplified one at that. You did something that, to the best of our knowledge, has never been done before, and we must make sure that no one outside of this room ever knows of this."

"I don't really have any plans to go shouting about what happened here."

"I'm serious. There are some who would try to use this knowledge to bring about the end times."

"The end times? I mean, don't get me wrong, it's pretty fucking horrific, but there's a bit of a difference between anarchy ensuing in a small town and the end times."

"Lev," Taleen began. "Imagine this being broadcast. Imagine this being played on the radio or on TV. Imagine an end-of-the-world cult believing this would give them the stairway to heaven that they have always craved, no matter how ludicrous and misguided that would be."

"Holy shit."

"Exactly. It can't ever leave this room what happened here."

"No … no, of course. So, you were saying about how we close this portal."

"How we try to close it." Xavier took over once again. He reached into the inside pocket of his jacket and retrieved a small parcel wrapped in string. He untied it and folded the grey cloth out to reveal five carved oval wooden tablets. On each of them, a symbol was engraved.

"What are these?"

"These are how we try to close the portal, or at least render it inactive." He looked across to Delane who pulled an archaic-looking book out of her bag.

"If what we believe is correct," she started, opening the book to a marked page, "this incantation, followed by the dropping of each of these tablets in order, with the simultaneous utterance of these words"—she pulled a strip of parchment from the back of the book—"will close the gateway."

Lev glanced from face to face, finally coming to rest on Taleen's. "You guys have been studying this for like a long time, right?"

"Our fathers and their fathers accumulated knowledge that was passed on to us. We have built on that knowledge and chosen designates to whom we will pass on our learnings."

"That all sounds great, but what I'm getting at is this; what's your level of certainty with regards to this working?"

Taleen shook her head. "Genuinely, I have no idea. In all the books and scrolls and murals we've seen, this is the only place we've ever found so much as a hint that the portals can be closed. And I'll be honest with you. There are gaps in our knowledge when it comes to understanding these ancient languages and glyphs. It's not like you can run down to the local bookstore and get a Mesopotamian-to-English phrasebook."

"So, this incantation thing. Even if it is right, we can't guarantee that we're going to say it right?"

"We can't guarantee it, no."

"And those tablets. Where did they come from?"

Delane flipped the pages in the book. "We had them carved from the wood of a Judas tree," she said, pointing to a picture.

"A Judas tree? That's a real thing?"

"They're common in what is now Iraq but was once Mesopotamia. We have a carpenter there who is familiar with the methods they used back in those times."

"So, you're saying that not only are we not sure the spell will work, or even if all the words are right, but we're using some carvings that were knocked off a couple of weeks ago by some bloke in Baghdad?"

"Tikrit, actually."

"Well, that makes all the difference. Let's get this show on the road."

*

"Beth!" Naomi shouted, running through the crowded hallway towards her sister.

"Naomi!" The two embraced tightly, Bella catching up and throwing her arms around both of them. They held on for several seconds, then several more.

"Where is she?"

"They're operating now."

"Have you heard anything since she went in?"

"No. All we can do is wait and pray." The three of them walked down the hallway. "I just don't understand any of this. I don't understand what's happening."

"Well, I think somebody does."

"What do you mean?"

Naomi looked around. There was enough panic in the air without creating more. "Let's go outside."

"I don't want to leave. What if—"

"It's going to be a while before there's any news and they'll know you wouldn't leave here."

"Okay."

They drifted through the crowds, seeing familiar face after familiar face. They all shared the same troubled and fearful expressions. The trio finally made it to the entrance then headed to the small garden by the side of the building. Normally, it was where nurses might grab a coffee or bedbound patients were taken in wheelchairs to get a little bit of fresh air, but this morning it was empty.

The three of them sat down on a bench, the sisters immediately clasping hands. The air was heavy with foreboding as they both knew the dangers hanging in the balance as the medical team worked on Enola.

"It's like the whole world's just gone insane," Beth said, catching her breath for the first time since it all started.

"Some people Lev knows showed up. They looked like they stepped straight out of a Bela Lugosi film."

"Showed up where?"

"At the bar."

"You think they're something to do with this?"

"I don't know. I'm glad they appeared when they did though. Things were about to get bad with Barry Wilkins."

"What do you mean get bad?"

Naomi shook her head. "It doesn't matter. This tree trunk of a guy that was with them saved us though."

"What are they doing here?"

"It's something to do with the house, Beth."

"Our house?"

"No. The Black house. I didn't get the full story before I left, but I got the impression that all of this is somehow linked to that place."

"On any other day, I'd say that was ridiculous, but less than half an hour ago, I had to kill one of the sweetest men I've ever met. I just witnessed Millie White murder her husband in front of a ward full of spectators, including her kids. Ridiculous seems pretty tame at the side of all of that." She burst out crying and Naomi wrapped her arm around her. Bella stood and went to the other side of her aunt, embracing her too.

"It's okay, Aunt Beth."

"No, it's not. I can't.... I can't lose my little girl."

"No-no isn't going anywhere. She's strong. She's a fighter. She's not going anywhere." Tears began to pour down Bella's face too. She'd have given everything she owned for those words to be true.

*

"Stop the car," Taleen demanded. The three luxury motorhomes were little more than burnt-out husks as the Mercedes pulled up. Even twenty metres back, they could all feel the heat. "It's Jamie," she said, climbing out.

"How can you possibly know that?" Lev asked, following her.

"You know many people who'd hire three top-of-the-range Winnebagos and head up here in a convoy? I'm not someone who believes in coincidence, darling."

"What do you think happened?"

"We're less than a minute out of town. My guess is the same thing happened to them as happened to others." They surveyed the inferno a little longer, their eyes closing in on the foetal charred corpse on the road. "Well, Jamie was always fascinated by the infernal pit of Hell."

"Nice."

"You may think he was your friend, Lev, but he was never a friend to anyone but himself. Jamie was damaged goods long before he fell in with that satanic cult. He never knew the meaning of altruism. If he did something nice for someone, it was by accident. It was because there was something for him at the other end."

"Maybe you should give the eulogy at his funeral."

"If I went to his funeral, I'd be too busy dancing on his grave to deliver a eulogy. Besides," she said, gesturing to the blaze, "I doubt there'll be anything left."

"We should get back in the car," Viktor said, coming up behind them. He pointed to the several trees that had already caught fire. "It may be that this stretch of road becomes impassable soon."

"Yes. Yes, you're right."

They returned to the vehicle and set off once more. Viktor gave the burning motorhomes as wide a berth as he could, but the heat was almost unbearable as they passed by. Lev looked on solemnly. Despite what Taleen said, there was a part of him that would always have a soft spot for Jamie.

Several minutes later, they pulled up at the fallen tree blocking the road to the Black house. Lev was still busy revising the notes he'd been given. He wanted to memorise the incantation as best he could. He had little doubt that reading pages in the basement would be difficult for a number of reasons. When he finally looked up from the papers, he focused on the trunk that had heralded the start of this fateful journey.

"Yeah," Lev said. "We need to get out and walk from here."

They all exited the car and Viktor walked around to the boot, opened it up, and proceeded to grab a sports bag along with two long reels of rope. "You will help carry, yes?" he asked, handing Lev the ropes.

"Yeah. But what's all this for?"

"Insurance," Taleen replied.

"Insurance?"

"We don't know how any of this will play out. We don't know what's going to happen. The only thing we do know is that the four of us need to go down into that basement to perform this ritual."

"Don't you mean five of us?"

"No. Viktor is part of our insurance policy."

"I don't understand."

"You will."

They continued over the fallen tree and up the hill. "Do you think what happened in town could have had an effect on this place?" Delane asked.

Xavier exhaled a long breath and scratched his whiskered chin. "On the one hand, the events were all localised. I mean, the quake didn't even reach us on the outskirts. On the other hand, we're talking about something that is, in essence, a kind of dimensional gateway. We don't truly know anything about it other than it exists. We can't really be sure of any of the writings we have read. We don't know how much is truth or simply the hypotheses of the most advanced minds of the time."

THE DEVIL'S FACE

"Please, by all means, keep on talking, you're really helping to put my mind at ease," Lev said as the house finally came into view.

They all looked at the shimmering lake beyond for a moment before focusing on the building itself.

"You can feel the energy," Taleen said to no one in particular.

"Yes," Delane agreed.

"I can't feel anything," Lev replied. "I didn't really feel anything the last time until we went into that basement."

"There's something here," Xavier said, holding both his hands up as if warming them in front of a fire.

Lev glanced towards Viktor who remained seemingly unflappable. "So, what now?" Lev asked.

"Now we go inside."

*

"Tulip!" Beth said, jumping to her feet as the doctor appeared in the garden. The tension in the air could be cut with a knife as the three family members waited for her to speak.

"Okay. They've extracted the bullet and the good news is that it missed any vital organs."

Beth, Naomi and Bella all exhaled deep, relieved breaths. "Thank God," Beth said.

"But there's been quite a lot of internal bleeding and that's what we're currently trying to stop."

"Tell me truthfully. What are her chances?"

Tulip didn't answer for a moment. "She's young, she's strong. Her signs are good. That's all in our favour, but I'll be a lot happier when we get the bleeding under control. You've got the best doctor in the place looking after her, Beth. And the surgical team with him is first class. Enola couldn't be in better hands."

Beth didn't sit so much as her legs gave way and she flopped back down onto the bench. "This is like some nightmare, some horrible, horrible nightmare."

Tulip shook her head. "In my life, I've never seen anything like this. I've never even heard of it. It's like half the town's gone mad."

"Sheriff!" They all turned to see Eddie, one of her deputies, appearing in the garden.

Beth slowly climbed to her feet. "Eddie."

"I just heard about Enola." Eddie was the youngest of the deputies and tended to be quite emotional. He wouldn't have lasted five minutes in any other town, but Beth protected him quite a bit. He threw his arms around her, which was a little surprising but welcomed at the same time. "How is she?"

"She's in the theatre now."

"What do you want me to do?"

"Do you know where Carl is?"

"I ain't seen him. I tried to call him, but nothing."

"Okay. I need you to go back to town and—"

"What's happening? It's like the whole place has gone—"

"I don't know, Eddie. But the state police have been called in and I need you at the office. Don't touch anything. Ultimately, it's a crime scene and I'm guessing, when all this is over, there are going to be a lot of questions, but when they get here, my guess is that's where they're going to be heading and you'll be the liaison. If you can, get a radio out to me so we can stay in contact, but I'm going to stay here. I've got to stay here."

He nodded. "I understand, Sheriff. I won't let you down." He walked away looking more like a child playing cops than he had ever done. Her heart sank a little, knowing that whatever this disaster was, her department hadn't been able to manage it on behalf of the town. A reckoning for this would have to be paid at some stage, but today wasn't that day.

24

The five of them stood at the basement door. Now they were inside the house, Lev conceded there was something he hadn't felt before. It was as if the property was one pole of a magnet and they were another. It felt like there was something in the air repelling them.

"You're serious?" he asked, looking down at the length of rope that Viktor had given him. "You want me to tie this around my waist?"

"Yes," Taleen said, taking the stretch of rope she'd been handed and wrapping it around herself before securing a knot. "The last time you went down there, by your own admission, you lost time. We have no idea what might happen this time, but at least—"

"At least Viktor can pull out our dead bodies if the worst comes to the worst?"

"My hope is maybe he can pull us out before such an event occurs."

"You do realise it's not a straight line? You go down the staircase, you turn right, and it's not as if it's a small basement. It's a bloody big basement."

She shrugged. "It's a long rope."

"Yeah, but my point is—"

"I know what your point is, Lev. And this is a long way from ideal, but we're winging it right now, and this is something, isn't it?" she said, holding the rope up. "And something's better than nothing, right?"

Lev started laughing. "This is mental. The whole thing is just…. A couple of days ago, I thought this was going to be an easy gig to pay my rent for a couple of months until the band went back into the studio. And now there's a fucking town tearing itself apart, the guy who got me this job is currently doing a pretty fucking great Guy Fawkes impression, one of the sweetest kids I've ever met is fighting for her life, and we're about to head down into a basement to try to close some kind of gateway to Hell using an incantation constructed from best guesses and some fucking carved tablets that some twat in Tikrit probably sells to the fucking traders in Marrakesh as souvenirs for tourists."

"I'm sensing that you're not a hundred percent on board with the plan."

Lev laughed again, and this time, it was in slightly better humour. "This is crazy, Taleen."

She reached out and took his hand. "I know, Lev. It's beyond crazy, but it's all there is. Whether it was Jamie or your recording that unleashed mayhem on this town, it doesn't matter. If it happened once, it can happen again, and we can't risk that. It's not hyperbole when I say that in the wrong hands and with the right know-how, what's in that basement could bring about the end times."

It's true. He knew it wasn't Jamie who did this. He knew it was his recording, but he also knew that if someone else got hold of this knowledge, if someone with malicious intent learned of what had happened, then Taleen's prophecy of it somehow being broadcast could bring about events that he couldn't even imagine.

He took the rope and tied it around his waist. "Oh, well. I suppose if this does go tits up, at least we'll have front-row seats."

"For what it's worth, darling, I have no intention of this going tits up as you so delightfully put it."

"We'll see soon enough, won't we?"

"Yes. I suppose we will."

Lev reached out and took the door handle. He pulled it open and it immediately slammed shut as if there was someone on the other side pulling it. Delane and Xavier both jumped.

"Well," Lev said. "That didn't happen before. I thought this Azelophet thing could only possess people. How the hell did it slam the door?"

"I dare say little of what you experienced before will be like this time," Taleen replied. "You've got to feel it, Lev. The Azelophet doesn't want us here. You've got to feel it."

He nodded. "Have you ever read about this kind of thing?"

She shook her head. "The events that have occurred today have never occurred before. We're in completely uncharted territory. I don't know what's going on, but it's linked to what happened in town."

He opened the door again, and again it slammed shut. "Well, this is going to make things difficult," Lev said.

"I fix this," Viktor said, dropping the heavy sports bag on the floor and pulling out an axe.

"Um ... they let you carry that on the plane?"

"I went to hardware store last night. Is good for small town. Wide range. I open shop like that one day, but for now, I take door off hinges." Without another word, he swung, driving the blade of the axe through the jamb. The wood around the hinge splintered. He struck again and again, finally separating the hinge from the wood before shifting to the lower segment of the door. Lev leaned against it, holding it in place. Four more deafening crashes and the frame and the door were separated.

Viktor dropped the axe and pulled the handle, grabbing the spine of the door too as he lifted it away. He threw it down the hall, leaving the cold, gaping darkness beyond.

"The lanterns, Viktor," Taleen said and the big Russian reached into the sports bag to retrieve four battery-operated camping lanterns.

"These came from Jones Hardware too. It is good store."

"Yes, yes, yes. It's a good store, we've figured that out. Thank you, Viktor. Now, you know what to do?"

"Viktor knows."

Taleen flicked on her lantern and began to descend the stairs then stopped suddenly. She turned to the others. "I almost forgot one of the most important things. She reached into her pocket and handed each of her companions a pair of noise-cancelling earplugs. "These work in factories and around heavy machinery. Let's see if they work for demons."

They took the packets, opening them up and placing the small plastic plugs in their ears, blocking out one another's sounds, the sounds of the house, the sounds of everything but their own breathing and thoughts. They continued down the staircase as Viktor released more slack on the ropes.

The temperature seemed almost Arctic as they reached the bottom step, and a short, sharp gust of foulness rushed towards them. They weren't able to hear the cries of disgust the others exclaimed, but it was clear from their faces that the stench of decay riled the bile up inside of them all.

They placed their lanterns down in a line casting as wide a ray of light as they could in the expansive, dingy basement. Suddenly, the four ropes fell slack and the quartet shot concerned glances towards one another.

Taleen turned to the staircase. "Viktor? VIKTOR?" She wouldn't be able to hear his reply but hoped the ropes would become taut again or she might receive some sign at least, but there was nothing. She started back to the bottom of the stairs but stopped suddenly, something inside compelling her to turn.

Lev stared towards her, concern seizing him as he saw the concentration on her face, targeting a defined spot above the crevice. There was nothing there.

Suddenly, all four ropes began tugging at the same time, not a gentle tug to say, "It's alright, I am Viktor and still watching over you." This was something else. Delane immediately fell back on her buttocks, Xavier collapsed like a felled tree, and both started sliding across the floor, their fearful screams filling the room and even managing to pierce the protection provided by the buds.

Taleen was jolted from her trance, almost falling over like the others, but then an expression of understanding flashed on her face and she leapt, outpacing the drag. She swooped down, grabbing the fabric pouch that Xavier held as he and Delane continued to be dragged.

Lev had spent most of his adult life lugging heavy equipment in and out of studios and concert venues. He was a different specimen to the others, and although the force at the other end of the rope felt like the first pull of a full tug-of-war team, he leant against it, remaining upright, his boots giving him enough purchase to provide a pause to undo the knot and shake free of the nylon line.

He charged across to Taleen as she put up a similar fight. She wrapped her right arm around him, using him as an anchor as he unfastened the rope around her waist. They both stood there out of breath as they watched the lines disappear, closely followed by their two companions. The frightened cries were suddenly replaced by pained ones as Delane and Xavier seemingly bent back against the thick wooden post at the foot of the staircase before disappearing out of view.

Five seconds later, the air shook around the remaining pair and, as impossible as they knew it was, a surety clutched them. They both walked side by side to the bottom of the staircase and looked up to see the door in place once more.

They didn't need to walk up the stairs and try it to know it wouldn't open. They looked towards each other and Lev reached up, taking his earplugs out.

"What are you doing?" Taleen asked, pulling one of hers out just a little to hear the reply.

"Taleen. This thing did something to Viktor. It just pulled Delane and Xavier across the floor and up the stairs. It put a destroyed door back in place to stop us getting out of here. You honestly think it can't get past these?" he asked, holding up the small buds.

"But the whispers?"

"I let them creep up on me before. I wasn't prepared. Each time this thing has come at me, I've managed to beat it back. I'm not going to let it win, Taleen."

She nodded, taking the other earplug out. "I suppose life always comes down to a few moments in the end."

"Yeah. Well, let's make these count."

The pair retraced their steps to the gaping crack in the floor and, again, Taleen became entranced by the space above it. Lev was about to ask her what it was when he suddenly saw too.

It's every fleeting glimpse.

They played in rapid succession, causing icicle fingers to run down his back. Starting from that night, the night that changed his life forever. The devil's face hung there in mid-air before him while he was trapped in the car while his father bled out by his side.

Then, a few months later, he walked into the kitchen, simultaneously switching the light on. The image froze. He remembered, simply because it had always stuck with him, that in that split second he had seen that face again. He had denied it a thousand times since, but that's how personal demons worked. Subliminal suggestions, sounds, fleeting images. And here it was. Proof in this freeze-framed broken shard of time. The devil's face, staring through the window. With a single pace, the refraction of light slightly altered and it was gone.

Another. Taking a bus back from a friend's house. It set off from the stop with a queue of people waiting for another number. A split-second image burnt into his mind's eye. The face—again, the face. He swivelled in his seat, but it was gone. Once more, he put it down to his mind playing tricks. Once more, it had been real.

Scene after scene played out above the gaping fissure in the basement like some filmed-to-order horror movie. *They follow us. We never know when they're there. There's no predicting when or where. They just appear for moments in time. Are they always there? Are they always with us? Is it simply an accident when we catch sight of them or is it deliberate? Do they want us to know? Do they want to sow the seeds of doubt in our minds, haunting us with their presence even in absentia?*

Dozens, hundreds of times he'd thought he'd seen this thing, and now he was sure. Every chill down his spine. Every door creaking. It had all been the Azelophet?

He reached out, grabbing Taleen's arm, and she dragged her eyes away, tears running down her face. She knew he knew. She knew he'd just come to the same revelation she had pondered for so long.

"Let's get this done, Taleen."

She nodded, wiping the tears away. "I'm sorry."

With those two words, she betrayed a vulnerability he had never witnessed before. Something in him felt compelled to hold her and he took a step forward, throwing his arms around her. She reciprocated. Neither could explain the need for it, but they both shared it.

He kissed her gently on top of her head. "For what it's worth, there is no one I have more faith in to get this done, or, y'know, damn us to suffering for all eternity. One of those."

Taleen sniffed, letting out a laugh and pulling back. "Thank you, darling. I don't think anyone has ever given me such a vote of confidence." She clutched the pouch she'd grabbed from Xavier tightly and walked up to the fissure once more, this time averting her gaze from the cinematic odyssey of her demonic encounters.

"Before we start," Lev said, pulling out the tape from his jacket pocket. He was about to throw it into the crack when Taleen cried out.

"No!"

"What do you mean?"

"I mean whatever is on that tape has power. Look what it did in town. Let's not give that power back. We haven't heard the whispers, Lev; maybe you trapped them in that recording. Maybe you took away their voice, imprisoned them on that celluloid."

"Have you any idea how mad that sounds, Taleen?"

"Do you have a better explanation as to why the same thing that happened to you and Anna the other day hasn't happened to us again?"

"Because we're ready to fight it this time."

Taleen shrugged. "Sure. That might be the reason. You want to risk it though?"

"You seriously think something could be imprisoned in here?" he asked, holding up the tape.

"Is it any more unbelievable than hoping these carved tablets and a spoken incantation are going to bring all this to an end?" They both stared above the crevice where their past lives continued to play out.

"I suppose not."

He put the tape away and the pair took a final breath before starting. The temperature in the room had dropped further and they could see their breath as they exhaled.

"Remember five by five. We speak the incantation twenty-five times in total before the ceremony of the tablets."

"Do we both have to speak it simultaneously?"

"Really, only one person needs to say it."

"What did we all come down here for then?"

"Insurance. Which was probably just as well, considering what happened to Delane and Xavier."

"Do you think they're dead?"

"I don't know. But I feel…."

"Like it's scared of us?"

"I think it's scared of you. From what you've told me, each time it's tried to possess you, you've fought back. Even though the whispers entranced you when you were here before, they didn't possess the power to do anything else. I doubt if your cohort was as lucky. Like I said, Jamie would have selected each of you for a reason. He probably didn't realise that you were the exact opposite of what he wanted."

When Lev didn't reply, she turned towards him to see him glaring into a darkened corner. "It's staring at me."

"What?"

"It's here. It's staring at me, Taleen. I can see it. It's just standing there. Its head lowered a little, peering through the darkness."

"Don't look at it. Look at me. It will try everything to stop this."

He dragged his eyes away and looked at Taleen. "Let's get on with this."

"Azela cofura menak ick ophet.
Belata hypora klieg um sabet.
Azela cofura menak ick ophet.
Belata hypora klieg um sabet.
Azela cofura menak ick ophet.
Belata hypora klieg um sabet."

A sudden bang followed by a loud clatter made Taleen pause for a second and both their heads turned to the staircase. Lev glanced towards the corner to see the menacing shape of his tormentor had vanished. He looked back to the stairs and saw Xavier and Delane standing there. They were statuesque, simply regarding their two former companions like curious animals.

They suddenly broke into a run. "Just carry on," Lev ordered. "Don't let anything stop you, Taleen."

"Azela cofura menak ick ophet.

Belata hypora klieg um sabet."

He kicked out and Xavier shot backwards, his feet leaving the floor. At the same second, the slight figure of Delane became airborne too as she flew at Lev. He ducked away, but she was lightning fast and pivoted, leaping on his back, wrapping her arms and legs around him, screaming like a banshee. It was deafening, disorienting, but he knew that under no circumstances could he allow the ritual to be interrupted. He shoved and writhed, running backwards towards the wall, smashing Delane against it, causing her to scream even louder.

Then it was his turn to cry out as she sunk her teeth into the nape of his neck. "FUUUCK!" The pain was almost incapacitating. He could feel the blood already running down his spine as he saw Xavier scrambling to his feet and starting towards Taleen.

If ever Lev needed to tap into the bar-fighting glory days of Blazetrailer's early years, it was now. He threw his head back, feeling it crack Delane's nose and causing her to instantly release her grip as she slid down the wall, howling in pain this time.

He set off at a sprint towards Xavier, tackling him to the floor before he reached Taleen.

"Azela cofura menak ick ophet.

Belata hypora klieg um sabet."

He unleashed one, two, three punches in quick succession, bloodying the other man's face as he fought and flailed. Lev hammered his fist down a fourth time and there was a hollow crack as Xavier's head bounced off the hard floor.

He was out cold, but Lev could hear Delane starting to rally again. He grabbed Xavier's scruff, starting to drag him away just in case the unconsciousness was momentary when he stopped suddenly.

"Oh fuuuck!"

Taleen paused, turning to where Lev was looking. In the glow of the four camping lanterns, she could see Viktor's outline at the bottom of the staircase. He carried the axe in his right hand and, even from this distance, she could identify the malevolent intention in his gaze.

Shit!

"Don't stop, Taleen. Don't stop!"

"Azela cofura menak ick ophet.

Belata hypora klieg um sabet."

He let go of Xavier as Delane, bloody face and all, charged towards him. Viktor began to move, too, the axe blade making a chilling scrape against the floor. Lev was old-fashioned. He wasn't someone who liked the idea of men hitting women; in fact, he railed against it, but for all intents and purposes, Delane wasn't Delane at that moment. She was the Azelophet. He launched towards her as she leapt at him. She met his right hook in mid-air and he watched as one of her teeth flew from her mouth.

The animalistic growl rising from the back of her throat fell silent and she dropped to the floor. Without pause, Lev turned towards Viktor and ran at him.

He's going to chop me into sushi.

Such was the speed of the attack that Viktor didn't have time to strike; instead, raising the axe only to be taken by surprise and rugby tackled. There was an almighty thud as the two figures hit the floor and the axe scuttled across the surface, disappearing into the shadows beneath the stairs.

Winded but well aware of what was at stake, Lev jumped to his feet as Taleen continued to chant behind him. The big Russian was a little slower in his ascent, but whereas Lev was out of breath, bleeding and clearly shaken, there was not a hint of Viktor being flustered. He strode towards Lev, his eyes fixing him with an icy glare.

Lev understood there was no point trying to talk him down. He knew that he was just a puppet and the puppet master was probably in one of the dark corners, watching on with that unsettling smile. Lev kicked out hard, connecting with Viktor's stomach, but the big man barely flinched.

He did it again, but this time, Viktor caught hold of his leg before he made contact then reached out his massive right hand, grabbing Lev by his jacket and flinging him at the wall as if he was an empty shot glass.

"UGGHHH!" He could feel every bone in his body rattle as he smashed against the stonework and dropped to the hard floor. But despite the pain, he jumped to his feet as Viktor made a beeline towards Taleen.

"Azela cofura menak ick ophet.

Belata hypora klieg um sabet."

Lev ran, diving through the air, powering his shoulder into the Russian's thigh, wrapping both his arms around his victim's legs and bringing him down to the floor with an echoing thump. This time, he didn't wait. He scaled Viktor's body while the other man tried to get up and started punching him. He got in two good hits before the big Russian swatted him away, and Lev went flailing, only to spring again and dive onto Viktor's back as he rose.

He wrapped his right arm around the Russian's neck, squeezing with everything he had. Viktor sunk his fingers into Lev's arm. It was like they were thick drill bits boring into his bones. The pain was intense, but Lev kept his grip then reached round with his other hand, clawing his middle and index fingers into the huge Russian's eye.

An angry growl left Viktor's throat and he spun around and ran back towards the wall, crushing Lev's frame with his own and forcing his assailant to let go. Lev slid down the cold stonework, struggling to find the energy to get up again but knowing he'd have to. Before he could rally himself, however, Viktor turned and released an almighty kick. Lev heard and felt his ribs breaking.

"SHIT!" The pain was extraordinary, but he clenched his eyes shut and dived to the side just as Viktor's boot narrowly missed him and smashed against the wall. Lev jumped to his feet again, lunging towards the big man once more who this time punched his would-be attacker in the ribs. "NAAAGH!" It was a whole new level of pain and as Lev staggered away, doubling over, he looked towards the darkened corner of the room where he had seen the face earlier and, sure enough, there it was again, the smile broader now as victory edged closer.

Lev turned to see Viktor heading towards Taleen again. He raced after him, leaping onto the big man's back, this time reaching around and clawing at his eyes with both hands. A deep cry of pain left the Russian's mouth and it was his turn to double over and stagger away as he desperately tried to shake Lev off. He twisted and turned and writhed, and when none of that worked, he ran backwards towards the wall as he had before, but just before impact, Lev let go and dived to the side, causing Viktor's head to smash hard against the stonework.

Lev regained his footing and swung at the Russian once more, knocking the big man's head back against the wall again, dazing him further. Lev was about to punch a second time when Viktor unleashed a powerful, backhanded strike and his victim was catapulted sideways.

One. Two. Three. Four.

This time, he didn't rise and the mighty Russian staggered forward again.

Seeing what was happening out of the corner of her eye, Taleen jumped to her feet. She wasn't sure if Lev was dead. She wasn't sure if any of this would work. All she was sure of was that Viktor was coming for her now and that she had reached twenty-four.

"Azela cofura menak ick ophet.
Belata hypora klieg um sabet."

Twenty-five. She backed away as her bodyguard-turned-Azelophet-minion approached and she opened the cloth pouch, looking down, making sure to pick up the correct first tablet.

"Kassum!" she said, throwing the first of the oval carvings into the gaping hole. "Pelotro!" She dropped in the second as Viktor shot towards her.

In turn, she sprang across the giant crack in the floor, clutching on to the remaining tablets with all her might and just avoiding Viktor's reaching fingers.

"Sumserro!" she said, depositing the third tablet.

Viktor charged, and she side-stepped again, leaping to the other side of the fissure.

"Philak!" She threw in the fourth tablet, but before she could speak the final lament, she felt Viktor's cold hand grab her hair and drag her head back. She fell down and he knelt over her bringing his fist back. A blur of movement swept into her field of vision and Lev's booted foot connected with Viktor's temple, making him collapse sideways. She briefly glimpsed Lev to see his face was bloodied; he was clutching his ribs and she knew in that instant it was now or never.

She scrambled to her knees, grabbed the remaining tablet and almost shouted, "Phet-Azel," at the top of her voice before dropping it in. For a few seconds, nothing happened; then a thousand, ten thousand, ten million agonised screams filled the room. Taleen collapsed onto her side, covering her ears. Lev did the same, their faces just inches apart, each feeling the other's pain and fear as the sound dragged on and on. Then—

Silence.

They continued to look at each other for a moment before Lev's eyes fell shut. "Lev? Lev?" Taleen said, reaching out and grabbing his arm, tighter and tighter, but to no avail. "Lev?"

"M-Miss Zakarian?"

She turned to see Viktor lumbering to his knees. "Viktor. Viktor, is that you?"

"Is me. Who else is it going to be?" he asked, looking around the basement in confusion. "How I get down here? What happened?"

"It doesn't matter. We need to get Lev and the others to hospital."

"Yes. Yes." He reached up, touching his head and bringing away bloody fingers. There was an expression of puzzlement on his face for a moment and then he turned back towards his employer. "Miss Zakarian, this thing … it worked?"

Taleen looked towards the fissure in the floor then above it. There was no cinema show of her past life playing now. There was just thin air. "Yes. Yes, Viktor, I think it has."

CHRISTOPHER ARTINIAN

25

When Lev finally woke, it took him a while to figure out where he was and what was going on. His eyes squinted at the brightness of the room, eventually focusing on the figure in the chair near the end of his bed. She was reading a magazine and had her booted feet raised, resting on his mattress. Several empty coffee cups sat on the small table next to her.

"Jodie?" he croaked and an almost joyful smile lit her face.

"You're awake," she replied, immediately lowering her feet and going to sit next to him, taking his hand in hers.

"What's going on?"

"You've got three broken ribs, a bite out of the back of your neck, a head wound, and apparently the tiniest dick the doctors have ever seen."

A pained smile cracked on his face. "I bet it took you all morning to think of that, didn't it?"

"All morning? I was working on it all day yesterday too."

"What do you mean?"

"You've been out of it for two days."

"Jesus."

She brought his hand up to her mouth and kissed it gently. "And it wasn't true what I said about your dick. They have seen a smaller one. Last year, there were quintuplets born prematurely. Apparently, they all had smaller dicks than yours. Of course, three of them were girls." She giggled to herself and kissed his hand again. "I'm sorry. I'm just giddy to see you awake. You had me worried."

"Is Taleen okay?"

"Taleen and Delane and Xavier and Mr Roboto or whatever he's called."

"Viktor?"

"Yeah. Shit, he's big."

"You should try getting thrown across the room by him. So … did it work, the incantation or whatever it was?"

She shrugged. "You're best speaking to—"

"Darling! You're awake." They turned to the door to see Taleen standing there. She stepped into the room and walked straight up to the bed, kissing him gently on the head before sitting in the chair Jodie had vacated moments before. "My hero."

"You have low standards for heroes," Lev replied.

"Nonsense. You managed to stop Viktor from ripping me to pieces and you gave me the time I needed to deliver the incantation."

"So, it's done? It's over?"

"It's over. The gateway is closed."

"So, now you can close the other ones you know about."

A huff of a laugh left Taleen's mouth. "We've made all the other ones we know about as inaccessible as possible, and closing this one was hardly a walk in the park, but yes, over time, we have the know-how to do that now."

"What happened with Delane, Xavier and Viktor? I thought you'd only bring—"

"Bring people with me who would be unsusceptible? This isn't a science, Lev. Viktor was never meant to set foot in the basement and as for Delane and Xavier, I thought they would have been okay. If it hadn't been for you, however, this would all have ended in disaster. It is proof that no amount of preparation and planning is ever enough. There are no sure things."

"So, what now?"

"Now I go back home and have a well-deserved rest," she said, climbing to her feet and kissing him on the forehead again. She hugged Jodie and kissed her too. "You'll both come over when you're back in LA. We'll celebrate."

"Miss Zakarian. The car is waiting."

"Ah, Viktor, darling. Our friend Lev is awake. Come and wish him well."

The giant Russian stepped into the room from the doorway and walked up to the other man, grabbing hold of his shoulder roughly. "When you are back in LA, you and I will go for drink. Will have good time."

Viktor's fingers felt like a vice around his shoulder. "That sounds … good."

"Yes. It will be good. We will share many stories. Have laugh riot as you say. Very good. Very good," he repeated, relinquishing his grip and nodding before heading back out of the room.

"I don't think I've ever seen him so emotional," Taleen said.

"That was emotional?"

"For him, yes. Well, darlings, I'll go gather Delane and Xavier and we'll be on our way. Oh, and by the way, Lev, we had a little bonfire before leaving the house. I took care of that tape for you," she said with a wink. "Toodle pip, darlings. See you soon."

The two friends stared towards the doorway for a moment as the bustle continued outside. "How's Enola?" It was the first time Lev had the wherewithal or chance to ask since waking up.

Jodie's face lit up. "She's a sweetheart is what she is."

"You've seen her?"

"When I first got here, Bella was in the room with you. I got talking to her and met Beth and Naomi. Enola woke up late last night and Bella came to get me. She thought it would be a cool surprise for her. The poor kid's heart rate nearly went through the roof."

"But she's okay?"

"She's going to be fine."

"I need to go see her."

Jodie jumped to her feet. "Lev, I really don't think you should be moving."

He started to climb out of bed and let out numerous pained grunts and groans as he did. He disconnected the heart monitor, immediately turning it off in order to silence it. "Besides. When they figure out that I don't have insurance and I can't pay for any of this, I'll need to be mobile to try to outrun their security, at least."

"Taleen's picking up the tab your medical bills. I was going to, but she insisted. She said it was the very least she could do. Here, let me help you," Jodie said, rushing around to the other side of the bed and offering support.

"Thanks."

"You want a wheelchair?"

"You having me on?"

"No. You got put through a blender by Viktor. A wheelchair doesn't seem unreasonable. Plus, y'know, you're a lot older than me. I should probably get used to how it's going to be a few years from now."

"Cheeky fucking bitch. I'm three years older than you."

"Yeah, but let's face it. Those three years haven't been kind."

"Unbelievable. I've been conscious less than ten minutes and you're already taking the piss."

She wrapped his arm around her shoulder and placed her left arm around his waist, guiding him out of the room and down the corridor. The previous night, when she had stepped out, she had been asked for her autograph multiple times, but this time, people had the good grace to leave her alone while she helped her friend.

The nurse who had last been in to check on Lev arched an eyebrow as she saw the pair of them slowly moving down the hallway, but every member of medical staff in the hospital was run off their feet, and provided Lev wasn't screaming in pain or taking his last breath, then she wasn't really too concerned.

"You, okay?" Jodie asked as the pair continued.

"Yeah."

"You want to stop?"

"No. I'm good. How did you actually get here?"

"Flew then drove."

"Brian's with you?"

"No. I mean I actually drove."

"You?"

"Yeah. Why?"

"You?" he asked again.

"Yeah. Why?" she repeated.

"'Cause the last time you drove was in Germany and you crashed us into a ditch."

"True. But I had been drinking most of the day and I'd just done a line of blow. Plus, I hadn't been behind a wheel in years."

"All great reasons why you should never think about climbing into a driver's seat again. I still have nightmares about that day."

"Well. I didn't really have a choice. You were down here. All hell was breaking loose and it's not like I can do that album without you, is it? I wouldn't know where to start. And who else would put up with my bullshit?"

"Good points, all."

Jodie giggled. "Arsehole."

They paused outside of the closed door to Enola's room. "Thanks, Jodie."

She tiptoed up and kissed him on the cheek. "Seriously. I don't know what I'd do without you, Lev. You're my best friend. You're the guy who always makes things right."

"I don't have any intention of going anywhere, so you don't need to worry."

They were about to enter when Jodie paused. "Oh, err, I phoned Lottie."

Lev had managed to make the journey from his room without too much discomfort, but the thought of Jodie talking to his soon-to-be ex-wife made him buckle at the knees a little. "I bet that went well."

"I thought your kids should know that you were in hospital."

"What did she say?"

"She was cool with it. We're going shopping the next time I'm in town."

"Uh-huh."

"She was cold at first, but when she heard you were in a bad way, she softened a bit."

"I bet she did. I don't have any assets. If I die, she can say goodbye to child support."

"No. I think she was genuinely concerned. She said she'd tell the kids and get them to phone the hospital when you came around."

"Well, thanks. Two potential apocalyptic events in the space of twenty-four hours and I'm still standing."

"I can be diplomatic as fuck when I need to be."

"You prove it every day."

"Arsehole," she replied with a grin before opening the door. "Brought someone to see you," she announced, guiding Lev into the room.

Beth was sitting by Enola's side, holding her hand, and a broad smile cracked on her face as the two visitors walked into the room. She climbed to her feet and went to

THE DEVIL'S FACE

the door. "Come and take a seat," she said, supporting Lev on the other side as Jodie was doing.

When they'd parked him in a chair, Jodie went over to the bed and gave Enola a gentle hug and kiss, lighting up the girl's face further. "I've asked Bella to bring her camera back when she comes. Nobody is going to believe Jodie Starr came to visit me in hospital."

"Yeah, well. Wait until you and your mum come to see me. We'll make them weep with jealousy," Jodie replied before ruffling Enola's hair and sitting down beside her.

"How are you feeling?" Enola asked, looking towards Lev.

"Don't worry about me. How are you doing?"

"Sore. But the doctors are pleased."

"Yeah," Beth replied, sitting down next to Lev. "The operation went better than they'd hoped. They stopped the bleeding, her vitals are good, and the wound's looking like it should."

"That's great news."

"But what about you? You were out cold when I came up to see you this morning."

Lev shrugged. "I'm fine. Fuckin' hard, I am. You don't need to worry about me."

"Okay, hard man," Beth replied with a smile and reached out, taking his hand. She gave it a squeeze. "It's good to see you up and about, anyway."

He suddenly noticed she was back in her uniform. "How are things in town?"

"Getting back to normal. Someone burnt the Black house to the ground, but being unconscious and all, you probably wouldn't know anything about that, would you?"

"Like you said, I was unconscious."

Beth smiled and looked across to her daughter as she fired question after question at Jodie. "What happened up there?" Beth asked quietly.

"Even if I could put it into words, I doubt if you'd believe me. Hell. I barely believe it myself."

Beth nodded slowly. "I doubt the town will ever recover from this. I doubt if any town could. The state police are going to be here for some time. My job's largely ceremonial at the moment."

"There's nothing to say you have to stay in this town, y'know."

"It's my home."

Lev turned towards Enola then looked back at Beth. "The way I see it, Enola, Naomi and Bella are your home. This town is just a place."

"I can't think about anything at the moment other than getting my baby back to health."

"She seems to be doing pretty well."

"Having Jodie at her bedside when she woke up definitely helped. So, what now?"

"I don't know how long they want to keep me in here, but then I'll probably head back with Jodie."

"Oh. Okay."

"Then I was thinking maybe the weekend after next I could come back and I could see you and Enola. Maybe we could have that picnic we talked about."

"You're serious?"

"Yeah. I'm serious, Beth. It's not the stuff you do; it's the stuff you don't do that you regret the most in life."

"And the guy with less than two hundred bucks in his wallet is going to keep coming back to see us just like that?"

"Jodie's floating me an advance. I'm going to have co-writing credits on her solo album as well as production credits on that and the next Blazetrailer album. Money's not going to be a problem. I've worked with Jodie for a long time and we tend to do it best in bursts. We'll probably eat and sleep at the studio for days at a time then have a few days away so we don't end up knifing each other."

Beth laughed. "Nice."

"My point is I can make this work. I want to make this work. And, y'know, if after a while it's not doing it for either one of us, then at least we'll have tried. But there's a spark here, Beth. And I want to see if I can start a fire."

She took his hand and raised it to her lips, kissing it gently. "That's beautiful. Please tell me it wasn't a lyric."

It was Lev who laughed now. "No. But I might make it one now you come to mention it. So, what do you say?"

Beth glanced across to her daughter and happiness remained etched on her face as Jodie talked to her. Then she turned back to Lev. "I say when I leave here, I'm going to go out and buy a picnic basket."

It was Lev's turn to beam now. "Good then."

*

Anna had been in a coma for two weeks after the crash, and when she woke, she was still in a state of virtual catatonia. The doctors and her family had spoken to her and, other than the odd blink, there had been little response. Occasionally, a tear would run down her face, but it was impossible to tell if it was a reaction to aural stimulation or simply that her lacrimal glands were going into overdrive.

There had been bleeding on her brain after the accident, but scans had shown that this had stopped. The cuts and bruising she had sustained had healed, and physically it was hard to tell there was anything wrong.

She had been transported by ambulance from the hospital to her sister's home in Pilot Point and the family had rallied around. Linda, her sister, had trained as a nurse, and although she couldn't give Anna twenty-four-seven attention, she took on board the main chunk of the workload while other family members filled in the gaps in her care.

Initially, Anna's sustenance had been provided through a drip, but then she moved on to soup, protein shakes and other forms of nutrients. All this was in the hope that, one day, she would simply snap out of it.

Her mother, father, brother and extended families all took their turns visiting, reading to her, putting a straw up to her lips so she could drink, and taking her for walks in the wheelchair. Even friends and one-time work colleagues dropped in to see how she was getting on.

However, as time passed and Anna's condition showed no signs of changing, their enthusiasm waned, gradually leaving Linda with more and more responsibility. It eventually became too much for her husband, and when their kids left for college, he left too.

When Linda's parents passed and her brother moved away, Anna became her responsibility and hers alone. It was a long, lonely, bleak path. But each day Linda would continue to help Anna exercise, if you could call it that. She would move her legs and arms in an attempt to keep her joints supple and at least give her muscles some activity. She would feed her, although, as time passed, Anna became little more than skin and bone. Her once rosy cheeks drained of colour; her eyes became hollow brown marbles. Linda would change her sister's nappies, talk to her, do everything other than live her life. Occasionally, the doctor would pay a visit, identifying a new malady to add to the list of things that were wrong with her—heart arrhythmia, the early stages of kidney disease, anaemia. But still Anna somehow continued.

Despite the hardship, despite everything, Linda battled on, steadfast in the belief that, one day, her sister would return. She tried her hardest to shield her heartbreak, her depression, and her tears. She had made a vow to look after Anna and it was one she had no intention of breaking, whatever the cost.

Five years became ten. Ten became twenty. Twenty became thirty. Both their best days had been and gone, but that didn't matter. A promise was a promise.

Often, she would say, "I miss you, Sis," or, "I'd give anything to hear your voice again," but there would be no response, despite how much she wished it. Occasionally, she'd see an eye twitch, a blink or a hand movement that gave her a little hope, but when nothing else came, the hope soon dissipated.

THE DEVIL'S FACE

*

"LINDA! LINDA!" The scream came from deep within Anna, just like it did every day, every day since she had come out of the coma. She heard every word said to her. Her heart broke when she heard of her sister's divorce because of her. It broke again when her parents passed. So many years she had been stuck in this body as a prisoner. "LINDA! LINDA! LINDA!" She hoped that, one day, her brain would activate her vocal cords. She hoped that, one day, she would be able to speak to her sister again. Plead for her to end this eternal suffering. Tablets. A pillow over the face. Anything. Anything but this. "LINDA! LINDA! LINDA!"

The familiar shriek of cellophane made her clench her eyes shut tight. Every day for the last thirty-three years, she had been a prisoner in this bed and a prisoner in that basement simultaneously. Every day for the last thirty-three years, she had suffered the indignity of being bathed by Linda, having her nappies changed, being fed. She had tried on numerous occasions to refuse food, but each time, they simply hooked her up to drips and feeding tubes and she lost even more control of who she was.

She waited. The last echoes of her scream were long since dead in her head as she felt the clear plastic wrap encase her naked body. She felt the Red Man's hands lift her, pull her, shape her as the cellophane weaved and covered her flesh. Finally, she was bound like a mummy, her skin suffocating as she felt the Red Man's frame drape over her. She could feel the contours and the bulges, causing bile to bubble in the back of her throat. *Powerless.*

She felt and smelt his warm, rancid breath, prickling over her ears and cheeks as he repeated the whispered words, "You're all mine. You're all mine," over and over and over again. *Powerless.*

Occasionally, his hand would pass over her encapsulated body, gently running around the outline of her breasts, her stomach, her hips, her thighs. *Powerless.*

Thirty-three years. Every day, he would come, just like he had for those six months when she was trapped in that basement. Every day for thirty-three years. Her screams went unheard, her pleas unanswered. She could do nothing but let it happen.

Thirty-three years.

*

One morning, Linda walked into Anna's room. Sometimes, her sister's eyes would be open; sometimes, she'd wake soon after her entry, but on this day, something was different. Anna's right arm was out of the covers. Linda always tucked her in. "There we go, sweetie. As snug as a bug in a rug," she would say each night without fail, gently kissing her on the forehead. She would wait, hoping for a response, but one would never come. Often, she wondered if Anna heard anything, whether there were any processes going on in her brain at all, but unless she woke up, woke up properly, she would never know.

Today, though, her arm was outside the covers. *That's got to be something, right?*

As she approached, she noticed the thumb, forefinger and middle finger of her right hand beaked together and moving. *It's like ... it's like she's writing or something.*

Even when Linda rushed to grab a pen and paper, there was a part of her that knew it was wishful thinking and that what she was hoping was impossible.

But then the impossible came true. They were never complete thoughts, only single words or pairs of words, and often they were in a kind of shorthand, but for the most part, Linda got good at filling in the blanks. These scribblings were confined to thirteen minutes each day, between the times of six thirty and six forty-three, but they were something. They were proof her sister was still there.

The first thing Anna wrote was "Kill me." "Red Man." On the second day, it was "Pills" and "Red Man here." The third day was "Smother." Each time, Linda had cried floods of tears. She had sacrificed her life for the care of her sister only for her to ask for death.

She had got angry. "There's no one here. There's no one here but you and me. Jesus. I only wish you could see how much that was true. You're all I've got and I'm all you've got."

For several days after, she refused to put a pen and paper in her sister's hand. When she had finally succumbed once more, the messages had read, "Sorry," "Luv U," and "Twirly grl." The last message made Linda cry tears of happiness. This was Anna's nickname for her all through growing up on account of how she used to twirl her long hair around her finger.

These thirteen minutes each day became like a drug for Linda, but more than that, they were a way she could make life slightly better for her sister, too. "Lvnder bad." Linda had brought in a small bowl of dried lavender to freshen the room, but obviously it wasn't to Anna's liking. "Lilies good." On the other hand, she appreciated the fresh flowers. "Classical radio." Every morning, when Linda had walked into Anna's room, she'd turned on the TV and let that run in the background all day until saying goodnight to her. Now she tuned the radio to a classical station.

Little things. Lemonade instead of cola. Pumpkin soup instead of chicken. Little things. All the time little things interspersed with "Luv you," "Thank U," "Twirly grl." All the time little things, but they made everything worthwhile.

Then, one day, the notes became more cryptic. "Tape," "Lev," "Cam." Either Linda couldn't make out what the scrawls said or she couldn't quite understand them. The next day, there were three more messages, and this time, Linda managed to piece the jigsaw together. "Sctland," "Camra," "Tape," "Lev."

Lev had visited once soon after the accident and he had phoned every now and again to find out if there was any improvement in Anna's health or if there was anything he could do. As far as Linda knew, he and Anna had only worked together for a short time, so it was a little strange that he had so much interest, but he was thoughtful, warm, and always listened, so she was grateful for the contact.

It had been a long, long time since Linda had delved into the cupboard in Anna's room. It contained what was left of her worldly possessions and right at the back was the sports bag retrieved from her car. The cracked compact mirror in her make-up bag, the smashed reading glasses and the broken camera. All had been damaged due to the crash, and as useless as they were, Linda had kept them. She wasn't quite sure why, but they were Anna's and to get rid of them would be like admitting that Anna was gone too, whereas the last few weeks had shown her that she was simply broken, like these things, and who knew, one day she might get fixed.

Anna looked at the camera. It was practically an antique by today's standards. She remembered how impressed she'd been when her sister had shown her the top-of-the-range eight-millimetre Sony camcorder all those years ago, but a lot had happened since then. She hit the eject button and the spring-loaded casing opened. She looked at the tape. "Anna, I doubt if Lev's even got a way to play this. It's ancient."

Anna's pen started moving again. "Send Lev."

"Okay," Linda said, placing her hand over her sister's. "I need to go to the post office anyhow. I promise I'll send this to him."

"Luv U."

"I love you too."

The digital clock clicked to six forty-three and Anna's hand fell limp.

*

The visits by the Red Man played in a loop. They had done ever since Anna had awoken from the crash, and often the anticipation of his arrival was more terrifying than the event itself. It catapulted her into a heightened emotional state and that's when she had experienced the first reacquaintance with her motor functions, albeit very limited. It was this exacerbated state of anxiety that gave her system the boost it needed to communicate with her sister.

She didn't know how it worked or why it worked, but it was something. It was something beyond being trapped in this eternal hell with the thing that had started all her night terrors. At first, she had pleaded for death, a quick way out, a way to stop the suffering. However, that had done nothing but upset her sister, who had sacrificed so much already.

Just having contact with her was something. It was something more than she'd had for the last thirty-three years, but it wasn't enough. It wasn't enough to make up for all the torment, the endless crushing torture of every single day but for those thirteen minutes, which somehow the Red Man knew nothing about, had no control over.

Linda had spoken of how Lev had phoned to find out how things were. She had heard his name from time to time. Linda had always kept her up to date with who had called and who she had run into, but up until recently, Anna had been unable to respond. Now, though, Lev's name lit a small beacon of hope. If anyone could possibly understand what was happening to her, it was him. They had experienced something inexplicable together and in the absence of her words, the tape would be a reminder. She hoped it would still play. She hoped it would spark the memory of the terror they had both felt that morning. She hoped he would be able to fill in the blanks as to why she wanted him to have it.

Because, in the absence of hope, all she had was this. All she had was a lifetime of terror and suffering played back in a loop, day after day after day, punctuated by just thirteen minutes.

EPILOGUE

NOW

Lev took another drink and looked at the Post-it note once more. "She wanted you to have this."

He looked at the address again. Pilot Point.

"Jesus!"

Goosebumps ran up and down his arms and the echo of the laughter he'd heard a few moments before came back to haunt him. He looked around the room. This was the one place in the house that he had really made his own. There was still a lot to do, but it would be worth it when it was finished. The idea was for him and Beth to spend six months in the US and six months in the UK.

This house was perfect and came with a good amount of land. There was a loch as well as woodland on the property. The house was stone-built with plenty of character. Beth and Enola loved it. Freddie and Sal loved it, too, and he had visions of having extended family get-togethers here and enjoying semi-retirement.

After the success of Jodie's first solo album and the subsequent Blazetrailer release, Lev had become a hot property with other bands lining up for him to be their producer. The years had been good to him ever since the big showdown – *the unleashing* – that nearly ended his life.

But in all that time, he hadn't considered that the trial wasn't over. In all that time when he'd been living the good life, Anna had been paying the price. He'd been due to return to the US the following week, but in good conscience, he couldn't delay his return any longer with the knowledge he now possessed, or at least thought he possessed.

His system was used to the booze and it wasn't as if there was an army of police in the Highlands anyway, so he threw a few clothes into a carry-on bag, headed out to the car and set off.

He looked in the mirror, regarding the magical white building he was leaving behind for a moment, and wondered if what he was about to face would mean it would be the last time he ever got to see it.

There were no streetlights out there and it was half an hour before he noticed bars appear on his phone. He would drive to Inverness Airport, get the first available flight to Heathrow, and then fly on to Dallas. He wanted to see Beth. He'd kill to see Beth and hold her right now, but if what he thought to be true was true, it would be like leaving a wounded animal on the road and slowly letting it die.

He'd spent a good portion of the last thirty-three years of his life in airport lounges and on planes. He'd learnt to grab sleep where he could and while away the endless hours of travelling.

He chose not to call Beth as much as he wanted to. He didn't even call Taleen or Jodie. This was his burden and

THE DEVIL'S FACE

his alone. He and Anna had walked into that house. He and Anna had walked out, but he was the only one who had found freedom.

He choked up a little as he pulled up in the rental outside Linda's home. Thanks to flight delays, it was eight thirty in the evening. He had contacted her to tell her he would be arriving and she had been quite excited to receive him. He would be the first person to communicate with Anna other than her. It seemed only fitting as she had been the one who wanted him to have the tape.

Linda had made him dinner and the pair of them had gone upstairs to sit with Anna for a while. He was more than a little horrified to see the hollow shell that she had become.

He left a little after eleven to head to the hotel, but he didn't sleep much, nervous about missing the thirteen-minute window the next morning to talk to her.

Linda had come to relish that small fragment of time she spent with her sister each day, but she was willing to forego it in the hope that Lev, the man Anna had specifically sought contact with, might somehow provide the next evolution in communication.

He was already by her bed at six twenty-five. It seemed strange talking to someone who was seemingly in a state of sleep, but nevertheless, he did it anyway. He spoke about his life and what he'd been doing and then he moved on to the crux of why he had shown up.

"When I got the tape, I didn't know it was you. When I played it back, I…. God, Anna. I hope it's not true. I hope this isn't what I think it is. I came to see you when you were actually in a coma. I so wanted to speak to you. You and I were the only two people in the basement that day and something happened after that. It was something crazy and terrifying and I really, really wanted to share it with you.

"I hope this isn't what I think it is, Anna."

He saw the digital clock flick to six thirty. The pen was already resting in Anna's hand and the paper was underneath it. Suddenly, the nib began to move.

"Gud hear U."

"It's good to see you, Anna."

"Long."

"Yeah. It's been over thirty-three years since that day. One day, and ever since, I've always felt a bond with you. I suppose that was inevitable after what we went through."

"Y. U unstand."

"Unstand? Understand?"

"Y."

"What do you think I understand, Anna?"

"Here."

"What about here?"

"In here?"

"Yeah. I'm in here with you. In your room, now."

"N."

"No, what?"

"He in here."

All the air left Lev's lungs and he was sure he felt the temperature drop.

"He?"

"He."

Lev knew who it was and it wasn't the He who plagued his existence. The Azelophet tailor made torture. He and Anna had never specifically spoken about their histories, but it was almost as if there was an unspoken understanding between them. Lev had seen the devil's face in that basement when he had returned there. *Had Anna's demon been with her since the crash? Could that really be true?*

"The thing from the basement? The thing from the Black house?"

There was a pause before she wrote anything else and Lev looked up at her face.

"Y."

"Oh, fuck, Anna." He removed the first piece of paper and put another one in its place.

"What do you want me to do?"

"U kno."

THE DEVIL'S FACE

Lev looked at the clock. They still had a few minutes. "There's got to be another way."

"N."

"I know someone. There's this woman called—"

"N."

He stared at her face. It was gaunt, drawn, tired, pale. Linda had warned him of how Anna's eyes could only ever stare straight ahead, but they were looking towards him at that moment and a shudder ran down his back.

"Please. Let me—"

"N. N. N. N. N. N. N. N."

Lev closed his eyes and exhaled deeply. Somehow, a part of him had known this all along, ever since he had received that tape. And there was a part of him that knew he would have to do the unthinkable to end Anna's torment. *Thirty-three years*.

He took away the piece of paper and replaced it with a fresh one.

"Are you suffering?"

"Y."

"And it's because of what happened in that basement?"

"Y."

"You've been like this ever since the crash?"

"Y."

"You don't want to go on?"

"N."

"He's in there with you every day?"

"Y."

A long pause. "You want me to end your suffering?"

"Y."

"You want me to kill you?"

"Y. Y. Y."

Lev looked at the clock. Six forty-two. It was no small risk. He could end up on murder charges for this. He could lose everything he'd worked for. He could lose Beth, his family, everything. On the other hand, Linda had told Lev about the laundry list of health problems Anna suffered in addition to this horrific catatonic state she was made to endure day in, day out. She had already confounded her doctor by surviving as long as she had. Would her death raise any questions beyond inevitability finally playing its hand?

He reached out and squeezed Anna's wrist. "I owe you at least that." Her eyes stayed fixed on him as he stood and took one of the pillows from underneath her. He bent down and kissed her gently on the forehead. "I hope you find peace." He gently placed the pillow over her mouth and nose. There was no struggling, there was no thrashing; there was nothing, until…. The entire house began to shake as a deafening rumble erupted.

The face that had visited him so many times before hung over him now, its expression fixed in a furious snarl as a scream sounded from downstairs. Lev met its gaze, matching its anger for what it had made Anna suffer through. A thunderous, booming yawp of hate billowed from its open mouth, then silence but for the sound of footsteps charging up the stairs.

Lev quickly replaced the pillow as Anna's head lolled to the side. He looked towards the paper to see "Thank" on it then turned to Linda as she stormed into the room.

"She was in the middle of writing something and then she just…."

Linda tentatively walked up to the bed. She knelt down by her sister's side and reached out, placing a hand on Anna's face, which inexplicably bore the tiniest of smiles. "Oh, sweetness," she said as tears immediately formed in her eyes.

"Somehow, I knew," she said, turning to Lev. "Somehow, I knew that you coming would either be the end for her or the beginning. Somehow, I knew. She wanted you to have that tape. She wanted to reach out to you. Whatever it was she wanted to say, she got to say it." More tears than ever rolled down her cheeks and her body began to shake.

"Whatever peace she wanted to make, she made it. I've always said the Lord works in mysterious ways, and if sendin' her off with that earthquake ain't one of the most mysterious, then I don't know what is."

She climbed to her feet and stepped into Lev's arms. He held her as she sobbed hopelessly. "I'm sorry, Linda."

"You've got nothing to be sorry about. You gave my sister peace. After all these years, she's finally got the peace she wanted."

"I hope so. I really hope so."

The End

A NOTE FROM THE AUTHOR

I really hope you enjoyed this book and would be very grateful if you took a minute to leave a review on Amazon and Goodreads.

If you would like to stay informed about what I'm doing, including current writing projects, and all the latest news and release information; these are the places to go:

Join the fan club on Facebook
https://www.facebook.com/groups/127693634504226

Like the Christopher Artinian author page
https://www.facebook.com/safehaventrilogy/

Buy exclusive and signed books and merchandise, subscribe to the newsletter and follow the blog:
https://www.christopherartinian.com/

Follow me on Youtube:
https://www.youtube.com/channel/UCfJymx31VvzttB_Q-x5otYg

Follow me on Amazon
https://amzn.to/2I1llU6

Follow me on Goodreads
https://bit.ly/2P7iDzX

Other books by Christopher Artinian:

Safe Haven: Rise of the RAMs
Safe Haven: Realm of the Raiders
Safe Haven: Reap of the Righteous
Safe Haven: Ice
Safe Haven: Vengeance
Safe Haven: Is This the End of Everything?
Safe Haven: Neverland (Part 1)
Safe Haven: Neverland (Part 2)
Safe Haven: Doomsday
Safe Haven: Raining Blood (Part 1)
Safe Haven: Hope Street
Safe Haven: No Hope in Hell
Safe Haven: War Zone
Before Safe Haven: Lucy
Before Safe Haven: Alex
Before Safe Haven: Mike
Before Safe Haven: Jules

The End of Everything: Book 1
The End of Everything: Book 2
The End of Everything: Book 3
The End of Everything: Book 4
The End of Everything: Book 5
The End of Everything: Book 6
The End of Everything: Book 7
The End of Everything: Book 8
The End of Everything: Book 9
The End of Everything: Book 10
The End of Everything: Book 11
The End of Everything: Book 12
The End of Everything: Book 13
The End of Everything: Book 14
Relentless
Relentless 2
Relentless 3
The Burning Tree: Book 1 – Salvation
The Burning Tree: Book 2 – Rebirth
The Burning Tree: Book 3 – Infinity
The Burning Tree: Book 4 – Anarchy
The Burning Tree: Book 5 – Redemption
The Burning Tree: Book 6 – Power (Part 1)
Night of the Demons

CHRISTOPHER ARTINIAN

Christopher Artinian was born and raised in Leeds, West Yorkshire. Wanting to escape life in a big city and concentrate more on working to live than living to work, he and his family moved to the Outer Hebrides in the north-west of Scotland in 2004, where he now works as a full-time author.

Chris is a huge music fan, a cinephile, an avid reader and a supporter of Yorkshire County Cricket Club. When he's not sitting in front of his laptop living out his next post-apocalyptic/dystopian/horror adventure, he will be passionately immersed in one of his other interests.